Summerland Cove

ALSO BY ELLEN BAKER

The Hidden Life of Cecily Larson

Keeping the House

I Gave My Heart to Know This

ELLEN BAKER

Summerland Cove

A Novel

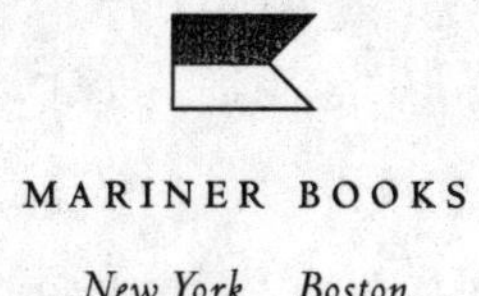

MARINER BOOKS

New York Boston

HarperCollins books may be purchased for educational, business, or sales promotional use. For information, please email the Special Markets Department at SPsales@harpercollins.com.

The Mariner flag design is a registered trademark of HarperCollins Publishers LLC.

hc.com

FIRST EDITION

Designed by Chloe Foster

Map by Noah Springer. Copyright © 2026 Springer Cartographics.

Library of Congress Cataloging-in-Publication Data has been applied for.

ISBN 978-0-06-344877-3

Printed in the United States of America

26 27 28 29 30 LBC 5 4 3 2 1

I will arise and go now, and go to Innisfree,
And a small cabin build there, of clay and wattles made;
Nine bean-rows will I have there, a hive for the honey-bee,
And live alone in the bee-loud glade.

And I shall have some peace there . . .

"The Lake Isle of Innisfree," W. B. Yeats

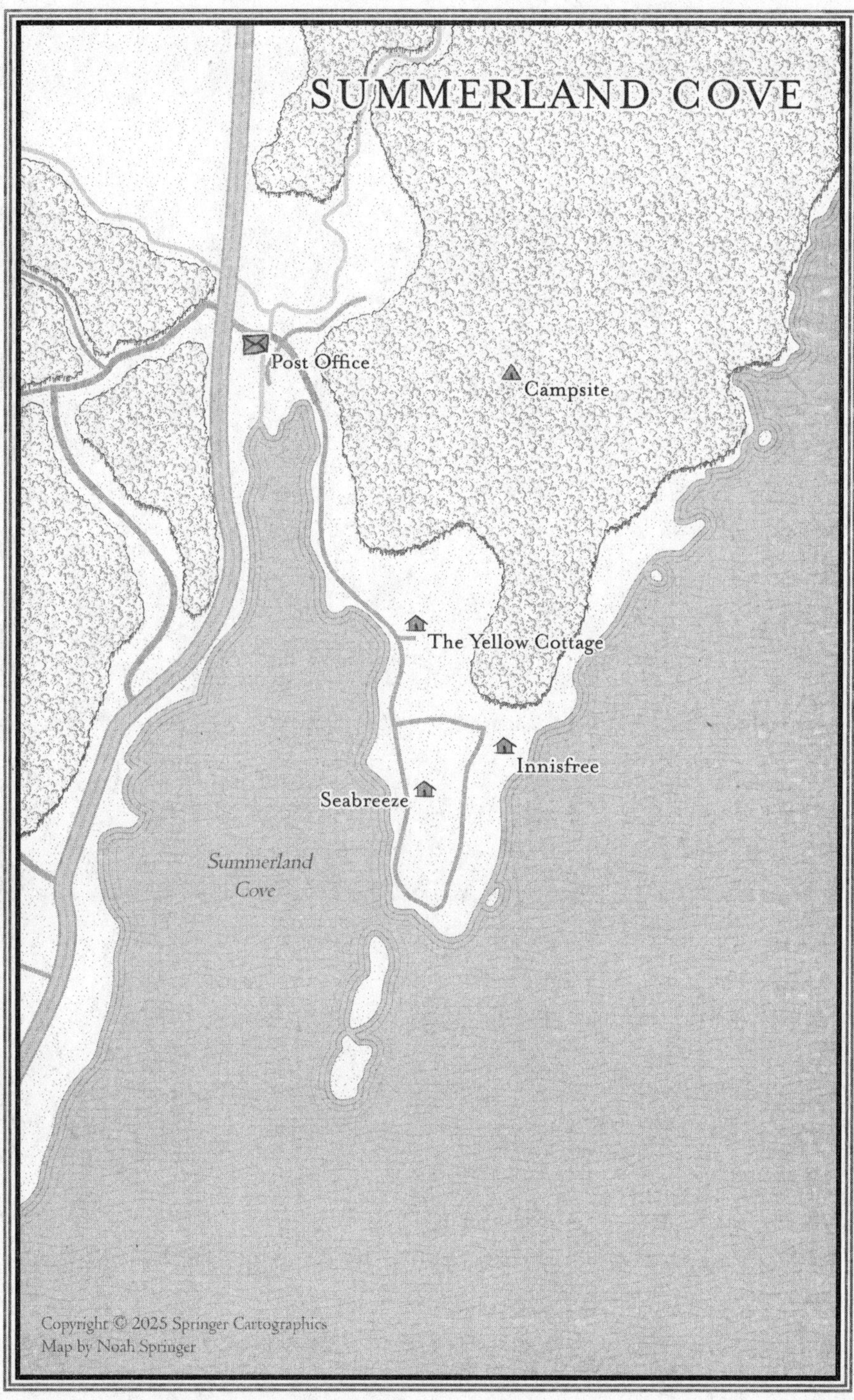
SUMMERLAND COVE
Post Office
Campsite
The Yellow Cottage
Innisfree
Seabreeze
Summerland
Cove
Copyright © 2025 Springer Cartographics
Map by Noah Springer

PART ONE

Even in the Quietest Moments

CHAPTER 1

Lindy

Saturday, July 24, 2010
2:45 p.m.

David had said he didn't want a big party for his fiftieth, but Lindy had blazed ahead planning one, anyway. The inspiration had struck one cold night in January, at home in Cranston. Their daughter Hailey's wedding was set for August 7 in Maine. Lindy's parents' fiftieth anniversary happened to fall the week before, and David's birthday was the week before that. "The summer of a lifetime," she'd told David as he'd crawled into bed. "Three parties, three weekends in a row. We'll get all the kids to spend two full weeks in Maine." He'd slipped off his glasses and sighed, kissed her good night, and switched off the lamp. She'd taken that as a yes.

Now it was go-time, D-Day, David's Day, as she'd been referring to it in her mind. The weather, thank God, was glorious—eighty-two and sunny, not a cloud in the sky. It was the perfect late-July-in-Maine day that people dreamed about all winter long.

"Where do you want the cake?" said Kate, David's younger sister, banging in the front door of the yellow cottage with a giant box from Hannaford, sunglasses nestled in her curly salt-and-pepper hair.

"On the table," Lindy said, finishing folding away an afghan from potential red wine spills. David's family had changed nothing about the yellow cottage's interior since the '70s. It was all knotty pine, threadbare mustard couches, and old rocking chairs, plus doilies and afghans crocheted by David's grandma, who'd been dead thirty years. Lindy didn't know how you could seriously go four decades without updating a room, but the soul-lifting view of the cove out the old single-pane picture window overshadowed both the outdated décor and the musty smell that lingered.

"I could've made a cake," Kate said, as she set the box down and pushed up the sleeves of the light L.L.Bean flannel she wore open over a grubby T-shirt and shorts.

If Kate had made the cake, it would've ended up sugar-free, gluten-free, entirely devoid of any semblance of birthday-cake-ness. Lindy and Kate had been best friends as kids, from the ages of ten to fourteen, but, since then, they'd never quite seen eye to eye.

"Oh, no, you're doing so much already!" Lindy said. "Thank you for going to town to pick it up. And, again, I really appreciate being able to hold the party here."

David's parents had bought the yellow cottage in 1973, when David was thirteen. Now that they were gone, David technically shared ownership with Kate and their younger brother, Josh, but since together the three siblings had twelve kids, it had always just made sense for David and Lindy and their four to stay at Lindy's family's nearby cottage, Innisfree, with Lindy's parents. They'd done so as much as they could every summer while the kids were growing up.

Lindy had been summering at Innisfree since before she was born, just as her mother had done before her.

But Innisfree would be the site of the anniversary party next week, and base of operations for Hailey's wedding the week after that. Lindy's mom, Greta, who was eighty-one now, had said that was "more than enough for one summer."

She had a point. Sometimes Lindy didn't know what she'd been thinking, to attempt to pull all this off at once. "It's really great of you guys," she emphasized to Kate, then laughed. "I think my mother might've had a breakdown, otherwise."

Kate shrugged and gave a little smile as she opened the cellophane-topped box. "The lettering sucks," she said. *Happy 50th, David!* was written in blue icing, drastically off-center, in lettering that appeared to have been crafted by an eight-year-old drunk on Kool-Aid. The attempt at a trio of balloons, off-center to the opposite side, more closely resembled a triumvirate of swimming sperm.

"Oh, God," Lindy said.

Kate laughed. "They said there was nothing they could do, given that the party's in a couple hours. Don't worry, he'll probably think it's funny."

Would he? Lindy still didn't know, she realized, after all these years.

The first time Lindy met David, she was ten years old.

Well, "met." More like "spotted" from the seat of her pink Schwinn Fair Lady as she rode past the yellow cottage.

Their enclave of summer cottages was known as "The Cove," but it was, more accurately, Summerland Cove Point, a small, rocky point lined on one side by a tidal cove and on the other by the Atlantic Ocean. The point was accessible only by turning off the main highway onto Summerland Cove Point Road, which, though not wide enough for two cars to pass, was officially "two-way" for its first half mile, before becoming a counterclockwise one-way loop, tracing the tip of the point, then connecting back up with itself again.

At ten, Lindy was allowed to ride from Innisfree all the way out to the highway, almost three-quarters of a mile. When she reached the post office on the corner there, she had to turn around and pedal back. As the damp, cool breeze ruffled her ponytail, to her right was the deep blue cove, rimmed in seaweed-covered rocks. On her left, she passed a half dozen cottages set back on large lots, then the Summerland Cove Point Association or "SCPA" clubhouse, a small one-story shingled building with a single clay tennis court out front. (As on all sunny mornings, Mr. and Mrs. Hastings were there, swatting a ball around and laughing.) Gulls swooped over the cove, crying. A heron stalked for fish in the shallows. In the distance across the water, the cars going past on the main highway were tiny, soundless, irrelevant, as if part of another world.

Lindy's tires crackled over gravel. At the inward bend of the road, barely visible below a rim of dark rocks, was the community beach, a tiny stretch of gritty sand just wide enough at high tide to lay out a towel, and across from that was the yellow cottage, which ten-year-old Lindy knew had recently sold. "To a family from Chicago," was the word around Summerland Cove. "Three kids—boy, girl, boy." (*David, Kate, and Josh,* in that order, Lindy would soon learn.)

She'd seen a station wagon with Illinois plates parked in front before, and now she spotted a skinny boy carrying a heavy box up the front steps. He was ignoring the younger girl who trailed him with a smaller box. Normally, Lindy might've stopped to try to make friends with the girl, but her eyes had fastened onto the boy. He had curly, dark brown hair and long legs, and he was wearing running shorts, a white T-shirt, Adidas sneakers.

It wasn't as if she had a feeling right then that she would marry him. It was just that he looked interesting, that was all.

After the yellow cottage, she'd usually have taken the cut-through part of the loop that led directly to Innisfree. Today, feeling wrought up or thoughtful or both, she rode the whole loop in the direction that cars traveled, skirting another half dozen old cottages—these were far more closely spaced—then curving around to pass the tall pine that stood watch over the rock formations and crashing waves at the point's end. Relishing the dampness of spray on her face, she curved again and stood on her pedals to power her way up the hill past five more cottages and into the woods. Innisfree was at the end of the loop, on the high ground, looking out at the ocean and Monhegan Island.

She leaned her bike against the porch rail and banged in the screen door. In the farthest room, her mother was practicing Chopin on the piano—as usual.

Lindy mulled it over till dinnertime, then suggested to her parents that they should probably invite the new people from Chicago over for drinks. (Her father had grown up in Chicago, and that was where Lindy's parents had met. Certainly, Lindy told her parents, they would have a lot to talk about.)

Greta put out deviled eggs. David's parents brought Kate along, so that Kate and Lindy—their mothers must've discussed it—could become friends, which they did, bonding over Boggle on a rainy afternoon. ("You two are the exact same age!" Mrs. Kauffman had told them excitedly, but Lindy was two months younger, a fact Kate never let her forget.)

Not until the summer David turned seventeen did he notice Lindy as more than his little sister's friend. Lindy, who was fourteen by then, knocked on the door of the yellow cottage to get Kate to come to the beach, but David answered and said Kate was sick in bed with a sore throat.

"Oh," Lindy said, wondering instantly if Kate had made good on her threats to kiss Andrew Thompson and ended up with mono as a result. Lindy's mother was always warning her about mono, calling it "the kissing disease," though Lindy had never kissed anyone yet. "Okay."

David looked Lindy up and down and swallowed. She liked the depth of his dark eyes, the handsome shape of his nose, the unruly curls of his mop of dark hair. "I'll come with you," he said.

Her heart made an involuntary little leap. Truth be told, she'd always had a tiny crush on him, which she kept deeply buried on account of Kate. If Kate ever talked about him (Lindy took care never to ask), Kate would say dismissive things like, "Oh, he's always off in his own world." Or, "He thinks he's so much smarter than the rest of us!" But, hanging around the Kauffman family's yellow cottage, Lindy had observed that David was kind to his mother, had excellent table manners, and told quiet jokes under his breath, though never at anybody else's expense. He took time to play tennis and go to the beach with his little brother, Josh. He took Josh and Kate out in the rowboat three times a week.

And, over these past few summers, Lindy had witnessed him with his nose buried in *The Red Badge of Courage, Walden, The Catcher in the Rye.* Were these assigned summer reading for school? No matter. He was clearly smart. Ambitious. One rainy day, when Lindy and Kate were playing Boggle in the yellow cottage's front room, she'd seen him, engrossed in a copy of *The Human Condition,* walk all the way down the stairs and to the kitchen, grab a box of Frosted Flakes out of the cupboard, fill a bowl, splash milk over top, put everything away, grab a spoon, eat the bowl of cereal while standing at the counter, rinse the bowl at the sink, and walk back upstairs again, without ever stopping reading.

She was certain he had never observed her in return.

Needing time to get her bearings now, Lindy gave a little toss of her waist-length blonde hair, which she'd taken to ironing flat each morning and which, somewhere deep down, underneath all her typical fourteen-year-old-girl's prosaic (as her mother put it) insecurities, she knew was her best feature. (This despite the shock of her best friend's older brother suddenly regarding her as a real girl—could that be true? Or was she misinterpreting? But no, because already she imagined she could hear Kate: *Ewwww.* For once, she decided not to care what Kate would say.)

Finally, she'd shrugged. "Whatever," she'd said, though she hadn't been able to hold back a smile.

"Hey, Mom!" Cody said, all six foot two of him bursting in through the yellow cottage's front door. The youngest of Lindy and David's four children, Cody had recently turned twenty-one. He took after Lindy's father physically, big and blond and athletic, but while Lindy's father had always been circumspect, Cody entered every room like a cheerful hurricane.

Lindy forgot the horrible cake, grinned at the sight of him. "Hey, sweetie!"

"Where's Dad?" Cody gave Lindy a quick, warm hug, then was off for the kitchen. "What have we got to eat?"

"Check with Aunt Kate." Kate had insisted that she and her five kids, who ranged in age from eight to eighteen, would take over in the kitchen for the evening so Lindy could mingle. Kate's whole family, including her husband, Matt, were in for the party from their farm, which was inland just an hour. All summer long, all of them came and went as they pleased from The Cove, though due to their work they didn't usually spend long stretches. Kate raised goats and sold artisanal cheese—not at all what Lindy would've predicted for her when they were young.

Now Lindy, overhearing Cody and his aunt and cousins greeting each other enthusiastically in the other room, frowned down at her watch.

Nearly three o'clock.

David had called her at nine this morning and said he was on his way, so he should've been here by 1:30. Two, at the latest, if there was traffic—which there no doubt was on a summer Saturday.

But three o'clock? Could there have been *that* much traffic?

Maybe he'd stopped somewhere. Even a meant-to-be-quick stop at the New Hampshire liquor store invariably led to him getting lost in the wine selection for an hour.

She looked up to see Eli, who was making his typical quieter entrance in Cody's wake. Two years older and four inches shorter than his brother, Eli took after David: curly dark hair, thoughtful dark eyes, and very thin, the exact way David had been when he was young. "Hey, sweetie," Lindy said. "How was traffic?"

Eli hugged her awkwardly. "Not that bad."

As they pulled apart, Lindy frowned again at her watch. "Then Dad should definitely be here. And where are your sisters?" Her oldest, Hailey, had been assigned to pick up Eli's twin, Emma, at the bus station in Portland.

"Em's bus doesn't get in till three," Eli said. "About now."

Last Lindy had heard, Emma had been scheduled to arrive in Portland at one. Today of all days, Lindy thought, Emma could've done the unpredictable thing of *not* changing her plans. "You mean they won't get here till four thirty? The party starts at five!"

"She had to take the train from New York to Boston first, then wait for the bus." Eli always defended his twin. It was sweet, really. Predictable. Emma had always been the more troublesome of the pair, Eli the more inclined to follow the rules. Eli liked to try to make everything make sense, even things that didn't.

Emma liked things to be messy.

Lindy sighed. At least Emma and Eli had both been able to get the full two weeks surrounding the parties and wedding off, Emma from her job as an assistant designer for a fashion line in New York, Eli from his research assistantship in Cambridge. Both were planning to spend the whole time at The Cove, and so was Hailey. Cody would be traveling back and forth to Newport, where he'd gotten his dream job as a lifeguard this summer.

Cody came back into the room, his mouth full of half a slider, the other half of which he held in his hand. "Dad probably stopped off for a hike."

"Those are for the party, Cody. And that would show poor judgment on your father's part, which he is not known for, in general."

Eli chuckled under his breath, as if to disagree. Lindy hadn't seen her older son in three months, and now she remembered he'd recently developed a way of making her feel like she wasn't as smart as he was. Harvard could probably be blamed, but she wasn't going to stand for it. "Do not disrespect your father, Eli. Yes, he sometimes loses track of time, but he's not irresponsible."

Eli smirked, seemingly okay with being corrected on this point. "I know, Mom."

Cody swallowed his huge bite of sandwich. "But, Mom, you know Dad's, like, constitutionally unable to drive all the way here without stopping somewhere to 'breathe in' the Maine woods." This was true. David, a runner when he was young, had injured his knee in his mid-twenties. He could no longer run, but he went hiking at every opportunity and found the woods, especially in Maine, irresistible.

Eli pounded his chest and held out his hand, an imitation of David's favorite dramatic gesture. "'Smell that salt air, kids!'"

Lindy stifled a smile at the spot-on mimicry and gave her best disapproving-mom shake of her head. "Boys, go to Innisfree, get cleaned up, and say hi to your grandma and grandpa, then walk back. I need your help."

"Sure, Mom." Cody disappeared into the kitchen again, drawing more cheers from his cousins. Eli and Lindy barely had time to exchange glances before Cody was back with another slider, already half eaten. "See you soon!" he called, banging out the door. Eli, with another amused smile, shrugged, gave Lindy a little wave, and followed his brother.

Lindy looked at her watch again. Where *was* David, honestly?

CHAPTER 2

Hailey

Saturday, July 24, 2010
3 p.m.

Hailey leaned against her Mazda Protegé in the sunny lot at the Portland bus station, biting her pinkie nail.

Damn it. She had to stop biting her nails. There would be hand photos for the wedding.

If there was a wedding.

All right, of course there was going to be a wedding, she thought. A glance at her oval solitaire diamond ring reminded her of the reality, though the three-inch binder stuffed with contracts and samples and to-do lists currently in the trunk of her car should have been enough.

She was just irritated that Noah wasn't coming to her father's birthday party tonight at The Cove. The date had been on the calendar for months. Now he said he couldn't get time off. "A Saturday night in July, babe? Seriously? When I've already put in for our wedding two weeks from now?"

Hailey thought he should've made the party a priority. It wasn't every day her father turned fifty, and even though his actual birthday wasn't till tomorrow—a smaller dinner with just family was planned—Noah wasn't coming up then, either. He worked three to eleven, the party and the dinner were both planned for five o'clock, and Summerland Cove was an hour and a half drive from Portland. "So, no, I can't just 'pop in,'" he'd told Hailey.

The restaurant where he worked was called Bleu, for reasons unknown to Hailey. It was an "up-and-coming" place, according to a review that had run last month in the *Portland Press-Herald,* which had also called it "intimate" and "pleasing." It seated only thirty people at a time. Hailey had never eaten there; it was booked out for months. Noah was the sous chef, underneath the head chef, Robin. They had no backup other than the horrible "Alexandra," whom Hailey had never met but who, according to Noah, would steal his job the second he showed weakness. Hence why he could not take a night off for the party. "I'll be lucky if I still have my job when I get back from our wedding, babe."

Hailey had recently discovered that every Friday and Saturday night, Noah, Alexandra, and Robin all had drinks together after work "to bond," "to strengthen the team," which explained why he often didn't get home till after one a.m.—and was a bit drunk when he did. Hailey did not like Alexandra, needless to say.

She'd only just learned about the late-night drinks because she had only moved in with Noah two weeks ago, after leaving behind both her legislative aide job and the apartment in Augusta where she'd lived since finishing college two years ago. She'd had it all planned out like clockwork: Move to Portland in early July, get settled in at Noah's apartment before heading up to Summerland Cove for Dad's birthday party. Mostly hang out there for a full two weeks, both to make her mother happy and to prep for the wedding. (Her mom had been making a *huge* deal about how this would be "the last summer for them all to be together" and had basically insisted that all the kids stay the entire two weeks. Only Cody had been unable to get the time off work.)

So, Hailey would be at The Cove through Grandma and Grandpa's anniversary party, then all the way through to her own wedding. She and Noah would spend two nights in Bar Harbor for a "honeymoon"—he'd promised Bali when "things settled down a bit"—then head back to Portland, where Noah would go back to the grind at Bleu while Hailey started law school at the University of Southern Maine.

She didn't think things would ever settle down a bit.

She knew she should be excited, but she'd been nauseous instead, barely able to eat, the entire last two weeks. Noah would bring home extraordinary-looking leftovers from work, and she wouldn't be able to stand even the smell of them. Her migraines were worse than ever, too.

Biting her pinkie nail again, she decided maybe the problem was that Noah was just too good-looking now. He'd been squarely in her league when they'd met, but, after moving to Portland, he'd started going to the gym six days a week and now bragged he'd lost fifteen pounds of fat and gained thirty of "pure muscle." It was hard to trust a man who looked like an underwear model, even if you'd known him back when he didn't.

Who was this Alexandra, anyway? Noah'd been working with her for a year. Why hadn't he introduced her to Hailey?

Okay, well, probably because Hailey hadn't been around. Finding time to spend together this past year had been a challenge, between her working long hours during the week and his insane weekend schedule, plus the hour drive each way. Not to mention, she'd been swamped with wedding to-dos! She and her mom had been working for a year off a seven-page checklist they'd grabbed from the internet, marking each task with an *H* or an *L* to indicate which of them would run point. With the wedding now only two weeks out, they were down to the last page. *Prepare toasts. Finalize shot list. Hair and makeup trial!*

In other words, Hailey's dedication to planning the moment when her life and Noah's would become one had made him feel more distant than ever.

Ironic.

On the bright side, Hailey had loved how happy planning the wedding seemed to make her mom—which was why she had told her mom exactly zero percent of how she was feeling currently.

She was also *not* about to confess to her dad. An unfortunate side effect of the wedding-planning madness (as her siblings had started calling it; Hailey didn't know which of them had started it) was that she'd talked to her dad a whole lot less this past year. The last time she'd called his cell, he'd answered with, "Hello, this is Wallet Central," which made Hailey feel terrible, because it was true that every time she called she needed another check for another deposit (flowers, tents, chairs, officiant, caterer, DJ, the list went on). Things would be crazy tonight—her mom said there were, like, a hundred people coming—but tomorrow Hailey would carve out some time to really talk with her dad, try to bridge the gap that had formed between them these past months. She knew he'd just been joking with that wallet comment, and she missed him.

She glanced at her phone for the time. *Shit,* she thought. Where was Emma? Their mom was gonna kill them, if they were late for Dad's party.

But when she looked up, there was her sister, strolling coolly out from the glass double doors of the station. Emma, good New Yorker that she was now, was decked out head to toe in black—tank, short skirt, fishnet tights, combat boots—and, with her petite frame, spiky dark, short curls, and tattooed little arms, she looked adorable, as ever. "Such a little pixie," their grandma always said of Emma, the implication (to Hailey) being that Hailey, at five foot nine, was gargantuan.

("You just have bigger bones, like your grandpa!" Greta had told her, which hadn't exactly helped.)

Suddenly feeling very Laura-Ashley-frumpy in her floral sundress from Gap, Hailey waved. "Emma! Hey!"

Emma nodded and gave a cool smile, then turned to a gangly, glamorous young woman with a curtain of straight black hair who was walking just behind her, rolling a big metallic black suitcase. Emma said something to the woman, then reached for her hand.

A ping of pain sounded in Hailey's temple. She hadn't heard anything about Emma bringing a guest. She didn't even know Emma was *seeing* anybody. And if Hailey hadn't heard about it that meant their mom didn't know, either.

Wait. Maybe they'd just met on the bus? Emma did work pretty quickly sometimes.

Either way. There was already barely room enough at Innisfree for everybody to sleep. And, while most of the family had grown used to never knowing who'd be the next romantic lead in the revolving-door drama of Emma's life, since Emma'd been bringing home girls *and* boys for years, Hailey was pretty sure that Grandma and Grandpa still didn't know that Emma was bi. Sure, they'd probably end up being fine with it, but it seemed like a lot to spring on a couple of octogenarians right when hundreds of people were about to descend on them for Hailey's mom's crazy series of parties.

Emma, halfway to the car, stopped, turned, and stood on her tiptoes to kiss the woman, who passionately kissed her back—it didn't seem they had just met on the bus—and another problem dawned on Hailey. At Innisfree, she and Emma shared a bedroom.

The other two bedrooms, the ones that faced the water, were occupied by their parents and grandparents. Their brothers slept in the attic. Grandma didn't like for anyone to sleep on the couch in the living room, because she didn't want "the peace of my treasured early mornings" interrupted, so anyone who dared to, she'd shake awake at four a.m. or something ridiculous to watch the sunrise with her.

That meant the only halfway reasonable alternative for sleeping was the room they referred to as "The Closet." Next to the girls' room, it was windowless, with barely enough room to walk past the lumpy twin cot that was wedged inside.

Hailey had planned to ask Emma to sleep in there so she and Noah could have the girls' bedroom. Now that they were only two weeks away from getting married, this would surely be allowed? (Last summer, the one night Noah'd visited, Grandma had made him sleep in The Closet, even though he and Hailey were already engaged. Emma had hounded Hailey relentlessly to sneak over and join him, but Hailey hadn't wanted to get in trouble with Grandma. "You are *so lame*," Emma had declared, before flopping over and going to sleep.)

Come to think of it, maybe last summer's debacle explained why Noah "couldn't get off work."

But now that he wasn't coming, and Emma had brought this woman—

whom Emma would probably pretend was "just a friend" to get past Grandma's no-unmarried-lovers-in-the-house rule—no doubt Hailey would wind up relegated to The Closet.

She sighed. Still, she was happy to see her sister—it had been since Christmas—and, as Emma and the woman approached, holding hands, Hailey moved forward, poised to reach out for a hug.

"Hey, Bridezilla," Emma said, with an impish grin.

Hailey felt that like a jab to the stomach, but she laughed, hugged her, and said, "Hey, brat," even as a weird certainty dropped onto her with what felt like an actual thud: This weekend was not going to be *anything* like what she'd hoped.

CHAPTER 3

Greta

Saturday, July 24, 2010
3 p.m.

The thing about life was, you had to control it.

Especially when you were at Innisfree.

Greta had never truly liked it here. Her mother had named the place after the Yeats poem, but to Greta it had not lived up to the promise of peace—not for the past sixty-nine years, anyway.

But if the beds were made with tight corners and quilts you could bounce a quarter off of, the porch corners swept free of cobwebs, the table set with a vase of hydrangeas, the kitchen spotless, her extensive perennial gardens thoroughly weeded—she did love the way the hummingbirds and butterflies flitted among the liatris, the salvia, and the purple coneflowers in the mornings—then she could feel she had regained dominion over the place. Strange that, after all these years, trying to control it all was still a thing she felt the need to do, not just upon first arriving for the summer, but every single day she was here. But maybe it explained why she'd kept coming back, summer after summer, all these years. That odd satisfaction she got just from keeping the place in order. The triumph of showing that it could not defeat her.

The ocean, which ceaselessly caressed the rocks below, was always there to remind her that even things you thought would last forever never actually did.

Not even—it turned out—Innisfree itself, which Greta was planning to put on the market the day after Hailey's wedding.

Lindy didn't know a thing about that.

There were a lot of things that Greta'd been keeping from Lindy lately.

"Tom?" she said, looking across the table at her husband. They were eating lunch at three o'clock, because things were slipping out of her control more and more every day.

Lindy had been over at the yellow cottage since late morning getting ready for the party, and Greta had gone out to the garden. She'd lost track of time! (She never used to "lose track of time." Even the notion had felt impossible; she'd always been suspicious when people made the claim.) Then she'd had to arrange some fresh hydrangeas. Put in another load of wash. Note down the messages that had been left on the answering machine while she was outside. (Fortunately, Tom never answered the phone anymore.) Three people had called to say they were going to be late for the party, and two weren't coming. One message was just static—people never understood that their cell phones didn't work in this part of Maine—and she deleted it. Only then, with everything in order in her mind, could she tackle making lunch.

Not that its lateness truly mattered. Neither she nor Tom had much of an appetite these days. He might forget to eat entirely, if she didn't remind him.

Even now, seated at the table! He was staring into the distance, out across the living room toward the windows and the ocean, blue eyes watery behind his glasses. His white hair was neatly combed, his L.L.Bean shirt and khakis pressed-looking. All Greta's doing. She had made an entire platter of BLTs, which he loved, and she had set the big sturdy barnboard table in the dining area for just the two of them with new bright blue dishes and paisley cloth napkins, a mixed bouquet in a blue vase. Lindy liked to keep Innisfree "freshened up" and was always buying dishes and napkins, lamps and tablecloths and sheets, plus the occasional end table or little desk at a yard sale, which she'd spend a sunny day or two refinishing outside. A couple years ago, she'd gone to the L.L.Bean Home Store in Freeport and picked out a new couch and chair for the living room in a pretty blue-and-white pattern, with coordinating throw pillows and blankets and even a large, braided rug. Greta didn't mind—she knew how happy these small tasks made Lindy—but she was glad that Lindy had never suggested switching out this table, which had been Greta's mother's, long ago.

Tom didn't appear to notice the half sandwich growing cold on his plate. He didn't respond to his name, either. "Tom!" she said again, louder, and finally he looked at her, mildly startled, and she felt terrible. It was so hard to stay patient, as the kids would say, *twenty-four seven.* She inhaled, took a gentler tone. "Eat your sandwich, please, darling."

Obediently, he picked up his BLT and took a bite. He began chewing, and a look of pleasure came over his face, as if he was remembering the surprising fact that this was something he liked—or perhaps he was experiencing the pleasure of the taste without actually remembering ever having eaten a BLT before.

Greta suddenly wanted to cry. She ached for the music which was absent from her life these days. The arthritis in her hands made it too painful for her to play piano, and she didn't have the wherewithal even to put an album on the stereo. Even the *choosing* of one felt like too much.

She busied herself cutting her own sandwich into bite-size pieces—though, oh, she *was not* hungry—blinking back tears, hoping today, for the party, would be a good day for Tom. Hoping Lindy still wouldn't notice how bad he was getting.

He'd always been quiet, polite. His natural sweetness seemed only to have increased with the progression of the disease. So had his desire to immerse himself in research, in writing. He seemed to take such comfort in these familiar acts that Greta no longer complained—"You're *retired,*" she'd been reminding him for the last decade—when he spent most of his days at his desk in their bedroom, which he'd piled high with his favorite books and notebooks. Every night he reported great breakthroughs, and every morning it broke her heart to glance at his notes and see that few of them even made sense. "It goes this way sometimes," the doctor had said. The alternative, Greta understood, was rage.

She could tell, this past week, that it had puzzled him sometimes when Lindy walked into the room and said "Hey, Dad!" and kissed his forehead, but he would pat her hand (oh, thank God for that steady, good-natured way he'd always had) and Lindy would head for the coffee, or the refrigerator, rambling on about one of her parties or one of the kids. Greta wasn't trying to keep track of details, not on those particular subjects, not right now. All she was trying to do was keep Innisfree, herself, and her husband under control so that her daughter could have these parties she wanted to have, because, after this summer, nothing was ever going to be the same.

He'd been diagnosed in March. The party plans had already all been set. Hailey's wedding had been the first thing on the calendar, then Lindy had added the fiftieth anniversary party for them (a sweet thought back in January; a nightmare to imagine now), and the birthday party for David. In March, Tom was still well enough to talk it over with Greta. "We can't ruin Lindy's plans," he'd said. "I don't think we should even tell her. Not till afterward. All right?" He had looked at Greta with such love and pleading, how could she even begin to think otherwise? And truly Greta had agreed, whole-heartedly! She'd actually believed that by late July—only four months away—he'd still be fine. She'd thought they'd have months and months, possibly years, to discuss their old favorite albums, concertos she'd played on the stage, the news, the constellations, the gardens, the grandkids, the latest exhibit at the Met and what was playing at the movies at Lincoln Center.

Things had progressed much more quickly than she'd imagined possible.

Yet, it had seemed—to her alone now, because Tom could no longer weigh in—too late to tell Lindy that they needed to change their plans.

He still had good moments. He'd had at least two conversations with Lindy that Greta had overheard from the kitchen, and yes, Lindy had done most of the talking, jabbering on about the parties, but Greta thought he'd seemed to understand everything that was being said, and

Lindy (it did seem unbelievable, but she was quite distracted with these parties) evidently hadn't noticed a thing.

He would remember their grandchildren, Greta had to believe.

Not a minute later, though, Cody and Eli banged in the side door, and Greta saw panic in Tom's eyes as he dropped what was left of his sandwich back onto his plate. Cody (my word, he was a *giant* now) came toward them, grinning, bellowing, "Grandma! Grandpa!" Greta hopped up and went around to stand beside Tom, draping her arm over his shoulders. She could feel the tension in him, but he evidently trusted her enough to realize that the young men who'd just barged in must not be a true threat.

"Tom," she said. "Look, it's Cody! And Eli. Why don't you give your grandsons a hug?"

In this way, she managed the greetings, then quickly suggested to Tom that he go upstairs for a nap or a bit more work on his book. He shuffled off, seeming relieved, as Cody grabbed a sandwich from the platter.

"Is Grandpa okay?" Eli said, with a worried look.

"Yeah, he seems off," Cody said, with his mouth half full.

Greta would've scolded Cody's manners, but she didn't have it in her just now. "He's just tired. He's been working so hard on his book!" she said, bustling to clear away the dirty plates, and she didn't know how she was going to get Tom through a party, let alone these next two weeks, if the sight of his grandsons—whom he clearly did *not* know—had unnerved him so.

CHAPTER 4

Lindy

Saturday, July 24, 2010
5:30 p.m.

Lindy's parents weren't there yet by 5:30, which was weird, but what was even weirder was that David wasn't there yet, either.

His birthday party was happening without him.

Everyone *else* was there. As predicted, pretty much the whole Cove had turned out, filling the downstairs of the yellow cottage and spilling out onto the lawn, into the sublime evening. It was a perfect seventy-eight degrees now, with a light breeze, the reflection of the lowering sun skipping and rippling across the cove, all the way to where the highway lined the wooded mainland. The tide was going out, leaving rocks and mounds of seaweed exposed, the smell of salt and lobster in the air. Ducks paddled. A cormorant dove for a fish. A few small, brave boats bobbed on moorings, though the cove was notoriously vulnerable to storms. The American flag that the Seversons always flew at their large cottage across the way—the only house on the water side of Summerland Cove Point Road, at the slight bend that made room for it—snapped in the breeze.

The happy crowd's laughter and conversation surely carried throughout The Cove, even across to the mainland.

Was David seriously not going to *show up*?

Lindy had tried his cell phone three times from the yellow cottage's landline. No answer. She'd left one angry voicemail and one worried one. The third time, she'd just hung up. She'd even tried their Cranston house phone twice, in case somehow he'd never left home, but there was no answer there, either.

Had he planned to stop somewhere on the drive up? She had no idea. They'd talked for only a minute this morning, and that qualified as their second-longest call of the ten days she'd been here. There was no cell signal at The Cove, not for miles around, and Innisfree's landline phone was beside the stairs in the middle of the living room, which meant anything said there carried to every room in the house. And although it wasn't as if, at her age, Lindy kept secrets from her parents, it had always been understood at Innisfree that long phone calls were impolite.

Also, she never wanted to give her mother any whiff of even a chance that David had displeased her. Greta had it in her, if the mood struck, to poke and prod him, to blow things totally out of proportion, and it was his birthday, for heaven's sake. That was why, when David had called last night to say he was too tired to drive up as planned and would come this morning instead, all Lindy had said was, "Okay, honey," even though she didn't really think it *was* okay. She'd wanted to have a night with him before all the kids showed up. She'd planned to give him one of his birthday presents, though his actual birthday wasn't till Sunday.

It was also why, this morning, when he'd called at nine to say he was just about to leave, all she'd said was, "Great!" although she'd thought he should've been on his way at least two hours earlier.

Lindy, deep down, had known he didn't want this party.

But not to show up wouldn't be like him! Even when they both knew she was charging ahead with something that maybe she ought not to, he always ended up supporting her in it.

She tried to tell herself again: Maybe he really had just stopped off somewhere, lost track of time. Or maybe the traffic really had been terrible. Yes, the boys had arrived on time, traveling the same route, but Cody drove much faster than David, as a rule, weaving in and out of lanes to skate through traffic. David stayed steadfast in the center, going just below the speed limit in his Subaru.

She tried to occupy her mind with other, smaller concerns. Noah hadn't come with Hailey, which didn't seem good, while Emma had brought a new girlfriend, Reese. The tall, gorgeous young woman had shaken Lindy's hand with an unnerving level of earnestness, and when she said, "Reese Kobayashi, ma'am, I've heard so many good things about you," it was with the air of a journalist about to ask a series of soul-destroying questions, which made Lindy worry that Emma might not exactly be in safe hands. But before she could think what to say, Kate had tugged on Lindy's arm and dragged her off to the kitchen with an urgent question about the fruit. Kate said her kids had been driving her crazy—hindering more than helping, when it came down to it—so she'd sent them outside.

That the kitchen crew had abdicated gave Lindy an excuse to busy herself with the food. She put out fresh platters of sloppy joes and a fresh bowl of pasta salad, as Kate cut up another watermelon. The giant crockpot of baked beans was still half full. Marjorie Westfield arrived bearing one of her famous cookie cakes, a thick chocolate chip concoction topped with a drizzle of caramel sauce, large chocolate chunks, and a scattering of toasted almonds. Lindy had to rearrange the food table to make room for it, while Marjorie stood by in her summer uniform—only the colors varied, day by day—of crisp blouse and capris, statement necklace, ballet flats, and Chanel No. 5, her hair in an artfully tousled silver bob. Today's ensemble was white with black accents—black jewelry, belt, and flats; white shirt and capris. "Oh, dear," Marjorie said. "I didn't mean to cause a problem, but I know everyone expects the cookie cake."

It was true that Marjorie had brought a cookie cake to every party at The Cove for at least the last twenty years, even when the party wasn't officially a potluck. According to Lindy's mom, the contribution was more officious than gracious, but Greta's view was tainted by a longstanding feud she had with Marjorie. It was a feud older than Lindy, which Greta had never been willing to explain.

By 6:30, the crystal fruit salad bowl contained only dregs and pink juice, and Marjorie's cookie cake was reduced to crumbs. "I've never been at a birthday party where the guest of honor wasn't!" Lloyd Ralston said, elbowing Lindy, grinning and laughing to show a mouthful of pasta salad. Lindy had known Lloyd all her life—he and his wife, Anne, were friendly with her parents—and had never liked him less than in this moment.

The fact was, "traffic" couldn't really explain why David still wasn't here, could it? Neither, it seemed to Lindy, could losing track of time.

When she retreated to the kitchen again, Kate met her eyes and said, "I'm getting worried."

David and Kate's younger brother, Josh, had followed Lindy in. Josh and his wife, Marielle, lived in Chicago with their three young boys. Marielle, a teacher, drove out with the boys every summer to spend most of it at The Cove, while Josh flew in and out, managing to spend at least a couple of weeks every July. "I just tried his cell again," Josh said now, brown eyes soft with concern, tugging at the collar of his white polo shirt as if it was choking him. Six years younger than David, he was a shorter, stockier version of his brother, and his dark hair hadn't yet started to go gray. "No answer."

"I'm getting worried, too," Lindy admitted, though, when she looked out and through the crowd to the front door, her parents, at least, were walking in.

At seven, she decided to cut the cake. Cody had just returned from checking the answering machine at Innisfree and reported, "No messages." The food was almost gone, and people were getting tired. There was a general air of confusion—"He's *still* not here?"—bemused laughter. Everyone had known David a long time. "We always knew he was an odd duck," Winnie Taylor told Lindy, in what seemed the best summation of the crowd's sentiments. "But this seems *very* odd."

So Lindy lit the candles—just an oversized five and zero, because to put fifty candles on even a large cake had seemed to Lindy a little cruel. She led everyone in singing "Happy Birthday," managing to act as if the whole thing—David not being there (and, God, the terrible-looking cake)—was a giant joke, even as her stomach ached. Cody blew out the candles, and everyone cheered. Slicing and serving the cake onto tiny blue paper plates took her a good twenty minutes.

Afterward, he still wasn't there. Outside, the sun was beginning to set, angling to cast a spotlight across the water, shifting it to a darker shade of blue.

Her mother came up to her, looking worried. "Honey, we're going to go home now."

"David still isn't here!"

"I know, but your father's tired. I'm sure David will be here soon. Your father and I will celebrate with him at the family dinner tomorrow."

Lindy huffed out a frustrated sigh. "Fine." It wasn't her mother she was mad at, after all, not this time. She waved goodbye to her father from across the room. He did look tired; her waving didn't even catch his eye. Her mother looked tired, too, come to think of it. Greta's long white hair was straggling—highly unusual—from its customary elegant twist. But her pink button-up shirt and white linen capris (undoubtedly from Talbots) were still crisp and wrinkle-free, while Lindy's white jeans were spattered with watermelon juice and her black T-shirt had a smear of white frosting across it. She'd never been able to live up to her mother when it came to being flawless.

She watched as Greta wove her way toward the front door through the crowded room, smiling at everyone but shaking her head slightly whenever anyone tried to stop her to talk. That seemed unusual, too—except in the case of Marjorie Westfield, of course, whom Greta had avoided at all costs for Lindy's whole life.

As for the rest of it, Lindy had to remind herself: Her mom was eighty-one now, and her dad was eighty-three. Of course they might get tired a little easier than they had even last summer. Lindy watched her mother take hold of her father's arm and willfully lead him out, then felt a stab of regret that she hadn't said so much as hello to him all evening, busy as she'd been with the food, with saying hello to everyone else.

With trying to keep her panic at bay.

She sneaked into the back bedroom, where there was a telephone, and tried David's cell again.

No answer.

Eight o'clock.

The sunset was painting the sky over the cove in swaths of orange and purple, the air was cooling, and the crowd was drifting away. The garbage can was full of paper plates with remnants of white frosting. Everyone said the cake, despite its appearance, had been delicious. Lindy hadn't wanted any. She'd gone into the kitchen, tried to focus on tidying up. The kids must've been keeping an eye on her, because they followed her in.

"I bet he stopped for a hike, then got hungry and stopped to eat," Cody said, as he grabbed a leftover slider from the platter nearby.

"That doesn't even make sense," Hailey argued, with a toss of her long blonde hair. "He wouldn't *do* that."

"He might," Emma said, tugging at a thread at the hem of her black miniskirt.

"But even if he did, he would *call*," Hailey insisted.

"That's true," Eli said. He ran a hand through his dark curls.

"Yeah, why hasn't he called?" Cody said, through a mouthful of slider.

In that moment, Lindy wanted to kill David. How dare he do this to their children? Not show up, leave them all to worry!

But Hailey was right. He *wouldn't* do that.

Oh, God. He'd been in an accident.

That was the only explanation. Incapacitated, unconscious, he wouldn't be able to call.

(Dead? No. Lindy would not allow herself to think that.)

Yes. He had to be at some hospital somewhere between here and

Cranston—Providence, Boston, Portsmouth, Portland?—unconscious! Hurt! And she was here serving *cake*?

She needed to check her cell phone for messages. A hospital might have been able to find her number in his cell. Or access his medical records, where she was listed as his emergency contact. (Though, God, probably with just the Cranston phone number!)

"I've got to check my cell phone," she told her kids.

"He wouldn't call your cell phone," Cody said, folding his big arms. "He knows you don't get signal here."

"I know, but—"

Understanding dawned on Hailey's face. "Oh!" Her eyes filled with sudden tears.

Lindy hugged her tightly. "I know we don't want to think the worst."

"Crap," Emma said. Then she said the word five more times. Lindy saw Eli take a step closer to his twin, and it wasn't clear which of them needed comfort more.

"I'll drive you to town, Mom," Cody said. When she looked up at him, his jaw was square, and he seemed more grown-up—like a man, not a boy—than she'd ever seen him. "So you can check your phone."

Everyone wanted to come along and check their own phones, too, just in case. Kate and her husband, Matt, and Josh and his wife, Marielle, all wide-eyed now that they were coming to terms with the idea that this might not just be "David being David," said they'd hold down the fort, see the dwindling party through. Cody ran over to get his Jeep from Innisfree, and within five minutes they were on the road, Lindy riding shotgun, Hailey and Eli in the back. Emma, not wanting to leave Reese behind in a crowd of strangers, had given Eli her phone and passcode. They drove in silence in the twilight through the woods, windows down, wind whipping their hair, phones in their hands. Fifteen minutes later, as they drove into signal range, the phones started to ding, ding, ding, ding. Each of them dove into retrieving their messages—there were voicemails, texts!

Lindy had two voicemails, and she dialed in.

Both were spam. Goddamn it.

"I don't have anything from him, Mom," said Hailey.

"Me, either," said Eli. "Neither does Emma."

"Hold on," said Cody, and he pulled off onto a side street and stopped the Jeep. (Lindy couldn't contain a flare of pride at what seemed uncharacteristic behavior for her youngest: *So safety-minded!*) In the lowering darkness, his phone lit up in his hand as he activated it and scrolled through. Then he let out a sigh. "Nope."

They all sat in silence a moment, then Eli's voice came from the back seat. "What do we do now, Mom?" he said, sounding small.

She had no idea.

She heard Hailey sniff back tears. Felt the tension of Cody and Eli, too.

She had to think of something.

She told Hailey and Eli to take turns calling David's cell phone. He would answer for them, if he could. Somehow, she thought there was still a chance: He just hadn't wanted the party, he'd decided not to come, he was avoiding her calls because he knew she'd be mad at him. It was certainly preferable to thinking he was dead in a ditch somewhere. And, yes, she would be furious.

She told Cody to drive to the hospital.

"He's not answering, Mom," said Hailey from the back, and Lindy straightened her spine to keep from starting to cry.

She didn't expect to find him there—at the small local hospital ER—but somehow her heart was still in her throat as she ran inside the whooshing double glass doors and up to the glassed-in reception desk, asking breathlessly if by any chance they'd had a David Kauffman come in.

And somehow her heart still sank when the answer was no.

The helpful lady behind the desk, after a painfully slow search through an old-fashioned filing cabinet, handed over a printed list of all the ERs in New England. The kids had parked the car and come inside, and, as they gathered around, Lindy shaking her head gently to tell them, *No, not here,* she noted vaguely that this was the quietest ER waiting room she'd ever been in. It was empty, in fact. Just further proof, as far as she was concerned, that Midcoast Maine was heaven; just another reason why she couldn't wait to retire to Innisfree year-round with David someday—God, she hoped, hoped, hoped. They'd been talking about it for years. He just had to be okay.

"I have a list!" she told the kids, holding it up, and they huddled together to look.

"That's a lot of hospitals," Cody said.

"Here," Eli said, grabbing the pages out of Lindy's hand. He borrowed a highlighter from the receptionist and sat down. It took him one minute flat to highlight all the hospitals along the route from Cranston and tear the list into four pieces. Mechanically, they called every highlighted number, one by one by one, the beeps of their dialing and their voices filling the waiting room. "David Kauffman? . . . No?"

"No?"

"Are you sure?"

"No? Okay, thank you."

Finally, they sat there, defeated, and looked at one another.

"Well, this is good news, right?" Lindy managed to say, but the truth was reflected in her children's eyes. No matter how perturbed David might've been with Lindy, he would not have just not shown up for his own party, knowing that everyone was waiting for him. Especially knowing that his kids were waiting for him.

Even if he wasn't lying in an ER anywhere between here and Cranston that they could find, something had gone terribly wrong.

And now the man Lindy had loved since she was fourteen years old was missing. And they had not the first idea of what might have happened, or where to start looking for him.

CHAPTER 5

Lindy

1977

That week that Kate was sick, that summer Lindy was fourteen, David and Lindy went to the beach together twice more. After Kate was up and about again, David invited Lindy to come out in the rowboat with him and Kate and Josh. There was plenty of room, he insisted.

"I wake up to an altered reality," complained Kate, though, to Lindy, the rowboat invitation only confirmed that David still thought of her as just another little sister. Only once, at the beach, had he touched her at all. "You're sandy," he'd said, tracing a two-inch line through grains that had stuck to her upper arm in a gritty patch. Her skin was hot from the sun, the wind was whipping her hair, and a dozen other people were sharing the curved forty-yard stretch of sand, when, on a not-so-hot day, you might have the place to yourself. It was the first of August, and David had turned seventeen a week earlier. Lindy, who would be fifteen in November, felt her face flame, and David had looked away like he was embarrassed, too.

But, a few days after the rowboat outing, he arranged to borrow a Sunfish from a neighbor. Lindy had mentioned in an offhand way, one of the days at the beach, that she would love to learn to sail. Now he said this would be a perfect time: light winds in the right direction for sailing in the cove, almost high tide, and the neighbor wasn't using the boat. "I have *no interest* in that," Kate said, flouncing off to read a book, and, anyway, only two people could go out at once.

The Sunfish was on the beach, and David told Lindy to sit toward the front on the side of the tiny cockpit, and to watch out for the boom. He shoved the boat into the water and clambered aboard from behind, rocking it atop the glassy blue surface of the water. Lindy was already laughing, trying to find something to hang on to. "You're going to capsize it!"

He grinned, getting himself situated on the other side of the cockpit, grabbing the tiller and the line to control the sail. "Am not," he said.

Each time he tacked, they both had to duck under the boom to switch sides. Her knee kept brushing his. "Sorry," she would say, blushing, and he would give her a shrug or a wink.

He explained how to judge the direction of the wind. How to adjust the sail. How the slightest motion of the tiller would cause a big turn. He made it all look easy. "Want to try?" he said, after a bit. She liked the way he looked squinting against the sun. She'd never thought of him as graceful, but he had a nice way of moving around the boat. His arms were long and lean and muscular.

She wanted the moment to last.

She wanted an excuse for another lesson.

"Not today," she said. "Just keep showing me how it's done, okay?"

He smiled and said okay.

But there were only three weeks left of the summer, and the couple of times conditions would've been right for sailing, the neighbors were using the Sunfish.

One drizzly morning, Lindy knocked on the door of the yellow cottage, ostensibly to see Kate. But Kate answered the door and said, "David's not here." The instant assumption that Lindy was looking for him (had she been so transparent?) startled Lindy, but at least Kate didn't shut the door in her face. She simply left it hanging open and turned away so that Lindy might follow her inside. Lindy did so with some trepidation, closing the door quietly behind her, because it was clear that Kate was unhappy with her.

Kate flopped onto the couch, arms folded. Lindy sat carefully on the opposite end, just as Kate and David's mother sailed through the room with a heaping basket of dirty laundry, calling out hello to Lindy. Lindy said hello back, but Mrs. Kauffman had already gone outside, the screen door banging shut behind her. She must have decided the drizzly day would be a good one for the laundromat.

"I know you want to know where he is," Kate said. She had grown taller and thinner this summer, and her dark, curly hair was long and wild. Freckles dusted her nose. She was wearing a yellow Moody's Diner T-shirt and cutoffs, and her elbows and knees were pointy. Her bare feet were dirty, as if she'd just come in from a long walk outside. "It's so *obvious,* the two of you."

"What's obvious?" Lindy said, because nothing felt obvious to her. She hadn't come here looking for David, she told herself, although now she was undoubtedly curious where he was.

Kate rolled her eyes. "He's camping."

Lindy had understood previously in a vague way that David and his friends, Toby and Mike, liked to hike up into the woods and make camp. Last summer, they'd stayed up there six days and nights in a row, only returning home for the colossal picnic baskets their mothers packed for them each day—stacks of PB&Js, giant bags of Ruffles, entire packages of raw hot dogs for them to cook over the fire, marshmallows for roasting, homemade cookies—which Kate said entirely voided their claims of "surviving in the wild."

Lindy had never before felt personally betrayed by David's decision to spend a night away from the yellow cottage.

So, okay, maybe she had been coming to see him.

She didn't want Kate to know. Also, even if she wouldn't have been able to put words to it, she could sense that the dynamic of her life was shifting, and she wanted to keep her childhood—and her best childhood friendship—intact for at least a moment longer. "Wanna play Boggle?" she asked Kate.

But Kate just looked at her, eyes narrow, skinny arms still folded. "Not really," she said.

When David's first letter arrived in New York in early October, Lindy was astonished. In late August, she had helped the Kauffmans pack the big station wagon for their drive back to Chicago. She had been standing beside it when Mrs. Kauffman and all the kids piled in. (Mr. Kauffman was long gone, having managed to spend just two weeks around the Fourth of July at The Cove, traveling back and forth by airplane.) David had only waved to Lindy from a distance as he'd climbed in on the passenger side, while Kate had given her a tight hug and promised to write, which, honestly, was a relief, though Lindy couldn't help but feel a knot in her stomach watching the station wagon disappear around the bend of Summerland Cove Point Road, reentering the world. Had Kate been wrong to say it was "obvious" about Lindy and David, when that seemed to imply that David had as much of a crush on Lindy as she did on him? Or, possibly worse, had Kate told David something that had put the kibosh on whatever inclinations he might've had toward her?

She'd tried to put both possibilities out of her mind. To tell herself it didn't matter. Summer things didn't matter at all once you got back to New York, that was what her mother always said.

But now, a letter. She and Kate had always exchanged intermittent letters over the winter, but David, obviously, had never written to her before. She stuffed the envelope with the familiar return address in unfamiliar handwriting inside her backpack for the elevator ride up to the apartment, hiding it away like it was something shameful. "Your father and I would not be very happy if you started spending too much time with that Kauffman boy," her mother had told her back in August, and when Lindy had asked why, Greta had said something about him being seventeen while she was only fourteen, but Lindy was sure there was more to it than that.

Upstairs, though, as she turned the key in the lock with a click, she heard the familiar sound of her mother playing intricate notes on the piano, back in her studio with the door closed. When not out on tour, Greta practiced seven hours a day, eight in the morning till four in the afternoon, with an hour off for lunch. When she was done, Lindy was granted access to the studio and required to practice from four to six. Her father joked that theirs was the only piano he knew that worked longer hours than he did.

One of the best things about summers at The Cove: Lindy was required to practice only one hour per day. Greta still practiced for four or five, which she swore to Lindy's father *was* "taking it easy." Lindy might've thought this would give Greta more time to notice Lindy was alive, but in fact it seemed she had even less, since she did all her own cooking and housekeeping and entertaining at Summerland Cove, not like in the city where she had help come in. And because Lindy's father was always up in his attic office writing his boring academic history books—he did his research throughout the winter in New York, and said Summerland Cove was the place where he could really *write*—Lindy was left more to her own devices in general.

But today her parents' absence worked in Lindy's favor. Lindy went into the narrow U-shaped kitchen and grabbed a Tab from the fridge, then retreated down the hall, passing her mother's studio just in time to hear a wrong note, a pause, her mother swearing, then the complicated passage beginning again. Lindy went into her bedroom and closed the door, shutting out as much of the noise as possible. Without taking off her jacket, she sat cross-legged on her white canopy bed and pulled out David's letter from her backpack. She set it on her green and pink patchwork quilt. She examined her name—*Lindy Sanderson*—in his crooked handwriting and decided she liked the way it looked.

She cracked open the Tab and took a bracing sip, the bubbles tickling her throat and nose. Then she ripped open the envelope. *Dear Lindy,* the letter said, and her heart beat faster.

But after that it was really just small-talk-type stuff. He wrote about how he had recently placed second in a regional cross-country meet, how Josh was playing quarterback in peewee football, and how, when his family had arrived back home after the summer in Maine, his father had noticed that David had grown two inches and insisted on marking his new height on the kitchen doorjamb.

Lindy realized now that, although seeing the envelope from David had, at first, been a huge surprise, she had leapt immediately to expecting that inside would be some kind of declaration. A statement of interest in her, at least. But all he'd written at the end was: *Write me back and tell me what's going on with you. Sincerely, David Kauffman.*

She huffed out a sigh, even as she got up, crossed to her desk, and sat down to write him back. She used her pink stationery, her favorite blue pen.

Dear David,

If we're going to be pen pals, I'd prefer that we get to the bottom of important things right away. To start, I would like to know three things.

1. *What are your biggest dreams?*
2. *Where do you want to live when you grow up?*
3. *Why did you ask me to go out sailing with you?*

Sincerely,
Lindy Sanderson

All her friends later said she was lucky he'd written her back at all, but it had never occurred to her to prevaricate. She came by that honestly from her mother, she guessed. Anyway, two weeks later, his answers arrived.

1. *Run a four-minute mile.*
2. *Not in a city. Probably the woods in Maine.*
3. *Because I think I like you.*

If he'd written, "Because I think you're cute," the way she imagined most boys would, she might not have bothered to write him back. But somehow, "I think I like you" made her feel not just seen but taken seriously, the way David clearly took most things in life. And to be regarded in this thorough and serious way by David Kauffman seemed suddenly like something Lindy had been hoping for since she was ten years old, although she hadn't exactly known it until now.

CHAPTER 6

Hailey

Sunday, July 25, 2010
1:30 a.m.

We need to retrace his steps," Hailey said into her cell to Noah, as the whirring of tires on I-95 filled the Jeep and the headlights swept the black night. "We'll do that in the morning, starting from Cranston."

Cody was driving, and Eli was in the back. Their mom had already called the state police, almost four hours ago now, from the hospital waiting room. Hailey'd listened as Lindy argued. No, he wasn't disabled; no, they couldn't prove he was in danger. Yes, the last she knew he'd been not in Maine but in Rhode Island, and it was true she had no proof other than his saying so that he'd *actually* been in Rhode Island, or that he'd *actually* set out driving to Maine. Even Lindy's swearing that she'd been married to him for decades and never known him to lie didn't help, but she finally got them to concede to one point. "They're going to keep an eye out for Dad's car," she'd reported upon hanging up. Hailey, exchanging looks with her brothers, had known that wasn't nearly enough, especially as there seemed a good chance the officer had said that just to get their mom to let up. They'd driven back to The Cove, and Lindy had wanted to call the Cranston police, ask them to do a welfare check at the house. She had *not* wanted Hailey and her brothers to go, though she'd wavered when she remembered there was some chance a hospital might have left a message on the answering machine there, and they'd insisted. Without saying the words, Hailey had known Cody and Eli agreed: They needed to see for themselves.

"We'll check the house tonight to make sure he didn't, like, hurt himself before he even left," Hailey told Noah now. She knew she wasn't the only one who had the unspeakable image in her mind of her dad laid out across the garage floor, car key abandoned near his open hand, dead from a heart attack or injured by some ladder or something falling on him.

Noah yawned. It was 1:30 a.m. She'd woken him up when she'd called. Earlier, she'd been afraid she wouldn't be able to say the words *My dad's missing* without totally breaking down. And yes, it had felt strange to blow past Portland without getting in touch, but Noah had surely been out for drinks with Alexandra and Robin. If Hailey had called, she'd have had to compete for his attention, and maybe she hadn't been sure she'd win out. To learn that would've been more than she could take tonight.

"Babe," Noah said, "he probably just, like, decided to stop at a hotel. You said he wasn't crazy about the idea of that party, right? I can't believe you're, like, driving to Rhode Island tonight. That's insane."

Hailey felt the wrongness of each of his words lodging in her chest. "You don't know my dad. He wouldn't do that."

Noah sighed. Yawned again. "All right. Well. You're with your brothers?"

"Yes. Like I told you."

"Okay. Well. Good luck. Keep me posted. I've gotta get some sleep."

"Sure." Hailey clicked off the call, too furious to say goodbye or that she loved him, and she immediately regretted that, because now the blackness of the night and her fear about what could've happened to her dad rose to the surface, turning general unease into something closer to panic, despite the solid presence of her brother beside her. Cody was looking straight out at the highway, but he would've heard every word of her conversation with Noah. At least Cody was good at—well, it wasn't exactly making excuses for people, but maybe just having empathy for everybody's point of view. *Noah's tired,* he would surely be thinking. *Hailey's upset. Of course it wasn't going to be a perfect conversation.*

A moment passed—the headlights, the tire noise, a couple agitated twists of her engagement ring around her finger—then Eli's voice came from the back. "Nice he could be so supportive."

"I thought you were asleep!" Hailey glanced over her shoulder. Eli was leaning against the door behind Cody, his legs stretched out so that his feet were behind Hailey. His eyes were barely open. He gave a little shrug.

She swatted his knee. "Don't you dare give me shit. This is hard enough. How long ago was it you called Mom?"

Eli yawned. "About thirty minutes."

"All right, I'll call again."

Their mom had demanded progress reports every thirty minutes. "At minimum! If you're going to insist on venturing off into the night like this." The words *When my husband is already missing* hung unspoken in the air, especially when Emma said she and Reese wanted to ride along to Cranston, too, and Lindy had all but shouted, "You are not *all* going to leave me at once!" Lindy couldn't receive texts without signal, of course, and Grandma and Grandpa were asleep at Innisfree—they'd left the party so early that they'd surely gone to bed thinking David would show up any minute—so Hailey and her brothers had been instructed to call the yellow cottage's landline. Their aunt Kate and uncle Josh had promised to sit up with Lindy, while Emma and Reese had been assigned to wait by the phone at Innisfree in case David called.

Hailey clicked to dial. The phone rang in her ear just once. "Eli?" said their mom. The yellow cottage had no caller ID.

"It's me, Mom."

Cody and Eli called out in unison: "Hi, Mom!"

Lindy gave an audible sigh of relief. "How's it going?"

"Fine. We just crossed into Massachusetts. Any news?"

"No. Nothing."

Hailey had never heard her mom's voice sound so hollow. She blinked back tears. "Okay, well, we'll call you again in half an hour."

"Okay, sweetie. Be safe. I love you."

"Love you, too, Mom." Hailey ended the call and wiped away her tears. If her mom could be calm, so could she.

But there was no smart-ass comment from Eli, no good-natured ribbing from Cody, which meant the world was tilted off its axis for sure, and Hailey felt the darkness descending again, the highway vibrating through her body. She glanced at the speedometer and saw Cody was going eighty-five. There wasn't much traffic this time of night.

They drove a mile in silence before Cody spoke up. "I would think," he said, in an oddly gentle tone, "that a person's fiancé would want to be with them in a time like this."

Hailey looked over at him, surprised. What had happened to *Noah's tired, Hailey's upset*? Cody's profile in the darkness looked sharper than she'd have drawn it from memory, if she could draw.

He glanced over with a half-smile and said, "Just saying," as if to soften the blow.

The Cranston house was dark. The big maple in the front yard cast a shadow across the two-story white 1940s faux colonial in the moonlight. Hailey swallowed nervously as Cody pulled the Jeep into the driveway.

Just because the house was dark didn't mean that her dad wasn't inside, laid out hurt since yesterday morning, or even—she could not stand to think it—dead.

None of them had thought to grab the garage door opener from their mom's car, so Eli hopped out and ran around to unlock the back door. Cody drummed his fingers on the steering wheel as the bright headlights reflected on the white garage door. Hailey tried to breathe, her stomach in a tangle, her head beginning to ache. Their family had lived in this house since Hailey was sixteen months old and Eli and Emma were newborns. Every inch of it was familiar, as much a part of her as her own body.

Now being here felt strange and wrong. What if Dad really was just on the other side of that door, laid out on the ground? If Eli yelled in alarm when he walked into the garage, would she and Cody hear him?

Her stomach flipped again as the garage door whirred, beginning to slowly lift. The light came on, and the door retracted. The stall was empty, except for Eli, who stood in the middle of it, hands splayed out in a kind of shrug. Their father's car wasn't there.

Cody let out a relieved sigh. "That's good, right? He got out on the road yesterday!"

Hailey climbed out of the Jeep. "Come on, we have to check inside." Suddenly, she didn't think they could rule out the possibility of a home invasion, someone breaking in, hitting their dad over the head and driving off in his car, although it was hard to think who would target their modest home in this modest neighborhood—or want a 2003 Subaru Outback. Still, she hurried to where Eli stood on the step that led into the house from the garage. A series of beeps sounded as he punched in the code to deactivate the alarm.

"I checked," he said. "The code was activated yesterday morning at 9:15. Right after Dad called Mom to say he was about to leave."

"Okay," Hailey said, but as he got the door open, she pushed past him and rushed inside, calling, "Dad?"

Cody and Eli were right behind her, calling for him, too. Hailey flipped on lights as she barreled through the rooms, all perfectly decorated, clean, uncluttered, most of them updated recently by her mom, who believed that a fresh pair of curtains or a fresh coat of paint could make your whole life feel new. Kitchen, dining room, living room, Dad's office. "Dad?" Hall light. She ran up the flight of stairs. "Dad!" She looked in her parents' bedroom first. It was totally neat. Bed made. An orderly stack of books on her dad's nightstand. "Dad?" The door to her parents' bathroom was open, and she peered inside. Nothing. She flipped on the light to be sure. A used towel hung on the rack, but the counter was clear of any of the usual shaving cream or her mom's face creams, and both toothbrushes were missing from the holder, which just meant they'd been packed to take to The Cove. Hailey flipped off the light and, after quick peeks in her and Emma's old room, in Cody and Eli's old room, and in the bathroom they'd all shared—everything looked untouched everywhere—she trudged downstairs.

If her dad wasn't here, he could be anywhere.

Her brothers were in the kitchen, standing by the counter, and turned when they heard her coming. Quickly, she lifted the lid of the kitchen garbage can that stood beside the door. It was empty, a fresh bag lining it. That settled it. Taking out the garbage was always the last chore her parents did before leaving on vacation. That it was done could only mean that her dad had left this place under his own power, without any trouble.

"He's not here," she told her brothers, though of course they already knew. The house had a too-quiet feeling.

"There's nothing on the answering machine," Cody said.

"Look," Eli said, holding up a flip phone.

"Is that Dad's?" Hailey reached for it.

"Typical Dad," said Cody. "He left it in the drawer."

Hailey flipped it open. *22 new voicemails, 44 missed calls,* read the screen. That must've been her mother calling, yesterday. Well, they had all called, multiple times; her aunt and uncle had, too. Why had it not occurred to any of them that he might've forgotten his phone at home? It was a typical move, no matter how much his family teased and scolded him. "We might need you!" they would tell him. Or, "Dad, you've got to learn how to send a text message, seriously!" He was unphased, unflappable, on the subject. He wasn't used to being tethered to a device, he'd tell them, and he forgot to check it even if he did remember to carry it, so what was the use? Even the old "What if your work needs you?" argument never made inroads. He would just shrug and say that people had functioned without cell phones for centuries, he didn't mind being a Luddite (he would use air quotes when he said the word), and he was sure the office could figure out how to reach him if they were desperate enough. "And so can you," he would say.

Hailey was really glad that her father was not lying dead on the kitchen floor, but, assuming they found him unharmed, her mother was definitely going to kill him.

CHAPTER 7

Lindy

Sunday, July 25, 2010
3:30 a.m.

After the kids called to say they'd reached Cranston to find the house empty, David's cell phone forgotten in the kitchen drawer, and no helpful messages on the house phone's answering machine, Kate said they'd better try to get a little sleep. Lindy started to argue, but it was true there was really nothing else they could do at this hour. She'd told the kids to be sure they got some sleep, too, before even thinking of turning around and driving back to Maine.

Most of the people in the yellow cottage—Josh's wife and three boys, Kate's five kids—had gone to bed hours ago. Even Kate's husband, Matt, had gone upstairs with apologies around 1:30, saying somebody was going to have to be up to make the blueberry pancakes for the kids in the morning. Lindy supposed that was true, though it was hard, just now, to imagine the arrival of morning at all, let alone the continuation of old summer traditions.

"Maybe he just stopped at a hotel," she found herself saying to Kate and Josh, as Kate took another sip from what had to be her third glass of wine—extremely unusual for clean-living Kate. Lindy, who hadn't been drinking at all, wondered if Kate could possibly feel as woozy and strange as she did. "Maybe he just really didn't want the party?"

Kate patted her hand and nodded, as if trying to believe that, too.

"Although I still don't know why he wouldn't call," Lindy said, voice faltering, because when she thought of the lack of a phone call, all she could imagine was David, having stopped off for a quick hike, lying in the woods somewhere, hurt, helpless, cold. What would it be—a broken ankle, his knee blown out again? Or had he hit his head?

"Lindy," Josh said, "I'll walk you back to Innisfree."

Kate startled, went pale. "I'm going, too! I don't want you alone, Josh, walking back here." They all looked at each other, taken aback, acknowledging it: They were in a new reality now. One where it didn't feel safe to let anybody venture out alone, not even just over to Innisfree. They could get lost. Vanish. Someone could hurt them . . .

Lindy shook her head to clear it of the thought. She'd go crazy if she started to think that.

They walked in silence in the moonlight, Kate and Josh flanking Lindy like bodyguards around a dignitary as they made their way up and over the crest of the slight hill, listening for the crack of twigs in the woods lining the narrow road and to the breeze rustling the oak and birch leaves. The damp air smelled lush with summer blooms, fallen pine needles, the salt of the sea.

Lindy had walked this small cut-through section of Summerland Cove Point Road between the yellow cottage and Innisfree thousands of times over the years. As a child, heading to and from the beach. As a teenager, sneaking over to the yellow cottage to see David. As an adult, carrying casseroles and salads for family dinners at the yellow cottage and community potlucks at the SCPA clubhouse. She had chased her children through here, all of them laughing and running. She had watched them grow taller and taller among these trees.

"Lindy, I hate to ask," Josh said, and the sound of his voice was startling in the enveloping darkness. "But have you, uh, noticed David having any trouble lately?"

She knew instantly what Josh meant, and the knowing fell like a rock into the pit of her stomach. The truth was, she hadn't noticed anything. Not a thing. Had she missed something? She hated to think so, but, with her focus on the parties and Hailey's wedding, God knew she could've. "No," she managed, swallowing back a lump of guilt.

"How's his work going?" Josh asked.

"I have always thought that job was too stressful for him!" Kate interjected.

"I—I don't know," Lindy said, trying to remember the last time David had told her anything about a case he was working on. He was a lawyer for the Northeastern Innocence Project. Every case he worked on was a matter of life or death, of an apparent wrong needing crucially to be made right, within a labyrinthine system that made fixing mistakes very difficult. It *was* stressful. She'd never liked that it was what he'd chosen to do. Not that it wasn't noble. It was. But he was her husband, the father of her children. If he wanted to put his law degree to work on behalf of humanity, why not child protective services? Environmental protection? But no. He made visits to the maximum-security prison instead, trying to get the stories of the murderers who lived there, who all said they were innocent, and he believed nearly every one of them, and, often, took up their fights as his own.

But had she really stopped asking? Settled for "fine" as an answer to the old "how was your day" question? *Probably*, she realized. He was naturally circumspect. Had to be drawn out. And of course, much of his work was confidential, so he couldn't talk about it at all. And yes, Lindy had been preoccupied these last few weeks (okay, who was she kidding, months), and she'd probably been doing most of the talking, because it was easier, and because she always had so much to tell him. Also, she'd been having so much fun! She hadn't felt such clarity of purpose in years. Every day brought a new decision to make: venue, flowers, caterers, menus, tents, music, a cake. Hailey's dress alone had required seven shopping expeditions—they'd tried Portland, Boston,

Providence—and, after the choice had been made, there'd been three fittings in Portland, and Lindy had driven up from Cranston for each one. The other two parties had been easier to plan, but not nothing. Not even close to nothing.

So, yes, she'd been distracted. Not paying David much attention at all. "I really don't know," she said again.

"It hasn't even occurred to me in a long time." Kate's voice sounded young and frightened now. "To worry, you know? I mean, he's seemed fine all these years! You don't think he could've gotten into a bad state without you noticing, do you?"

"I don't . . . think so?" Lindy swallowed. "Have you guys talked to him?"

"Not much, no," Josh said, sounding choked.

"Not in a few weeks," Kate said. "We said we'd catch up when we saw each other." Her tone turned harder, then. "Have you not been paying *attention*, Lindy?"

"Hey," Josh scolded.

"I'm just saying," Kate went on, and the wine she'd drunk was showing, reminding Lindy of when they were young, in their twenties, when Lindy had often worried that Kate was drinking too much, that it was going to get her into trouble. Ever since Kate's first pregnancy, nineteen years ago now, Lindy had rarely seen her drink at all. "We've *trusted* her with him all these years," Kate went on. "We've trusted you, Lindy, to take care of him!"

"Stop!" Lindy said, trying to rein things in. If Kate regressed to her younger self, to who she'd been back when everything had happened, Lindy might start slipping, too. And slipping was not an option. "I have been taking care of him. I'm his *wife*. Just . . . don't say anything to the kids. Okay? Promise? They don't know anything about what happened back then, and I don't want them to know."

"Fine," Kate snapped. They were at Innisfree now. "But if you missed something, Lindy, I swear—"

"That's enough, Kate." Josh took hold of his sister's elbow and steered her away. Lindy walked up Innisfree's porch steps, pulling the screen door open with a creak, knowing that any hope of getting sleep tonight was gone.

In the shadowy living room, Emma was asleep on the couch sitting up, looking small and innocent, like a child again. Reese was asleep on her shoulder, long legs stretched out, and the old rotary phone sat on the coffee table before them, the cord snaking across the floor.

Lindy shook them awake gently and sent them upstairs, then sat down on the couch herself and looked out the picture windows to the ocean beyond. The moon had swerved around the end of the point by this time of night, but she could still discern the slight motion of the black water in its distant, refracted light. She knew her mother would be up in an hour or so, before sunrise. She should go upstairs to bed—she did not want to have to tell her mother the news at four in the morning—but she didn't want to leave the phone.

Would Greta say she'd always known it would come to this? God, Lindy hoped not. But Greta might.

Lindy stretched out and pulled the throw blanket down over her, trying to think what to do once it wasn't too damn late or early to do anything. Just a couple hours from now. Should she call the hospitals again? Try again with the police? Go out looking?

But where?

She tried to remember David's voice this morning, when he'd called to say he was leaving Cranston. (Or, God: yesterday morning.) She hadn't noticed anything unusual about it. Maybe he'd sounded tired . . . but wasn't everybody tired?

David's not just anybody, she heard, as if Kate and Josh were still there talking to her.

Kate and Josh hadn't forgotten: David was fragile. Lindy—even as she knew in her bones that that fact stood as a foundation, or maybe a basement, to their life—had spent the last two-plus decades trying to forget it.

She didn't think she should be faulted for that.

Because, to build a life, to build a family, you had to decide what was true. You had to decide what you would accept. You had to decide who you were.

You didn't have to venture into the basement. Or even think about what was down there.

Not often, anyway.

CHAPTER 8

Lindy

1978

They wrote back and forth throughout the winter and into the spring. At the bottom of one of her letters in February, she drew a cartoonish sketch of herself bundled up and leaning into a howling wind. He raved about it, so she began illustrating each letter. She usually never shared her sketches with anyone, but when she remembered the way his brown eyes looked hazel in the sun and how it had felt when her knee brushed his in the Sunfish, she wanted to make him smile.

In May, he wrote that he'd had a dream about sailing with her again, and when summer came, the first time she stopped by the yellow cottage, on a foggy, cool, early June day, he answered the door. She saw Kate standing behind him in the living room, and Kate, surprisingly, grinned and gave Lindy two thumbs up, which Lindy guessed amounted to her giving her blessing. This seemed an odd change of heart from last year, but maybe they'd all grown up over the winter. (Kate, Lindy knew from a letter, had lost her virginity to a boy she'd met in her biology class. *Seems fitting, I guess, even though we were just learning how to dissect frogs,* she'd written.)

David stepped out onto the front porch and shut the door behind him. Lindy was barefoot, wearing a navy-blue sweater and cutoff jeans.

Her legs were freezing, covered in goose bumps, and her hair was frizzing unavoidably in the dampness. She tilted her chin to look up at him. She had written to him about things no one knew—her hatred of her leering piano teacher; her fascination with wandering the period rooms in the American Wing at the Met; her dream of going to art school. It was strange to think, looking at him now, that he knew all those things about her. And the sketches! She might as well have let him see her naked. He would be turning eighteen soon, and he was broader in the shoulders, and taller, too.

"Did you grow another two inches over the winter?" she said, and he smiled, reached out, and casually looped two of his fingers around two of hers.

"I've been looking forward to seeing you," he said.

Lindy'd had a casual boyfriend named Kent in New York for the last three months, because who even knew what David meant by writing her things like, *Sometimes when you look at the stars don't you just feel so small?* Half the time, she didn't know how to respond to what he wrote. *What's the use in having big dreams when you're just going to turn into a cog in the machine?* Or, *Did you know the average human spends five years of their life waiting in line?* She asked him questions that were more prosaic—*Are you going to prom? What are you most looking forward to about summer?*—and though she really wanted to know his answers, he rarely responded directly. He seemed to like to tease her with his mysteriousness, and he would sidestep and write something slightly philosophical instead. (*Dating is just a ritual to give the bored something to pretend to look forward to,* did not tell her whether he'd had a date to prom!) Sometimes Lindy even thought her mother—it had turned out to be impossible to keep the exchange of letters a secret—had been right when she said that, once they spent more time together, David would quickly see that Lindy was too young for him. "You can pretend all kinds of things at a distance," Greta would say.

Now, though, Lindy gave both Kent and her mother's opinions the old heave-ho in her mind. She would write to Kent later today; she would ride her bike to the post office to make sure the letter went out immediately. "You have?" she said. David nodded. Smiled. He squeezed her fingers slightly, and she felt warmth flooding her as she gazed up into his dark eyes, unable to keep from smiling. She was fifteen and a half years old, and suddenly she knew two things for sure.

One: Her mother was wrong about David. (Just as, it lately seemed, Greta was wrong about most things.)

And two: If he was a mystery, he was one that Lindy wanted to solve.

She still had to practice the piano for an hour a day, and David ran for two or three. At least, in Summerland Cove, Greta let Lindy have the piano first, early in the morning, so Lindy could have the rest of the day free. "It's summer. I'm not heartless," Greta would say. (Lindy suspected Greta just wanted to be sure the piano room, which was the big room on the other side of the stairs from the living and dining rooms, would be available in the evenings. Greta and Tom liked to listen to their LPs—David Bowie, Fleetwood Mac, Janis Joplin, Bob Dylan—on the stereo in there, drinking their martinis and dancing when they got "loosened up" enough.)

David got up early to run first thing in the morning, too.

But it wasn't straightforward, at first, how the days would go, or when or how often Lindy would see him. In the past, she could go knock on the door of the yellow cottage any time for Kate. Now it seemed crucial to ensure she didn't seem too eager to see David. Everyone over there knew now that, if she knocked, it wouldn't be to see Kate.

The first week, the weather was cool, damp, and cloudy. There were chores to do at Innisfree, helping her mother get the cottage ready for the season. Greta liked to have everything "shipshape and in Bristol fashion" before Lindy's father arrived, so that he could "just relax and not worry about a thing." And Lindy got engrossed in a novel she found on the shelf, *Windswept* by Mary Ellen Chase. The book, an old family saga set in Maine, had her mother's name written in pencil on the flyleaf, though Lindy found it hard to believe that Greta had ever sat still long enough to read it, or that, if she had, she'd have liked it enough to keep it all these years. Lindy couldn't ask, though, because she'd found it up in Greta's old room—now Lindy's father's office—in the attic, where Lindy wasn't supposed to go.

For years now, Lindy had been begging to be allowed to have the attic be *her* room, but Greta refused to consider it. Even when Tom said he wouldn't mind switching, Greta simply said, "I won't hear of it," using her *and-that's-final* tone. Tom could only give his daughter a rueful shrug, and Lindy had to stay in the room next to her parents, which had belonged to her mother's brothers when they all were young. Greta said it was the far superior room, but Lindy, snooping around and checking out the view from the attic this week, with her father absent and her mother not paying attention, didn't agree.

Finally, the sun came out, and Lindy took her sketchbook out to the porch. The warmth of the sun on her skin as she sat in one of the Adirondack chairs was a relief after the chill and fog of the last few days. From the piano room came the sound of her mother playing a Chopin nocturne, one of the complicated ones that was beyond Lindy ("For now," according to Greta). Lindy sighed at the thought of all the years she'd have to practice before she'd ever be as good as her mother and looked out at the blue of the ocean, the frame of pine trees, the rock ledge below that was visible only at low tide. As much as Lindy loved Manhattan, she loved this place just as much. Even playing the piano here wasn't so bad, because here you got to look at the ocean while you did it, instead of being stuck in a tiny square room in a small apartment. That she could love such disparate places equally was a fact about herself that didn't seem to make much sense, but her father said you couldn't always expect things to make sense. (Her mother said you could try.)

A squirrel leaped onto the porch railing and sat looking at her. She smiled. "Oh, you want to be my subject, do you?" It didn't answer, just sat there working its little mouth and blinking. She began sketching it, enjoying the feel of her pencil gliding over paper, making lines. After a moment, she thought she heard a knock on the door. As she got up, the squirrel scampered away and clambered up a nearby tree. She peered around the corner of the porch, and, to her surprise, there on the steps stood David, tall and handsome in a white T-shirt, jeans, and sneakers, sunlight glinting on his dark curls. When he saw her, he smiled. "I thought about writing a letter," he joked.

"The post office is way down at the end of the road," Lindy observed coolly, hiding the way her knees had started to hum at the sight of him.

David's smile deepened. "That's why I thought I'd just come over."

They were the talk of The Cove, after that. They were seen walking together at all hours. Arriving at the season-opening potluck at the clubhouse together. (Leaving together, too.) They played tennis at the SCPA court. Went out sailing in the neighbor's Sunfish. They went to the beach, where he rubbed Coppertone on her back and they talked about their families and the transcendentalists and urban crime rates and Louis Comfort Tiffany's theories of light, all of which made her feel that they'd already gotten to a deeper level than a typical teenage romance. This was a satisfying feeling, even if the level of romance in their romance was not yet satisfying.

Lindy knew all the adults were talking to her parents about her being seen with David so often, and she overheard Greta at the wine and cheese party at the clubhouse the following week saying, with her typical flair, "It will burn itself out, the way these things do."

Lindy disagreed, but of course she didn't say so.

On the other hand, what was there to burn out, when he hadn't even kissed her yet?

She wished she could ask Kate's opinion on what on earth he might be thinking, the way she would've if he were any other boy, but obviously, she couldn't.

The only halfway clear sign that he was even interested was the way he kept showing up on the steps of Innisfree, wanting her to come for a walk or to the beach, wanting to talk with her about everything. He asked her to tell him all about Central Park and the Upper West Side and the natural history museum. (It was nearly inconceivable to Lindy that he had never been to New York; even more inconceivable was that his principal reaction to her tales of its marvels seemed to be suspicion.) He told her how his second-biggest dream, after running the four-minute mile, was to attend Brown University to study philosophy and epistemology, which he said meant "the nature of knowledge. What do we know and how do we know we know it?" He said his biggest hero was Henry David Thoreau. "Life in the woods, the citizen's responsibility to resist evil, all that." He also declared that, if he'd been of age to be drafted for Vietnam, he definitely would've moved to Canada. Lindy could all but hear her mother saying the words *too idealistic for his own good,* but Lindy found that she admired idealism.

However, with David always caught up in pondering lofty notions, she realized that, if she ever wanted him to kiss her, she was going to have to nudge things along.

So, one night in late June, as sunset painted the sky over at the beach—they had the place to themselves, this time—she tucked her hair behind her ear, cocked her head, and said, "I've been wondering if you're ever going to kiss me."

He laughed and teased her. "Yeah, well, I've been wondering if that would be a good idea."

"I think it might be," she said, giving her voice an optimistic lilt.

"I guess that settles it," he said, but he just sat there smiling softly at her, his arms looped around drawn-up knees. The water lapped gently at the bunchy swirls of seaweed that lined the low-tide shore. The smell of old salt was in the air.

"Well?" she said, after a moment.

"Oh. Now, you think?"

She scoffed and looked away. "Never mind." She watched a cormorant dive, the silver water ripple.

And then his hand was on her elbow, and she turned toward him, still miffed, but he was close, leaning in, smiling a little, and then his lips touched hers. They were soft and warm in a way that felt surprising. And it wasn't that she'd never been kissed before, but it had never made her feel like this: at home in her own body in a way she'd never been. As if her heart had finally settled into her own chest.

When he pulled back, he said, "It's about time you kissed me."

"It's about time you kissed me," she retorted, and then they smiled and kissed each other again.

On Summerland Cove Point, people said that to leave it was to "go back to the world." This had always seemed true to Lindy before, but now Summerland Cove Point *was* the world.

On the Fourth of July—Mr. Kauffman had finally arrived—David invited her to join his family for the community lobster bake at the clubhouse. Plastic gingham tablecloths draped the picnic tables that filled the small room, which was noisy with a hundred conversations. On each table stood rolls of paper towels to use as napkins. Lindy, behind David in the long line, spotted Greta up ahead serving the corn, using tongs to place the steamed cobs on everyone's trays as they passed. After serving Marjorie and Thorndike Westfield with a scowl on her face, though both Marjorie and Thorndike had smiled at her in a friendly way, Greta nodded as she served David, then, uncharacteristically, gave Lindy a wink as she dropped a piece of corn onto her tray. (Lindy's dad must've mixed her a couple of martinis earlier, back at home.) "Don't stay out too late, sweetie," Greta whispered then, quietly enough that no one else would hear, but Lindy still shook her head, embarrassed, and moved quickly on past—only to encounter her father serving the lobsters.

One thing about The Cove: You couldn't go anywhere without your parents seeing you or at least knowing exactly what you were doing, because, if they didn't see you themselves, someone else would tell them where you'd been. Fortunately, her father simply said hello to David and served him a lobster, then made a show of trying to find Lindy the biggest one. "They're all the same size, Dad," she objected. His search was holding up the line, and David was waiting. Tom finally selected one and set it on her tray—he, too, gave her a wink—and David led her over to where his family sat.

Lindy soon found herself sitting crammed between David and Kate, joking with both of them as they all fought over the elbow room needed to crack open the lobsters' claws and tails, dipping the sweet meat into melted butter, gnawing corn off the cob.

And yet, the entire family seemed to acknowledge that Lindy was there as David's guest, not Kate's. To her surprise, they even seemed happy about it. Lindy kept catching Mr. and Mrs. Kauffman shooting warm looks at her across the table.

Just as Lindy was finishing up her last bite of coleslaw, with David distracted by Josh on his other side, Kate nudged her and said in a tone so low that no one else would hear, "I think you make him happy. That's good." Lindy looked at her old friend quizzically, trying to discern why Kate would say such a thing. Most mysteriously of all, Kate had said it with an air of bowing out, of leaving David to the better person. But Kate was already talking to her parents.

Lindy looked across at Mr. and Mrs. Kauffman then, wondering if what David had said—how they didn't like each other very much, and it was by design that they spent the majority of their summers apart—was true. It was hard to imagine that it *could* be, not just based on how happy they seemed now, surrounded by their children, but also because Lindy's parents were just the opposite. Tom always came up to The Cove as soon as he possibly could after turning in his grades for the semester, and Greta always said that the only reason she liked having a week or two on her own with Lindy at the start and end of summer was that it made reuniting with him that much sweeter. "Ewww, Mom!" Lindy would predictably say, though secretly she couldn't help being pleased to know that her parents' love was solid, and even though, more secretly than that, she sometimes thought they were so caught up in loving each other that they nearly forgot she was part of the family, too.

Later, David's family stayed back at the beach to wait for the fireworks, while Lindy and David walked out to the end of the point, making their way across the striated rocks that jutted out into the ocean. The sky was softening into evanescent bands of pink and orange. Gentle waves rolled in, and a gull swooped past, screeching. Lindy, preoccupied with trying to think how to share her thoughts with David, finally ventured, "What do you think—"

David tugged her hand, interrupting, and gestured to where they were standing. A question. She nodded, and they sat down close together on a cool, sharp rock. He draped his arm across her shoulders. "What do I think what?" he said.

She swallowed. The sky was darkening now to vivid shades of coral and purple. She knew it was a strange and bold question to ask, but they'd already talked about so much, and she had to know. "What do you think love looks like?"

He smiled as if he thought the question was strange indeed. "A better question might be: Does love exist? Is love a thing we can know exists?"

She got frustrated then. Why couldn't he ever just be a normal boy? "Oh, stop it with your epistem-whatever. Look around you." Lindy gestured widely to the clusters of people—families, groups of friends—gathered on the rocks under the painted sky, then back to the row of three cottages across the tip of the point and the two columns of cottages behind that lining the road on the flat cove side and all the way up the hill on the ocean side. "Look at this place. These families. Lucky us! We're *part* of this."

"*You* are. Your family's been here for generations. Mine's only been coming a few summers."

She frowned. She wanted to say, *For how smart you are, you're really a fool.*

His eyes were very dark in the dusky light. She wanted to say, *Can't you see that all you have to do is decide to make all this yours?*

But she couldn't seem to make her voice work, so she just leaned in and kissed him briefly, then angled toward him, pressing her nose into his neck. He leaned his head on hers and pulled her closer, seeming pleased to hold her. The clean scent of his skin mixed with the salt-and-seaweed smell of the air somehow made her frustration dissolve, and a feeling of hope began seeping through. Gulls swooped and keened overhead. His T-shirt had ridden up slightly in back, and she hooked her thumb inside the back waistband of his jeans.

On the opposite side of the cove, someone set off a firework, and it whooshed into the sky, and she looked up in time to see it explode in a red bloom in the twilight. She and David met eyes and grinned. He kissed her, then she pulled back to look into his eyes, wanting to dive inside them. *Mine,* she thought. *I'm going to make you see.*

CHAPTER 9

Greta

Sunday, July 25, 2010
5:15 a.m.

As she did every morning, Greta put the kettle on to boil and made a cup of pour-over coffee in her favorite mug to take out to the deck for the sunrise. Usually, this act provided a moment of peace before her daytime thoughts intruded, but today she couldn't stop rehashing last night's party. Tom had really seemed not to recognize *anyone,* and though he'd been unfailingly pleasant, she'd seen him getting frustrated—frustrated with her, really, because he clearly understood that *she* was the one who'd dragged him to this house full of strangers. All evening, she had struggled, trying to conceal these realities in each interaction with neighbors and friends they'd known for years or decades.

How long before everyone would know the truth? Would she be able to keep Tom's condition secret through Hailey's wedding, two weeks from now?

It was getting harder to imagine that she would. Especially since Marjorie Westfield, the worst gossip of The Cove, had been at the party last night, along with her insufferable "cookie cake." Greta had managed to avoid her, but that didn't mean Marjorie wouldn't take any observation she'd made and simply run with it. Tom had unquestionably seemed out of sorts, probably even from a distance.

Greta picked up her mug, the warmth a comfort to her hands. Walking past the dining table and into the living room, she noticed, in the half light of dawn, Lindy asleep on the couch.

What on earth? Why wasn't she upstairs with David?

Greta noticed then that the phone had been moved from its usual place by the stairs to the coffee table in front of Lindy, the long cord stretching across the floor.

David? she thought.

She quickly shook Lindy awake, and Lindy groggily told her it was true: David never showed. "There must be something really wrong, Mom," she said, tears forming in her eyes. She said Hailey, Cody, and Eli had driven to Rhode Island last night, but all that told them was that he wasn't there, either, and that he'd forgotten his cell phone at home.

Greta set her mug on the table and hugged Lindy tight, unsettled to think that, on top of everything else, her grandchildren had gone to Rhode Island in the night while she'd been asleep and totally unaware that anything was wrong. Why hadn't they awakened her and told her? Getting old was so bizarre, an abdication of former responsibilities without ever quite agreeing to the downshift. "Oh, honey. I'm so sorry." Greta had a gut feeling Lindy was right—something was definitely wrong for David not to show, not to call—but tried to pretend otherwise. "Let's not count our chickens, though, okay? Today's a new day. I'm sure he'll arrive with some funny story to tell. Car trouble or something! Can you get some more sleep?"

Lindy was already nodding off, her body's need for rest shrouding over her mind's alarm. *Good,* Greta thought, tucking the blanket around her, then picking up the mug again. A long-ago gift from Emma, it featured a complicated few bars of music framed by the words, *What part of . . . don't you understand?* It usually made her smile. Not a chance, today. She quietly went outside into the cool morning and sank into one of the Adirondack chairs. She sipped her coffee, worrying, watching as the red globe of the sun poked above the silver horizon.

Normally, she tried to clear her mind during sunrise, make it a moment of meditation. Another thing that was impossible, today.

Because there was some possibility, she realized, that David's failing to arrive last night could be her fault.

She had laid too much on David recently, without Lindy knowing. Without at all meaning to!

The possibility had opened up two years ago, really, when Lindy'd had a lump in her breast. Lindy hadn't wanted Greta to know, evidently, but David had phoned Greta and, after making her promise not to tell Lindy he was doing so, kept her informed along the way. The lump turned out to be a benign cyst, thank heaven, but the series of calls it spurred had normalized direct communication between Greta and David. Previously, their phone contact had been limited to quick hellos on holidays, with Lindy and the kids lingering and chattering in the background. During the period of the lump, David would call Greta from work, and she could call him at the office, too, to check for updates.

So, it had not seemed as strange as it might have to call him at work two months ago.

What she didn't say: Tom had started working with a lawyer right after his diagnosis, but things had just moved too quickly, and she didn't understand anything about it, and now this lawyer was saying that the only way she was going to have money to pay for Tom to go into the memory care facility where she believed he'd get the best care was to sell Innisfree, and something about how Tom had put it into a revocable trust a few years ago but that didn't mean she couldn't sell it now that she needed the money.

Though she knew this wasn't David's exact area of expertise, she still wished she could ask him to help guide her through the legal aspects of it all.

Obviously, she couldn't, not while keeping Tom's diagnosis from him and, most importantly, from Lindy.

So, what she had said to David was, "I'm wondering if you would be willing to buy Innisfree. We'd wanted to leave it to you and Lindy, of course, but we've run into an unexpected wrinkle."

And what David had said was, "A wrinkle?"

She'd spilled out far too much, without meaning to. She did manage not to tell him about Tom's diagnosis. But the money trouble, yes. "It's hard to understand when we've been so careful all these years, but we've had some unexpected expenses, and we need to move to Florida."

"You're not making sense, Greta. Florida? Anyway, Lindy and I don't have the money to buy the cottage. We just sent our kids through college, and there's Hailey's wedding . . ."

Greta almost cried out—it had been such an effort to keep the cottage, to keep the summers at The Cove, all these years, for Lindy, who loved it so, and now it would all be for nothing? But Greta caught herself. "Just forget it. Don't tell Lindy, all right? I'll figure something out!" and hung up.

But he had called her back the next day. "Do you need *help*, Greta? Is everything all right?"

"You didn't say anything to Lindy, did you?"

"No. I didn't."

"Good. Don't. But . . ." She'd had another conversation with the lawyer. "We are going to have to sell Innisfree. We'll wait till after Hailey's wedding."

"But you can't do that! Lindy—Lindy talks about nothing but wanting to move up there when we retire. She *lives* for summers up there. The kids do, too! I mean, we met there, we had our *wedding* there . . ."

"I'm so sorry, David. But listen, there's still your family's cottage, right?" Greta knew this was a thin argument. Lindy loved Innisfree; the yellow cottage was owned in equal shares by David and his siblings, and it was always crowded with the innumerable cousins. Retiring there would be out of the question. Even visiting would be a chore to work out.

"Just . . . just wait, okay?" David said. "I'm going to try to figure something out."

"Well, I would hope so. To think you ruined my daughter's ambitions, and then you can't even afford to buy Innisfree?" Greta knew the words were wrong the instant she said them. But she had been saying wrong things all her life, and if she'd learned anything, it was that there was little you could ever take back. It seemed no use even to try.

David sighed. Greta imagined he was rubbing his temples, leaning his elbows on his desk. "How much do you need for it?" he said.

She straightened her shoulders. "The real estate agent said it would sell for six hundred thousand. I'm afraid I need the full amount." The memory care facility in Florida was fifty-five hundred dollars a month, Tom could live for years, and Greta needed to buy a condo for herself nearby. They had no equity; they'd been living in the same rent-controlled apartment on the Upper West Side since Lindy was six years old.

It was amazing how little they'd managed to save.

Equally amazing to Greta was that her father's wealth, the wealth she'd been born into, was simply gone. Her one brother who'd survived the war, Harrison, had inherited the Connecticut house, and, when he died—decades ago now—it had gone to his two sons, who had long since sold it off. All Greta had left was Innisfree, which her father had purchased in 1925 for a hundred dollars from the developers who'd named the place Summerland Cove. Then he'd lost a good deal of money in the crash of '29, and they'd lived a middle-class life ever since. And God knew, she and Tom had never accumulated much money, pursuing their passions for music and academia and giving whatever they could to people and causes they loved. To Lindy, the grandkids, the Lincoln Center and the New York City Ballet, the Manhattan School of Music and the Met, the Summerland Cove Point Association (replacing the roof on the clubhouse three summers ago had not been cheap). Tom gave the doorman in their building two hundred dollars every Christmas, for God's sake!

And they had enjoyed their monthlong vacations at Delray Beach each winter for the last decade since Tom had retired, and since Greta had had to retire, too, due to the arthritis developing in her hands. She hated that she could no longer play—sometimes she sat down and noodled for a few minutes, but it didn't take long before the pain overwhelmed her—and yet to cease doing so had meant a kind of freedom she had never experienced. Oh, how they loved their long walks in Florida on the endless sandy beach! Maine had always seemed to her so cold, so rocky, so rough; life in Florida seemed free and easy and, above all, warm.

Then, as it happened, their neighbor Sue at the condo where they'd always rented had gotten dementia. She'd gone into this memory care place, Sunset Acres, and her husband, Stan, said he trusted them with her life, he couldn't imagine her getting better care anywhere, and God knew he'd have cared for her at home if he could have, but it was a fool's errand to try.

So, maybe Greta was acting on reflex, but what else did she have? She was in a panic, on behalf of Tom, on behalf of herself, because things were happening so fast, and she could not stand to think of the day when he would wake up beside her and not know who she was. That day was clearly coming at her as fast as an express train, and she was frozen in its headlight, just waiting for it to strike.

"Six hundred thousand?" David said. "Jesus Christ. And you need to sell it this summer? Right now?"

"I'm so sorry, David." She was blinking back tears, and the tears made her feel surprised, as she had lately felt surprised by almost everything. She needed to button back up, get things back under control. But thinking of how disappointed Lindy was going to be, she couldn't. The tears streamed. She tried wiping them away. "Don't tell Lindy, okay?" she said to David. "Please. I don't want it to ruin things for her . . . all her parties this summer. You know?"

There had been a long pause. Greta blinked, swallowed back more tears. Then David had said, "Okay. But listen, I *am* going to try to figure something out. You're not going to put it on the market till after the wedding, right?"

She'd hung up feeling hopeful that day. He would figure something out. He would save the cottage for Lindy.

But now, sitting here on this July morning, on the fiftieth anniversary of the day that David had been born, Greta knew. It had not been fair to lay that on David, and especially not to ask him to keep it from Lindy. It had not been fair, and it had not been right. And now David had left home in Rhode Island but had not come to The Cove, probably because he couldn't face Greta, couldn't face Lindy, couldn't face knowing what was coming just two weeks from now: Lindy getting her heart broken in the worst imaginable way.

Because, clearly, if he'd figured out a way to buy the cottage, he would've told Greta by now.

And David didn't know the half of it. He didn't know about Tom.

And David wasn't strong enough to handle all of this, was he? To handle Lindy's heart being broken in so many different ways at once?

Though, in fact, he had not been as bad a husband to Lindy as Greta had feared he would be. In many ways, he had been a *good* husband—better and better over the years. And then, two years ago, of course, Greta had fallen in love with him once and for all, when he'd had the goodness, the decency, to share Lindy's health scare with her.

But now, caught up in her own panic, she had done the unforgiveable. She had forgotten the things she'd known to be true about David. The things that had made her fear so much for Lindy when they were young. The things that had made her and Tom try, all these years, to keep Lindy and David sheltered in whatever ways they could.

Worse yet, she had forgotten the lesson she had learned when she was twelve years old: Things that had once seemed perfect could, in an instant, be ruined completely.

CHAPTER 10

Lindy

1978

Lindy's father insisted they have David over for dinner, though her mother complained that imbued a mere summer romance with a significance it didn't deserve. "They're going to forget all about each other the minute summer's over," Lindy's mother said, ignoring the reality of last winter's letters, plus the fact that the Kauffman family appeared to be taking Lindy's presence in David's life seriously, at least. But Tom said nobody could predict the future, and he wanted to get to know this boy that his daughter was spending so much time with.

"Have you thought about academia, son?" he said, swirling the ice in his whiskey sour, as Greta circled the table serving up the beef stroganoff. She was wearing an apron printed with cartoonish lemons over a starched red cotton dress, plus full makeup and pearl earrings. Lindy was pretty sure the entire get-up could only be an ironic gesture of protest against putting on this dinner for David.

"Dad!" Lindy said. She worried that her father's question was insensitive, that it only pointed out how little choice David had in the matter. David's father owned a giant machine shop back in Chicago, which David didn't like to talk about because he was dreading having to work there next summer, after he finished high school. Mr. Kauffman had told him that it would be time to "join the real world for good" then. No more summers at The Cove. (Hearing this had been a knife twist in Lindy's gut; she tried not to let on.) Salt in the wound, David said, was how unfair it was that he'd be starting out "learning the ropes" in management, when men who'd worked there twenty years would never get such a chance. "Nepotism," he scoffed. "I'm sure I have less talent for this than any one of them." But even less than he wanted to work in management did he want to work on the shop floor.

Now David smiled at Lindy a little to let her know the question was fine. "Can't say that I have, sir."

"Best job in the world, in my view."

"Though not the most lucrative," teased Greta, and Tom laughed and gave her a wink. They were so embarrassing, flirting with each other like teenagers. Probably, to embarrass Lindy even further, they'd end up putting on *Rumours* after dinner and try to get David up dancing. She shook her head and rolled her eyes at David to convey her mortification, but he just gave her one of his cute half smiles, which made her heart give a little flip, and for a second, her parents might not have even been in the room.

The period room at the Met that always figuratively grabbed Lindy by the lapels and shook her in a way that was almost entirely unpleasant—yet she couldn't look away, either—was the one from 1680s Massachusetts, with its low ceilings and canopy bed and brick fireplace, diamond-paned yellow glass windows, scarlet coverlet and bed curtains, the cradle at the foot of the bed. It gave her a feeling of cold mornings, crowdedness, the threat of death. Of not wanting to get out of bed.

Her favorite, the Powel Room, from 1760s Philadelphia, had high plaster ceilings with intricate molded designs, a dazzling cut-glass chandelier holding eight tapers, and elaborate hand-painted green-gold Chinese wallpaper featuring stately birds posing among the branches of flowering trees. This room felt made for teatime and good manners, women in corseted gowns making plans for revolution they would never tell their husbands about. Lindy would spend an hour or two in the Powel Room at a time. She'd attempt to sketch the chandelier if she was feeling up to a challenge, or the tilt-top tea table if she was not. It was a room full of hope and beauty, ideals and optimism.

"But wouldn't the first room be more representative of regular people's lives?" David said, when she told him about the contrast. "Of how regular people feel, most of the time?" It was dusk, and they were sitting on a log beside the campfire up in the spot in the woods that he and Toby and Mike had set up. Toby and Mike had gone home for dinner, but David and Lindy had roasted hot dogs and now were cuddled together, holding hands, as the night grew cool.

"That's what I love about you," she blurted, without thinking of the implications. "Your optimism," she joked.

Usually, he would laugh at her jokes. But now there was a silence, as if she'd dropped a boulder into the center of a pond and they were just watching the ripples fan out. "Do you love me, Lindy?" he said then.

The question and the answer both surprised her, though maybe they shouldn't have. "Well. Yes. I think I do!"

He sighed like this was disappointing, but then he kissed her harder than he ever had, twining his fingers through her hair. She let herself get swept up, dissolving under the sweet-tasting pressure of his mouth, forcing herself not to think of how he hadn't said "I love you" back, and when he slid his hand underneath her T-shirt, she didn't object. Soon, he laid out the sleeping bag on the ground beside the flickering fire, and she lay down and let him unbutton and half unzip her jeans. He kissed her belly right down to the waistband of her cotton panties. She lifted her hips, wanting him to take off her jeans, but he groaned and shook his head before moving up to kiss her mouth again. "I really don't want to hurt you," he said. "I'm sorry."

"You're not going to hurt me, David." Under his weight, her whole body was humming now, not just her knees, and she didn't know what would happen next, but whatever it was, she wanted it.

"Listen, Lindy, there are things about me you don't know, okay?" He sat up, raked a hand through his hair. "I shouldn't have—"

She sat up, too, aggravated now. "Well, then, tell me! We've been talking all this time! What is it you think I should know?"

But he shook his head, stood up and held out his hand. She took it and let him pull her up so she was standing close beside him. "David?" she said, looking up at the square of his chin in the near-darkness, as if divining its exact shape would help divine the answers she needed, too.

He withdrew his hand. "Come on, I'll walk you home," he said, averting his gaze, kicking dirt on the fire. She wished she knew what had gone wrong. That she could say something to rewind.

But from the slump of his shoulders, it was obvious he'd turned some corner, one that led away from her, and that he wasn't going to turn back. She buttoned her jeans. She thought, *Well, if he doesn't love me, then . . .*

She couldn't finish the thought, couldn't even try to convince herself that any small consequence of him not loving her would be okay, not the whole trek home through the woods, with him walking silently beside her, his sneakers quiet on the pine needles of the forest floor.

Three days passed, and he didn't stop by Innisfree, and she didn't go to the yellow cottage. It rained almost nonstop the first day, which was an easy excuse to give her parents, but days two and three were gorgeous, and she sat out on the deck and sketched for hours, skirting their questions about why she wasn't seeing David. It wasn't as if she understood it herself! What she did know for sure: She didn't want to leave Innisfree, in case he'd gone to the beach or the clubhouse or out sailing without her. That would be just too humiliating, to see him moving on with his life, after what had happened.

When she woke up on the fourth morning, it was raining again, and she suddenly felt certain that he did love her. She tallied the evidence in her mind: Their conversations; the way he touched and held her; even the way he'd stopped himself the other night before taking off her jeans, instead of plowing ahead the way an opportunistic boy with an uninvested heart might've.

She thought of the way he looked at her. The way he sometimes kissed her gently on the forehead, seeming most times to surprise even himself with this, as if it was an impulse not quite under his control.

She remembered the way he pointed out every cormorant because he knew how much she loved to watch them dive.

Yes! He loved her. Right?

So what was wrong? What was he afraid of? What was it that he thought she didn't know about him that would get in their way?

She washed her hair, dried it, and ironed it flat. She put on jeans, a T-shirt, sneakers, and her yellow raincoat and walked over to the yellow cottage, swallowing back her nerves.

Kate answered the door. "He's up at the campsite. We thought he'd be home by now, with this rain, but I guess they're sticking it out." Oddly, she seemed a little worried. Preoccupied, anyway. But, knowing Kate, she was probably just in the part of a Sweet Valley High book where it seemed like nothing was going to work out the way you wanted it to.

Lindy was too embarrassed to go up to the campsite when she knew Toby and Mike would be there. Now she wasn't feeling so certain that David loved her, and he might have told them how she'd said she loved him, and they'd probably all laughed about it and called her a little fool, or worse. She walked down across the road to the beach and sat on a wet rock at the edge of it. The rain had stopped, and she watched the tiny gray waves lapping the shore. She traced lines with her fingernails in the damp sand nearby, wishing she had her sketchbook. After a few minutes, she heard some boys talking back and forth, bike tires crunching on the wet gravel road above. She craned her neck to look and saw Toby and Mike riding by. Which meant David was by himself in the woods. Avoiding her, clearly.

Well, she wasn't going to stand for it.

She marched through the woods at a good clip, motivated at first by anger and then by what began to feel, strangely, like fear. Setting out, she'd been sure she could find the place again without much trouble, but it took her longer than she thought it would to get there, and soon she was almost running, though why she was in such a hurry, why her heart was in her throat and she couldn't catch her breath, she didn't know.

And then she got there, and the campsite looked empty. She paused in the quiet to take in the scene as her own heavy breathing echoed in her ears. Charred, damp embers smoldered inside the rock fire ring. The green canvas tent was soaked and drooping. Old rain dropped from leaves on the surrounding trees. "David?" she ventured. Then, through the half-open entry flap, she saw a slight movement—a flash of white fabric, maybe. "David?" she said again, more loudly, moving closer.

She leaned down to peer inside, and he was sitting cross-legged in there, his face pale. He looked back out at her with wide, dark, frightened eyes. And then she saw the hunting knife in his right hand, the blood pouring from a slice in his left wrist. "David!" she screamed. She lunged for him, grabbed the knife handle without thinking. He didn't fight for it, just let his hand fall open, and she flung the knife outside, backward toward the fire ring. She snatched up a hunk of sleeping bag and pressed it hard to where his wrist bled, watching as the fabric began to stain.

"I don't know why I did it," he said, in a strained, odd tone of voice.

"Stop, stop, stop, stop!" she screamed at the blood.

CHAPTER 11

Lindy

Sunday, July 25, 2010
9 a.m.

Tiffany?" Lindy said into the phone at Innisfree, pacing, arm crossed over her stomach to try to keep from shaking. She'd called Hailey, asked her to look in the address book in the Cranston telephone table for David's assistant's cell number. When she'd dialed it, Tiffany's voicemail had picked up. "It's Lindy Kauffman. I'm so sorry to bother you on a Sunday morning, but I really need to know if you've heard from David at all since yesterday morning. And if you've noticed anything about his . . . state of mind, lately?" She explained vaguely that he hadn't shown up, gave the number at Innisfree and her cell number, and asked Tiffany to call as soon as possible and to try the Innisfree number first.

Lindy hung up the phone and said, "Damn it," just as her mother walked past, heading for the kitchen with a worried look. Her father was passing in the opposite direction. "Dad?" Lindy said, but he didn't turn or answer. Was he getting that hard of hearing? She wished she could lean on him for help, but it was clear he was so much older than he'd been last summer, so much older than he'd been even at Christmas, when she'd seen him last.

Emma came running down the stairs trailed by Reese, who was

glammed up for the day in smoky eye makeup, a black romper, and tall gladiator sandals. When they reached the bottom and faced Lindy, Emma looked frightened, and Reese was wearing an appropriate look of concern. Why did Lindy get the weird feeling she was maybe an actress, though? Lindy hadn't had time to ask, but the girl just seemed to lack sincerity. "We're ready to go," Emma said, and Lindy told them to head out to the car, that she'd be out as soon as she gave Hailey another quick call.

Earlier, Lindy had phoned the police again, only to be told again that she needed to prove David was really in danger before he could be listed as a missing person. She had called all the hospitals again, too, plus the customer service line of her and David's joint credit card, the one they used for everything. No new charges. A call to their bank's automated line revealed just one new transaction on their debit card: a three-hundred-dollar cash withdrawal, which he'd made on Friday after work from the ATM near their house in Cranston.

This seemed like exactly what he'd do to prepare to go out of town, and it meant he could've paid cash for gas or anything else he bought after leaving home. He would've paid cash for tolls along the highway, too, because he was anti-E-ZPass, saying that the way it tracked your whereabouts was an invasion of privacy.

If only he felt differently about that! Having a record to check could've given them an idea of how far he'd gotten, plus told them if he had actually been headed for The Cove.

But Lindy simply couldn't believe that he would've called and told her he was on his way if he'd had some other plan. The more she thought it through, the more she convinced herself the only feasible explanation was that—as Cody and Eli had theorized yesterday—he'd stopped off for a hike. Fallen in the woods. Without his phone, he'd have to just wait for someone to come along.

So, Hailey and the boys were setting out from Cranston this morning, planning to check all David's favorite stops to ask if he'd been seen, to try to track his movements and figure out how far he'd gotten. He was almost religiously opposed to stopping before he'd crossed the Massachusetts state line into New Hampshire, so they would start there and visit the places he tended to frequent. The two gas stations he preferred. The New Hampshire state liquor store. The popover bakery in downtown Portsmouth. The Nike outlet in Kittery. The Starbucks at the service plaza in Kennebunkport. Then they would check the Audubon sanctuary in Biddeford. And whatever other trailheads they could find.

Just searching from the New Hampshire state line up to Portland would take them all day.

So, Lindy had decided that she, Emma, and Reese would tackle the rest of the route, see if they could turn up any trace of him. They would go to town first to check their phones, then visit every trailhead between there and Portland, every place where he might've even thought of stopping off.

Meanwhile, when Lindy had called over to the yellow cottage this morning, Kate had said she was heading to town to use the library computer to make *MISSING* posters, which Lindy thought and hoped was premature. But Kate was going to have two hundred printed, if she could find a print shop that was open on a Sunday, then she and Josh would start posting them. Kate said she'd sent her husband and kids back to the farm. There were animals to take care of, the older kids had summer jobs on top of that, and Matt had taken the younger kids so Kate could focus on the search for David.

Now, overhearing Greta in the kitchen offering Emma and Reese coffee and food as they passed through, and the girls politely refusing and going out, Lindy dialed Hailey's cell. The *whir-click-whir* of the rotary dialing seemed to go on forever. Finally, Hailey answered on the first ring, and Lindy filled her in on everything that was new since they'd talked an hour ago. "Okay," Hailey said. "We're just leaving now. We'll stay in touch over your cell phone."

"Good. Listen, honey, I'm so sorry. I know we had things we needed to do today—this week—for your wedding. I don't want to say that—"

"Stop, Mom," Hailey interrupted. "Let's not even think about the wedding right now."

Lindy hated to hear the strain in her daughter's voice, but what could she do? She and Hailey had been operating off their giant, seemingly all-important wedding checklist for almost a year, and Lindy off an additional huge one for the other parties and every day in between. Now those lists had become trifling, irrelevant, replaced by a new, terrible list in Lindy's mind: *Call Tiffany. Call police. Call hospitals. Check trailheads. Cancel birthday dinner.* "Okay," she said. She made Hailey promise to be in touch frequently, and they hung up.

"Mom?" she called and went to the kitchen to find Greta. Greta was making a fresh cup of coffee and looked guilty, like she'd been caught at something. Lindy couldn't imagine what could be on her mind to make her look that way; didn't even have the bandwidth to try.

"Coffee, honey?" Greta said. "For the road?"

"No, thanks, Mom." Lindy couldn't stop trembling, as it was. "Can you call down to Shaw's and see if we can cancel the lobsters for tonight?" They'd ordered two dozen for David's birthday dinner. On Lindy's old to-do list for Sunday morning, July 25: *Pick up lobsters.*

"Oh, honey," Greta said sadly. "Do you really think he won't be here by tonight? Let's just wait awhile longer."

This was so far outside the possibilities Lindy had been considering that it took her a moment to make sense of it. "Do you really . . . think there's a chance he'll just . . . show up?"

"I do!"

Lindy hoped Greta was right, but she couldn't believe it. Still, she said, "Okay." It would be terrible if David showed up expecting a birthday dinner and she'd canceled the lobsters.

Absently, she went out to the back hall to look for her purse and keys. She still didn't want to believe that David would've put his family through the last twenty-four hours intentionally. *Couldn't* believe it, knowing what she knew about him after thirty-plus years.

Unless, somehow, he'd just . . . broken? Again? After all this time?

CHAPTER 12

Lindy

1978

"This is strange," David said, in that same odd tone of voice. Inside the musty tent, he was watching his blood seep through the sleeping bag as calmly as he'd have watched a duck swim past the beach—as if it had nothing to do with him.

"Shut up!" Lindy's mind felt scrambled as she tried to remember a first aid filmstrip from school last year. She needed to stop the bleeding. Glancing around the tent, she spotted an extra T-shirt in the corner. She grabbed it, tried to tear it into strips. It wouldn't rip. Quickly, she folded it, steeled herself, moved the sleeping bag away from his wrist, and wrapped the folded shirt around it. She yanked a shoelace out of his nearby sneaker, wound it tightly around the shirt, and knotted it.

"Hold your arm above your head," she snapped, imagining she remembered that necessity from the filmstrip, and she half forced his arm into the position, as he half complied. He still seemed mostly bewildered, calm. In the tent was the tinny smell of his blood mixed with the musty, damp canvas and lingering smoke of the smoldering campfire.

"Come on. We have to get you out of here." She wedged herself under his raised arm, grabbed him around the waist, pushed him out of the tent, and pulled him to his feet. "Keep your arm above your head!"

He raised his arm higher again, and now he looked ashamed. "It's okay," she said, because she was sorry for him then, though she was furious with him, too. "You're going to be okay."

She tucked herself back underneath his arm and held his waist as they walked, feeling the heat of his skin under her hands through his T-shirt. A drop of something wet landed on her neck, and she wondered if it was blood or old rain falling from the trees. His weight was heavy across her shoulders, and his feet were bare, and as she watched them stumble along next to her sneakers, she thought she should have put his sneakers on for him, even though she'd taken the lace out of one, but she didn't want to go back. She didn't know how much time there would be before he would pass out.

"I don't want to do this, Lindy," he said.

"I don't care," she said, though she didn't know exactly what he meant. "You're doing it." They didn't talk anymore after that. They were both breathing hard, and when Lindy saw the opening in the trees revealing the road, and the basin of the cove beyond that, her heart beat faster.

When they got to the road, he was very pale. He seemed rueful now, but he still wasn't saying anything. She thought she could run to the yellow cottage in about a minute; trying to make him walk would take ten. "Sit down," she said, and he crumpled to the ground, as if her will had been the only thing keeping him on his feet. "Keep your hand above your head."

He looked up at her, a question in his eyes.

"Promise me!"

He blinked, raised his hand higher. Red seeped through the T-shirt around his wrist. "Okay."

"Don't you dare move. Don't you dare do anything!" He gave her another quizzical look, but she didn't have time to stay and argue, and there were so many ways she could lose, so many wrong decisions she could make. "Stay here!" she said again, and she wheeled and took off running, her shoes pounding the gravel road, her heart and throat filling with tears, as the cove lapped peacefully beside her.

~

She banged up the porch steps of the yellow cottage and in through the screen door to the living room, yelling for his mother, crying. White-faced, Mrs. Kauffman grabbed the keys to the station wagon and was gone, peeling out onto the road, sending gravel flying. Lindy wanted to go with her, but it was too late. She had barely caught her breath, and Mrs. Kauffman was gone.

Kate came running downstairs, looking shocked. She must've overheard what Lindy had yelled to Mrs. Kauffman, because all Lindy could manage to say was, "David . . . David," and Kate just came over and hugged Lindy tight, and she was crying as hard as Lindy was.

"I'm sorry I didn't warn you," Kate said a little while later, tugging at a thread on the bottom of her cutoffs. They had finally collapsed onto opposite ends of the sofa. Lindy still felt short of breath. "My parents told us not to say anything to anyone. We all just hoped he would be better. He seemed so much happier here. He seemed really happy with you!"

Kate had been telling Lindy about how, for a couple months over the winter, David had had a hard time. First, he'd run away from home for a full week and, when he got back, refused to say where he'd been. After that, he slept too much, couldn't go to school sometimes, carved strange designs in the walls of his bedroom, and even punched a hole in one. Their mother had taken him to a doctor and everything. David had refused to take any medication, but when spring came, his track coach helped him get into a routine of running, and he seemed to bounce back, to seem almost like himself. "And then we got here, and he *did* seem like himself," Kate said. "We never dreamed he'd . . ." She shook her head and started biting a fingernail.

Lindy had been writing to David all winter and had spent nearly the entire summer with him, and she'd never had a clue about any of this.

Over the winter, if a reply took longer than usual to arrive, she'd stew in self-doubt, wondering if he was still interested in her at all, and when it finally appeared in her mailbox, she'd feel redeemed.

Now to find out he'd been . . . *unable* to write sometimes? On the run from home? Sick? Incapacitated by the workings of his mind?

She didn't know what to make of this information, or of the terrible turn of events. It was impossible to think that he'd *meant* to slice his wrist open, even though, the instant she opened the tent flap, she'd understood that he had. The intent had been evident in his eyes—mixed though it had been already with regret.

Remembering him with the knife in his hand and the blood pouring from his wrist made her nauseous, yet she couldn't stop seeing it, and now she realized there'd been fear in his dark eyes, too. She couldn't stand to think what would've happened if she hadn't gotten it into her head to march up into the woods and confront him.

Had their fight the other day been part of the reason why he'd harmed himself?

No, she couldn't think of that, either.

She wanted to cry and cry and cry—but what good would that do? She blinked and reached for Kate's hand. Kate gripped her hand tightly in return, and they sat there, waiting.

Two hours later, the phone finally rang. By then, Josh had come in from a bike ride, and all of them were sitting together, silent, terrified. Kate jumped up to answer.

She listened for a moment, then said, "He's going to be okay?"

Lindy instantly started crying. They all did, even Josh, who tried to hide it, wiping his eyes, looking away. "They're admitting him to the hospital?" Kate said, wiping her eyes, too. "Okay. Okay. Don't worry, Mom. I'll watch out for Josh. We'll be okay. Okay. Okay."

Kate hung up and looked at Lindy, then at Josh. She lifted her chin, even as she blinked back more tears. "I'm in charge now," she said.

~

Lindy didn't want to tell her parents, but when she walked in the door at Innisfree, they were in the kitchen laughing and fixing up their five o'clock martinis, as a disconcerting Dizzy Gillespie jazz tune blared from the distant stereo in the piano room. To see them acting so normal was startling. It also made clear that there was a before and an after, and that her parents were still living in the before. She wished she could go back there, too—never tell them, keep the horror outside of Innisfree forever—but when her dad, seeing her, grinned and said, "Hey, pumpkin! We were wondering where you were!" she simply burst into tears. He rushed to hug her, asking what was wrong. She asked him to go turn off the music, which he did, and when he came back, he hugged her again, and then it all came spilling out into the quiet, through tears she tried and failed to hold back.

"He did *what*?" Greta said. "And you found him like that?" She was pinching the skin at the base of her throat. She pushed her martini glass slightly away across the counter, a tiny movement that said, *No, I don't accept this, no.*

Lindy wiped her eyes with her sleeve. She had to get a hold of herself. She needed to help David, if she could. "Dad, will you drive me to the hospital so I can see him?"

"I don't think that's a good idea, Lindy." Greta's tone was not unsympathetic, but it was unyielding.

Lindy looked to her father. "Please?"

Tom glanced from Lindy to Greta and back again. It was always this way—him being forced to choose sides, or at least to place a fulcrum so some sort of balance could be achieved. "Why don't we call and see if he's up for company?"

Lindy looked back to her mother, who gave a tight nod. Her father went to the living room. Lindy leaned her head on her arms on the counter, listening to the sounds of the phone book being pulled out of the drawer, thin pages flipping, the rotary telephone dialing. Greta picked up her martini and took a big sip. "Summer shouldn't have things like this in it," she said.

"Mrs. Kauffman says it would be better if we didn't come today, pumpkin," Lindy's dad reported gravely moments later. "I'm sorry."

After that, he wouldn't let her out of his sight, insisting on a game of Monopoly in the living room. He was always the hat; she got to be the dog, her favorite. Today, she sat hunched over, feeling mute and slow. She kept seeing the blood streaming from David's wrist, and her dad said he'd be the banker, for a change—a single acknowledgment that things weren't as they'd always been.

Except then he refused to buy anything, saying he was saving his money for Park Place, which he never landed on. Lindy dumbly compiled stacks of properties, built rows of little green houses, traded them in for red hotels. When they stopped for a quick supper of Greta's crab rolls, Lindy's usual favorite, Lindy could eat only three bites, and even that made her nauseous. Afterward, when Tom landed on Boardwalk and went broke, it was Lindy who felt hollow, done in.

Greta was sitting on the sofa nearby, legs crossed elegantly, reading the latest *New Yorker,* sipping her fourth martini, when she typically limited herself to two. She'd put Supertramp's album *Even in the Quietest Moments* on the stereo in the other room, and her foot bobbed along to the distant beat. Lindy wondered what it was like at the hospital, what David was thinking, if he was lonely, if someone was sitting with him, watching him so he didn't do anything bad to himself again. Her dad was putting the game away, the money back in the bank, saying he'd beat her next time. "You didn't even try, Dad," she said, and he looked surprised, as if he'd thought he'd been fooling her. She kissed him good night—the crisp scent of his aftershave had been blunted by the day—and hugged her mother, who smelled of alcohol and the celery she'd put in the crab salad, then trudged upstairs to get ready for bed, thinking maybe she'd write David a letter tonight, maybe she'd be able to see him tomorrow.

Fifteen minutes later, a knock sounded on her bedroom door. She was already in bed, light on, pen poised above a blank piece of stationery, because what did you say to a boy who'd just done what David had?

Both of her parents came in. They hadn't done this in years, not since she was a little girl, afraid of monsters in the closet. Her mother sat beside her on the edge of the bed, while her father perched on her little white desk chair, leaning his elbows on his knees, brow knit above soft blue eyes. He looked this way sometimes when he thought there was about to be a fight, and Lindy wasn't in the mood to fight with her mother tonight, but she would if she had to.

"Listen, sweetie," Greta said, patting Lindy's hand. Lindy, wanting to cry again, swallowed hard and studied the tiny pink flowers inside the small white squares of her yellow-bordered quilt. The window was open a crack, letting in salt-scented air, and she heard the ocean lapping against the rocks in the darkness outside. "Your father and I discussed it."

Lindy looked up. This did not sound good. Her mother was wearing a tiny, rueful smile.

"We know you care about David," Tom said.

Greta gave Lindy's hand a little squeeze, probably intended as sympathetic, but to Lindy it felt like a vise tightening. "But we think that he's . . . he's going to need some time apart from you."

"Apart?" Lindy sat up straighter. "What does that mean?"

Her father broke in. "When a person gets in a bad state like that, you want to help them, but there's not really anything you can do. He needs professional help."

Lindy couldn't believe her dad was saying this, let alone anything like it. He had spent all night playing Monopoly with her! He had spent all night pretending to be her friend. "He needs people who love him!"

"Sweetheart." The sadness in Greta's eyes said, *Poor child—you poor, ignorant child.* "A boy like that, he's not . . . he's not going to be able to have a normal relationship. Not right now. Maybe not for a very long time."

"We like him," Tom insisted, as if Lindy had accused them of the opposite. "We don't want to see anything bad happen to him. But you're our first concern, pumpkin. It's our job to keep you safe."

In no world had Lindy expected to have to fight with *both* of her parents. "He's not going to hurt *me!*"

Greta shot her another sad look. "Sweetheart, you just can't affiliate yourself with a boy who's unstable. You have too much going for you."

Lindy looked to her father. "Dad!" But he averted his eyes, got to his feet, and leaned over to kiss her forehead. She wanted to think it was her mother who was making him act this way. It seemed nonsensical for them to make these pronouncements now, after they'd gone all night without even talking to her about what had happened or asking any questions. How could they be so sure of themselves when they knew so little? "Try to get some sleep," her father said, and it was all she could do to keep from saying, *Ha.*

Her mother kissed her forehead, too, then her parents met at the foot of her bed, took each other's hands, and told her good night. She folded her arms and frowned. They shot her sad looks in stereo, then went out.

It was final: They had betrayed her. Abandoned her. How could they not understand? How could they say that she needed to let David go, that she couldn't help him, couldn't be with him?

Watch me, Lindy thought, as the door clicked shut behind them.

CHAPTER 13

Hailey

Sunday, July 25, 2010
4 p.m.

Nothing. Nothing. All day long, Hailey and her brothers were finding nothing and getting nowhere, for all the miles they drove, all the stops they made. Each time the three of them went inside any place, Hailey took the lead, showing a photo she had on her phone of the whole family, zooming in on David's face. The first couple times, it was the weirdest thing to say the words, "Our dad's missing, and we were hoping you might've seen him in here?" After that, she got inured to it, almost, and everyone was kind, asking concerned-sounding questions. When? Why? Really? *Yesterday, his birthday party, traveling from Cranston, yes.*

Every stop began with a soaring hope, camaraderie with her brothers. "This is the place!" Cody would say, jogging ahead to open and hold the door for her and Eli, and Hailey would glide into the cool of the air-conditioning, the falseness of fluorescent lights. She would tip her sunglasses up on top of her head, scanning for the person who looked like they might be in charge, who might know something.

Each stop ended in the sinking feeling of fresh defeat, and she would exit to the shock of the burning sun, baking pavement, traffic noise, the heat of the black leather Jeep seat through the thin fabric of the sundress she'd grabbed out of her old closet in Cranston.

No one had seen him. Not at the state liquor store, Popovers on the Square in Portsmouth, or the six other places they tried in New Hampshire. At the "Welcome to Maine" rest stop, she took one of the prescription pills in her purse for her pulsing headache, and they grabbed maps showing the locations of all the Audubon trails and the state and local recreational trails. Then they searched for his car at every trailhead in southern Maine, making stops in Kittery, South Berwick, York, Saco, and on and on. At the Starbucks inside the Kennebunkport service plaza, where their dad often stopped, they were met with blank stares.

Out on the road, they saw dozens of older-model green Subaru Outbacks. They even saw a couple at the trailheads. But none of them had Rhode Island plates, and none of them was David's.

Her headache had gotten worse and worse, causing stars in her vision, nausea.

"I can't get it," Eli snapped now, tossing their dad's flip phone onto the back seat beside him. "I've tried all our birthdays, Mom and Dad's anniversary, everything! It locked me out now." He leaned back, spread-eagled, and shut his eyes behind his sunglasses, letting out a frustrated sigh.

"This sucks," Cody said, and Hailey could think of nothing to add, and nothing to say to the contrary.

"I'm just heading to work, babe, what's up?" Noah answered the phone sounding slightly out of breath. She guessed he was walking the mile to work, which he did most days, citing both the environment and the cost of parking.

Aware of her brothers listening, and of the tire noise again as Cody barreled north on I-95, she rubbed her aching temple and told Noah they were almost back to Portland, they'd found no trace of her dad, and she'd just talked to her mom, who, searching with Emma and Reese, had found no trace of him north of Portland, either.

Then Hailey got to the point. "I don't see how . . ." She stopped. Her head had hammers inside it. "I mean, Noah, we're going to have to put the wedding on pause for now."

"Pause? What does that mean?"

The tension—and his cluelessness—finally broke her. "It means I don't know where my dad is! And I can't go through the motions of getting ready for our wedding when—"

"What do you mean, go through the motions? Is that all it is to you?"

He got this way sometimes. She knew how to handle it. You couldn't blame him; he'd snap. "That's not what I meant. It's just—" She had to get her bearings, remind herself of what was really going on, what was important. She had to remind Noah, too. "I mean, it's Dad's birthday today! Something has to be really wrong for him to not show up, not be in touch with any of us. He could be hurt! He could be *dead*, Noah!"

Noah sighed. Had he realized he was being unreasonable? "Okay, look. I'm tense, all right? I wish you were here."

"Yeah. I wish everything was normal, too."

Noah sounded like he was running now. Maybe crossing a street. "Look, he's gonna turn up, okay? I'm sure it's just some big misunderstanding. I mean, I just think you're gonna be sorry if you cancel the wedding for no reason. It's still almost two weeks away. Eight-seven-ten, right?"

She and Noah had made the planned date of their wedding, 8/7/10, into kind of a mantra, something they said when one or both of them got overwhelmed or frustrated, and they joked that repeating it so often would make remembering their anniversary easy, years from now. She let out a breath. "Yeah. Okay."

"Okay, good. I gotta go, babe. I'll talk to you later. Love you."

"Okay. Love you, too." She ended the call.

"Did you just agree to keep the wedding on?" Eli said from the back seat.

"Well . . . yeah. I mean . . . Dad could show up any minute!"

"Let's hope so," Cody said grimly, not sounding convinced.

Hailey bit her lip, squinting through her sunglasses at the hot concrete out ahead, twisting her ring around her finger. She couldn't believe she'd said it, in front of her little brothers: that their dad could be dead. She was supposed to hold it together for them, take care of them, protect them.

At least, she'd always managed to before.

Back at Innisfree, Grandma was boiling lobsters as the sunset colored the sky pink and orange outside the windows. The kitchen was full of steam, and Hailey's mom was there telling Eli, Emma, and Reese to take some of the cooked lobsters over to the yellow cottage for the cousins. "This is weird, Mom," Cody snapped, gesturing to the steaming pot, Greta in her apron and oven mitts, the big bucket of uncooked lobsters tumbling over each other inside it like bait worms.

"I know," Lindy said, "but we didn't want to cancel the lobsters this morning in case he showed up, and then it was too late to cancel them. So, we've got two dozen!"

"I'm not hungry," Cody said, and it was probably the first time in his life he'd uttered that sentence. A fresh hammering started up in Hailey's head, and she exchanged looks with her mom as Cody grabbed a Sam Adams from the fridge. Not meeting anybody's eyes, he crossed the cottage in six long strides, went out the front door, and flopped into the Adirondack chair beside Grandpa on the deck. The room felt suddenly empty, off-kilter. Emma, Reese, and Eli were walking out the back door, each carrying a platter stacked with cooked lobsters.

Hailey rubbed her pounding temples again. She was sweaty, needed a shower. Badly. But *could* you just "go take a shower" when your dad was missing and your mom and grandma and maybe your brother were apparently losing their minds? It didn't seem like the right thing to do, but Hailey had no idea what she *could* do. The fishy smell of the lobster was making her nausea worse. She hoped the people at the yellow cottage were hungry, because nobody at Innisfree was going to eat these things. Lindy was frowning at her, as if preparing to say something, but then just turned back to Greta, who was telling her to set the timer for the new batch, which Lindy did.

Hailey knew her mom had planned on making a special birthday cake for tonight. The store-bought one had been fine for yesterday's party, but tonight's was going to be a chocolate whiskey cake with ganache meant to replicate one that Lindy and David had had at some restaurant in New York years ago, which he often talked about as the best cake he'd ever tasted. The restaurant was no longer in business, but Lindy had tracked down the former chef and convinced him to share the recipe. It called for a special kind of Irish whiskey that cost $150 a bottle, and Lindy had sprung for it, saying the chef swore it made the difference between acceptable and sublime. Hailey wondered where that bottle was now. Her mom hadn't actually made the cake, had she? Hailey massaged the back of her neck, hoping to ease the pain in her head. The steam from the lobsters was making the kitchen so hot, and she was seriously about to throw up, but she thought she should stay and try to do something to help.

She heard a knock at the door and went to answer it, wiping the sweat off her face, figuring it was some well-meaning neighbor wanting an update.

When she saw who was standing on the other side of the screen, her breath caught. She recognized him instantly, though he'd been gone from The Cove since they were seventeen. Seven summers ago.

"Jack?" She pushed open the door and stepped outside into the cool evening.

She had never imagined she would see him again. He looked like a grown man now, his jaw squared, his eyes narrower. He was a couple inches taller than her, and his light brown hair was shaggy, bleached blond at the tips by the sun. In a blue Quiksilver T-shirt, khaki shorts, and OluKai flip flops, he looked at ease, in shape—he must've kept up his surfing and tennis—and his smile was bright even in the dusky light.

"Hey, Hailey! I just got in, and my grandma told me . . ." His smile faded. "She told me about your dad."

Jack's grandma, Marjorie Westfield, who was Hailey's grandma's least favorite person in The Cove, was from Connecticut and had been a driving force behind the SCPA for as long as Hailey could remember. Her cottage, "Seabreeze," had belonged to her family, the Tennysons, from the time she was a girl, and it sat on the cove side, four cottages down from the end of the point. If you drew lines between Innisfree, the yellow cottage, and Seabreeze, you'd get a triangle that was just slightly askew. Jack was from San Diego, and for three summers, when he was fifteen to seventeen, he'd come to stay with Marjorie—his father's mother—at The Cove. By the second summer, it had become obvious that his parents had shipped him, their only child, off because they were going through a nasty divorce. By the third summer, he was estranged from his dad.

The fourth summer, Marjorie said that Jack had opted to stay on the West Coast. (Marjorie had a way of discouraging questions, even as she invited you in for tea and perhaps a slice of her famous cookie cake, which she always seemed to have recently baked, "just in case someone stopped by." She would sit across from you in her spotless granite-and-glass kitchen, lean in like you were all that mattered in the world, tuck her silver hair behind her ear, gaze at you with her soft blue eyes, and gently pry out every secret. But she was *nice,* honestly. Hailey didn't know what her grandma's problem was with her.) After that, Hailey had learned through the grapevine that Jack was in school at Stanford, and, much later, working in Silicon Valley. She'd been careful to pay only enough attention to these reports to glean one thing for sure: He seemed destined never to return to The Cove.

She *had* thought once or twice, when she was younger, about friending him on Facebook, but finally decided sending a request could seem pathetic. They had never stayed in touch over the winters, not even after what happened between them when they were seventeen. *Things that happened in the summer didn't matter at all,* that was what Hailey's grandma always said, and, on the subject of Jack Westfield, Hailey tried to believe that was true.

But now he was standing on the steps of Innisfree, brow furrowed with concern, acting like no time had passed since they'd last kissed goodbye seven years ago, and she wished she'd taken a shower, put on a better dress.

"I was wondering what I could do to help," he said.

PART TWO

Big Girls Don't Cry

CHAPTER 14

Hailey

Monday, July 26, 2010
5:15 a.m.

Jack said he was sure his grandma would let him use her Z3 roadster—he'd flown in from California, so he didn't have his own car—and, sure enough, at 5:15, there came the rumble of the BMW's motor headed up the hill toward Innisfree. Inside the dimly lit kitchen, Hailey's grandma had made Hailey a cup of pour-over coffee and was now making one for herself. Hailey took a last hurried, bitter sip and thanked her. "Be careful out there, sweetheart," said Greta, with a frown. She had never liked Jack, simply because of who his grandmother was. Hailey said she would, grabbed a stack of the *MISSING* flyers that Aunt Kate had made yesterday, and banged out the screen door into the damp, pink dawn. She hurried to the road to meet Jack beside her grandma's burgeoning garden, since Innisfree's driveway was full with Hailey's mom's Volvo, Hailey's Protegé, Cody's Jeep, and her grandparents' old Camry, which they always stored in Maine over the winter rather than driving it back to New York City.

Last night, when Jack had offered to help, Hailey had been so surprised and off-kilter that she'd simply blurted, "Want to help me search in the morning?"

He'd given her a little smile. "We'll leave no stone unturned."

He'd easily agreed to go at first light, and, though he seemed to want to say more or be invited inside, she'd just said thank you, good night, see you at 5:15.

She'd spent a rough night studying the contracts in the wedding binder only to find that, almost without exception, the window had closed on getting any money back if they canceled. She'd tossed and turned on the lumpy cot in The Closet, trying to imagine where her dad could be and coming up with not a single positive scenario she could believe in. Finally, she'd fallen into nightmares of drowning, being chased by a shark, seeing Noah at a bar with some beautiful girl and slinking away so he wouldn't see her, and a few times in the middle of it all she'd half woken up and wondered, *Jack Westfield? Really?* But at least this morning she'd gotten a shower, the smell of lobster wasn't plaguing her, and her headache was no longer excruciating enough to make her nauseous.

"Hey, Hailey," Jack said, smiling as she opened the passenger door of the gorgeous silver convertible and sank awkwardly into the low leather seat. He had the top down, and she was glad she'd tied back her hair and worn a cardigan, because the morning was still cool.

"Hi, Jack," she said, and the way he looked at her caused a small thrumming in her heart, which she tamped down. Pinning the flyers printed with her father's picture and the word *MISSING* under her hands, she absently twisted her ring. Noah would still be sleeping. She hadn't heard from him since yesterday afternoon.

But there's no signal, so he probably did text or call and it just hasn't come through yet, she reminded herself. Being pissed at Noah did not seem like a good idea right now, not given everything that was going on, and definitely not with Jack Westfield smiling over at her like he could still see straight through her the way he used to do, like seven years hadn't passed at all.

"Ready?" Jack said. She gave a little nod, he gunned the motor, and they were off.

~

"Law school? Really?" Jack raised his voice to be heard above the wind as they skirted along the winding highway. Hailey stuffed the flyers under her leg and pulled her sweater tighter around her. Jack reached down without comment to press the button to turn on her heated seat, which, honestly, amazed her. That he was paying attention like that. "What about your writing?"

Hailey's stomach hitched. "Oh, that was just a silly thing I did when I was a kid! I haven't really kept it up." This wasn't entirely true. She was, technically, still "working on" a story (she didn't dare call it a "novel"), writing it longhand in a spiral notebook that was, at this point, almost full. She was on chapter twenty-two. It wasn't nothing. But she'd added only two chapters this entire past year, between the wedding planning and work and everything else, and she knew she'd have zero time for it once she started law school.

So, it wasn't like she was telling him a lie. That part of her life was pretty much in her past, an old childhood dream.

"What about you?" she said above the wind. "I thought you took some big job in Silicon Valley."

"Key words, exit package. My company got bought out a couple months ago. I've been pondering next steps."

"A.k.a., surfing?" Hailey smiled.

"Uh, yeah." He gave her a wicked little grin, shifting into a higher gear. "Then my grandma called last week and said my dad's being a dick about her being here by herself. Wants her to sell the place since he never comes here. And she fell. Back in February? Didn't get hurt too bad, but still."

"Oh! I hadn't heard that."

"She's been trying to keep it quiet. I don't think anybody here knows about it. But . . . she's eighty-one. It could happen again, right? So, I came out here to stay with her to piss him off. So she can spend the rest of the summer, and he can't complain about her being here by herself."

Hailey's smile had faded; her headache sharpened to a point beside her eyebrow. She inhaled. "You're going to be here the rest of the summer?"

The same wicked grin, this time with an added tilt of an eyebrow. "Yep."

He hadn't asked about her engagement ring, though it was winking in the early morning light.

Last night, Hailey's mom had admitted to having totally forgotten about the couple dozen forest preserves, all owned and maintained by a single land trust organization, that were within a dozen miles of Summerland Cove, scattered around the broad peninsula that was bounded by tidal rivers and ended at the ocean. Hailey couldn't believe no one—not even her—had thought to consider that her dad might've stopped at one on his way to The Cove on Saturday.

"We should go check the parking lots right now!" Hailey had told her mom. They'd been finishing cleaning up the kitchen, just the two of them. Grandma and Grandpa had gone up to bed, and Lindy had ordered the other kids to take an hour to themselves and do something that "felt halfway normal." Emma and Reese had disappeared up to the girls' room; Eli had taken a shower. Cody had gone for a walk and would end up either at the yellow cottage playing video games or visiting Kelsey Grimes. (Every summer for a decade, it had been obvious there was something between those two, though Cody swore they were just friends and he had no interest in more, especially since she was now in school in Wisconsin and that was "too damn far away.")

Lindy had looked up from scouring the lobster pot, eyes snapping. "I don't want *anyone* going out tonight to look! I want you here, under this roof. Safe. It's bad enough Cody insisted on going out for a walk."

"We need to be doing everything we can, Mom."

Lindy frowned, returned to scouring the pot. "I think someone would've reported it, if a Subaru with Rhode Island plates was parked for two days and a night at one of those places."

"But what if nobody came along?"

"Lots of people use those trails every day. If he'd hurt himself, someone would've found him. Probably right away. It's not like they're labyrinthine trails, you know? They're pretty short."

Hailey folded her arms, feeling petulant. She didn't want to think that her dad hadn't made it at least to their peninsula. She didn't like to think of him lost out there in the wider world. Nor did she want to remind her mom of what the whole family knew: When David was by himself, he sometimes ventured off the beaten path. "Okay, so it's not likely," she snapped, "but it's *possible*. Like, say he drove all the way here and made good time and figured he could just spend, like, an hour in the woods before he had to show up here and face everyone at the party."

Lindy cocked her head but kept scrubbing.

"He *would* do that. You have to admit. And you know he doesn't really like parties."

Lindy turned to her, aghast. "Your father likes parties!"

"Okay, Mom. Whatever." Hailey realized then that neither of them had said a word about the wedding, or about all the things they still needed to do to get ready for it. The question of whether they should cancel loomed, despite what she'd promised Noah. But then, she felt like admitting this out loud to her mom would be like conceding that her dad was seriously *gone*—and that they might be in this horrible search-mode limbo for days, even weeks. Forever?

Impossible.

And then, even though Lindy had seemed totally done in and claimed not to want anybody to leave the house, and even though it was after nine by the time they had finished with the kitchen, she rounded everybody up, sending Eli and Hailey over to the yellow cottage to get Kate, Josh, and Cody, and the six of them—two carloads—drove to town to check their cell phones, while Emma and Reese again stayed at Innisfree next to the landline.

No one had gotten a message from David.

At least, Hailey thought now, checking the local trailheads was a clear mission for her and Jack to tackle this morning. The closest one was just a few miles from Summerland Cove, and it was one of her dad's favorites, so she had to think it was where he'd have been most likely to stop.

As Jack turned in among the tall pines that shaded the parking lot, the roadster bumping over the uneven dirt, Hailey's stomach twisted. The lot was empty. No Subaru. No Dad.

Yes, it had been a long shot, but—

Do not wallow, she told herself. She plucked a *MISSING* flyer from the stack, asked Jack to stop, then jumped out and pinned the flyer to the large wooden kiosk that featured a map of the trail and information about the wildflowers and animals you'd be likely to spot on your hike. She grabbed a land trust brochure from the wooden holder that was mounted nearby and hurried back to the roadster, sinking into the seat again. She unfolded the unwieldy brochure, which was printed on plain white paper with blue ink and provided a map of the peninsula showing the locations of all the land trust trails.

"Okay, there are thirty trails," she reported, tugging the big paper straight, studying the legend. "We know he's not at this one."

Jack spoke quietly. "We're going to assume the car didn't get stolen after sitting here for a couple days?"

Hailey winced. If you allowed for the possibility that her dad and his Subaru could've become separated, that made the search for him even more impossible. "It's not that nice of a car," she said, and if she was in denial about the infinite number of places that her father could be after almost forty-eight hours missing, she was going to stay in denial. She would limit the number of possibilities she'd allow in her mind, at least right now, to these thirty trailheads on the peninsula.

Or, twenty-nine, since he wasn't at this one.

Jack gave her a small, sympathetic smile, as if he understood. "Okay, Hales. Where to next?"

CHAPTER 15

Lindy

Monday, July 26, 2010
9:15 a.m.

"She's on vacation?" Lindy said into the phone at Innisfree. She had called David's office looking for Tiffany, who'd never called her back yesterday, even after Lindy left a second message in the evening and sent three texts throughout the day.

Which was really weird, Lindy thought. They'd always been friendly enough. Not that Lindy had ever had much to do with Tiffany. The occasional hello on the phone when Lindy called David at the office, that was about it. Though the girl *had* come to their holiday party at the house last December, wearing a slinky gold sequined dress and lipstick the color of a bruised plum, downing Prosecco and talking on about what an *amazing* boss David was, and how *inspiring* it was to work at the Innocence Project, and how she'd come to Providence from Chicago looking for purpose and *found* it. With her long lashes, glowing copper skin, and Pilates-toned body, she looked like she could've been Halle Berry's hot twenty-two-year-old sister, though she was, according to David, twenty-seven.

Lindy, who could *not* go sleeveless in winter, had primarily worried that the girl had to be freezing in her short spaghetti-strapped dress, and twice offered to loan her a sweater, but Tiffany had laughed prettily each time and refused, the second time adding an, "Aren't you sweet?" in a tone that Lindy couldn't help but feel, on reflection, was a bit condescending. Tiffany had not brought a date to the party, and everyone there was nearly twice her age, so who was she trying to impress with that dress?

David? No. Couldn't be.

At least, that was what Lindy had thought at the time.

Now it all just seemed weird. Not only had the girl not responded to Lindy's calls or texts yesterday, but she had taken vacation at the same time as David?

Shouldn't she be there to handle things while he was away?

"Just today?" Lindy asked the woman who'd answered the phone, who'd identified herself as "Shawna." Lindy had never met a "Shawna," had never even heard David mention the name.

"She's out for the week," Shawna said, in a clipped way. "May I take a message?"

"Uh, no. No, thanks." Lindy said goodbye and hung up.

She tried Tiffany's cell again. Again, the call went to voicemail. "Tiffany, it's really important," Lindy said. "*Please* call me."

As she replaced the old phone in its cradle, she felt hollowed out, alone. This morning, when she'd asked her dad for ideas on what more she could do to search for David, he had only looked at her blankly. Her mom had quickly broken in to say she was sure David would arrive today, then hustled a confused-looking Tom into motion and out the door for their morning walk. Cody, meanwhile, had gathered all the kids—except Hailey, who was already out with Jack—to go out searching in the Jeep again. When Lindy placed another call to the state police, the officer she spoke to had said there'd been no sightings of David's car and that his case still didn't meet the criteria to be added to the missing persons registry. "Legally, an adult has the right for people not to know where he is," the officer said, then suggested that, if she was really concerned, she could call the local TV and radio stations. Heart in her throat, she had. The TV stations wanted pictures; driving to Portland and Bangor with them would be her next step. Maybe she'd ask Kate to help.

But right now, Lindy was alone with her thoughts. And, as if considering Kate's and Josh's worries about David's mental state hadn't been bad enough, now she couldn't help recalling all the times this past year that he had come to bed chuckling over something.

Lindy knew he always checked his email last thing before crawling into bed, and when she would ask what was so funny, he'd say, "Nothing," still smiling to himself. A couple times, he'd actually said, "Oh, Tiffany sent me this joke. It would be too hard to explain. I'll show you in the morning." Both times, he'd just leaned over to give her a peck goodnight on the temple and flipped off his lamp—and neither time had he shown her the joke in the morning.

She also couldn't help recalling the tender way he had helped Tiffany with her coat after that Christmas party—and how Tiffany had reached up and pressed her hand over his against her shoulder for a moment, giving him a warm smile.

And then there were all the times he'd worked late these past few months. Tiffany had certainly been spending far more time with him than Lindy had. Plus, Tiffany was in on all his confidential cases. The two of them could talk about everything! Everything that was important to David.

Whereas, for David and Lindy, there was so much they *couldn't* talk about.

God, it would be such a cliché, wouldn't it? *Man runs off with his assistant because they've bonded over shared "important work," while his wife has been too distracted to pay him any attention for the last six months?* (Yes, Lindy was instantly blaming herself that this scenario even seemed possible.)

She didn't want to think that her imagination was being unduly influenced by Kate. Last night in the Volvo on their way to town to check their phones, Kate had told Lindy about a friend whose husband had disappeared for a few days, only to call and confess he'd run off with his assistant. "That's what fifty-year-old men do, I guess!" Kate had declared. "And they've got five kids! Been together thirty years."

"Hey," Josh had broken in from the back seat, sounding offended. "David wouldn't do that."

"Oh, yeah, no," Kate said. She'd obviously had a couple glasses of wine again, which was bizarre. Was Kate off the rails because of David? Or was she just letting loose because her husband and kids weren't around? "Of course not, he wouldn't," she went on, but by her tone Lindy couldn't tell if she was being sarcastic.

Either way, a bad feeling had started whirring in Lindy's gut the instant Kate had told the story, and now the image came to mind again of beautiful young Tiffany in that sparkling gold dress, pressing David's hand to her shoulder, smiling up at him.

Was Lindy about to find herself in the same situation as Kate's friend? Five kids, four kids, twenty-five or thirty years together. Was there no point at which you could just relax and know that you were safe? That your family would survive intact?

She tried to boot this line of thinking out of her mind. It wasn't that it was preferable to think of David lying injured in the woods somewhere—she'd *always* worried that his knee would give out on him again—but . . . well, it kind of was. Because maybe Hailey would find him at one of the local trails this morning! Maybe the other kids would find something!

Maybe.

Lindy went to the kitchen and made a fresh cup of coffee—she'd need to be alert for a full day of driving—and, as she drank it, tried to worry about other things. There were plenty, including the fact that Hailey was out with Jack Westfield this morning. Lindy would've been glad to have seen the last of Jack Westfield. The summer Hailey was seventeen, he'd had her in tears more times than Lindy had seen Hailey in tears before or since. And to think he'd show up less than two weeks before Hailey planned to get married! If Lindy was on speaking terms with God right now, she'd be asking, *What is this, some kind of joke?*

And, yesterday, driving around with Emma and Reese, Lindy had learned that what she'd assumed in Reese to be an actor's cool veneer was actually that of a fashion model—perhaps even more concerning? Then, though the girl had sat mostly silently in the back seat, seemingly asleep, head leaned back, mirrored aviator shades on—Lindy kept an eye on her in the rearview—suddenly, two hours into their searching, she'd sat up straight, flung off her sunglasses and exclaimed, "Lighthouse!"

"Pardon me?" Lindy had said.

"Lighthouse?" said Emma in the passenger seat, turning eagerly toward Reese.

"Yeah! Lighthouse!" In the mirror, Reese sagged, frowned. "Or, light. House. Two words? Or, White House? Give me a piece of paper. I'll write it down."

Emma nodded and turned to face front, opening the glovebox to root for paper and a pen, saying to Lindy, "Reese is clairaudient. Psychic, but she hears things rather than sees them, you know? She's been trying to get information about Dad."

"Oh!" Lindy said. "Wow! Really?" She paused, taking it in. "Lighthouse?" She tried to be open-minded.

"Yeah," Reese said, busily writing.

Emma was Googling on her phone. "Oh, God. There are sixty-five lighthouses in Maine." She whirled to face Reese. "Is he at one of them?"

Reese shrugged, handing the piece of paper to her. "No idea. I'll keep trying." She sank back into her seat and replaced her sunglasses. Lindy glanced over to read the paper that Emma held in her hand:

Lighthouse?
light house?
White House? (D.C.)
white house?

At least the girl had pretty handwriting, but was this the kind of partner a mother wanted for her daughter? Crazy? No. It was not. And now Lindy had to consider whether they ought to take the girl seriously and start searching the sixty-five lighthouses that were, according to Emma and Google, strewn along the length of Maine's coast, which, Emma said, when you included inlets and islands, ran for 3,478 miles. Or should they check the White House? Or a white house? Their house in Cranston was white, but the kids had already looked there!

For God's sake.

And one more thing Lindy almost couldn't stand to think of: the empty look in her father's blue eyes this morning. Wasn't he worried about David? Was there something else wrong? Or was he just that involved in the new book that her mom had said he was writing now, the one that was keeping him at his desk in the bedroom pretty much all the time so far this summer? Because, typically, he would've done or said *something* to help her . . .

None of these thoughts stopped Lindy's mind from circling back. *It's what fifty-year-old men do.*

The gold dress. The late-night emails. The warm smile. The hand on the shoulder.

She stepped out onto the deck, taking in the deep blue ocean and a lobster boat motoring past, relishing the salty breeze on her face, letting the beloved scene strengthen and console her, even as she tried again to clear her mind.

Then she remembered: Tiffany had been on their Christmas card list last year, and Lindy had written her mailing address in the family address book, beside where David had earlier written her cell number. And, at Lindy's request yesterday—she hadn't known who she might end up needing to call—the kids had brought the address book back from Cranston.

Maybe Tiffany had a home number that would be written in there, too?

Lindy hurried back inside to where she'd left the address book beside the phone, set down her coffee, and flipped to the J page. There was the girl's name—*Tiffany Jeffries*—and cell phone number in David's handwriting, plus her mailing address in Lindy's. A Providence apartment.

There was no landline number.

Lindy would call Information!

Quickly, she dialed 411 and supplied the operator with Tiffany's name and address. Quickly, the operator found the number. Lindy's hand shook as she scratched it with pencil onto her mother's notepad beside the phone.

She hung up and sipped her coffee again, pacing. Why was she so nervous about calling this number, after all the other, potentially more consequential, calls she'd made?

David was *not* having an affair. He was not at Tiffany's apartment—or with Tiffany anywhere—right now.

But Tiffany might be privy to some information about him that Lindy was not.

She set down her coffee and dialed.

In her ear came the ringing. *One. Two.* Lindy's heart was in her throat again; she told herself to get a grip. *Three.* (Involuntarily, she saw tangled white sheets, David's pale body, the woman's golden legs kicking off the sheet—to get up and answer the phone?) *Four.*

A bored-sounding woman answered. "Hello?"

Lindy cleared her throat, collected herself. "Is this Tiffany Jeffries?" She tried to sound stern, though she didn't think the voice sounded like Tiffany's at all.

The woman yawned. "No, she's not here. Can I take a message?"

Lindy exhaled. Explained who she was and why she was calling. "I tried my husband's office, and they said Tiffany is out on vacation all week. I really need to speak with her."

"Oh! She's on vacation? I thought she was at work when I got home this morning. I'm a resident at the hospital. I'm there more than I'm here. I never see her."

Lindy wondered if all of this was really true. "You have no idea where she is? Or who she's with? Or why she wouldn't be answering her cell?"

"No." The woman seemed unconcerned. "I'll leave a note to tell her you called, for when she comes back. Good luck." The woman hung up.

Lindy pulled the phone away from her ear and stared at it.

Okay, it was ridiculous to think David might be having an affair with Tiffany.

Wasn't it? When he and Lindy had been each other's one and only for so long?

CHAPTER 16

Lindy

1978

David was in the hospital in Boston for three weeks. Lindy wasn't allowed to go see him. Her parents and the Kauffmans agreed, claiming his doctors agreed, too. Her father, with uncharacteristic sternness, added, "So, don't you dare think you're going to hop a bus and go down there, young lady. They will not let you in."

Lindy boycotted the piano. At first, out of sadness; then, out of protest. Her mother was onto her. The first three mornings, Greta brought her cinnamon toast in bed. After that, she said Lindy needed to get up and at 'em. "No," Lindy said. She didn't know why. She just felt like the sound of the piano, the feel of the keys under her fingers, would make her scream.

The weirder thing was, she couldn't bring herself to draw, either.

She said almost nothing to her parents and came downstairs only when they insisted on it for meals, and then her mother got angry when she would barely eat—but what did she expect? Finally, even Lindy's father snapped, "Goddammit, we're trying to do what's best for you!" As if that was supposed to be some consolation.

When the sun came out, she went to the beach and lay on the sand with her eyes closed for entire afternoons. Her mind felt blank. But on the other side of that blankness, she felt, would be a new Lindy.

"What are you going to do?" Kate asked tentatively, finding her there. In a floral pink bikini top and cutoffs, her curly, dark hair twisted up in a straggling bun, Kate looked twenty, not fifteen. Sand grains frosted her knees. Lindy didn't remember her looking grown-up two weeks ago.

"I don't know," Lindy said, but within the range of possibilities circling her sun-drenched mind—she felt she was waiting for a corresponding door to swing open, to let the right one inside—was not the thing that Kate thought she might do.

"When you go back to New York," Kate said, "it would be easy for you just to forget all about him. If you wanted to?"

Lindy sensed a hopeful lilt in her old friend's voice. Why did everyone seem to think that Lindy was bad for David? That Lindy was the cause of David's despair? (Or, in her parents' case, vice versa.) Lindy knew the opposite was true.

She also knew that, as of that rainy day when she'd found him in the tent, she was the entire reason he was even still alive.

When David got back, there were only three days left in the summer, and Mrs. Kauffman wouldn't let him out of her sight. Greta spoke to Mrs. Kauffman on the phone, making her promise that she wouldn't leave Lindy alone with David, then finally let Lindy walk over to the yellow cottage to visit him. The late-August sun was shining, Greta's garden was in full bloom, and the ocean was a radiant deep blue. Lindy had ironed her hair and put on a new top her mother had bought her in town at Renys last week. It was a cap-sleeved button-up made of thin cotton in an orange-and-purple plaid. She would never wear it in New York, but today she wanted to look cheerful. Her toes felt numb with nerves as she walked the wooded gravel cut-through from Innisfree toward the yellow cottage.

Approaching, she saw him sitting in the rocking chair on the front porch. As she hurried toward him and up the steps, he stood, seeming taller and paler than ever, and she ran into his arms, burying her face in his black T-shirt. She'd promised herself she wouldn't cry, but it was hard work to swallow back the tears that welled. The clean white cuff of a bandage encircling his wrist shouldn't have been as shocking as it was, but seeing it made her realize she'd spent three whole weeks hoping that what she knew to be true would end up having been false, a joke, a gag, a nightmare—but it was all real. At least the scents of laundry soap and maple syrup that she picked up from his T-shirt were a comfort, because these smells meant his mother was taking good care of him, and he was letting her.

David squeezed her arms to push her slightly away and smiled down like he felt sorry for her. "My mom said we can be out here alone, but she's going to check on us every five minutes."

Lindy nodded, looking up at him, overcome with a swell of love not just for him but also for his mother, and for the fact that Mrs. Kauffman was not following Greta's instructions to the letter. David's face looked angular, unfamiliar, and her stomach lurched at the sight of a scratch on his face. She reached up and touched it before she could think.

"They still let me shave myself, but I have to be watched," he said. "It's weird."

Lindy's father had instructed her not to question or push David, just to demonstrate acceptance. Now she had to bite her tongue to keep from asking why he'd hurt himself, if he was feeling better, if there was any chance he might do it again.

"I missed you," she said instead.

David gave a rueful smile. "I figured you wouldn't want anything to do with me ever again."

"Don't ever think that." She'd promised herself she would be bold. "I love you."

David pulled away and sat down in the rocker. He squinted out across the road at where the sun cast glitter across the cove. "I'm a losing bet, Lindy. That's one thing I've come to understand."

She folded her arms. Again, it was hard not to cry. "I don't believe that."

"I have to go back to Chicago. We're leaving day after tomorrow."

Her stomach lurched; she'd thought they had one more day than that. She watched the toe of her beat-up sneaker digging into the porch floorboard.

"I'm sorry," he said, and when she looked up at him, she could see he meant for more than just having to leave.

Her father's advice was drowned out by her desperation to make David see. "What if there was something to look forward to?" she blurted, because, though she wasn't sure she believed in God, she had to think there was some reason other than her stupid wounded pride why she'd hurried into the woods that day in time to save David. If there was a God, it seemed clear to her now, He had made her rush into the woods because He had big plans for David, who was obviously extraordinary.

David squinted out at the cove again, drumming his fingers on the arm of the rocking chair. Lindy thought of him punching a hole in his bedroom wall back home. Had anyone patched it? Had his father? "Like what?" he said.

"Brown University! Epistem—whatever!"

David shook his head. "That's out of reach."

"It's not! You would just have to apply! Don't say it's out of reach if you haven't tried. And if it turns out to be out of reach, then apply to a dozen more schools. In New York, preferably, so I can be near you! It's your brain, David! You're so smart. It needs . . . it needs more out of life. It doesn't want to give up. It wants the opposite!"

He narrowed his eyes, suspicious—enough of a sign that he wanted to believe in her to make a tiny hope flame in her heart. "They say I'm really sick, Lindy," he said.

She stomped her foot. She felt she had nearly gotten through to him; that she just needed to push the rest of the way. "You can't give up! Tell your father no about the job."

He looked up at her. After a moment, he reached to take her hand. "Goddamn," he said, his eyes soft, and suddenly he was like the old David again, the David of last summer. "I really love you."

She squeezed his hand hard. It was all she could do to keep from crying, hearing those words for the first time. And—he was still in there! She had gotten through. "Then you have to try! On days when you don't feel like trying for you, try for me."

He squeezed her hand in return, studying her, still looking as if he was trying to decide whether to trust her. Finally, he gave a slow nod. "They said running is good. I'm supposed to keep running. They put me on some medication. They didn't give me a choice. Doesn't it make you scared?"

"Of course it does!" she said. "But you're . . . David, *I* don't have a choice. My heart is yours. It always has been, and it always will be."

Tears welled in his eyes then, and she felt him fully surrender, though the only signs were slight: A twitch of his mouth, a tiny new slope to his shoulders, a soft exhale. "Mine's yours, too," he said, squeezing her hand a little tighter.

CHAPTER 17

Hailey

Monday, July 26, 2010
12:15 p.m.

So, you're getting married?" Jack said finally, pointing his chin toward Hailey's ring, and her stomach did a little nonsensical flip. This was the first time he'd said a word about it, after they'd been side by side in that tiny car for the last seven hours. They were face-to-face now, though, at a weathered picnic table on a waterfront pier of a restaurant overlooking Pemaquid Harbor, and she was holding up her menu, trying to decide what to order, so maybe this was his first time noticing it.

The menu didn't seem to make sense; she set it down. That the day should be so gorgeous—seventy-eight degrees, a pretty sailboat cruising among the lobster boats and skiffs moored in the tree-rimmed harbor—seemed wrong. The red umbrellas over the dozen tables lining the pier rippled in the light breeze; the sapphire of Jack's eyes matched the water, or the other way around. She didn't want to be lulled into forgetting about her dad. "I don't think we should be eating lunch," she said. "We need to keep looking."

"Hales, as I already argued, and you agreed, you're exhausted. We searched all thirty trailheads. You need a break. You need food. If you want, right after this, we can head back to The Cove and see if there's any news. Maybe they've found him. Maybe he showed up." Unlikely. An hour ago, they'd driven to town for signal to check messages. Hailey'd had a voicemail from her mom saying she was driving down to Portland to drop off photos of David at the TV stations and post flyers, while Kate was going up to Bangor to do the same. Lindy expected to be back by seven, but she'd stay in touch. There was also a message from the caterer wondering about replacing the shrimp cocktail with smoked salmon crostini, and one from the bakery saying they needed the rest of the money for the cake. From Noah, there'd been a text: *How r u? U coming home today?*

Clueless, at best. Hailey hadn't replied.

"But first," Jack went on, "you need to eat. Because once you get back, it'll be all family and demands and everything, and you won't take a break."

She checked her phone for the time. "What's today?"

Jack cocked his head. "Monday."

"He should've been here forty-eight hours ago. It doesn't feel right to take a break."

Jack reached out and laid his warm hand over hers. She was too surprised to pull away. "Hales," he said. "Let it go. Just for one second. This isn't under your control right now, okay? You can't fix it right this minute. You need to put your own oxygen mask on right now." He smiled. "You need to eat a giant mound of french fries. Dr. Westfield's orders."

Despite herself, she smiled back. Wow, her emotions sure were all over the place. Was she going crazy from the stress? She'd thought she'd been going crazy before, about the wedding, but that was nothing compared to this. Still, she didn't think she should be enjoying the feeling of Jack's hand on hers quite as much as she was. She extracted her hand just as the waiter came. Being hungry felt ridiculous, too, but she was starving. She still hadn't really read the menu; she ordered a burger and fries. Not on the approved pre-wedding diet, but whatever. Jack ordered fish tacos, grabbing the menus and handing them up to the waiter with a smile. She hoped the smell of the fish wouldn't make her nauseous again.

She sipped her Diet Coke, watching a gull circle over the boat-studded harbor. "I am getting married."

Jack's face lit up with a genuine smile, and she felt a twinge, which made her want to laugh at herself. Had she hoped he'd be unhappy?

"Or I'm supposed to be!" She twisted her hair up into a quick bun and let it fall again, thinking of her wedding dress. After all the lacy, beaded, off-the-shoulder mermaid styles she'd tried on, she'd ended up going with a plain, classic satin V-neck ball gown that had felt like her the minute she'd put it on. She remembered: Her last fitting was supposed to be tomorrow in Portland; she'd need to reschedule. She thought of the stacks of boxes in the corner of Noah's apartment containing the vases and candles and sea glass for the centerpieces, the place cards, the guest book and programs. She'd planned on grabbing them tomorrow and bringing them up to Innisfree. *The best-laid plans,* her dad always said. "In two weeks. Less than two weeks."

Jack frowned. "Jesus. Really?"

"Yeah." She took another sip of Diet Coke, as he looked at her, his mouth slightly agape, like she'd shattered his sunny worldview. Was it wrong that she felt a little satisfied at that? It wasn't easy to hang around with someone who had a sunny worldview when your own world was basically falling apart.

"Okay," he said finally, appearing to gather himself. He leaned on the table, hands folded, and looked at her intently, like a cop negotiating with a suspect. "So, what are you going to do?"

Hailey swallowed. Her headache, which had eased for a while, pinged again like a timer going off. "I don't know. I've got, like, this crazy to-do list I'm supposed to be tackling right now. But my dad—"

"Well, yeah, obviously you can't keep on doing all the shit for your wedding when your dad's missing," Jack interrupted, seeming angry about it now. He caught himself, took a breath. "What does your fiancé have to say about all this?"

"I don't know. He's, like, not here. He wants to keep the wedding on."

Jack leaned back. Reached for his water and took a sip, the spark back in his eyes. "Well, who could blame him for that?"

Hailey laughed, though her face heated up. Okay, so Jack was still a charmer. Whatever. "He thinks my dad'll show up." Her headache was coming back in force, tinging like a metal hammer above her eyebrow. "He doesn't realize this is really, really not like my dad."

"Why isn't your fiancé here?"

"He's working."

"Hmm." Jack sipped his water again.

"What?"

He set down his water and resumed the good-cop posture. "It's just I think if my fiancée, if I had a fiancée, was going through something like this, I'd want to be there."

Hailey didn't want to talk about Alexandra, the purported threat to Noah's job. Just for a second, she decided, she would forget everything and just lean in to Jack's company. It would probably be her last opportunity in this lifetime! She smiled and teased him. "You don't have a fiancée?"

He sat back like she'd pinched him. "No way. I'm too young to get married."

"You're the same age I am!"

He shrugged. Grinned a little, relaxed again. "You know what they say. Guys and girls mature differently. I'll get married when I'm thirty-five to some girl who's twenty-two, and we'll actually be at the same maturity level."

Hailey's stomach did another little flip—in protest? Whatever. She ignored it. "That is both insightful and disgusting. Not to mention unfair. Are you seriously going to marry somebody who right now as we speak is, what, ten years old?"

He laughed. "Twelve. But don't worry, I haven't met her yet."

Hailey frowned, plunging her straw up and down through the ice in her Coke. "The whole biological clock thing. So unfair."

"So, wait, you're getting married because you want kids?"

"No! Oh, God. No. I don't want kids. Not right now." In fact, Hailey'd found herself terrified of getting pregnant, especially since moving in with Noah. She was on the pill, but still. Getting pregnant would *not* be good right now. "I told you—I'm starting law school."

He leaned back and looked down his nose at her, light glinting on his sun-bleached hair. "Okay. So why get married? It doesn't seem like there'd be a need for it."

Hailey paused. She'd honestly never thought like that. "Well, I love him. We've been together three years!"

Jack laughed. She wanted to kick his shin, but just then the food arrived.

"Oh my God, I'm so full," Hailey groaned, as they headed out to the parking lot. "I haven't had a meal like that in six months." Also, weirdly, this was the first time in weeks she hadn't felt nauseous before or after eating. Even the smell of Jack's fish tacos hadn't gotten to her. At least she could be confident she wasn't pregnant right now. "Let's walk for a minute and make a game plan." A better view of the harbor was a short distance away. "Are you up for more searching?"

"Sure, but don't you want to go back to The Cove and check in?"

She shrugged. "My mom's not even there. They'll call me if there's any news. Maybe we should head for town again. Check messages and search around there. I think there are a few more trails north of Route 1."

They were beside the harbor now, and Jack sat down in the inviting-looking grass. "Is there some other explanation that's possible, other than that your dad stopped off for a hike? Do we need to think outside the box here?"

She was impatient to get going, but Jack was being so decent. He deserved a full explanation. She sat down beside him cross-legged, pulling her skirt over her knees, and told him everything: The expectation that her dad would arrive for the birthday party; the call he'd made to her mom that morning; how the house in Cranston had looked normal, down to the fresh bag in the kitchen garbage can; all the places her mom had called; what they knew of her dad's usual habits; how he always said hiking in the woods was the thing that kept his head on straight, and how he insisted on doing it even though it sometimes tweaked his old bad knee. "Him stopping off for a quick hike and falling or hurting his knee is the only logical conclusion," she finished, brushing dirt from the grass off her hands.

"Sometimes people do things that are illogical," Jack said, then lay back in the grass, folding his hands over his belly, looking up at the sky. "And unpredictable."

Hailey's heart thudded. She could not start thinking things like that. "Don't be an ass," she huffed, and lay back beside him. The grass was cool and soft. "Anyway, I don't think my dad has an unpredictable bone in his body."

"Lucky you."

She heard the note of pique in his voice. Had he ever resolved things with his dad? From what he'd said about his reasons for coming to stay with his grandma this summer, it sure didn't seem like it. She was trying to think how to ask, when he broke in.

"Does your dad have feelings about you getting married?"

"Well, I'm sure, uh," Hailey started, before realizing she had literally no idea what her dad felt about her getting married. He'd wished her well, he was paying for everything, he hadn't complained. But it was true he'd never seemed . . . *enthusiastic.* She propped herself on her elbows to look at Jack. "Wait, you're not suggesting that he could be trying to, like, sabotage my wedding?"

Jack shrugged, a question in his eyes.

"No way. He would never do anything like that."

Jack's mouth quirked. "Okay, Hales," he said, and even though his words agreed with her, in his voice she heard his questions: *Why isn't your fiancé here? Why get married?*

"Shut up," she said, and lay back down. There was at least a foot of open grass between them, but suddenly she was remembering the afternoons, back when she was seventeen, in his uber-comfortable bed at his grandma Marjorie's cottage. White sheets, white comforter, throw pillows in shades and muted patterns of gray. His grandma didn't care, said she'd rather they were safe and not "getting eaten alive by mosquitos back in the woods," as she put it, promising not to tell Hailey's parents about the extent of the privacy that was being offered, either. All she cared about was that they were using birth control, although they really weren't doing anything that required it. Except for that one time, the last day of the summer.

Hailey heard Jack sigh, and when she turned her head to look, he was gazing over at her with soft eyes. "Hales," he said. "It's good to see you again."

She blinked. Tried not to show her alarm. Had he been thinking about those long-ago afternoons, too? "It's good to see you, too, Jack," she said, in what she hoped was a very formal tone of voice.

He smiled a little, turned his face back toward the sky. She turned to look up, too, watching the clouds float past. The warmth of the sun lulled her eyes into drifting closed. *Just for a second,* she told herself.

When she woke up, she could tell the light had changed. The sun had swung around the harbor, casting different shadows. Her head, for a moment, was pain-free. "Shit!" she said, sitting up. "Shit, shit, shit!"

"Good morning, sunshine," Jack said laconically. He was sitting with his elbows hooked around drawn-up knees, looking out at a beautiful sailboat cruising past, pure white sails fluttering.

"Why did you let me sleep? We need to use the daylight hours!" She rubbed at her cheek, which she could feel was imprinted by swirly patterns of grass blades, like pillow marks after a long night. Nice.

He smiled a little. "I just woke up myself. We must've needed that."

She exhaled, as reality came flooding back: Her dad, gone without a trace; thirty fruitless trailheads; Jack saying they might need to think outside the box; the text from Noah she hadn't answered; the giant wedding checklist, getting longer and longer with things that weren't done. *Why get married? Where's your fiancé?*

Her headache was back. "Let's go to town, okay?" she said. "I need to check my messages."

"Sounds like a plan." Jack got to his feet and held out his hand to help her up.

"I got it!" she said, getting up on her own. She brushed off her skirt. "Thank you."

He grinned.

CHAPTER 18

Lindy

Monday, July 26, 2010
8:00 p.m.

As the sunset began to tint the sky outside the windows of Innisfree, everyone gathered in the living and dining rooms. Lindy had called a family meeting after getting back from Portland, where three TV stations had promised to run stories on David and show his picture.

Kate, back from Bangor, sipped from a large glass of Cabernet and sat at the dining table with Josh and his wife, Marielle, their heads bowed together as they reviewed the list of where flyers had been posted. Cody bounced on his toes beside the staircase like a boxer before a fight. Emma was seated in the blue chair in the living room, and she and Eli, who was perched on the chair's arm, were trying again to unlock David's phone. Reese sat on the other arm with a pen and paper, looking toward the ceiling and occasionally making a note. More channeling? Lindy had to assume. She wondered briefly what would come through, then realized she had to be truly desperate to be wondering that.

Greta set a plate of cheese and olives on the coffee table and sat down beside Lindy on the couch, a bit too close. "Your father was tired," she whispered. Lindy bit her lip to keep from saying, *Seriously?*

The screen door swung open and in walked Hailey, with Jack Westfield trailing. Hailey had a big paper sack in her hand, and Jack was carrying a stack of five pizza boxes. So strange: There was an ease about Hailey that Lindy hadn't seen in at least two years. Not that she was smiling. She looked appropriately concerned, as she apologized that it had taken them so long to get there. When Lindy'd called two hours ago, Hailey and Jack had been an hour away, posting flyers at gas stations and shops in Brunswick, and they'd offered to pick up pizza on their way home.

"We got a few pints of gelato from Gelato Fiasco, too," Hailey announced, moving toward the kitchen with the paper bag, as Jack set the pizzas on the dining table beside where Greta had put out plates and napkins, glasses, wine, sodas, and beer. "I'll put it in the freezer for now." Hailey truly did look . . . lighter somehow? Very odd, given the circumstances.

"Hey, man!" Cody was saying, going to hug Jack, who looked astonished at how Cody had grown. Jack had been taller than Cody seven years ago, and now was six inches shorter. "Good to see you!" Eli also got up to greet Jack, giving an uncomfortable half hug the way boys did. Lindy had forgotten how much her two sons had idolized him back in the day. Even Emma looked up from David's phone and gave Jack a little wave and smile, and Emma didn't favor many people with her smile.

Well, Lindy couldn't worry about Jack Westfield now. "All right, everybody! Grab some pizza, then we've got things to discuss."

"Okay," Lindy said loudly, waving for everybody's attention as they settled in with their pizza, beer, and wine. Lindy wasn't drinking anything in case a call came and she needed to drive somewhere. She gave a quick update on the TV stations, the police, the hospitals, and the various searches they'd all done, concluding, "All we know so far is where there's no trace of him. So, next steps. Tomorrow, I'm going to drive to Cranston and see if I can find anything in our financials."

She wasn't going to say this out loud, but the thing was, she still hadn't had a call or text back from Tiffany.

And she'd started to think, if David was having an affair, maybe he'd been stockpiling cash for a getaway? If he had been, Lindy would've had no idea. She really didn't keep close track of their finances. More accurately, she didn't keep track at all. David managed everything on his PC at home. He also kept paper statements in files in his desk drawer, she was pretty sure. They—or he—might have whole accounts she knew nothing about.

And he *could* have lied to Lindy when he'd called Saturday morning and told her he was on his way. If he was running off with some woman, spurred by a fiftieth-birthday midlife crisis, it seemed unlikely he'd have come right out and said so.

"Eli," Lindy said, "I was hoping you'd come with me and help me search the computer." Her kids were all way better with computers than she was, and Eli was the best researcher.

"Sure, Mom."

"I'll come, too," Emma said. "Reese needs to get back to New York for work, so can we drop her at the bus station?"

Lindy couldn't help feeling relieved that Reese and her "clairaudience" would be leaving, and she was glad to think of Emma coming to Cranston. Eli and Emma always felt better when they were together, and Emma tended to see things that the rest of them missed, or at least to see things differently. "Of course."

"Jack and I will keep searching and posting flyers," Hailey piped up, and Jack gave a nod to confirm—almost like they were a couple! Annoyed with how quickly Jack had parachuted back into her daughter's life, Lindy also noted, really for the first time, Noah's glaring absence. He lived an hour and a half away. He owned a car. And he hadn't bothered to come check on Hailey? Or offered to help search for David?

"Me, too," said Cody.

Lindy shook her head to bring herself back to the present. She noticed Cody hadn't taken any pizza. He still wasn't eating? *Goddamn it, David.* "You three go together. I don't want anybody going anywhere by themselves."

"You guys should check lighthouses," Emma said, with a glance at Reese. "We have reason to believe he may be at a lighthouse."

"We do?" said Hailey.

"Not *really*." Lindy couldn't hold it in.

"Mom," scolded Emma, then turned to Hailey. "Reese is clairaudient, and she got the word 'lighthouse.'"

"Really?" Kate said. "That's amazing!"

Lindy, still not buying it, was surprised by Kate's enthusiasm. How much wine had Kate had tonight?

But it wasn't like they had much else to go on. "Fine." She turned to Hailey, Jack, and Cody. "Kids, if there's a lighthouse, or a trail by a lighthouse, that it seems like Dad might have stopped at, it won't hurt to take a look. Let's not tackle all sixty-five right now, but Pemaquid, the Portland Head Light, you know the ones he's aware of." Lindy realized then that tears were streaming down her face. She tried wiping them away. They just kept flowing, like blood. Emma looked alarmed at the sight, then cut her eyes over at Reese, who let out an exasperated breath.

"It's not her fault!" Lindy said, still swiping at her tears with the back of her hand. Emma never needed an excuse to break up with anyone, but Lindy, even if she wasn't Reese's biggest fan, didn't want to be the cause of another fracture. "It's nobody's fault. We're all doing the best we can."

Reese coolly tore off the piece of paper she'd been making notes on and handed it to Emma, who looked down to read it.

Lindy was hot with embarrassment, even as her tears still flowed. A room full of people. She glanced around, saw eyes welling in sympathy or fear. "Agenda item one: Let's all try not to lose it," she said, trying to laugh, wiping her face again. Her mother squeezed her hand so tightly it hurt. Kate came over with her wine glass, sat down on Lindy's other side, and took her other hand. Lindy was grateful.

Emma was shaking the little piece of paper at Reese. "What does this mean?"

Reese shrugged. "Just what it says."

"I'll go to the police in person tomorrow," Josh broke in, as if to rescue them all from Lindy's tears, from the fear welling in the room, from the tension between Emma and Reese. "State and local. I know it's a lot of jurisdictions all along the route, but maybe if I show up in person . . ."

"Good idea, Joshie," Kate said.

What went unsaid, Lindy realized: Police generally figured that a fifty-year-old man was fine—and nobody's victim—even if his family didn't know where he was. A couple of the TV stations had told her as much today and wouldn't run the story as a result. That police officer had said it, too: *Legally, an adult has the right for people not to know where he is.*

"I'll stay by the phone at the yellow cottage," said Marielle.

"I'll stay here at Innisfree," Greta said, squeezing Lindy's hand again. "I'll make sure there's plenty for everyone to eat."

Lindy happened to catch Hailey's eye then. Seeing the worried way her daughter was looking at her, she immediately tried to telegraph that she was okay. Then she noticed the softness with which Jack Westfield was gazing at Hailey, and she remembered the wedding to-do list, all the things she and Hailey should be doing this week instead of what they were doing now. *The best-laid plans,* David always said. She thought again of Noah's absence. It plain did not make sense that he wasn't here. Lindy had always liked Noah! (He brought Lindy flowers whenever he and Hailey visited!) David didn't, not really, though he tried. "There's just something I don't trust about the kid," he'd said.

"You haven't really spent *time* with him," Lindy had argued. "He's offering our daughter a *life*. He's going to be very successful, you know? He's smart, talented, and handsome! Bleu was a semifinalist for the James Beard Awards. And that's mostly Noah's work, even though he doesn't always get the credit."

"According to him, it's mostly his work," David had said skeptically.

Now Jack Westfield was here instead, the wedding was probably going to need to be canceled, and Hailey's whole future could be in jeopardy—

Agenda item one, don't lose it, Lindy reminded herself. She wiped away more involuntary tears and met Hailey's eyes again across the room.

They were going to get through this. And if they found David alive, if it turned out he'd run off with this little Tiffany girl, or otherwise intentionally ruined their daughter's wedding plans—not to mention her parents' fiftieth anniversary—she was going to divorce him so fast his head would spin.

Although, unfortunately, just thinking of needing to divorce him made *her* head spin. She'd never once imagined such a thing, not in all these years.

As soon as Lindy declared the meeting over, people began chatting in small groups. Kate patted Lindy's knee and got up to refill her wine glass. *David,* Lindy scolded internally, because his absence *had* to be the reason Kate was suddenly drinking so much. Lindy had privately always thought Kate's issues with alcohol as a younger woman had been brought on by worry about David. The pattern seemed to be repeating itself now.

Then Lindy noticed Emma and Reese quietly arguing, just as Greta touched Lindy's arm and said softly, "I think we should cancel the anniversary party. Your dad and I don't want—"

"No!" Lindy said. So many of her parents' old friends—the ones that still traveled—had planned their summers around coming for the party, swearing not to let it slip to Greta or Tom that they'd be there. One of the joys of the planning had been imagining how surprised and thrilled her parents would be to see so many old friends. "Not yet. Everything is pretty much set."

"But I really don't think—"

"Mom, please. We all need something to look forward to, right? I mean, today's only Monday. I'm sure David will turn up by this weekend." Though, as soon as the words were out, Lindy realized she wasn't sure of that at all.

Greta looked skeptical, but just pursed her lips, nodded, and got up to go help Kate, who'd started clearing plates, as Hailey came over to Lindy.

Across the room, Emma said loudly to Reese, "That's not true!" She jumped up, crying, and ran upstairs. Eli, alarmed, hurried after her. Reese stood, hands on hips, and glanced around the living room, sending angry darts everywhere, then stormed upstairs, too.

Lindy's mom-antennae were on high alert—what could Reese have written on that piece of paper to make Emma so upset?—but she felt strangely powerless to move.

"Eli's got it, Mom," Hailey said quietly.

And how strange to realize: Hailey was right! Lindy didn't need to get involved. Emma was a grown adult, plus she had Eli to help her, and Emma had always preferred his help to Lindy's from the time they were two years old.

Lindy squeezed her daughter's arm, then went to the dining table, looking over Josh's and Marielle's shoulders at the list of where flyers had been posted. Cody, without a word to anyone, pulled a chair over to the phone and sat down, pulled out the list of hospitals, and started making calls.

Ten minutes later, Reese was hauling her suitcase downstairs, and Kate, who'd been helping Greta in the kitchen, was telling Reese there was no taxi but she'd be more than happy to drive her to the bus station in Portland right away.

Josh, overhearing, stood up. "I'll do it, Kate. You're drunk."

The room froze in shocked silence—at The Cove, people didn't *say* such things. "I am not!" Kate said, as tears sprang to her eyes.

But Josh was moving for the door. An angry-looking Reese and her suitcase trailed him. "How many glasses of wine have you had?" he asked his sister, who put her fists on her hips as he walked out.

Goddamn it, David, Lindy thought again, hating him for a moment. *Where are you?* He had never understood what she always, always had: That without him to hold the center, everything would fall apart.

It was her mother's favorite Yeats poem, other than the one about Innisfree: "Things fall apart; the centre cannot hold . . ."

CHAPTER 19

Lindy

1982

My head just gets crowded sometimes, Lin, you know that," David said, throwing his sleeping bag into the back of his ten-year-old Corolla Wagon, which was parked sideways across the yellow cottage's lawn. The June breeze was cool, though the sun was warm. In the cove, a pair of eider ducks—a male and a female—floated on the high-tide waters. David slammed the hatch shut. His tent and other gear were already in there. "It's nothing personal. Don't worry. I'll be back in three or four days." He grabbed her arms, kissed her forehead with a smack, then headed for the driver's seat.

Lindy crossed her arms over her stomach. "But we just got here. I was looking forward to spending some time together."

It had been a busy year. On top of trying his utmost to qualify for the Boston Marathon, David had just finished up his third year at Brown and, at the urging of his favorite professor, decided to apply to attend law school right away after graduation. He had promised Lindy he would try for NYU, where she had just finished her first year. Her parents had refused to allow her even to apply to Brown. She got free tuition at NYU due to her father; besides, they didn't want her "distracted." (They still seemed to believe, deep down, that David was someone they needed to protect her from.) So, Lindy and David had been limited to seeing each other one weekend a month, when one or the other of them would take the train the three and a half hours between Penn Station and Providence. This year, Lindy had been the one to do most of the traveling, since her parents finally permitted her to, and so Lindy and David could finally have some privacy. David's first two years of college, the only way they'd been allowed to see each other was if he took the train to New York and slept on the couch in her parents' apartment. Lindy couldn't seem to break it to them that she hadn't been a virgin since the summer of '79, so she and David had kept up the charade.

"I'll be back in four days," he said now, with a cute smile, folding himself into the driver's seat. "I'll take you for lobster." She always found it hard to be mad at him, even when she wanted to be. Anyway, she'd promised herself she would make his life easier, not harder.

She kissed him goodbye through the open window, and he waved out the window and tooted the horn as he drove away around the bend in Summerland Cove Point Road.

Four days passed. Lindy slept and read, tuning out the music her mother was always playing on the piano or the stereo. Lindy had not touched the piano since she was fifteen. Not since August 1978, when David had cut his wrist. She still didn't know why or how she'd held firm, when her mother had spent the months afterward railing, cajoling, instituting punishments, and making demands, all of which had only escalated after they'd returned to New York. Finally, one night at dinner just before Christmas, her father had said mildly, "It seems like she doesn't want to play the piano anymore, love," and Greta surrendered in disgust.

Lindy hardly ever drew anymore, either, unless it was a small cartoon in a letter to David to amuse him, and she was too busy to visit the Met. She was majoring in English and minoring in Political Science. She was trying to take life seriously, the way David did, and hoped not to follow in her parents' footsteps, though she wasn't sure yet exactly what that meant. She wore black most of the time. Her friends at school were thin women who smoked and talked about injustice and the importance and impossibility of making a difference. She was starting to think she might go to law school, too, though she hadn't told her parents yet, fearing her father's disappointment and her mother's dramatic reaction (a four-day faux breakdown, Lindy predicted). Her mother thought only music mattered; her father believed in the study of history like it was an actual religion.

"David's not back yet," Kate said, answering the door at the yellow cottage at sunset on the fourth day. "Want to come in?" She didn't seem worried. Lindy's stomach, on the other hand, had done an immediate flip. She'd known his car wasn't out front, but still.

She tried not to worry about David all the time, but a lot of the time—even hundreds of miles apart, the way they usually were—she still did. He'd had good doctors back in Chicago. His father had said it was fine for David not to take the job at the machine shop. (*His face was pale, and my mother was sitting there with her hands folded, biting her lip,* he'd reported to Lindy in a letter. *I guess I scared them, although that wasn't my intent, and I feel bad about it, actually.*) They'd supported his efforts to get into Brown and even helped pay his tuition, in the end. They just wanted him to be happy, they said.

Lindy was pretty sure they were still as scared, deep down, as she was, and as Mrs. Kauffman came up behind Kate now, Lindy could see it. Mrs. Kauffman's hair was iron gray; four years ago, it had been a soft brown. "Lindy!" She gave her a warm hug. Mrs. Kauffman never forgot who had found David in the woods. She never forgot who had suggested that he apply to Brown, giving him something to live for. "Come in! I just made cookies!"

Mrs. Kauffman soon went upstairs to bed, leaving Lindy and Kate alone, and they sat at the kitchen table eating cookies and drinking milk like children, talking about their first years of college. Kate, at Northwestern, had had one boyfriend, then another, then another. She was on the pill, so she didn't have to worry about getting pregnant. She was thinking of focusing on women's studies—no major was offered, just a certificate—but it didn't seem practical, not to her parents and not even to her.

Josh, seventeen now, came in after a while from being out with friends. He acted happy to see Lindy, but she could see worry in his eyes, too, when Kate told him David wasn't back yet, even as he said goodnight and thundered up the stairs.

After that, Kate got out two glasses and pulled a bottle of red wine from where it was hidden among the cleaning products under the sink. Lindy wondered if Kate had been hiding it from her mother, or if Mrs. Kauffman had been trying to hide it from Kate. Either way, Kate said it would dull the edges, and it did, without truly helping anything.

Lindy and Kate sat at the table till midnight, but David still wasn't home. Kate's eyes had blurred, with the wine, and they darted nervously as she saw Lindy to the door. She grabbed Lindy's arm, and Lindy realized Kate was drunk, which seemed oddly surprising. Lindy had never seen Kate drunk before. "He'll be back tomorrow," Kate said, but she didn't sound very sure.

By the next evening, Mrs. Kauffman was considering calling the police. "He didn't even say where he was going!" Lindy and Kate convinced her not to, communicating with their eyes to each other that Mrs. Kauffman could not be allowed to think the worst, because, if she did, then they would have to think it, too.

The next day, Kate got into a fight with her latest Northwestern boyfriend over the phone and broke up with him. Josh crashed his bike, scraping up his leg and hand. His mother pulled the gravel out piece by piece with tweezers while he clenched his teeth and swore.

Back at Innisfree, Lindy yelled at her mother to say she *had* cleaned the bathroom and washed the dishes, and what was she, some kind of domestic servant just because she was a girl? And would it be like this if she'd been born a boy instead? Greta threatened they could just go back to New York before Lindy's dad even got there; the entire family could just not spend summer at The Cove at all, and Lindy could forget about lobster dinners, lazy afternoons at the beach, reading on the deck, Monopoly with her dad, Boggle with Kate. She could forget about tennis at the SCPA club, the ice cream social, sailing in the Sunfish, crab salad, and fireworks on the Fourth of July. "Fine," Lindy snapped, and went to clean the bathroom again.

Lindy lay awake that night, her bedroom flooded with moonlight, her windows open to the cool salt air. Even the sound of the ocean lapping the rocks below didn't soothe her the way it usually did. She wondered where David was, if he was ever going to come back, if summer at The Cove meant anything to him at all. She was pretty sure he was excited about the prospect of law school, at least. But it was hard not to remember him in that tent four summers ago, blood pouring from his wrist, clenching the knife in his hand.

The next day, around suppertime, Lindy was sitting with Kate and Mrs. Kauffman on the porch of the yellow cottage when David's Corolla came sputtering up onto the lawn and parked.

Lindy ran for him, was breathless beside the car before he'd even stepped out. She wanted to scream, *That was six days, where the hell were you, how dare you, we've all been worried sick, don't you remember, please!*

She said, "Hi, honey! How was your trip?" and David climbed out smiling, taking her in his arms and kissing her like he'd been away at war.

CHAPTER 20

Greta

Tuesday, July 27, 2010
3 a.m.

Greta woke with a start from a dream of helping her mother, who had been dead for fifty-one years, set the table at Innisfree for Thanksgiving dinner. In the dream, her mother was instructing Greta how to fold the napkins into the shape of a turkey. In reality, they'd never had Thanksgiving at Innisfree.

Dreams, Greta thought, aware of Tom breathing quietly in sleep beside her, unsettled to have seen her mother, to have her feel so alive, so real, even though, in the dream, Greta had not been a child, but the age she was now—eighty-one. In the dream, her mother had looked the same as she had when Greta was a child, so Greta had *felt* like a child, even as she was trying to keep her mother from finding out about Tom's diagnosis and wondering if her mother could help convince Lindy to cancel the fiftieth anniversary party. Her mother had died four years before Lindy was born. "Darling, you have to pay attention," her mother had said, in the dream, and maybe that, in combination with the feeling of time all in a tangle, was what had woken Greta up.

The family she'd had when she was a child was all gone now. Her mother, her father, her three older brothers. Greta was the only survivor.

Why was it so unnerving to wake up and realize that, when it had been the case for more than thirty-five years?

Her two oldest brothers, Cary and Will, had died in the war, more than sixty years ago. Cary ("Henry Carrington Ashworth, if you please," he would say with mock importance, but he had been named after their father, who went by Henry, so they always called him Cary, which he ultimately liked because then girls crooned that he *did* resemble the movie star, and his friends and younger brothers took to calling him Grant, in jest) was a pilot in the Eighth Air Force, shot down on the Schweinfurt raid in August 1943. Will was a navigator last seen bailing out of his B-29 over the Pacific in 1944. Harrison had come home from serving as a paratrooper in the 101st Airborne but, honestly, had never been the same. The boy who'd left adored his family; the man who came back barely acknowledged that any of it was left. He moved to California, married a girl who'd danced in three Busby Berkeley films, fathered two sons, had little to do with Greta or their parents, and died at fifty-three of lung cancer, having taken up smoking two packs a day while in the Army.

The last time Greta saw Cary and Will, she'd been just shy of thirteen years old. It was December 1941, and it was a time in her life when she was nearly mute, after what had happened the previous summer at The Cove. None of her family seemed to notice her odd change in demeanor, or at least they didn't comment on it, not even when, shortly after the attack on Pearl Harbor, she went with her parents to see all three of her brothers to the train. Will, twenty-two at the time, simply promised her they'd win the war and be home in six months, as if he imagined her to be much younger and more gullible than she was. Cary, twenty-three, pulled her aside, gave her five dollars—an exorbitant sum then—and told her to spend it all on ice cream sodas, except to save a dime to buy him one when he got back. Harrison, twenty, was the only one who appeared to be upset about leaving, unsure whether he'd return. Cary and Will seemed to think the entire thing was a grand adventure, but that had been their general outlook on life, even before the war had come along.

"You have to pay attention." What did her mother mean by that, in the dream? What was Greta missing?

She shifted, and Tom woke with a start, half sitting up in bed. In the moonlight, she saw he looked alarmed, and she tried to soothe him.

"Betsy?" he said.

She didn't know who that was.

"No," she said, and though her heart had bolted like a zebra with a lion after it, she kept her voice calm. "I'm Greta."

"Who?"

On his face was a mix of terror and bewilderment, and her eyes filled with tears. She touched his cheek softly. She had known this would come, yet she hoped he was having a dream, too, and that when morning came, he would remember her again. "Go back to sleep," she whispered, and he lay back and closed his eyes like an obedient child, and she stayed slowly stroking his thin, soft hair until he was asleep again.

Two hours later, on the deck with her coffee, watching the sunrise over the ocean in the cool of the morning—it was unclear to her whether she was in denial about Tom forgetting her, or simply at peace with a thing she'd known was coming—she realized: Each memory was a key being pressed. Her mother, her father, her brothers. She could still hear their voices, see their faces. She could picture her brothers banging in the door at Innisfree, coming in from tennis or sailing, shouting playfully at each other about some ball that had been out of bounds. She could remember how she'd imagined they would always protect her, and her sense of betrayal when, long before they were actually gone, this turned out not to be true. She could remember nocturnes and sonatas she hadn't played in ten or twenty years and the lyrics to songs she hadn't heard in twice that long. She could see Lindy as a newborn baby at Mount Sinai, a little girl in pigtails and corduroy on the monkey bars in Central Park, a teen lining up for lobster at the SCPA. She could see Tom the day she met him, at the stage door of the Chicago Theatre on a bitter winter night. She could almost taste the cup of diner coffee he'd insisted on buying her that night, saying they had a mutual friend. (They didn't; he said later it was only her beauty that had made him so bold, that had made the lie feel requisite. She decided later that the entire incident had been so decidedly out of character for him, a taciturn Midwesterner, that she could trust his love for her was irrefutable.)

Every memory was a key being pressed to hammer a note, forming phrases, movements, the entire sonata of a long life.

In Tom, the action was muted now. Perhaps the damper was on, some hammers were entirely stuck.

He could no longer hear the notes of his life. He could no longer appreciate the sonata. It had been written, yet now could not be played.

Yes, she was taking the metaphor too far, and yet . . . *Pay attention.* Was this what her mother had been referring to? That Greta had to remember for both of them now? That Greta was the only composer, the only artist, still at work on the life that had been theirs?

Was beauty still accessible if memory was gone?

The beauty of the moment, yes. It was as if she heard her mother's voice.

She sipped her coffee. Dark roast—different than the diner coffee on the night she'd first sat across from Tom in that booth—and the taste brought her back to this moment, the sunrise. To David, missing three days now.

David. *Pay attention.*

Poor Lindy.

What did Greta know about David? She remembered him as a teenager—that ridiculous stroganoff dinner when she'd worn her pearls and Tom had said afterward, "I'm afraid I don't think he's going anywhere, love." She remembered David as a struggling young man, then as a dutiful young husband, a new father. Greta had been worried out of her head about Lindy marrying him, had lost more sleep over it than she could count, for almost a year. But as soon as the children came along, he'd—well, Greta could only think of it as that he'd grown into his own height, almost visibly filling with a strength and resolve that hadn't been evident before, just as Lindy had claimed he would. (Greta still didn't think Lindy could've known that outcome for sure; she still couldn't believe Lindy had gambled like that with her entire future, her entire life.)

Yet. Having been for the last twenty-plus years a man who put his children first, where would David have gone now, less than two weeks before his oldest daughter's wedding?

Greta should tell Lindy about Innisfree; that David knew of her plans to sell it.

But she could not imagine hurting Lindy with such terrible news in the middle of everything else.

And: three days gone. Even Greta couldn't believe that David would've avoided facing the music—facing Lindy and Greta and the impending sale of Innisfree—for that long. For the first forty-eight hours or so, Greta had believed this might've been what was keeping him away—but she didn't believe it now.

No, she did not need to tell Lindy about Innisfree, she was convinced. Not quite yet. Not until after the wedding, like she had planned.

It struck Greta then: Something really might've *happened* to David. What if he really wasn't gone of his own accord?

And—she hated to realize this, too—even if she did not, could not, tell Lindy about Innisfree just yet, she needed to tell Lindy about Tom. He had gotten worse over just the last few days—all the stress of so many people around, probably. Lindy was definitely going to notice that the excuses of him being "busy" and "tired" were wearing thin, were patently untrue. Greta felt it coming like a clock was counting down. Today? Probably—except that Lindy was going to Cranston today.

Tomorrow at the latest, perhaps.

Greta imagined, this morning after Lindy and the kids had gone, putting Tom in the Camry, driving him straight to Florida. She would go without stopping. She would drive all day and night, as if Time itself was in pursuit. She would never tell Lindy; she would protect Lindy from ever seeing her darling father this way: silenced, scrambled, vanishing. She would protect Lindy from the pain of being unknown, unremembered. Greta would simply drive and drive and drive, loving and remembering for herself and for Tom at once. (*Betsy?* she thought suddenly, interrupting her own reverie. *Who on earth was Betsy?*)

But that didn't matter, did it? Because Tom was hers, and she would drive him all the way to Florida, twenty-four hours straight, and then she would pull into the elegant circle drive at Sunset Acres and say, "Help us. Please."

But this was clearly a fantasy. Greta didn't know how to say those words. Did she?

CHAPTER 21

Lindy

Tuesday, July 27, 2010
1:30 p.m.

Typically, Lindy went into David's Cranston home office only to vacuum, so it was a bit strange to be in the room at all, let alone with Eli sitting in the big leather chair at David's PC, clicking the mouse to peruse David's internet search history, and Emma on her knees digging through files in the bottom desk drawer.

David hadn't had a password on the computer, so they'd been able to get right in. That had to be a good sign, right? That he wasn't trying to hide anything?

"What are we looking for here, Mom?" Eli said.

Lindy didn't know. She thought of Tiffany in that gold dress, the warm smile up at David. "Well, I know he hasn't used our joint credit card or our debit card in the last few days." She had called again about both this morning, and there were still no new charges. "Let's see if we can find out if he has another credit card that I don't know about."

As Eli clicked through screens, Lindy noted absently that the room's maroon walls and faux wood blinds felt dated and dark, and the Persian-style rug was threadbare. How had she let it go for so long? She was *always* tackling different rooms in the house; she liked to think she'd mastered low-budget "complete updates." She'd throw on a fresh shade of paint, pick out new curtains, rugs, lamps, throw pillows, "artwork" from the bins at TJ Maxx. "And voila!" she'd tell her family.

A couple months ago, when Lindy had hosted book club, her friend Samantha had so loved what Lindy had done in every room that she'd offered to create a job for her at the interior design studio she owned. They'd chatted about it for a while in the corner of the crowded kitchen as they sipped wine. Lindy had confessed wistfully about the hours she'd spent in the period rooms at the Met as a teenager, about her love for color, for the stroke of a pencil against paper, and for the satisfying feel of a pile of fabric swatches in her hand. But, she'd told Samantha, there was simply no way she could take on a job. She was far too busy with her family, and especially with planning the summer's events.

Now it seemed she should have been putting at least some of her recent time and energy into updating David's office. It was jarring to realize that, in her quest to create the perfect home, she had neglected her husband's space entirely. Had it been that she just hadn't wanted to horn in? Or was it symptomatic of a larger neglect—her overall failure to focus on *him*?

She hated to think it. Even more than that, she hated to think: Would David ever be back in this room again?

Ten minutes later, Eli found it in the history: David had visited a site for Chase Bank. "That has to be it," Lindy said. She knew nothing about any Chase card. "Em, is there a file for Chase Bank in that drawer?"

Emma, cross-legged on the floor with a pile of files in her lap, flipped through them. "No."

"Does he have his passwords written down somewhere?" Eli asked.

"I don't know," Lindy said, feeling foolish. How could she be so disconnected from her own life? So ignorant of its details? Had she imagined that nothing would ever happen to David, that he would just take care of this side of life forever?

If she had, it had been the epitome of wishful thinking.

Eli lifted the keyboard to peer underneath it. Nothing. He opened Excel and found that only one spreadsheet had been recently accessed, one titled "Movies We've Watched." (Lindy hadn't known David kept a record of that.) Eli opened Word and searched for a document called "passwords," but nothing came up.

"He'd probably write them down on paper," Lindy guessed. "Not on the computer." She opened the top desk drawer in front of her. A wooden insert kept the contents neatly organized: pens and pencils, paper clips, Post-its, batteries of various sizes, old phone cords and chargers bound with twist ties, a tiny tape measure. She lifted the insert, but there was nothing underneath except a blue Post-it with *32843* written on it. Could that be a passcode? If so, for what? She peeled the Post-it off the drawer's bottom and replaced the insert.

Eli was searching the middle drawer. It was less organized, a jumble of opened mail, takeout menus, brochures and maps of places they'd been. "Let me look at that stuff," Lindy said, and Eli gathered it up and handed the loose pile to her. On top was a car insurance statement and an envelope from Lifespan. A bill? Which one of the family had been to the doctor lately? Lindy couldn't remember any recent appointments—

"Here," Eli said. From the small drawer above where Emma was searching, he held up a tiny purple notebook. "This is it." He flipped through. "They're not in any order. Like he just jots them down when he opens a new account."

"Try toward the end, then."

He finally found it—*Crustacean25*—and typed it in. The Chase site opened. "Okay, this card has been open for about three months, looks like. It's got an intro zero-percent rate for twelve months and a balance of fifty-two-hundred dollars."

"Fifty-two hundred dollars?" Lindy's mouth was dry. That was almost as much as David made in a month, as far as she knew. "In three months? What are the charges?"

Though she didn't really want to look, she glanced over Eli's shoulder and saw that most of the charges were wedding-related. And then, she read the last, thrilling charge: "Thirty-two nineteen at the Kennebunkport rest area on Saturday, July twenty-fourth!"

"He stopped for gas in Kennebunkport!" Eli looked up, eyes bright. It was the first clue they'd found in all these hours and days that David was even still alive.

"Really?" Emma stood to look, a sheaf of papers in her hands.

"It means he definitely was heading for The Cove, and he definitely made it safely that far!" Lindy said.

"So, like, what does this mean?" Emma said. "Do we need to get back to Maine and keep looking up there?"

"We're here now," Lindy said. "Let's keep looking!"

But as Eli clicked through more screens and Emma sat back down to continue sifting through files, Lindy's excitement began to fade.

What was David trying to hide? Why did he have this whole separate, secret account?

He'd said not to worry about the wedding expenses, or the expenses for the other parties; to get whatever she and Hailey wanted. He had it covered, he said.

But if he'd had to open an interest-free account, it seemed that wasn't true.

What else had he been lying to her about?

Her stomach whirred. She grabbed the Lifespan envelope off the stack from the middle drawer and pulled out the folded paper from inside.

It was a letter from David's primary doctor, dated June 25, referring him to a cardiologist for an EKG due to heart palpitations and shortness of breath. The letter said not to delay, because the symptoms David had been experiencing could be a sign of a serious heart condition.

Heart palpitations? A serious condition?

David had said nothing about any of this to Lindy. She almost could not believe it could be true, and that she would know nothing about it.

Had he made a follow-up appointment? Had an EKG? She rifled

through the stack from the middle drawer but saw nothing else from Lifespan. *Goddamn it, David.* She'd gotten several notices in the mail from Lifespan inviting her to set up an online portal to access test results, but she hadn't taken the time. She was sure he wouldn't have set one up for himself, either, given his typical aversion to technology and his concerns about privacy. Plus, she usually managed that kind of thing for their entire family.

Even so, she asked Eli to pass her the little purple notebook—she didn't want to tell the kids that there might be reason to worry about David's health, too—and scanned through it.

No. Not a single note about Lifespan. That had to mean there was no online portal, no password, no way to tell whether David had had the EKG or not. Unless he'd signed a form at the office giving her access to his records? She should call and find out. She knew she was his emergency contact, so she probably did have access to his records.

Although that was a bit beside the point, because what this information actually told her was, if he'd stopped for a hike on his way up to The Cove, he not only could've fallen and hurt himself or injured his bad knee, but he could've had a heart attack somewhere back in the woods.

And if that had happened, and no one had found him by now . . .

She couldn't finish the thought.

"Hey, Mom," Emma said, standing with a paper in her hand. "I think you should take a look at this." Lindy, noticing how pale Emma looked, wondered again what had happened with Reese last night—what the girl had written in that note, why they'd fought, and why Reese had left so abruptly. Emma had refused to explain. Now she stepped over to Lindy, holding out a statement that said *Fidelity Investments* at the top. Lindy knew enough to know that this was her and David's primary retirement account. David had assured her that he had their retirement taken care of, too. At least, she wasn't to worry about it.

By the time Lindy had finished reading the statement, her hand was shaking.

A month ago, the account had had a balance of just over ninety-eight thousand dollars. Two weeks ago, David had cashed in the entire account. The remaining balance was zero.

The wedding wasn't going to cost nearly that much.

Where had David gone with ninety-eight thousand dollars?

CHAPTER 22

Hailey

Tuesday, July 27, 2010
2 p.m.

At Fort Williams Park, home of the Portland Head Lighthouse, Jack drove the Z3 slowly up and down the rows of parked cars in the tiered series of lots. Hailey shaded her eyes from the sun, zeroing in on the license plates, but, after fifteen minutes of low-gear rumbling, it was clear there was no green Outback with Rhode Island plates here.

As the roadster neared the map kiosk, she said, "Stop here, I'll post a flyer." Jack braked, and she hopped out. She pinned up a flyer, studying her dad's smiling face for a second as the paper and her hair fluttered in the breeze. *Where are you?* she asked him silently, but there was no answer. (Not that she'd expected one; she wasn't Reese.) In the distance was the postcard scene of the white lighthouse and blue ocean, tourists wandering, children asking for ice cream, and she wished for a second that she could be part of some other family, not her own, having a normal summer day.

When she got back into the car, Jack reached over to rest his hand on hers, surprising her again. She was conscious of her engagement ring, gleaming near where his thumb rested. She should pull her hand away.

But maybe not right this second.

"What now, Hales?" he said, and she quickly got her head in the game. What now? They'd been searching since six a.m. They'd gone to Pemaquid Point Lighthouse, checked twenty more trailheads, posted fifty more flyers at parks and gas stations and post offices from Pemaquid to Portland. Cody had gotten Kelsey Grimes to go out with him in the Jeep, saying they could cover more ground that way, while still sticking to their mom's demand that nobody go out alone. All day, Hailey had barely heard from any of her family. That had to mean they'd had the same luck as her and Jack: none.

So, what now? She didn't know. She was hungry and exhausted, sunburned and bereft. She'd rescheduled her wedding dress fitting for tomorrow, since the shop had said that was the latest she could schedule it and still hope to get alterations done in time for the wedding. But was she seriously going to go through with it? Hard to imagine, unless her dad suddenly showed up with some funny story about where he'd been. She was falling further and further behind on the rest of her to-dos, too.

And Noah hadn't offered to help. With anything. Not even with looking for her dad.

It occurred to her: Out of the entire wedding to-do list of a couple hundred items, there were only about five assigned to Noah, all relating to planning the honeymoon. He'd taken care of them months ago. The rest of the tasks had been assigned to Hailey and her mom.

Maybe that was traditional, but they were not exactly in a traditional situation right now!

That was it. If Noah wanted to keep the wedding on for 8/7/10, he would need to step up. Help her out. If not with the search for her dad, then with the wedding, at least.

And, okay, it was weird to be thinking all this with Jack Westfield sitting beside her with his hand on her hand, looking at her like she was a locker whose combination he was trying to remember. And it was weird that, in spite of everything, she was feeling not only content to be sitting in this car with Jack with his hand resting over hers, but also slightly fixated (though she didn't mean to be) on how a couple of his fingertips were spilling over, radiating heat through her skirt onto her thigh. And it was weird, too, that this heat was not unwelcome, and that she'd only managed to get to sleep last night by barring from her mind the realities of her present life and imagining she was seventeen again, snuggled into Jack's bed with him beside her.

"Maybe we should get something to eat," he said. "Regroup?"

Even that his eyes were so blue felt wrong. She extracted her hand, making sure his hand didn't collide with her ring. "I need to make a phone call," she said.

She paced on the grass in the shade nearby, her phone pressed to her ear. "You're at Fort Williams?" Noah was saying. "And you didn't bother stopping to see me?"

Yes, she was only minutes from the apartment. But showing up with Jack? That would *not* have made Noah happy. "You still don't seem to understand. My dad is *missing.*"

"I'd help out if I could, babe, but we're slammed at the restaurant. I'm working twelve days in a row. I mean, I told you. I can't take time off right now when I'm taking time off for the wedding next weekend."

"About that." She told him about the to-do list, her need for him to take over some of the tasks.

"Babe, I'm working twelve hours a day here, give me a break," he said. "Our plan was for you to take care of all that. That's why you quit your job early, right?"

Her teeth clenched. "We didn't know my dad was going to go missing."

"I can't do anything about that, babe. I'm sorry."

"Would you please just call the bakery and give them your credit card for the rest of the payment on the cake? And call the caterer and tell them that salmon crostini is fine? The phone numbers are on the list on the fridge."

A heavy sigh, like she'd asked him to give a section of his liver. "Yeah, okay, babe. Sure. That's fine. I gotta go."

~

"What is it you like about this guy, Hales?" Jack said, popping a potato chip into his mouth. While she was on the phone, he'd ordered them lobster roll lunches from the food truck that was parked nearby. Now they were sitting at a picnic table with an ocean view, and she was chewing a delicious mouthful of lobster drenched in butter and mayo complemented by a toasted brioche bun. Jack, apparently noticing that her face was getting burned, had found a floppy straw sun hat of his grandma's in the Z3's trunk and given it to her. She felt silly wearing it, but his thoughtfulness made her feel cared for, too, which was a nice change of pace. As before, it felt odd to be so hungry and not to be nauseous, but she wasn't going to question it. And, just for the moment, she was not going to feel guilty for enjoying the flavors of the lobster roll, the sunshine on her bare arms, the ocean breeze, Jack's smile.

And, yes, she had probably told Jack too much already about her phone call with Noah, but she'd been so frustrated after hanging up. She'd always known Noah was rigid in his routines and that he put his own needs first, but somehow none of that had seemed like a problem before. The first year of their relationship, they'd been in school (of course they both had deadlines they had to stick to). The second year, they'd been working (of course they both had obligations: hers to the legislative office; his to the upscale restaurant in downtown Augusta where he'd worked then). The third year, they'd been engaged and living an hour and a half apart. They'd never been through an emergency together—but she'd certainly never imagined that, when one arose, he would end up being so clueless, so selfish. She'd never imagined *anybody* would.

She swallowed her bite of lobster, feeling the need to defend her choices. "He has a lot of good qualities! He's smart, ambitious, talented, charming . . . What?" Jack had cocked an eyebrow like he thought she was bullshitting one or the both of them.

"Nothing," he said, with a little smirk, taking a bite of lobster roll, chewing thoughtfully.

"I'm serious," she said, reminding herself, too. "And he's fun!" She grabbed a potato chip out of the bag, flourishing it as she made her next point. "The first Thanksgiving we were together, senior year, there was a snowstorm, so none of us could go home, and he made this amazing feast for like ten of our friends. We had the best time." She bit into the chip and chewed, relishing the explosion of salt and oil on her tongue.

"I guess it's none of my business," Jack said. "I just want to see you be happy."

The corners of her mouth tipped up, even as she chewed, then swallowed. "I'm happy now," she said, because it was true, despite herself, despite everything.

The corners of his mouth tipped up, too. "Let's play the 'what if' game."

"Oh! Okay." She would've thought he'd have forgotten all about that. Those summers at The Cove, they used to take turns creating scenarios to make each other laugh or dream big. *What if you were a walrus; what if you had ten million dollars; what if you lived in Rome?* She sat up straighter, anticipating being amused.

"What if you're married to someone who's an unsupportive asshole?"

"What?" Her anticipation was punctured, a balloon popped. The spirit of the game seemed wrecked, suddenly.

"What if you have kids? What if one of the kids gets sick?"

"I don't think I like this game anymore."

"What if your husband won't take time off work to help out? What if he says it's all your problem?"

Hailey set down her lobster roll. "You're ruining our game."

"I'm not trying to," Jack said, but the look on his face was very serious.

She tried to laugh. "You're ruining my whole life."

"I'm not trying to," he said again. "I know it's none of my business."

"It is definitely not." Unfortunately, the minute he'd asked the questions, she could see the whole scenario playing out in her mind. It was the way the game always worked, even if you knew nothing about the subject. *If I were a walrus, I'd eat a lot of fish, I'd sun myself on any rock bigger than me. If I lived in Rome, I'd drink espresso, I'd spend more time appreciating art, I'd be aggressive in traffic circles.*

If I were married to an unsupportive asshole and our kid got sick, I'd have to deal with it alone. I'd feel guilty and resentful. My career would take a back seat, if I even had a career. We would stop making love. I would disappear.

It seemed the only real question to consider now was, *was* Noah an unsupportive asshole?

Or had he just been acting like one?

Maybe it was all the pressure he was under, at work, and with the wedding coming up . . .

She wanted to think that could be true.

Either way, Jack had just driven her fear of getting pregnant, which she'd managed mostly not to think about for three whole days, up another super-fun notch.

"What if you were on autopilot?" Jack said. "What if you were rushing into something just because it's what society tells you that, when you're twenty-four years old, it's what you should do?" He grinned slightly. "What if you were a victim of the aggressive marketing campaign the wedding industrial complex has been assailing you with since you were five years old?"

"Stop."

"I know it's none of my business."

"Says the man who continues to make it his business."

"It's just, I know you, Hales. I know who you used to be. And you're not acting like the girl I knew."

She sat up straighter. "That was a long time ago. I grew up. Unlike others of us at this table."

He smiled. "I'll tell you what I loved about you."

"What?" she said, not to ask for the accounting, but out of pure astonishment. He had never told her he loved her, not back then, not ever.

"Your sensitivity. You could always read my face and tell when something was wrong. And you always knew how to cheer me up. You're kind. Like, deeply, deeply kind, in a way that almost nobody is. I'm guessing that's what this guy, your fiancé, probably loves about you, too.

I'm guessing you're as tuned in to him as you were to me, and as kind and generous to him, in a world where a lot of us haven't experienced a lot of kindness."

"What a lot of rubbish," she said in a mock British accent, to deflect him, to try to pretend his words weren't basically arrowing straight into her soul. *Damn it.* Her headache was coming back again.

Jack kept going. "But for me, it was more than that. More than just how you related to *me.* It was . . . how you moved through the world trying to make sense of everything. Your singular perception of it all. Your ability to see shades of gray."

She leaned back, whipped off Marjorie's sun hat and rubbed the sweat from her forehead. She felt like he was chiseling through a shell she hadn't even known encased her, cracking it wide open. She kept up the British accent: "I practiced with the scatter cushions at your grandmother's cottage."

He smiled but wouldn't be thrown off-message. "I just really hate to think of all that being pounded out of you in some law firm where you have to make life into black and white. Or, you know, in some marriage where your husband fails to see you as a whole person with needs of your own."

She flopped the silly hat back onto her aching head and returned to her normal voice. "How do you even know all this stuff to say? Aren't you just, like, some surfer dude?"

He laughed. "I have some experience being the kid in a marriage like that, remember? Also, I've been in therapy for, like, nine years."

"Oh, right, you're from California and you're rich," she joked. She picked up a potato chip and contemplated it. "The rest of us just have to muddle through."

He shrugged slightly, his mouth quirked. "We all have our cross to bear."

She needed to gather up the pieces of her broken shell and reconstruct it, piece by little piece. She set the potato chip back down. "Okay, but listen. In all seriousness. My dad is missing! I can't . . . I can't make some gigantic change to the whole plan I have for my future right now.

Because he's going to come back. He's going to show up. Any minute now. And when he does, we're going to have a beautiful wedding that he's spending like twenty thousand real dollars on. I am *not* going to have everything go up in flames. I'm not going to have him come back to find out that he wasted all that money. Just because you . . . just because you think I should become antiestablishment or something."

Jack smiled. "I'll point out that I didn't say you should change your entire plan for your future." He took a bite of his lobster roll and chewed.

"Oh, please," she said. "Don't try to let yourself off the hook. You're disruptive. You always have been. I hate that about you."

Jack swallowed. "I know, Hales," he said with another little grin.

CHAPTER 23

Lindy

Tuesday, July 27, 2010
2 p.m.

Maybe it's in your regular savings account," Eli suggested, after Lindy and Emma told him about the missing ninety-eight thousand dollars. "Like, maybe he's planning to use it to pay off the credit cards?"

That didn't seem, at first, to make sense. Why would David cash in a whole retirement account that he'd end up having to pay a tax penalty on, just to pay off a smaller credit card balance that had zero percent interest for another nine months? Unless there were more outstanding balances they hadn't found yet?

"Okay," Lindy agreed. "Let's log in to Citizens and look." When she had called the automated line, the system had recited only the three most recent transactions on their checking account, not their savings account balance. She'd had no reason to wonder about that until now.

Eli found the information in the purple notebook and logged in. Quickly, he clicked to David and Lindy's savings account page.

The balance was only three thousand twenty-one dollars?

That couldn't be right.

All three of them were looking at the screen, but Emma saw it first. "Crap," she said, tapping a short black fingernail on the screen. Lindy blinked as she took in the numbers.

Back in March, David had withdrawn five thousand dollars from this small savings account. After that, every month he'd withdrawn another two thousand, always two days before the end of the month. There'd been no new deposits.

He'd drained the account of eleven thousand dollars in just four months.

Also, evidently, this was their entire life savings?

"I guess he didn't deposit the ninety-eight thousand here," Eli said dryly.

"Has he given you kids any money? Or do you know if he's given any to Hailey or Cody?"

Eli and Emma both agreed he hadn't, and they didn't think so.

Lindy bit her lip. "Click over to the checking account."

That ledger showed nothing unusual. No strange withdrawals, no charges she didn't recognize. But also no big deposits.

David had withdrawn a hundred and nine thousand dollars in the past few weeks that was now nowhere to be found.

"Look, Mom," Eli said, pointing to the screen. "He applied for a mortgage a month ago and was turned down. Debt-to-income ratio."

"A mortgage? That doesn't make sense. And what debts would we have? This house is almost paid off, I think. Student loans, I guess." Lindy looked over and noticed Emma was crying. "Oh, sweetie," she said, dodging around where Eli sat in the big chair to hug her, shoving her own fear and anger from her mind. "We're going to find him."

Emma, wiping tears away, dug into the pocket of her black miniskirt and came out with a tiny, folded piece of paper. "I didn't want to show you this. It's what Reese heard yesterday. It's why we fought. Why she left. I said there was no way, no way, and she got mad and said I didn't believe in her gift!"

Lindy took the paper, unfolded it, and read, in Reese's pretty handwriting:

Midlife crisis!!!
He is probably having an affair

Lindy, feeling strangely numb, looked back up at Emma, who was distraught. "Look, Mom, I know you don't want to think it, but—two thousand a month? Right before the end of the month? That's like he's paying somebody's rent, right? And, like, a hundred grand is gone? Like, it seems like he ran off? Like, okay, he went to Kennebunkport. But did he, like, get a hotel there? Like, with somebody? And maybe, like, that person is using their credit card and he's paying in cash, because, like, why else wouldn't there be any more charges for anything after that? That's, like, since Saturday, and he would've had to eat and stay *somewhere,* right? Or, like, if he had a hundred grand in cash, they could've gone anywhere! Taken a bus or . . . or a train . . . from Portland? Or if he's, like, applying for a mortgage, he could be, like, buying a house for someone, right?"

Eli, who had pretended not to be listening and now pretended not to have heard, drummed his fingers on the desk, picked up the little password notebook again and began flipping through it. "There's got to be something else we can find."

"I'm sorry, Mom. I just don't think there's any other explanation!" Emma said.

Lindy swallowed. She handed Reese's note back to Emma. "The scenario you're talking about would involve a person I don't know," she said stiffly.

And yet, she was tallying the evidence in her mind. A new interest-free credit card, a possible heart condition, a missing hundred and nine thousand dollars, a denied mortgage application. A hot young assistant who'd taken the week off at the same time.

If Lindy hadn't just seen that Kennebunkport gas charge and the letter from David's doctor, she would've been a hundred percent convinced that Reese was right: David was having a midlife crisis, and definitely an affair—and Lindy had noticed not a single sign of either approaching.

David's law office was in a giant old renovated mill building in Providence. Lindy left the kids at home to continue their searching and made the twenty-minute drive into the city, the traffic moving easily across the five lanes of I-95. She took the exit as if on autopilot, found parking on the street, and walked along the hot sidewalk and through a leafy courtyard to the building's entrance. She pressed the call button to get buzzed in, and, when the heavy steel door slammed shut behind her, the cool of the air-conditioning was a relief. As her flip-flops echoed in the stairwell, she realized too late that she probably looked disreputable. Her wrinkled yellow sundress was the kind of thing a person should wear only to the beach; her hair was a frizzy mess. Her mother would've been ashamed to see Lindy out in public looking like this. Hell, Greta herself wouldn't have gone around looking like this even in the privacy of her own home.

But had Greta ever been in a situation like this? Lindy, flip-flopping up the concrete steps, had to think not.

"Lindy!" Gina Vanzetti was David's closest friend in the office, as far as Lindy knew. At least, the two had been colleagues for a good fifteen years, while others in the office had come and gone. Gina and her wife, Laura, had come to dinner at David and Lindy's a half dozen times over the years, and vice versa. They'd always had a good time, though without ever growing truly close, which was how David seemed to prefer it. The receptionist, Shawna, had buzzed Gina at Lindy's request, and she'd come out right away, a wondering smile on her face. Petite with short salt-and-pepper hair, she wore red glasses, a conservative white blouse and gray pants, and surprising red-and-white Mary Jane pumps. "I thought you guys were up in Maine!"

"Hey, Gina. Can we talk in your office?"

"Is everything all right?"

Lindy gave a tight nod but gestured toward the office.

David always said that Gina was an excellent attorney and that he'd trust her with any case, but as far as office gossip, she was the worst. "She uses all her discretion on her cases, I'm afraid," he'd said, describing how Gina preferred to spend her lunch hours prying into the love lives of the young associates and staff. She offered advice and comfort as needed and justified her behavior to David by saying that, as an "old married lady," she needed some romantic intrigue in her life. As Lindy followed Gina into her office and Gina shut the door behind them, Lindy hoped she could count on the woman's lack of discretion now.

In the room with high ceilings and a giant Palladian window, Gina sat down behind her desk. Lindy perched on one of the armchairs across from her.

"You want some water?" Gina said. "You don't look so good."

Lindy swallowed and shook her head. "David's missing," she said. She explained in as few words as possible, while also conveying the searching they'd done and the theory that he might've gone hiking in the woods and hurt himself. She didn't mention the potential heart problem, the money that was missing, or her suspicions about Tiffany.

Gina's brow furrowed. "He was certainly looking forward to his time in Maine," she said, with what Lindy couldn't help but feel was an odd carefulness. "It really is concerning that he didn't arrive."

"Have you noticed anything . . . strange about him lately? I mean, how has he seemed?" Lindy was sure Gina would know nothing about David's long-ago mental health struggles, but there was still a chance she could have observed something.

But Gina shook her head. "Normal! He's seemed good! A bit stressed, but aren't we all? His caseload . . . well, I'm sure you know. It's especially difficult right now."

In fact, Lindy had not known that, but the information did bring to mind a possibility she hadn't considered: David worked with some clients who might be dangerous. Or who, even if locked up themselves, might have dangerous connections. "Is he . . . can you think of any reason why he'd be in danger? Is there anyone who's . . . you know, after him?"

Gina's eyebrows shot up. "No! No. It's business as usual around here. At least, as far as I know."

It seemed unlikely that anyone who was after David would have followed him to Maine, so, given the Kennebunkport gas charge, Lindy quickly decided the idea didn't make sense. Still, she asked, "Does he owe anybody money?"

"I can't imagine he would. He certainly hasn't said anything about anything like that."

Lindy, much as she hated to, needed to ask what she'd really come to ask. "Gina, this is awkward, but what about . . . what about Tiffany? She's out on vacation this week, too? I tried calling her and she didn't answer, and she hasn't returned my calls."

Gina's face lit up. She appeared greatly relieved to no longer be tasked with thinking about what might have happened to David. "Oh, yes! She's camping." Gina chuckled. "I mean, the girl isn't much of a camper-type, but she got involved with a guy who is, I guess. She's probably somewhere where there's no cell signal. I wouldn't worry about that."

Lindy's stomach had tied itself in a half hitch. "Have you met this guy? Do you know much about him?"

If Gina thought the question was strange, she gave no indication. She leaned forward onto her desk. "No, and she's been with him since just after Christmas! I can't pry a thing out of her. Except she's got a glow, you know? I mean, not that she's pregnant!" A laugh. "I don't mean that. Although I suppose she could be!"

Lindy felt like she might throw up. "You don't know, like, where she met him or anything?"

Again, Gina didn't seem to find Lindy's questions odd. Maybe she figured everybody was as interested in gossip as she was. "No! Weird, right? She said she's trying to keep her private life private. At least until she knows if things are going to work out." Gina shrugged and leaned back. "To each their own, I suppose."

Again, Lindy swallowed back a sick feeling. There seemed less and less chance that David was anywhere but off with Tiffany. Camping? Evidently so.

She thanked Gina for her time and left, stumbling out into the hallway in a daze. She stopped in the restroom and splashed water on her face, then looked into her own eyes in the mirror. *So this is where we are,* she said to herself.

It was a place she had never imagined she'd be.

As she stepped out of the building and back into the heat and sunshine, she pulled out her phone and dialed Eli. "Hey, sweetie." It took effort to keep her voice calm. Like a fisherman at sunset, she cast out one last hopeful line: "You guys find anything else?"

"Um, not really."

"What do you mean?"

"I mean not really."

She exhaled. Eli would tell her whatever it was when he was ready to, and not a minute before. Which left her with only her own theory, after all. "Okay. Listen, would you do me a favor and go look in the garage and see if the camping gear is there?"

A minute later, he was back on the line. "No, the gear's not here, Mom."

She closed her eyes, stopped in her tracks for a second. *Okay. I understand.* She opened her eyes again. The street was very bright and hot in the sunlight. She was only a few steps from where she'd parked the Volvo. "I'll be home in about twenty minutes," she said, "then I want to drive back to Maine tonight. We've got an anniversary party and a wedding to get ready for."

"What?" Eli's shock came across the line. She probably seemed to be changing courses. Maybe she was.

"I'll explain when I get there." She said goodbye, ended the call, squared her shoulders, and let out her breath, determined not to cry. Hadn't she cried enough tears over David in her lifetime?

"There's no way," Eli said, when Lindy told the twins the unfortunate truth that their dad had run off with Tiffany to go camping, skipping his own birthday party, abandoning the family at the height of their summer plans. *I have to think he'll at least show up for Hailey's wedding,* she'd told them, though she was past thinking she could predict what David would do. The fact that he'd applied for a mortgage seemed the deciding piece of evidence: He was setting up a new life somewhere else. He just hadn't informed Lindy yet.

Eli ran a hand through his disheveled curls, for a moment looking so like a young David that it skewered Lindy, made her hands clammy. "He wouldn't do that," Eli insisted. He was still sitting at the computer. Emma was cross-legged on the floor, surrounded by files she'd been sifting through. She looked up at Lindy, eyes welling with tears. It had been years since Lindy had seen Emma cry, until these past few days—

Lindy was struck with a fresh bolt of anger. That David would've done this to them! Bad enough he was doing it to her, but this, torturing their kids like this, she could not forgive.

She took another deep breath and managed to keep her voice calm. "I didn't think so, either, buddy, but that's where we are. Sometimes people surprise you."

Emma shoved the files aside and stood. "We'd better show her, Eli."

There was something else? Lindy didn't want to see it!

But she couldn't seem to make her voice work to say so. She closed her eyes and took another long breath, as Emma and Eli squabbled briefly in that twin way they'd always had, which involved few words and lots of meaningful looks. Eli finally grumbled assent, then Lindy heard the clicking of the mouse as he moved through screens on David's PC.

"Okay, here."

Lindy opened her eyes and saw on the screen Tiffany Jeffries' Facebook page.

Despite herself, she peered in to look as Eli scrolled down.

Tiffany didn't post often—she hadn't posted in four months, in fact—so there was nothing about a new relationship, a camping trip, or anything else current.

But, when Eli stopped scrolling, Lindy saw: Back at Christmastime, Tiffany had posted a picture that had obviously been taken at the holiday party at David and Lindy's home. It showed Tiffany in that sparkling gold dress, gazing up at David, who had his arm around her and was smiling broadly at the camera. It was the kind of smile that David rarely smiled. Tiffany had captioned the post, *BEST BOSS EVER!!!* And added a heart emoji.

"But I still don't think . . ." Eli said.

"We are going," Lindy said firmly, even as she felt her world start to spin, "back to Maine."

CHAPTER 24

Lindy

Tuesday, July 27, 2010
8 p.m.

"I just don't think it's worthwhile," Lindy said, gripping the steering wheel as the Volvo's headlights lit up I-95 in front of the darkening Maine sky. They were northbound, approaching the Kennebunkport service plaza, and Eli wanted to stop and ask to see the security footage from Saturday midday, to see if they could spot David. "It would take us hours to find anything, if they even agreed to let us have access. And we already know he stopped there. It won't tell us where he went after that." Truth was, Lindy did not want to see images of him. Especially, she did not want to see images of him with Tiffany. She also did not want to expose her embarrassing circumstances to even one more person, not even a security guard at the Kennebunkport service plaza.

"It's killing me that we were there looking for him on Sunday," Eli said. "Hailey and Cody and me. We asked at the Starbucks, but nobody remembered him."

Lindy swallowed at the pain in her son's voice. "I'm sorry, honey, but we know he just got gas for the car. It isn't going to tell us anything to find him on the security footage."

"We could see, like, what he was wearing," Eli said. "That might tell us something."

A sudden image popped into Lindy's mind of David in a Hawaiian shirt and lei—he'd never worn either in his life—on his way with Tiffany to the Portland airport to catch a flight to somewhere tropical. The girl could've charged airline tickets to her credit card, and he could've paid her back in cash. *With some of our hundred and nine thousand dollars.*

"I really don't want to see what he was wearing," she said.

"But, Mom, we need to be doing everything we can—"

Emma spoke up darkly from the back. "Give her a break, Eli. She's coming to terms with the fact that her husband's a fucking cheater."

Lindy clenched the wheel tighter. It was a shock to hear the sentence out loud, to know it applied to her. "Emma, that's enough." She let out a quick breath, trying to get her bearings. "Look, you guys, let's not say anything to the others, okay? The last thing Hailey needs is to go into her own wedding thinking . . . well, that every relationship is doomed." Lindy also didn't want Kate or Josh to know what David was really up to. She had the feeling he was going to need his siblings when this mistake of his blew up his life. Though why she was still trying to protect him, she had no idea. A lifetime of habit, maybe.

Lindy wished she hadn't given his picture to those TV stations. She wished she had never called the police. Kate was right: This was just what fifty-year-old men did! Even the police obviously knew it, though they'd been too polite to say so: *Your husband is likely having an affair, ma'am.*

God, if David was going to leave her for a younger woman, why did he have to do it in this entirely humiliating, devastating, public way? Couldn't he have gotten through two more weeks, put on a good face for the parties and the wedding, then told her privately that it had been his last hurrah? That would've been the humane thing to do. Didn't she deserve humane, no matter what mistakes she might've made over the years?

"It kinda seems like that's true, Mom," Emma said. "If this is what's happening with you and Dad, everyone else is basically screwed."

"We still don't know anything for sure," Eli argued. "A lot of other things could still be possible."

"Like what? Falling in the woods?" Lindy snapped. She didn't even want to think about the possible heart condition, and she was *not* going to tell the kids, but it was certainly another factor that had pushed David into full-on midlife-crisis mode. (God, and he was going to be *exerting* himself with Tiffany! Lindy quickly cut off that thought, blocked the image from her mind.) The timing of turning fifty must have just sent him over the edge.

"I have to think," she continued, "we've searched every trailhead between the state line and Portland. I have to think we've proven that theory is not true. In fact, you know what? Let's search the parking area at the train station in Portland. You're right, Emma. He could've parked there and taken off somewhere. We should search the airport, too." The idea of him with Tiffany on some tropical beach wouldn't leave her. They had all that money; they were making a real getaway of it!

The twins didn't answer. Eli simply sighed. It was true it would make little sense for David and Tiffany to drive to Portland if they were going to catch a flight, or even a bus or a train. They would've booked any trip out of Providence or Boston. And David wouldn't have taken the camping gear if they were headed to a tropical beach . . .

But wait. Gina had said Tiffany had a "glow."

What if David had taken the money not for some luxurious getaway, but because he was starting a new family with Tiffany? Of course! The mortgage application. He was buying her a house, a crib, a stroller. Maybe they were having a little camping-trip pseudo-honeymoon, before he told Lindy and took his permanent leave—

Lindy swallowed back bile. Glancing in the rearview mirror, she saw Emma bent over her phone, thumbing out a text. Was she writing to Hailey or Cody, telling them about the money, about Tiffany?

Lindy hoped not. She still had to believe that David was going to at least show up for Hailey's wedding. Even if he was setting Lindy aside in the cruelest way imaginable, there was no way he would miss the chance to walk their daughter down the aisle.

Besides, Tiffany had taken vacation for only a week, so she was clearly heading back to Cranston in time for David to attend Hailey's wedding—

But it didn't make sense that David and Tiffany would run off for a week together and then expect to go back to business as usual at work. Were they throwing it all away? Giving up their jobs and starting a new life with that hundred and nine thousand dollars?

Lindy didn't know. But she *did* know that she needed Hailey's wedding not to be ruined by everybody knowing about David's affair. (How would Hailey even *go through with* the wedding, if she knew?)

Yet, the more Lindy insisted on discretion, the more likely the twins would be to spill the beans. Emma especially, for whom being contrary was almost reflex.

Lindy decided, then: She would have to lie.

She would tell everybody that she'd heard from David, he was fine, he was camping, he was sorry he'd worried them. They would believe that. Especially Kate and Josh would. It would keep them from worrying, keep Kate from drinking. And it would keep David's affair, Lindy and David's marriage, as it belonged: private. For her to work out with him when he showed up again.

Although, after all this, the only thing that would be left to work out was a divorce settlement.

She flicked on her turn signal to exit at the Kennebunkport service plaza, and Eli perked up. "I'm not changing my mind about the security footage," she told him. "I just want a coffee."

Inside the large building, franchises of Burger King, Popeyes, Sbarro, C-store, and Starbucks encircled an atrium filled with tables and chairs where people were sitting and eating. The whole place was crowded, even at this hour, but that was late July in Maine for you—the busiest time of the year. Lindy told the kids to go ahead to the restrooms while she stood in the long line at Starbucks. Her hands felt clammy. She knew she had a good plan, but it still felt wrong.

When the kids came out and joined her, she gave Eli her credit card to place the order and made her way across the atrium and into the women's room, walking past a dozen stalls to one in the back corner. She stayed locked inside a couple minutes too long, listening to heels clicking in, faucets and hand dryers turning on, and heels clicking out again, as she tried not to breathe in the unpleasant smells of the cavernous room that had been used by probably thousands of people that day.

She hoped she was doing the right thing, though she had always taught her children there were no circumstances under which telling a lie was the right course of action.

But she had been wrong about a lot of things, it seemed.

When she went back out to the atrium, the kids were just gathering up the coffees. Lindy took her mocha latte from Emma and said, "You guys aren't going to believe this."

"What, Mom?" Emma said.

Lindy tried to form the words. They were in her head: *Your dad just called me.*

She couldn't say it.

She shook her head and started toward the exit, and the twins followed. "You guys," she said over her shoulder, even as she blinked back tears. So, she couldn't lie. She was going to have to stick with telling them the truth and appeal to them as adults, not assume they'd act like rebellious children. It helped to not be looking at them as she spoke; she was so humiliated, suddenly. "I—you know, guys. I need your help," she said. "Seriously. As I told you, all the evidence points to your dad being off with Tiffany for the week." She wouldn't mention her theory about Tiffany being pregnant, about how David was using their life savings to buy her a house, a stroller, a crib. "It's fucking unbelievable. But it's true. And it is going to utterly ruin your sister's wedding. And we really cannot have that. So much is ruined already."

"What are you saying, Mom?" Emma said from behind Lindy.

Lindy pushed open the glass door to go outside. The fresh air—a perfect seventy degrees now—was a relief. Beneath the smells of cooling concrete and traffic whooshing past on I-95 was the scent of distant pine trees, of Maine. Nearby stood the ten-foot-tall statue of a moose. Lindy and David and the kids had taken at least a dozen family photos with that statue over the years, part of their tradition each summer when they were heading up to Innisfree, and Lindy swallowed back a swell that came in her throat at the thought of happier times. "I think your dad's fine, Em, and he'll be back before the wedding. I just want—I don't want everybody to know what he's up to. Especially not Hailey. And I don't want her to know about the money, either. She'll think it's her fault—the fault of the wedding, I mean. And I don't think it is."

"But you can't know for sure that he's with Tiffany," Eli said.

Tears sprang to Lindy's eyes. "A wife knows." Besides, the evidence was so clear. "There have been some things going on that I haven't wanted to tell you kids about, and Gina told me some things at the office."

They had reached the Volvo, and she turned to face the twins. Emma had tears rolling down her face again. It was clear she, too, believed that David had run off with Tiffany, based on what Reese had written in that note, based on that photo on Tiffany's Facebook profile. Now Lindy just had to hope that Emma would take an adult view of things and understand why it was important not to let Hailey, especially, know the truth.

"So, what?" Emma said. "You want us to just, like, keep this information to ourselves?"

Just what Lindy had been hoping for, but, at the devastation in her daughter's voice, she had to swallow back more tears. She set her latte on the hood and pulled Emma into a hug. The girl was hot with anxiety and fear, and Lindy was struck with a fresh wave of fury at David, plus renewed conviction that it was definitely the truth: David was fine, he was just off having his midlife crisis with his little tramp. It was the only possible explanation. It was what fifty-year-old men did.

"That's right, honey." Lindy squeezed Emma tighter, stroking her spiky curls. "If you would. For your sister. And for Aunt Kate? She's been having such a hard time. Okay?"

Eli broke in. "We're not going to stop looking for him, are we?"

Lindy let Emma go and looked at her son. She didn't know what she was going to say until she said it. "I think he'll be back in a few days. Tiffany only took vacation through this week. Thanks to that credit card charge and the gear being gone, we know they're camping in Maine, and I know he won't miss your sister's wedding. I think it would be best just to let it be."

Eli frowned.

"So what are we supposed to tell everybody?" Emma said, wiping her tears away.

CHAPTER 25

Greta

Tuesday, July 27, 2010
9:30 p.m.

"So, the extra good news is we can go ahead with the party and the wedding!" Lindy, standing at the kitchen counter, took a sip of the wine she'd poured herself the instant she, Emma, and Eli had walked in from their day in Cranston.

Greta had waited up long past her usual bedtime for their arrival because Lindy had phoned from Kennebunkport and said David had called her on her cell. He was fine; he was camping in northern Maine. They could call off the search, and Lindy would phone the yellow cottage and let Kate and the others know right away, too. Greta had needed to know more.

"He's really . . . okay?" Hailey said now, hands clutched under her chin.

"Yes!" Lindy's eyes looked bright and a bit wild, but that was understandable, given everything.

"Seriously?" said Cody, excited. Beside him, Eli still seemed upset, and Emma had her arms folded and looked angry, which was surprising. Then again, she and her friend, Reese, had had that fight last night, and everybody was exhausted. It was strange that David had put them all through this, honestly. To go off camping on the day of his own birthday party, without clearly communicating his plans?

"No more need to worry!" Lindy took another sip of wine. "We can all get some sleep tonight!"

Hailey exuberantly hugged Lindy, and with that, everybody started hugging each other, except for Emma, who stood apart, arms still folded. Greta succumbed to a giant bear hug from Cody, even as she worried. The anniversary party. Now that they knew David was fine, Lindy would want to throw the party as planned. But how could Greta put Tom through that? He *had* remembered her today—a relief and a joy after the pain of the middle of last night—but Saturday was a few days away, and who knew how he would be by then . . .

"And tomorrow," Lindy said, pulling back from Cody and peering around to address Hailey, "we really tackle that wedding! We've got a lot to do!"

"Um, yeah!" Hailey said. "Fantastic!"

"Man, I'm starving!" Cody said, diving enthusiastically into the fridge, pulling out a box of last night's pizza and digging in.

"Lindy, about the anniversary party . . ." Greta managed to say, though she hated to break into this happy moment.

"That's almost set!" Lindy picked up her wine again for another quick sip. It wasn't like her to drink so much so quickly. *She must just be so relieved,* Greta thought. "The food's already paid for and confirmed for delivery. The cleaners are coming Friday, so we don't even have to worry about that." She frowned. "I did not want to end up saddling you with cleaning for your own party, Mom." Now she gulped the wine, draining the glass.

"Well, that was very thoughtful, honey," Greta managed. How was she ever going to tell Lindy they couldn't have the party when Lindy had been through so much?

And—though Lindy didn't know it yet—it would be their last party at Innisfree. Ever. Other than the people who would be in and out for Hailey's wedding, but that wasn't a party being *held* here.

Maybe Tom would be okay? It was just a few more days. He had seemed quite fresh this morning! As if calling Greta "Betsy" in the night had been only a bad dream. Everyone had bad dreams. Didn't they?

CHAPTER 26

Hailey

Tuesday, July 27, 2010
10 p.m.

Why aren't you happier?" Hailey said to her sister, upstairs in the girls' room. She was rooting for a cardigan in her suitcase, which she'd hauled in from The Closet and flopped open on top of the twin bed that hadn't been slept in. Their mom, after getting tipsy on wine—super unusual for her, but maybe she'd been inspired by Aunt Kate in recent days—had ordered everyone off to get some rest, but Hailey needed to go over to Seabreeze. Jack had already agreed to pick her up at 5:15 again tomorrow morning to go out searching, and she needed to tell him the search was off. "Dad's okay!" Then she reminded herself: That likely wasn't the only thing on her sister's mind. "I mean, I know you're upset about Reese leaving. What was that all about, anyway?"

Emma, stretched out on her rumpled twin bed, ankles and arms crossed, let out a heavy sigh. "I don't know," she said glumly. "She said she thought Dad was having an affair. I told her there was no way."

Hailey was glad, then, that Reese was gone. "Well, Dad's *not* having an affair. He's up in northern Maine camping."

Emma propped herself on her elbows. "Mom said he used to, like, go off by himself camping sometimes, back before we were born. Did you know anything about that?"

"No," Hailey said, still digging through her suitcase. Where was that damn sweater?

Emma lay back down and sighed again, staring at the ceiling. "I just wish we knew when he was planning to come back."

"Didn't Mom say end of the week?" Already their mom had called the police and the TV stations to say there was no need to look for their dad's car or run his story anymore. Lindy said she'd even assigned Uncle Josh to travel the coastline one more time tomorrow to take down the *MISSING* flyers that had been posted everywhere. That was more than enough to convince Hailey: their dad was definitely fine.

"Yeah, I guess," Emma said, not sounding convinced.

Hailey finally found her cardigan, yanked it out, and put it on. "Listen, Dad is fine, he's not having an affair, and he'll be back soon. I'm going over to tell Jack."

That got a little smirk from Emma. "Did you tell Noah yet?"

"Shut up," Hailey said automatically, stopping to look in the mirror by the door. She wondered if Noah would even be happy at the news, or if he'd just say, *Told you so.* She wiped a smudge of mascara from the outer corner of her eye, wishing she had time for a shower, a little fresh makeup.

She caught herself. Ridiculous. Also, she *could* just call over to Seabreeze, landline to landline—but that would probably wake Marjorie. Hailey knew she could get Jack's attention by tossing pebbles at his upstairs window, the way she used to do.

"Mom's not going to like you going out alone at night," Emma said. "Even if Dad's supposedly okay."

"Then let's not tell her."

Emma let out a mock gasp. "Hailey Marie Kauffman! What happened to being the perfect daughter?"

"Oh, for God's sake," Hailey muttered. In her mind, she saw a fractured shell. Wow, Jack better not have permanently *altered* her. She was not ready for that. But. "Just don't tell her," she said, and walked out, shutting the door quietly behind her. Through the closed attic door, she heard her brothers shouting and moving around up there—playing with their Nerf basketball? Most likely. Otherwise, the cottage was quiet and dark, and she tiptoed down the stairs, hoping the screen door wouldn't squeak as she pushed her way outside.

The night was starlit, black, and cool. Few lights burned in the cottages she passed as she made her way down toward the ocean, then around the point and back up the road toward Seabreeze. The moonlight shone on the water, and gentle waves lapped the rocks below.

She was trying not to think about what Emma had asked in mock alarm—*what happened to being the perfect daughter?*—but it had cut too close to the bone.

Because, yes, Hailey should definitely call Noah and tell him the good news about her dad. She should do what she could to try to appease him, repair things before the wedding, in which her parents had invested so much time and money.

Unfortunately, ever since Jack's game of "what if" this afternoon, she was having a hard time ignoring how badly Noah had been acting. She was also having zero luck keeping her thoughts from spinning out into what his bad behavior might portend for her future.

And now that Dad was okay, and Mom was hell-bent on going full-bore on the rest of the wedding preparations starting tomorrow, Hailey had no excuse to continue to think about postponing it.

As she approached Seabreeze, Hailey saw the light on in Jack's room upstairs.

She scooped a handful of mulch from the hydrangea bed below his open window and tossed it up to hit the screen, scooting away before the pieces rained back down. He came to the window, a dark shape framed in the light, wearing only a pair of shorts. She gave him a little wave, feeling sheepish suddenly.

When he spotted her, she heard him laugh. "Meet you at the front door!" he called, then disappeared.

So much for being circumspect. Also, she'd imagined he would have her come to the back, the way he used to. The back door led almost straight to a back staircase, which led almost straight up to his room—

Damn it. What had she been thinking, seriously?

She made her way around to the front and up the porch steps, feeling off-balance now, twisting her ring around her finger. She should have just called. Obviously, Jack wasn't going to invite her upstairs like no time had passed, like she wasn't engaged to marry Noah in ten days' time. Was she just out of her mind with relief about her dad being okay? That had to be it. Yes. She felt a fresh wave of solace at the explanation.

Jack didn't turn on the porch light. He opened the front door and closed it quietly behind him as he stepped outside. He had put on a blue T-shirt, and he didn't look surprised that she was there, which made her wonder how many other girls threw mulch at his window, here or back in California. She decided: She would tell him the news, then leave. Immediately.

"Hi," he said.

"Hi!" She spilled it all out quickly—her dad had called, he was safe, he was camping up north by himself, there was no more need to worry or search for him. "So, I just wanted to tell you that we don't need to go out tomorrow morning. And thank you!"

"Well, that is great news!"

At the sight of Jack's genuine smile, Hailey shoved aside a niggling thought of Emma's unease about when their dad would actually come back. She wasn't going to tell Jack about that.

Jack cocked his head toward the rocking chairs nearby. "Want to sit for a minute?"

"Yeah, sure! Great," Hailey blurted, then bit her lip.

Well, staying for just a minute would be okay.

She crossed the porch to sit in the farthest chair. "Won't we bother your grandma?" she whispered, imagining Marjorie would have her bedroom window, directly above them, open.

Jack sat in the other chair. "Don't worry. Once she takes her hearing aids out, she wouldn't hear an airplane crash into the cove."

Hailey sat up straighter. "You shouldn't say things like that. Don't you think it invites trouble?"

Jack shrugged, with a mysterious little smile that somehow took away Hailey's ability to form words. She looked out at the swirls of moonlight on the black, rippling water, twisting her ring again. It popped into her head to wonder where she'd be a year from now. It would be her one-year wedding anniversary, her grandparents' fifty-first, and her dad's fifty-first birthday. Maybe they'd be able to throw him a big party for that one. Maybe they'd all be able to spend time together at Innisfree again, despite the fact that her mom had made such a big deal about this being "the last summer" that they would all be together. (Would Hailey be pregnant by next summer? She almost shuddered at the thought.)

The two chairs were angled toward each other with a small table between them, and she was conscious of Jack's legs stretching toward her, his crossed ankles and large bare feet, even as she imagined Marjorie sweetly prying confessions out of one neighbor at a time here in these chairs, afternoon by sunny afternoon, over strong gin and tonics and generous slices of cookie cake. Maybe that was how Marjorie maintained dominion over The Cove—because she got everybody to dish their secrets not only in her kitchen, the way she'd always done with Hailey, but right here on her front porch.

"So, you're not doing *any* writing anymore?" Jack asked suddenly.

"Oh! Oh, well, actually . . ." Apparently, he took after his grandma when it came to prying information out of people, because Hailey *never* talked about her story, but within seconds she was divulging everything about her spiral notebook, the twenty-two chapters, her frustration over how little time she'd spent working on it the past year, her certainty that she wouldn't have any time for it once she was in law school.

"What is it about?" Jack asked.

Her face heated up. "It's a coming-of-age story, but also like a mystery." The truth was, it featured a teenage girl and boy in a small coastal village in Maine, falling in love one summer while they solved a cold 1930s murder case after finding clues in the guy's grandmother's attic. Hailey had not realized till literally this moment how much of the story had been inspired by her long-ago summers with Jack. She'd started writing it four years ago, imagining she was making the thing up out of whole cloth.

"Well, you can't give up on it." Jack grinned. "I want to be able to say I knew you when."

She laughed, as her face grew hotter. "Thanks for the vote of confidence." She hoped that, in the dim light, he couldn't see her blushing—

She caught herself. "I should probably get home," she said. "Lots to do for the wedding!"

Jack shifted slightly in his chair, then said, "Yeah, I guess it's getting late," which for some reason caused a pinprick feeling in her heart.

That was going to do nobody any good. She quickly stood.

He stood at the same time, and they ended up too close to each other. Whoops. Hailey tipped up her chin, studying his face, and the scent of him—his fresh-out-of-the-laundry shirt, the salt and heat of his skin—was all around. She felt the rise and fall of his chest as he breathed, and her eyes, without her wanting them to, traced the shape of his mouth.

"What if everything were different, Hales?" he said quietly.

She stepped back like he'd kicked her shin. "Jack," she scolded.

But he was looking at her softly. Almost like he was thinking about kissing her . . .

Okay, seriously. She hadn't wanted to ask—it would've felt too intimate, too suggestive—but it was impossible to imagine that he didn't have a girlfriend back in California.

Which meant he'd stand there and think about blowing up Hailey's whole life, without having any intention of sticking around.

And *she* would be seriously complicit, what with the whole throwing mulch at his window thing.

"I'd better go," she said. "Night, Jack." He opened his mouth, but she scooted around him and hurried down the porch steps and out to the road.

What if everything were different, Hales? she thought as she hurried toward the point, toward where the moonlight scattered across the rolling ocean, the familiar landscape feeling off-kilter now.

Well, everything *couldn't* be different. And that was that.

Okay. At least now that her dad was definitely okay, she and Jack wouldn't see each other except around the neighborhood. They'd have no reason to.

What a relief, she thought, even as part of her was tumbling headlong into a sorrow she could not name as she turned up the hill to head back to Innisfree.

She went inside and switched on the lamp in the living room, then tiptoed upstairs to grab her book bag—fortunately, Emma slept like a rock—and hauled it back down again. She had to remind herself of the facts of her life, she'd decided.

She sat on the couch and used both hands to pull out her thick wedding binder. The thing had to weigh eight pounds. She laid it flat on the coffee table, opened to the to-do list, and read: *Finalize seating chart. Confirm details and payments with all vendors. Confirm details and schedule with wedding party . . .*

She was feeling nauseous again.

She guessed she'd let Jack get into her head too much. But life with Noah was going to be great. They'd just had a rough few days, that was all.

She dug into her bag for a pen to make notes. She needed to find out exactly when Chelsea, her maid of honor, was planning to arrive from Rhode Island, and schedule a manicure for Emma to get that black nail polish off, exchange it for petal pink to match the bridesmaid dresses—

She found the notebook that contained her novel. Why had she even thrown it in there? It wasn't like she'd expected to have time to work on her writing. But she did tend to bring it with her wherever she traveled, and she'd also always done some writing during summers at Innisfree. So maybe it was just old habit to bring the notebook along.

Also, she hadn't wanted to leave it at the apartment for Noah to find. He didn't know she was writing a novel. (Or . . . a "story.")

She pulled the notebook out and opened to where she'd left off, to the last page grooved by the loops and lines and swirls of her ballpoint pen. She read the words they made, running her hand over the paper, loving the contrast between the textured page and the smooth blank one.

She dug into her bag again for the pen she knew was in there.

She found it, pulled it out, uncapped it, and, at the top of the blank new page, began to write.

CHAPTER 27

Lindy

Wednesday, July 28, 2010
3 a.m.

Lindy woke to the sound of someone tiptoeing up the stairs. For a second, because she knew she was alone in bed, she thought, *David?*

Then the realities all came whooshing back so quickly that they made her sit up in shock: David was gone; David was having an affair; David might have a heart condition; Lindy had lied to Hailey and Cody and her mother and Kate; she had lied to everybody and made Emma and Eli complicit.

And on the heels of these horrible recollections came a galloping stampede of terrors: What if she was wrong? What if David was out there somewhere, needing help?

Because he wouldn't do this to them intentionally, would he? To her, their kids, his sister and brother, his nieces and nephews? The crew of them had spent hundreds of hours searching, made and posted hundreds of flyers, driven up and down the coast a half dozen times, plus up to Bangor to alert the TV stations. They'd made a hundred phone calls and multiple trips to Cranston. Surely, he would've known that, if he simply *vanished,* this would be their response!

Wouldn't he?

Was she being foolish deciding that an affair with Tiffany was the only answer?

Or was she just *hoping* it was true so she wouldn't have to imagine other, even more terrible alternatives?

David finished his law degree in the spring of 1985, but by then he no longer talked about making a difference in the world, or even about philosophy. It was as if he'd lost his curiosity, his penchant for asking interesting questions. Maybe he was just worn out, or maybe his work in the public defender's office in Boston had discouraged him in general about humanity, about the business of being alive.

And yet, this summer, he would be studying for the bar, spending a little time at The Cove and a lot in Boston studying with his classmates, then going to Rhode Island to take the state exam there in July. In the fall, he would start a full-time job as a staff attorney with the Rhode Island Public Defender, which Lindy could hardly imagine would be any more uplifting.

She had been hoping he would come to New York. She would be starting law school at NYU, and she didn't see herself ending up in a public defender's office. She envisioned a downtown Manhattan firm where she would wear a very expensive suit and very high heels every day, which would please her all the more because they would seem gauche to her mother. Lindy had an apartment lined up with a roommate, but she would change her arrangements in a heartbeat to live with David, if he asked, though her parents would be scandalized.

She was just so tired of living so far apart from him. He'd chosen Northeastern because he thought the program there matched his interests better than any school in New York, so they'd spent the last three years, while Lindy finished up her undergrad, commuting back and forth from New York to Boston, which was an even greater distance than New York to Providence. (*A negligible distance,* David would say, and she would answer, in a tone as if she were teasing, *But not nothing!*) These past two years, they'd both been so busy that they'd seen each other only a couple times a month, if they were lucky.

That explained why she was completely surprised by the state he was in when he arrived at The Cove in mid-June. She'd been there nearly two weeks already, helping her mother with Innisfree. They were doing some painting and redecorating this year, and Lindy was painstakingly refinishing a pair of end tables she'd found at a yard sale, enjoying what she couldn't help but feel was her last summer before real adulthood struck.

She was hanging out with Kate on the porch of the yellow cottage when David drove up in his old Corolla, and when she ran down to greet him, she sensed instantly that something was wrong. He *felt* angry, though he said nothing. His curly hair was wild, too long; he had a three-day scruff of beard. He kissed her briefly, yanked his duffel out of the hatch of his car, and marched inside shouting to his mother that he was hungry. Lindy was surprised to see he was still limping. It had been months since he'd hurt his knee; the injury had kept him on crutches through part of the winter, and he'd been grumpy, to say the least, about being unable to run.

This was not the David that they had expected to see. This version of David had been gone a long time, and no one was happy to see him back.

Lindy hoped he was just worn thin by studying for the bar, and that, once he got a little rest and a few hours at The Cove under his belt, he'd relax into his more genial self again.

It didn't happen. Three days later, he and Lindy had a terrible fight. He couldn't believe she would even consider asking him to come to New York just to see if he could find some random job, when his old Brown professor had pulled some major strings to line up the job in Providence. David was registered and paid up to take the Rhode Island bar, he'd been studying his ass off, and he'd always loved living in Providence. Why the hell would he want to move to New York? There was no way in hell he was going to take the bar in New York! He'd have to study a whole extra year!

She couldn't believe that, after all this time, he still didn't make her or their relationship a priority, and New York was the center of the world and it was where they should start their life together, and certainly where he should start his career, not some public defender's office in a tiny city in a tiny state, from where he could expect to get exactly nowhere.

He packed up his camping gear and left, telling her not to expect him back anytime soon.

He does this all the time, she told herself. *He'll be fine. He'll be gone for a while, then he'll come back, and he'll be fine.*

Normally, she never scolded him, never told him he was doing the wrong thing, never indicated any dissatisfaction concerning anything about him or their relationship.

She didn't know how she had let herself lose control like that.

Five days—two of sun and three of rain—passed. She finished the end tables and painted the bathroom, but all she was really doing was worrying, waiting. Greta told her that no good would come of it.

"Of worrying?" Lindy said.

"Of being with David," Greta said. "It's time you grow up. Imagine a different life for yourself. Just *try.*"

And though typically Lindy reflexively did the opposite of what her mother advised, this time she found herself wondering, much as she loved David, if her mother could be right.

But then a call came in to the yellow cottage at noon on a Tuesday, and Kate ran over to Innisfree to get Lindy. "David's in the hospital in Blue Hill. He checked himself in."

Kate drove the family station wagon, Mrs. Kauffman rode shotgun, and Lindy sat perched on the middle edge of the back seat, peering nervously between the two of them out the windshield at the tree-lined highway, as if she could gain some control that way over where they were going or what was going to happen next. She was surprised and grateful they had invited her along—she'd had the sense both were miffed over her role in David's departure—but maybe they just needed reinforcements, with Josh and Mr. Kauffman both back in Chicago working.

David had checked himself in? Did that mean he'd harmed himself intentionally again, then changed his mind about his desired outcome? Or had there been some accident and he'd managed to drive himself to the hospital?

Kate and Mrs. Kauffman didn't know. The nurse on the phone had told them almost nothing. It was a three-hour drive to Blue Hill.

"We gave him something to help him sleep," said the doctor behind the desk inside the mint-green office in the center of the old hospital. David, the doctor had explained, had shown up wild-eyed in the ER saying he hadn't slept in four days and couldn't control the persistent, vivid thoughts he was having about ending his life. "A part of him was extremely cogent. A part of him wanted to save himself. Which is cause for optimism in my book," said the doctor, who had a very gentle, yet sure-footed, way about him. Lindy was relieved to the point of tears that David had found this man, that this man had been here for David. "Now we just need to evaluate if he has sufficient support at home to be released to his family. It certainly appears to me like he does." Lindy, her face hot with tears, glanced at Mrs. Kauffman, then at Kate. They were crying quietly, too, as the doctor said directly to Mrs. Kauffman, "He didn't hesitate to give me your telephone number, which is another good sign."

Mrs. Kauffman straightened, clutching her handbag in her lap. Her lip trembled slightly. "We will give him all the support he needs."

"I can see that," said the doctor, with a quiet nod. "I'd like to keep him here overnight so he can sleep. Tomorrow, you can take him home."

David, asleep half sitting up in the hospital bed, wearing a gown, looked as if he'd just fought a very hard battle. His beard had grown in entirely and made him seem a stranger, though the way his curls spilled over his forehead was familiar, as was the shape of his eyes, the curl of his eyelashes over his cheeks. The three women each kissed his forehead in turn—he didn't rouse; he smelled of sweat and campfire smoke—then sat by the bed for hours as he slept. Finally, Kate left to try to find a motel. When she came back two hours later, Lindy's nose caught the scent of wine. They each kissed his forehead again, and when they walked outside, it was the three of them against the world, and the sunset sky over the bay beside the ancient, white wood-frame hospital was a shade of lavender Lindy had never seen, and the taste of the cedar- and salt-scented air was sweeter than she'd remembered.

The next day, Lindy, Mrs. Kauffman, and Kate went to the hospital at the appointed hour. At the sight of David, groggy but awake in the hospital bed, Lindy's fear was a quick flare that she managed to tamp down as she went to hug and kiss him. Now she thought she smelled on his skin the old tinny scent of blood and a musty tent, though that didn't make sense and certainly couldn't be true. "Hi, honey," she said softly as she pulled back, and as he clutched her elbow and looked at her, there was regret and—she was sure of it—love in his deep, dark eyes.

Kate drove David's car, and Lindy drove the family station wagon, while Mrs. Kauffman sat in the back with David. They talked quietly to each other as if Lindy wasn't in the car at all, or at least as if she couldn't hear.

"I couldn't stop seeing it," David told his mother. "I saw my hand holding a knife and cutting my arms up and down and cutting my legs and I knew where the femoral artery was, even though I don't know, and I saw it gushing and thought how satisfying that would be, and the peace that would come, and the warmth before the cold, and then part of me knew I was just going crazy and I needed to stop it. I wanted to go home, and then I didn't know where I was, but then I was driving and I saw the blue *H* and I knew I should go there. And I don't remember what happened next. I don't remember arriving there, but obviously I did. How is it that the mind can divide itself like that? To know one thing to be true while at the same time another opposite thing is equally true? To remember things you'd rather forget and forget the things you want to remember?"

"I don't know, honey," said Mrs. Kauffman in a defeated tone, squeezing his hand, while in the driver's seat Lindy blinked away tears, because it seemed David was fully *back,* in a way he hadn't been in far longer than she had realized.

When they arrived at The Cove, it was late afternoon, and Mrs. Kauffman said she would allow David and Lindy to walk to the beach, but they had to sit where she could see them from the yellow cottage and be back in thirty minutes. She was going to make hamburgers, and they would be ready to eat by then. (Last night at the motel, Mrs. Kauffman had talked at length about how she was afraid David hadn't been eating properly, he had been studying way too hard, he had taken the weight of fixing the whole world onto his shoulders. What he needed was red meat and rest and a summer at The Cove, she declared, before flopping over and going to sleep. Lindy had lain awake a long time, thinking that to help him this time would probably not be that easy—the fact that his knee prevented him from running was especially worrisome—and she could feel that Kate, beside her in the bed, was awake, too, but there didn't seem to be anything to say.)

Now David held Lindy's hand. It was almost hard to believe he was really there. The misery of his absence was solved, only to be replaced with a set of circumstances that felt not only insoluble, but mysterious in an unlikable way. They went down and sat on the rocks, his gait uneven due to his painful knee. The day was cool and overcast but not rainy, and the sight of the cove, a silvery blue under the gray sky, caused Lindy's heart to lift, despite everything.

It was impossible to know what to say, though David seemed peaceful, as if his demons had been wrestled down, at least for now. Also, Lindy reminded herself, he was still under the effects of the medication he had been given in the hospital. (Upon his discharge, the doctor had handed Mrs. Kauffman a bottle of pills that he said would keep David calm starting right away, along with a written prescription for an antidepressant that should begin to work within a few weeks to make him better for the long term, provided he took it every day. They had stopped in town to have the prescription filled on their way back. David said he had not been taking any medication for a while, which none of them had known.)

"I don't know what happened," he said now, finally, in a gentle, sorrowful tone, stretching his painful leg out in front of him, propping his foot on a rock. She waited, hoping he would say more, and after a moment he sighed and looked out at the water and the boats on their moorings and continued in a slow, contemplative way. "I had this sense of hopelessness. Hollowness. I was born that way, I guess. It's tiresome. I hate to think of bothering you with it. Or my family. I thought if I could get away, I could clear my head. I don't know what's wrong with me. I don't know why it came to this again."

She studied the familiar contours of his face. She wished more than anything that he would just be all right. She wished she knew what to do.

She cupped his face in her hand; the unfamiliar beard was surprisingly soft. "Your mother thinks you need to eat more red meat," she said, which at least made him laugh a little.

Because of the trip to Blue Hill, Lindy got off track with her birth control pills. She and Kate and Mrs. Kauffman had hopped into the car so swiftly after the call from the hospital that none of them had brought an overnight bag, nor stopped to think they might need one. Since Lindy always took her pill in the morning, she didn't remember that she'd missed one until the following morning back at The Cove.

The slipup made her nervous, yet it opened up a possibility which stewed at the back of her mind. The front of her mind, as David liked to say about his own, was very crowded.

She was trying so hard to say the right things to him. To spend enough time with him, but not too much. He slept a lot. They went to the beach. They played board games with Kate, and he would watch Kate and Lindy play tennis. (In the evenings, Kate was always gone, out carousing with friends who drank too much. Lindy worried about her, but of course couldn't mention it to David, or even to Mrs. Kauffman, and the truth was she didn't have a lot of space to worry about Kate. Nearly her whole mind was taken up by David.)

He iced and rested his knee; he intended to rehabilitate it without surgery. His mother was trying to convince him to postpone taking the bar, to come back home to Chicago at summer's end. She would take care of him, she said. He wouldn't have to worry about money or a job for a while, and he could see his old doctors again, the ones who had helped him before. There was no reason to rush anything, she said; he needed time to recover.

So far, all he'd agreed to was stepping back from studying for a few days, but Lindy felt she could see the writing on the wall, and she didn't at all like what it said.

Whenever she wasn't with him, whenever she went home to Innisfree, the guard she didn't know she was keeping up simply collapsed. She cried in her bedroom. She was exhausted, went to bed early. Her redecorating projects languished; she was uninspired. She wandered through rooms, couldn't focus to read, kept asking her mother if Greta could possibly forego practicing the Tchaikovsky just now, if she could please turn the stereo down. Lindy craved quiet, the sound of the waves. Her parents cast worried glances after her like swooping butterfly nets that always missed their target. One night at dinner, her mother said to her, "You are not going to let this derail your plans," as a statement, not a question, and Lindy snapped, "Just stop, Mom," and her father laid a firm hand over Greta's with a quiet shake of his head.

Did Lindy know what she was doing? Maybe.

She didn't take her pill. Once. Twice. A half dozen times.

Maybe the back of her mind had decided—even if the front was too crowded to quite register the decision.

And yet.

It was hard to find any privacy at The Cove, but on the Fourth of July, when everyone was at the SCPA clubhouse for the lobster bake—Lindy's parents were serving, as usual—Lindy whispered to David after they were done eating that maybe his mother would let them go for a little walk, if his knee felt up to it, and he said it did.

Mrs. Kauffman, who seemed newly on the fence regarding whether Lindy was good or bad for David, consulted with her recently arrived husband with a glance, then gave a stern nod, cautioning them to meet the family in precisely one hour at the beach to watch the town fireworks. They promised they would, then got up to dump the contents of their red plastic trays—the broken lobster shells, the green liquid from the lobster innards, the devastated corn cobs, the empty silver-lined chip bags—into the giant trashcans. Holding hands, they walked out into the evening, away from the noise of everyone talking and laughing in the tiny clubhouse, out to the quiet lapping of the water on the shore.

Soon, they were upstairs in David's small bedroom in the empty, quiet yellow cottage, and quickly they were naked, in between the scratchy plaid sheets on his twin bed, which smelled musky and inviting like his skin, and quickly he slid inside her, and soon they both cried out in relief.

Afterward, she lay with her arm over his chest, her leg draped over his. With darkness falling outside, he held her and stroked her hair as the small fireworks around the neighborhood began to sound off intermittently and the breeze off the cove snaked in through the open windows. "I love you so much, David," she whispered, and he said he loved her, too, and she snuggled a little closer, hoping that now their life would change, that now he'd know for sure he had something to live for.

CHAPTER 28

Lindy

Wednesday, July 28, 2010
11 a.m.

Hailey?" Lindy tapped lightly on the girls' bedroom door. "Are you still sleeping, sweetie? We need to leave for your dress fitting in an hour."

Lindy hadn't slept much more after waking in the middle of the night. This morning, when she was sure her parents were out of earshot and the kids were all still sleeping, she'd called the hospital in Blue Hill.

David wasn't there.

And she'd decided again: She needed to stick to the story that she and Emma and Eli had agreed upon; carry on with the anniversary party and the preparations for Hailey's wedding; make sure that David's betrayal didn't completely ruin all their lives.

By sheer force of will, she needed to keep everything—including herself—from falling apart.

After Lindy steered the Volvo to town and onto the crowded Route 1 southbound, Hailey checked her voicemail. "Oh my god, I'm going to kill him," Hailey grumbled, then, without a word to Lindy, made two phone calls, giving her credit card number to the bakery for the final payment on the cake, telling the caterer the salmon crostini would be fine, telling both she was so sorry, there'd been a family emergency.

When Hailey ended her second call, Lindy said, "You should've used my credit card for the cake," though, as soon as the words were out, her stomach started to hum at the thought of the missing hundred and nine thousand dollars.

"That's okay, Mom," Hailey said. Lindy couldn't tell what Hailey was thinking, and the fact that she was wearing sunglasses didn't help. She'd seemed distant, quiet, all morning. Was she just sleepy?

Or was there some chance she was onto Lindy's lie?

Lindy, slowing for the traffic lining up to cross the narrow Wiscasset bridge over the sprawling Sheepscot River, didn't want to think so. Besides, everybody was exhausted after the long days of searching. Emma, Eli, and Cody had all just been waking up as Lindy and Hailey left.

Lindy felt fresh fury boiling at the thought of the damage David had done—

Enough. She needed to focus on Hailey.

"I'm really sorry about all this, sweetie," Lindy said. The traffic was barely crawling now. From experience, Lindy knew they could be here for a good twenty minutes, staring at the *HELL NO GMO* bumper sticker on the rusty Subaru in front of them. She thought she'd left enough time, but at this rate, they'd be late for the fitting. It was Red's Eats at the foot of the bridge in the pretty village of Wiscasset that was the problem. Tourists queued up at Red's for the lobster rolls by the hundreds all day long, crossing the highway willy-nilly in their haste to get in line. "This should be the happiest time of your life. Or one of them, anyway!"

Hailey gave a slow nod, drumming her fingers against her skirt. She looked at Lindy sideways from behind her sunglasses. "Were you happy when you were getting ready for your wedding? Did you really want to marry Dad?"

Lindy inhaled. The question seemed to come out of nowhere; she didn't know why it made her uneasy. "Of course I was! Of course I did. But, well, you know, it was different, too, because we didn't have a long engagement, and our wedding was so small. Out on the deck at Innisfree." Lindy knew Hailey knew this, but, feeling oddly nervous, she just kept talking, telling the story the same way she had always told it to the kids. She let up off the brake to let the Volvo inch forward another car length. Sunlight glinted on the broad river. "My mother and your dad's mother did all the food, and we had only about fifteen guests. My mother played the music, and I wore a crown of flowers, which I loved, and that prairie-style tea-length dress. Your father had just passed the bar, and we came up just for the weekend. It was a beautiful sunny September Saturday."

Another slow nod from Hailey, more drumming. "Were you sorry that you couldn't go to law school?"

"Oh, God, no! I've told you. You were the best thing that ever happened to me. To us. When I found out I was pregnant with you, we just couldn't wait to be a family."

"I always thought you had to be at least a little sorry not to go to law school. I guess I always felt a little bad about that. That you had to give up law school on account of me."

"Oh, no, honey! You shouldn't." Lindy remembered vividly how she'd felt then. How frightened David had been, at first. How angry Lindy's mother was. And how Lindy herself had simply felt *certain*. While she might not have previously been aware that she wanted a baby, now she wanted *this* baby more than she'd wanted anything in her life. She sent a letter to NYU immediately. She went to Providence to look for an apartment, while David went to Boston to study for the bar. In only about three weeks, he came around to saying he was happy about the baby, happy about getting married. He seemed lighter around the eyes. His knee was getting better, too. They were all going to be happy, he said. He was turning over a new, prosaic leaf, and he wasn't going to question things any longer.

"Honey," Lindy told Hailey now, crawling forward and braking again, "sometimes you can truly think you want something in life, and then when a new path presents itself to you, you realize that the new path is actually the right path, that it's what you really wanted after all."

"Hmm," Hailey said, twisting her ring around her finger.

Lindy thought she detected an odd tone in Hailey's voice, but she didn't have it in her right now to ask, and she found herself worrying, in a way she never had, what Hailey would think if she knew the truth about how and why Lindy and David's wedding—how Hailey herself—had come about. David's crises, Lindy's subterfuges and stubborn refusal to think anything other than that she could out-and-out *fix* him, simply by loving him, by giving him a home and family.

But of course, it hadn't been that simple, come to find out after all this time.

CHAPTER 29

Hailey

Wednesday, July 28, 2010
2 p.m.

In the mirror at The Wedding Shoppe in her satin ivory ball gown, Hailey looked . . . tired. Nothing like a Pinterest bride. She tried to smooth her hair. She shouldn't have stayed up so late writing, but she'd gotten caught up in her own world—

"It's lovely, honey!" said her mom. "I don't think you need any more alterations. I think it's perfect."

Hailey turned to assess the side view. She did love the smooth satin cummerbund, the deep V plunges of the bodice, and the ten tiny cloth-covered buttons that ran along her spine at the low back. The dark-suited attendant, a tall brunette named Tenley, stepped onto the stand beside Hailey smelling of floral perfume. Tenley pinched at the gown's waist, then tried to slide a finger down behind the cummerbund in back. Unable to, she pronounced her enthusiastic approval, too. "Would you like to take it home with you today?" she asked.

Hailey's head pulsed with fresh pain.

"That would be wonderful!" Lindy said.

"Here, let's try the headpiece and veil, too." Tenley stepped down to grab them from where they rested on a nearby chair, then quickly stepped back up, setting the tiara with its attached shoulder-length veil atop Hailey's head, reaching into her pocket for bobby pins and poking one in.

"Ow!" Hailey said.

Tenley giggled. "Sorry. Here." She poked another pin in on the other side, this time without doing damage.

Lindy, gazing at Hailey, clutched her hands together beneath her chin. "Oh, honey. You look so beautiful."

Hailey's headache was making her nauseous. She was shivering and sweating at once. "Please, I don't feel good," she blurted to Tenley. "I need to get out of this thing."

"Say no more!" Tenley said, whipping out the bobby pins and handing the headpiece to Lindy. "I got you," she said, fingers flying, releasing buttons. In seconds, she'd slipped the gown off Hailey's shoulders and down past her hips. Hailey stepped out of it. Now in just her backless champagne Spanx bodysuit, she was assailed by freezing air from the vents, and goose bumps popped out on her clammy skin. She dashed for the bathroom, hearing Tenley say knowingly to Lindy, "Don't worry. Happens all the time. Nerves."

"I just wish you would've, like, waited for me before you plunked down your credit card," Hailey said, with a glance over her shoulder at the voluminous white garment bag laid over the Volvo's back seat like some kind of sea monster. *For the happiest day of your life . . .* read the cursive across the front of it. "I wasn't ready to take it home today."

Her mom accelerated, weaving through traffic on I-295 heading north out of Portland. Hailey had decided not to bother calling or texting Noah. She didn't feel like stopping by the apartment, either, though she needed to grab the things for the wedding. He'd be asleep, then he'd be at the gym, then he'd be getting ready to go to work, then he'd be gone. And he hadn't called the bakery or the caterer, the two tiny things she'd asked him to do. *The happiest time of my life, right.*

"But, sweetie," Lindy said, "it's one less thing to have to worry about later! I thought you liked the way it fit—"

"I just . . . I wasn't ready." Hailey bit her lip, cutting herself off before she could say what was on her mind: That it was now too late to get any money back on the gown if she changed her mind about getting married.

She couldn't say that. She shouldn't even be thinking it.

Lindy switched lanes to pass a Honda and reached to turn on the radio. "Come on, honey, we need a little levity. Sing with me!" She turned up Fergie's "Big Girls Don't Cry" and started to sing along.

"Ugh, Mom," Hailey said, out of old teenager habit, but after a moment she joined in on, *Fairy tales don't always have a happy ending, do they?*

A glance over at her mom then showed Lindy was crying, and the sight stabbed Hailey. Seriously, how could Dad have gone camping right now? And not even bothered to say when he'd be back? What a jerk move!

Hailey decided. For her mom, for everything her mom had put into this wedding, and for everything her mom was going through right now, Hailey needed to one hundred percent get over her hesitations. She was simply too far down this road. There was no way she could cancel the wedding now. She was just having regular run-of-the-mill cold feet. Serious-feeling, but not, in the end, worth changing course over.

It happened to everybody, according to Tenley.

Back at Innisfree, Hailey wrestled the garment bag out of the Volvo, hoping despite herself that Jack wouldn't happen by and see her. The air was fresh and pleasant after the heat of the city and the manufactured, droning chill of the air-conditioning in the car. Quickly, she followed her mom through the fragrant garden and into the cottage, as Lindy sang out, "We have the dreh-ess!"

Hailey had to turn sideways to get through the door. "I don't know where I'm going to put it," she grumbled. She should *not* be thinking about Jack right now.

Greta was just coming down the stairs, smoothing out her red capris. "You can put it up in the attic for now, dear. The boys left and said they won't be back until Saturday. Emma, too. I can't believe I fell asleep upstairs. It's lucky I woke up. I have a quiche in the oven—"

"What?" Lindy said, not about the nap or the quiche. "Where did they go?"

Greta headed for the kitchen. "Back to Rhode Island. Cody said he has to work," she said, as she grabbed the kettle to fill with water, put it on the stove, and switched on the burner. "Emma and Eli just said they had things to do."

Hailey's mom looked pale. "Things to do?"

"Ridiculous," Hailey grumbled. She could not believe her siblings would do this to their mother when Lindy was basically still reeling from their dad being gone. True, Cody had originally planned to be here only for the weekend events, so it made sense he'd go back to his lifeguard job now that their dad wasn't technically "missing." But the twins? Neither of them had any reason to go to Rhode Island! And neither of them owned a car—neither of them even really *drove*—so, as long as Cody was down there, they'd be stuck down there, too. Why would they give up their time at The Cove?

Just then, Hailey glanced toward the front of the cottage. Through the sliding glass doors, she spotted the two green Adirondack chairs on the deck angled toward each other. Her grandpa was sitting in one, and in the other was a tall man who looked unfamiliar at first, until he turned his head, and she saw it was . . . Noah?

"Oh my God," Hailey said. Noah had taken time off work? And come to The Cove? "Will miracles never cease," she muttered. It was something her dad would have said.

Her mom spotted him, too. "Oh, Noah's here!"

"Oh!" said Greta, with a worried look.

Hailey hadn't seen Noah's Audi; he must've parked around the corner up the road. The driveway, occupied by her Protegé and her grandparents' Camry, would've seemed full to anyone who wasn't used to the fact that they usually parked four cars in it.

Lindy set her purse on the counter and came to take the garment bag from Hailey. "I'll take this upstairs, honey. We can't let him see it."

"I'd better check if they need anything!" Greta said, but just then the timer for the quiche dinged and the tea kettle started to whistle. Hailey headed for the deck, finding she was not exactly thrilled to see the guy who'd been so unsupportive about her dad, who'd failed even to make those two little crucial phone calls about the wedding.

As she stepped outside and slid the door shut behind her, she heard her grandpa saying, "It wasn't until you wrote that pathbreaking article on race in antebellum Louisiana that I truly understood how lucky I was to get to advise you, Howard."

What? thought Hailey, as a gull cried out in the distance and Noah cooly said, "Dr. Sanderson, it was my privilege to get to work with you."

Hailey gave him a *what-the-hell* look, even as her grandpa gazed at him with fatherly affection. "You're kind to say so, Howard. You get to the end of a career and you wonder sometimes if your work—if *you*—made any difference to anyone."

"Grandpa, no," Hailey broke in. "This is Noah, my fiancé—"

Noah gave her a quick, slight shake of his head, as her grandpa's eyes widened in confusion.

"Dr. Sanderson," Noah said calmly, "let me assure you that you did, and please go on." With that, Hailey's grandpa looked relieved, and she stood there another full minute, leaning on the rail in disbelief, turning away to watch a wall of fog creeping toward her from far out on the water, while her grandpa talked in detail about Howard's dissertation on postbellum New Orleans and where it fit in the scholarship that had come before and after.

Grandma poked her head outside, looking worried. "Everything okay out here? You fellows need some lemonade?"

"Doing just fine, Mrs. Sanderson," Noah said with a smile. Hailey turned to face him, folding her arms against the chill that had come into the air. He was wearing clothes that Hailey recognized—a fitted black T-shirt designed to show off his muscles, fitted chinos—but he really seemed to have become a different person. Even his posture was straighter, like a top-shelf graduate student of the past's would be. He sat with his feet planted firmly on the deck, his hands loosely fisted on the arms of the chair, an earnest, innocent look on his face. Hailey had never seen him sit this way in real life or wear this expression. He should be slouched back in the chair, his right ankle on his left knee, his chin leaned in his hand, grinning his sly little grin.

"Tom?" said Grandma. "Any chance you'd leave these young people to themselves?"

Grandpa looked at Hailey then, almost as if he hadn't noticed her before. "Oh, Howard," he said. "This must be your lovely wife I've heard so much about."

Hailey glanced at her grandma, saw the alarm on her face, and understood. She wanted to cry out. It took everything she had to keep from shouting, *Grandpa, it's me!*

She swallowed hard and spoke carefully. "It's a pleasure to meet you, Professor Sanderson. Howard has told me so much about you." Then she said, "Excuse me," and walked past her stricken grandma and inside.

Her grandma caught her by the wrist when she was on the third stair. "You can't tell your mother!" Greta said in a harsh stage whisper, because Lindy was right upstairs.

Hailey was crying. "*Mom* doesn't know?"

Greta looked abashed, sheepish—and so miserable that Hailey's anger collapsed, overcome by sympathy. She remembered Noah describing visits with his own grandma, who had since passed away, during which Noah would pretend to be his father so she wouldn't get upset. That must've been why he'd jumped right into character as Grandpa's old student—

Grandpa has dementia.

Greta clutched Hailey's hand. "It's been progressing very quickly," she whispered. "*Very* quickly." She looked into Hailey's eyes, as if asking for forgiveness. She took a deep breath and visibly swallowed. Hailey had never realized that you could physically feel someone else's heart breaking. And your own, too.

Greta continued quietly, speaking in a rush like the words were steam escaping. "Your grandpa and I agreed back in March, when we got the diagnosis, that we'd wait until after your wedding to tell everyone. We didn't want to interfere with your happiness. Or your mother's! And then it's just—it's just been getting so much worse, so quickly."

"Oh. Grandma." Hailey's heart cracked a little more. *She* had been the reason for the secret? For her *mom* not knowing about this?

Greta shot a nervous look up the stairs. "Let's just—I don't—"

Noah came walking inside then. "A little heads up would've been nice," he said.

Hailey felt herself go blank with the shock of his rudeness, as Greta bristled. "It isn't her fault. I didn't tell her. She didn't know."

Noah glanced toward Hailey, his face showing actual concern now.

Hailey's head pulsed with pain. Every other part of her had gone numb.

"I need to check on Tom," Greta said stiffly. "I'm afraid you've probably upset him." She headed toward the sliding glass doors and her husband outside. Hailey saw the fog was closer; that Innisfree would soon be encased in it.

Noah paced, seeming too big for the kitchen. He had moved quickly past the distress over Hailey's grandpa and onto his own grievances, and Hailey, who sat on one of the counter stools nearby, had gone from feeling numb to feeling steamrolled.

"Robin saw I was stressed," he was saying, "and I told her I hadn't heard from you and your dad was missing, and she made me take the night off to come up here and see what was going on with you. Now to find out your dad's fine, and you were down in Portland? And you didn't bother to let me know?"

Hailey straightened her shoulders. It was too much, really, this news about her grandpa, on top of everything else. And Noah had only come now because his boss had "made" him? "You haven't seemed all that interested in what's been going on with me."

Noah stopped pacing. "Don't pick a fight with me right now."

"I'm not picking a fight!" Hailey rubbed her temple, trying to ease its aching. She barely recognized him anymore. Was this the same man who'd charmed her by dramatically singing "Baby One More Time" under the lamp post outside her dorm on their second date, making her laugh so hard that she fell for him that instant? The same man who'd thoughtfully proposed on the second anniversary of their first date, sitting at the same table at Front & Main in Waterville where they'd had that first date? When had he become so . . . aggressive? Was it working in the restaurant business that had changed him? Or the drinking? Or was something else going on? Was *he* having doubts about their wedding? Were there things she didn't know about his childhood?

Well. Obviously. She'd met his parents only twice, once at graduation and once when he'd taken her to Virginia for a long weekend to stay at their beautiful brick colonial in Alexandria. Mr. Grayson had continually refilled his glass of Scotch and said he wished his son would become a lawyer like Hailey was planning to. Mrs. Grayson had talked plaintively about Noah's three sisters, who were scattered about the world, a yoga teacher, a travel blogger, an artist. "I suppose it's my fault that our kids are all so *creative*," she sighed, casting a sad look at a giant abstract canvas on the wall—a six-foot swath of shades and swirls of red was hatch marked with black lines—and admitting she was the one who'd painted it, "back in my idealistic phase." During dinner at the country club, everyone fawned over how fit and handsome Noah was now and seemed barely to notice Hailey. He had never invited Hailey home for Christmas, saying only that when his sisters were there, home was "a pinball machine." He considered his two older sisters "tyrants," his younger sister "spoiled rotten." Hailey was not required to make them bridesmaids in the wedding, and, as it turned out, the oldest had sent her regrets months ago.

With this, Hailey was reminded of the hundred and seventeen people who had RSVPed *yes,* selected the lobster or the chicken, bought things off the registries at Williams Sonoma and Crate & Barrel, made travel plans and hotel reservations. They would all be arriving in the area in just over a week, anticipating a perfect Maine weekend, Hailey in her gown, a lobster bake, a late night dancing underneath a big white tent drinking champagne.

What if everything were different, Hales?

"What is your problem?" Noah snapped. "You know I'm working my ass off for us, and you don't even appreciate my time and effort for coming up here to check on you. You say I'm not interested—"

"My dad was missing!"

"And I told you it was nothing to worry about. Turns out I was right, huh?"

"You had no way of knowing. Everyone else stepped in to help look for him."

Noah's eyes narrowed. "What do you mean, everyone else?"

She didn't want to let on about Jack, which seemed stupid, but there it was. "My—my aunt and uncle, cousins, friends, neighbors . . ."

"So, you didn't need me."

"You're supposed to be my *partner*."

Noah moved closer, towering over her. The look in his eyes was mean. "I told you, babe," he said. He reached as if to put his arms around her but instead rested his hands on the counter behind her on either side, enclosing her. Instinct made her shrink from him, even as her mind tried to tell her she shouldn't be afraid of her *fiancé*. "It is not the time to pick a fight with me."

Greta's voice broke in from the front of the cottage as she entered through the sliding glass door. "Young man. You do not threaten my granddaughter in my house!"

Noah gave a little uncomfortable laugh, but he didn't move away from Hailey.

"Grandma, it's okay," Hailey said, because she hated to see Greta looking so unhinged. Again, Hailey convinced herself she had nothing to fear. "He's not threatening me. Is Grandpa okay?"

Greta ignored her, homing in on Noah. "Young man, you move away from her right now."

"Ma'am, she's my fiancée," Noah said patiently, as if he thought Greta could be suffering from dementia, too. "All I'm doing is standing close to her."

"Move away from her," Greta repeated, but Noah didn't move. Hailey didn't know if her grandma was losing her mind or if Noah was.

"Why don't you just do what she says?" Hailey told him quietly. She couldn't move back from him because she was sitting on the stool, and with his arms surrounding her she couldn't get down. But all he would have to do was step back and Grandma would probably be fine. Hailey had never seen her act anything like this.

But Noah, too, ignored Hailey, speaking to Greta instead. "Ma'am, all due respect, you can't tell me how to be around my own fiancée. We're just talking."

Greta scowled, then abruptly headed for the stairs and marched up them.

Hailey let out a breath. Now Noah put his hands on her shoulders. He was acting casual, but the contact made her feel even more trapped. "Your whole family is fucking crazy," he said mildly.

"Maybe you should go."

"You think that's a good idea? To send me off before you've fixed this?"

"I haven't done anything wrong!"

"Neither have I. But it seems like we're having a problem, babe."

There was the sound of footsteps descending the stairs. Hailey looked to see her grandma, who rounded the corner to come toward them again.

"I told you, young man," Greta said. "Get away from her." She raised her arm. In her hand was an old-looking gun. She held it in both hands and pointed it at Noah.

"Grandma!" Hailey shrieked.

CHAPTER 30

Greta

Wednesday, July 28, 2010
5 p.m.

Still the young man was not taking her seriously, though she had a Colt .45 pointed generally in the direction of his head. He was laughing. A little nervously, maybe. Holding up his hands. He had taken one step back from Hailey. Only one. Greta was tempted to fire a round.

Oh, she wouldn't fire at his head. Maybe at the kitchen window. It would be so satisfying to watch the glass shatter and fall away.

But the gun hadn't been out of the attic cupboard in sixty years—she'd had it hidden behind a false panel—so she didn't know if it would function properly. She knew nothing about guns. She had only ever held one—this one—a couple times in her life, decades ago. Her brother Harrison had given it to her after the war, saying she could use it to protect herself. Only then had she realized that he must have known all along what had happened to her in the attic when she was twelve, the summer before the war, and somehow that felt like a bigger betrayal than the failure of her brothers to protect her. She wondered if Cary and Will had known, too, and if her parents had known, and if knowing was why Harrison had hardly spoken to her for the rest of his life;

why her parents had insisted on traveling with her on her concert tours until she was thirty years old; why her mother's dying wish had been that Greta promise to agree to marry Tom, who had been asking, so that Greta would not be left, as her mother put it, "without protection."

Now Greta held the gun in both hands, with her feet planted slightly apart the way she'd seen Benson and Rollins on *SVU* hold their guns.

"Grandma, put it down!" Hailey said.

"I want you out of my house," Greta told Noah. She craved the striking of a hammer, the sounding of a note. "I never want you in my house again."

Noah was still chuckling, his hands raised, but Greta was satisfied to see that he had broken a sweat and was backing away from Hailey. This was what Greta had wanted, but it was stunning to see that he had no impulse to protect Hailey. *Zero,* as the kids would say. "Fine, fine." It was the same tone in which he'd said, *A little heads up would've been nice.* She twitched to fire at him. Oh, not really, not really, she wouldn't!

"Grandma, please, put it down!" Hailey said again, but Greta continued to point the gun at Noah, following him with it as he moved toward the door. She felt she should've been using this thing all her life. It would have made her feel so powerful. It would have changed everything.

"Never come here again," Greta said to him.

Noah nodded. A glance at Hailey, as if accusing her. "No problem." He pushed his way out the screen door. A second later, through the kitchen window, Greta saw him running up the road, then he was gone.

Hailey was looking at Greta, aghast. Greta lowered the gun and said, "I suspect he won't bother you anymore."

Hailey covered her mouth and burst into hysterical laughter, even as her eyes filled with tears.

"Mother!" came Lindy's voice from the stairs.

"He was threatening her," Greta told Lindy, who stood at the foot of the stairs gaping. Lindy's eyes were red, as if she'd been crying, but Greta couldn't shift gears to ask why. "And it's not a far distance between taking a threatening posture and landing an actual blow, or an actual assault!"

Hailey had gotten her laughter under control and stood. "Grandma, he wouldn't have—"

Greta interrupted, insisting. "They all start off seeming wonderful, but most of them, unfortunately, are not. And I will not have that in my house!"

"Mother," Lindy said. "Put the gun down. Why would you *do* that to Noah?"

Greta moved toward the stairs. "I'll just go put it away. I don't think he'll come back."

"Where did you get that?" Lindy said. "You're not going to hurt yourself, are you?"

"Don't worry. I'm not David," Greta said, beginning to climb the stairs.

"Mother!"

"What does *that* mean?" Hailey said.

"I can't condone you marrying that young man, not anymore," Greta called to her.

"Oh, God, I'd better check on him," Hailey said, heading for the door.

"Mother, what is *wrong*?" Lindy said, as Hailey banged outside.

Greta kept climbing the stairs.

Greta gripped the rail as she ascended the steep steps to the attic, the .45 dangling from her other hand. Her heart felt clutched in a fist. Some summers, she managed not to go up here at all. She would send Lindy up to make the beds, or the grandkids up to grab this or that from storage. Nobody ever questioned it. They probably thought her too old to manage the stairs. They never seemed to remember that she attended Pilates twice a week, eight months out of the year, in New York City.

Greta heard Lindy calling after her, running up to the second floor, as if she'd taken a moment to see to Hailey, then decided to go after Greta instead.

Greta climbed faster. She still didn't like the attic, and she wanted to hold on to the gun—she enjoyed the heaviness of it in her hand—but she couldn't chance there being some accident, or Tom finding out about it. If he understood what she had done, he would be angry with her. He did not believe that violence or threats of violence were ever justified, not even in retaliation, not even for protection. He was a fan of Gandhi; he had traveled to Mississippi one summer with his students when Lindy was a baby. ("Don't you remember you're a *father*?" Greta had screamed at him, terrified, before he'd left.) He'd marched and sat in at a Woolworth's counter and been doused in ketchup and beaten by a police officer's truncheon, all without raising a hand in return, and he'd come home proud of his yellowing bruises. He would never approve of Greta having a gun, much less of her pointing it at anybody. He always thought there was a way to talk through to a solution, though Greta thought that, having been a student of history all his life, he ought to know better.

Of course, now, from this moment to the next, he might not remember that what she had done was something he would object to, or that it mattered to him what she did at all. He might not even remember who she was.

She swallowed hard, wishing suddenly that she had told him the secret of what had happened to her up here so that she might have the pleasure of knowing it was a thing that was now in the process of being forgotten.

She glanced over the room, the boys' unmade twin beds with their blue plaid sheets, the "updated" blinds Lindy had hung a few summers ago, replacing the old curtains with trains printed on them. It was a blessing, at least, that the attic looked nothing like it had in the days when it had been her room.

There was no reason it should have been her room. Since she came into existence, the bedroom at the back of the cottage, the one her granddaughters now shared, had been hers. But the summer she was ten, she'd gotten the idea that she needed a view of the ocean. Everyone else had one! (Greta and Tom's present room had originally belonged to Greta's parents, and Lindy's present room had belonged to Greta's brothers and contained two sets of bunkbeds, so they always had room for at least one friend.)

Greta's father had agreed. Greta's brothers liked to complain that Greta could ask their father for the moon and he would find a way to get it for her, but, in truth, they treated her the same way. She had been a "surprise," born eight years after the youngest of her brothers, Harrison, and the entire family had always been thrilled by her. Only her mother ever exhibited sternness, confessing later that she'd simply felt compelled to try to preserve Greta from becoming "one hundred percent spoiled rotten." (For one example: Greta's entire family considered her a "prodigy" on the piano, when in fact she was simply a capable student who had been started at age three, whose father didn't mind paying for three lessons per week.)

In any case, once Greta said the word, her father and brothers set about making over the attic's front half into a bedroom fit for a Connecticut princess. They added a wall to divide off the back section for storage. They put in a big picture window to give her a broader view. Her father, a stockbroker, had no idea what he was doing, but somehow managed to order his sons around with authority, and somehow none of them got killed in the process of putting that giant window in. Her mother ordered pink curtains, a pink-trimmed white bedspread, and a pink rug from the Sears, Roebuck catalog, and, four weeks after Greta's initial request, the family blindfolded her and led her up the steep steps for a grand unveiling.

It was perfect. Greta's original room was made over into a guest room, which her mother was extremely pleased to have. For the next two summers, Greta enjoyed closing the attic door behind her and climbing the stairs to her private lair. (Her brothers, having worked hard to create the space, were not allowed in it, a fact which they accepted with jovial ease.) She would retreat to the quiet with a book. She and her best friend Marjorie Tennyson, who would later become Marjorie Westfield, would hold elaborate tea parties, gossiping for hours over imaginary ladyfingers and Earl Grey.

Greta would've liked to have had her piano moved up there so she could practice without fear of interruption, but her parents had to draw the line somewhere. Will, who was the most scientific of her brothers, explained that the refusal was, more than anything, about the laws of physics, which even their father could not change, not even on Greta's behalf.

Heading for the back storage area now, Greta heard Lindy in pursuit. The gun felt very heavy in her hand. *You're not going to hurt yourself, are you?*

Such a thing would never have occurred to Greta.

Would it?

She didn't want Lindy to know where the gun was kept, so she hurried through the door that she'd left ajar in her haste to get back downstairs with the gun. It surprised her now that she had done such a thing, but, again, so many things had been surprising lately that she had almost lost the ability to become alarmed.

In the storage area were old tables, lamps, ancient suitcases, sets of dishes, a bureau that had belonged to her brothers when they were young. A trunk full of her mother's table linens, out of vogue for decades now. There had been an elegance to Innisfree when Greta's mother was alive—but of course one had to modernize. And Lindy's love of yard sales and decorating meant frequent "updates," so the detritus of the '70s and '80s was up here, too: the fondue pot, the plastic end tables, the VCR, the martini glasses, the floral armchairs.

They would have to have their own yard sale, Greta realized, before Innisfree was sold.

The big old wardrobe that stood at the back of the storage room had belonged to her father, and Greta had left its door ajar, too, when she had taken out the gun.

Quickly now, she fumbled past where her brother Harrison's old Army uniform and overcoat hung and pressed open the secret panel at the back. Carefully, she set the gun inside, not wanting to think any more about what Harrison might've known about what had happened to her in this attic nearly seventy summers ago, or whether such knowledge had been what had spurred him to give her the Colt. *Things that happen in the summer don't matter at all,* she had always told Lindy, mostly in an effort to convince herself.

Already missing the weight of the gun in her hand, and missing the person that holding it had made her into, she closed the secret panel, swung the wardrobe door shut and latched it, then hurried out into the boys' room, slamming the door behind her.

"Mother! Seriously, what are you doing?" Lindy, who had just arrived at the top of the stairs, jutted fists to hips.

"I put it away." Greta was having a hard time breathing, suddenly. "Let me by so I can go downstairs." Out the big window behind Lindy, only the treetops were visible, then a wall of fog, curtaining off the ocean.

"Mom, you pointed it at Noah!"

Greta pressed a palm to her throat. "I told you. He was threatening Hailey. I told him he needed to stop, and he didn't listen. So I came up here and got the gun. It's always been up here."

"What? Always? Up *here*? In the boys' room?"

Hailey came running up the stairs, wiping fresh tears from her face. Was she angry or just upset? Greta couldn't tell. Anyway, Hailey would thank Greta later. Greta had had no choice.

But now she needed to get downstairs. She would find Tom; she would sit beside him for a while. They would both feel better, then—at least, if he remembered her just now.

CHAPTER 31

Lindy

Wednesday, July 28, 2010
5:15 p.m.

"Are you okay?" Lindy asked Hailey quickly. Greta was moving toward the steps, though Hailey was blocking them. "Is Noah?"

"I couldn't catch him in time."

"He left?" *Oh God,* Lindy thought, *there's not going to be a wedding, is there?*

But Hailey's eyes had fixed on Greta. "Grandma, I'm worried about you. You need help! You need to tell Mom."

"Let me by," Greta said.

"Tell me what?" Lindy didn't know why Hailey would be confronting her mother with anything other than having pulled a gun on Noah. Lindy could hardly comprehend it, much less that Greta had "always" kept a gun up here where Lindy's sons slept.

Hailey folded her arms. "Grandma. Tell Mom about Grandpa."

"What do you mean?" Lindy shot a nervous glance toward her mother, who was still clutching her throat, pale.

"I don't like being up here," Greta said.

"Grandma," Hailey said. "You can't keep all this to yourself anymore."

In Lindy's mind, the idea that something might be the matter with her father simply did not compute, but her mother was clearly getting more agitated, her eyes darting toward the stairs. "All right, let's go downstairs," Lindy said. "Hailey, Grandma can tell me whatever it is down there. Okay?" Still not believing there could be anything to tell, she looked to her mother, who swallowed—*oh, God, there* was *something*—but nodded slightly in agreement.

Hailey gave a nod in return, its sternness a contrast to the concern in her eyes, then wheeled to hustle down the stairs. Lindy gestured for her mother to go ahead, then followed, feeling anxious, protective, confused, as Greta carefully descended, clutching the rail.

"We found out in March," Lindy's mother said, eyes watering, as she stood across from where Lindy sat at the kitchen counter. Hailey stood nearby, arms folded, feet planted, as if in an effort to keep herself still. "We . . . we decided we would wait to tell you, because we didn't want to ruin your summer plans. I know it sounds . . . foolish now."

Lindy's throat was swelling; she blinked back tears. She would not have imagined that any news could shock her, given everything.

And yet.

The distress on Hailey's face confirmed what Greta was saying. "Grandpa mistook Noah for one of his old students just now," she said quietly. "That's how I found out."

"Oh," Lindy said finally. "God." She glanced out toward the deck, where her father was sitting calmly in one of the Adirondack chairs, watching the fog creep closer.

Her father had been diagnosed with dementia.

Her father was "deteriorating rapidly."

Her father, the night before last, had failed to recognize her mother.

"This is why you wanted to cancel the party," Lindy said absently, though it immediately seemed like a stupid thing to say, and she thought of all the times, these last couple weeks, when she'd tried to talk to her dad and he hadn't answered or had seemed distracted. (She'd thought he was working on a book! Was that just a lie her mother had told?) She thought how miffed she'd been with him for not being more helpful about David. How blind and clueless and self-involved she'd been! Not to notice! That maybe he didn't even *know* her?

"I'm sorry," Greta said. "We thought we had time. Your father and I thought we would have a lot more time. We thought he'd be fine for the party . . ."

"You should've told me!" Lindy hated how she felt like, sounded like, a child, and she tried to straighten. "We need to make a plan. It doesn't matter about the party. I'll call everybody and cancel." Everything, everything, was falling apart. She heard David: *Sometimes you just push too hard, Lin.* But she couldn't stop. She started asking her mother questions. When did the symptoms start? *Last fall.* What doctors had they seen? *Five top specialists in New York.* What exactly was the prognosis? *Unpredictable decline.* And it had been rapid so far.

(And the book? "He believes he is working on one!" Greta said, in an odd, optimistic tone. "It keeps him calm.")

Lindy took a deep breath. Somehow, she was fuming at David: How dare he leave her to deal with this all on her own while he went off to start a new family with that little girl, Tiffany? Her parents had always been nice to him! At least, her father had! "Okay, we need to plan for the future," she announced. "Dad needs to get the very best care, twenty-four seven."

"Lindy, honey." Greta appeared about to say something more, then took a step back. She went to fill the tea kettle. She seemed to want to change the subject. As if any other subject existed. "You have enough on your mind right now. Even if we do cancel the party. There's still the wedding . . ." At that, she looked slightly guilty.

Hailey gave a little, unamused laugh.

"Mom," Lindy said sternly, "stop it with the tea. Let's set the question of the wedding aside for a moment. I'm sorry, Hailey." Hailey nodded once, twisting her ring around her finger, and Lindy turned back to Greta. "We need to talk about how we're going to take care of Dad."

Greta shut off the water, placed the kettle gently back on the stove, and turned to face Lindy. "*I'm* going to take care of your father."

Lindy quickly shook her head. "You're not going to be able to do it all on your own, Mom. You have to let us help you. We'll figure it out. You can move in with us! We've got plenty of room. We can travel to see his New York doctors. It's not too far!"

Greta stood blinking for a moment, while Lindy's gut swirled. "Your father loves you so much," Greta said. "All we've ever wanted was to protect you. It's all we still want now."

The sense that more terrible news was imminent sank through Lindy's skin. "Mom?"

Greta took a deep breath. "That's why what I've decided—what we've decided—is this."

Lindy heard her mother's words but couldn't make sense of them, not at first.

Florida?

A "memory-care" facility?

Sell Innisfree?

"Grandma, you can't *sell Innisfree*," Hailey said, aghast.

Right now, to Lindy, that seemed like the least of it. Her heart hurt like it'd had an electric shock. "Mom, you can't. Take him to Florida? I'll never—I'll never get to see him—I won't be able to help—"

"Believe me," Greta said, "I wish there was some other way."

"But we haven't even talked about this. You didn't even *tell* me."

"Grandma, there's *got* to be some other way," Hailey said, and Lindy hated to see her daughter standing there like she'd just been physically slapped, but she was feeling the same way.

"I understand you're upset," Greta said. "But please believe me when I tell you—"

Lindy couldn't withstand one more revelation, not right now. She got up and stumbled outside to where her father sat in the cooling evening. The fog, which had almost reached the deck of Innisfree now, and the rolling sound of the invisible ocean, all seemed part of some dream she wished she could wake up from.

She knelt beside the arm of the Adirondack chair, and when her dad looked down to meet her eyes, she could tell that, right now, he knew her. Thank God, today, right now, he knew her.

"Dad?" she said, and when he acknowledged her with a tiny smile, she threw her arms around his neck. He smelled of the same aftershave he'd always worn. Her mother had said that she had to shave him sometimes now and it wasn't easy to do. Lindy felt waves of sorrow overtaking her as she pressed her face to his crisp shirt, and she wished she could cry, that he would comfort her the way he always used to. But she understood now that they were past that, things were different now, so she stayed quiet, hoping he understood, too, that she would be the one taking care of him from now on, and she was sorry she was late getting about it.

"I guess your mother told you," he said, his voice rumbling through her as he gently patted her back. "I wish she hadn't. I wish she'd given you at least one more day."

CHAPTER 32

Greta

Wednesday, July 28, 2010
6 p.m.

"Grandma, I'm sorry," Hailey said. "This must be just terrible for you."

"Thank you, honey." Greta, watching through the window as Lindy knelt beside Tom in his Adirondack chair in front of the fog, felt as if a bandage had just been ripped off, exposing a gaping wound to light and air.

"I just wish there was some way you didn't have to sell Innisfree? I mean, what if you moved in with Mom and Dad, like Mom said?"

Greta blinked. Turned to Hailey. "I . . . I don't think so."

Hailey frowned, shook her head a little. "I have to try to call Noah." She turned and hurried to run upstairs.

Greta didn't know why Hailey would go upstairs if what she wanted was to make a phone call. She wanted to shout after her that she, Greta, had done her a favor regarding that young man.

But she supposed what she'd done instead was ensure that the entire family would think she was losing her grip and couldn't be trusted. Not with herself and her own decisions, not with the fate of Innisfree, and not with moving to Florida, let alone with caring for Tom.

Never mind that she'd been the one holding everything together all these years.

You're not going to be able to do it on your own.

Greta needed to sit down, but she just stood there, feeling like a fool, looking out to where Lindy still crouched beside the arm of her father's chair.

Greta wanted so badly for Lindy to understand.

But how could she have said all that she needed to say? How could she make her reasons understood?

I can't let this ruin your life.

I wanted so badly for everything you wanted this summer to go well.

I need to let go of the past.

I've tried and tried to keep you safe, and I'm afraid I've failed, as all parents are bound to fail—but I won't stop trying.

This is the only thing I know to do, even if I'm wrong.

Lindy never would understand, would she? About Florida and Sunset Acres. About selling Innisfree. (Greta would never, ever tell Lindy the whole truth about what had happened in the attic here. She would protect Lindy from that, at least!)

And now, Lindy wanted Greta and Tom to move in with her and David in Rhode Island. Just the scenario that Greta, in making the plans to go to Florida, had been hoping to avoid.

Greta could already hear the arguments Lindy would continue to make: *We have extra bedrooms now that the kids are gone! Or we'll make over David's office, if you don't want to do stairs! I'll handle Dad's medications, his appointments; I'll handle everything. You can just relax. I'm good at caring for people; it's what I've been doing for twenty-five years!*

But this would be a nightmare. Wouldn't it? Trapped in suburbia with her well-meaning daughter and overwhelmed, polite son-in-law, who would not want Greta and Tom there but would never say so, plus a series of intermittent, energetic, nearly grown grandchildren.

And it *would* ruin Lindy's life, having a front-row seat to her father's decline.

And Greta, God forgive her, had been picturing long solo walks on the beach in sunny Florida. Quiet when she wanted it; music, again, when she was ready. Either way, it would be a setting free from her own old memories, from who she'd always been. Even from the duties and responsibilities of being "Mom" or "Grandma." She would be simply "wife"—and this would be a more-than-full-time job from now on. (Not that she wanted to change places with Tom, not really, but sometimes she did think, *Why not me?* Why couldn't he be the one left to take care of everything? To remember for both of them? To continue performing the old roles, "Dad" and "Grandpa," which he had always relished more than she had relished her own.)

God forgive her, she simply wanted to put her entire focus on caring for Tom. And she wanted Tom, no matter what it took, to be fully *at ease* in the final chapter of his life.

If Greta let Lindy be part of caring for him, she would get none of that. And she would be failing her husband and her daughter—and herself—in too many ways to count. Even if Lindy believed the opposite, Greta knew this was true.

Hailey came running back downstairs, cell phone in hand. She went to the rotary phone and picked up the handset, pressed it between her ear and shoulder. She read off the screen of her cell phone as she dialed the rotary, and the clicking sound filled the room.

In Greta's day, people had known the numbers of the important people in their lives by heart.

Hailey stopped dialing and listened. After a moment, she announced, "He's not answering."

Good, Greta wanted to say, and it wasn't that she had meant to ruin her granddaughter's wedding. God knew she'd tried everything she could these last few months to avoid that very thing.

But here was the same old lesson that it seemed to be Greta's fate to learn over and over again: In a moment, even things that had once seemed perfect could be ruined completely.

She wondered if Innisfree *had* defeated her now, in the end. Despite all her efforts to the contrary.

CHAPTER 33

Hailey

Wednesday, July 28, 2010
7 p.m.

Jack! Jack!" Hailey shouted, tossing mulch at his window again, breathless in the damp and the fog, as the silvery cove lapped the seaweed-lined rocks nearby.

He came to the window. "Dude! Hales! What's wrong?"

"Come on! We need to go to town."

"Seriously?"

"Yes!"

He nodded and disappeared. The light went out, and a moment later he came out the back door, wearing his typical shorts, flip-flops, and T-shirt, plus a quizzical smile. "What's up?" He nodded toward the road. "You've got your car pointed in the wrong direction."

She let out a little, inappropriate laugh—she was full of those today—looking over her shoulder at it. Yes, she had driven her Protegé the wrong way down Summerland Cove Point Road to get to Seabreeze quicker, after her mom had come inside and started arguing with her grandma again, and now Hailey didn't care about the wrong-way thing, because at least she was pointing toward the exit. "Come on!" she told him, running for the car.

~

"Jesus," Jack said. She'd told him all of it as she drove faster and faster along the narrow highway through the forest, the fog encasing everything. Her grandpa had dementia, they had to sell Innisfree, Noah had been there and been a jerk and her grandma had pulled a gun on him, and he had gone and now Hailey didn't know if he would still want to marry her, and she'd tried calling him from the Innisfree landline but he hadn't answered. Then her mom and grandma had started fighting again, and she didn't know when her dad would be back, and her siblings had all gone to Rhode Island for reasons she didn't understand. So, Hailey needed cell signal to see if they'd called or texted, or if her dad had, or if Noah had, if he was furious with her or if he would possibly apologize for . . . well, for what? For not standing between her and the gun that had been pointed at them? For running away instead? And she guessed she hadn't really needed Jack to come along to town—except, for moral support, she *had*.

Her car was a manual, and every time she went to shift, her hand was shaking worse, and the peaceful farmhouses they passed seemed like jokes to her. Places where happy, normal families lived, where they put out coolers full of cartons of eggs from their chickens with a sign that said *$4* and trusted anyone who came along would leave the exact right change. Places where they were hammering on new shingles, tending to the lilies in the garden, letting the goats roam free. Her head was hurting like it was clamped in a vise.

"You need to take a break," Jack said briskly, in a tone like an army officer. "Pull over right here." He pointed to the side of the road up ahead where there was a small cemetery encircled by an iron fence filled with rows of crumbling gravestones. Hailey spotted a small driveway beside it and braked, managing to slow down in time to pull in and stop the car. She rubbed her head. "Let's take a walk," Jack said, opening the door and getting out.

"Jack, the ticks in here are going to be insane," Hailey called after him, but he was already making his way through the long grass toward the cemetery gate, so she turned off the car and got out and followed him. Whatever. Getting a tick bite would just be the icing on the cake, with everything else that was going on. Her headache was making her feel like she was going to throw up again, but that seemed almost normal by now.

Jack had stopped inside the gate and was looking at a gravestone. When she came up beside him, he said, "Here. Abigail Spoonhorn, beloved wife of Jacob. Born March 2, 1805. Died May 7, 1828. And next to her here is her baby. Harriet Spoonhorn. Born May 7, 1828, died three days later."

"Oh, God," Hailey said, rubbing her temple absently again. She didn't know what he was up to, but she couldn't help feeling drawn in. "That's terrible. She died giving birth, and then the baby died, too. I wonder what happened to her husband."

Jack shrugged, stepped over to the next grave, and read off the tall monument. "George Carpenter, born 1794, died 1850. His wife Mary Carpenter. Born 1799, died 1876."

Hailey found herself imagining the lives these people might've lived. She reached to brush her fingers over the letters of Mary Carpenter's name. "Is this supposed to be making me feel better?" she said, though in fact her headache had eased a bit, and the dampness of the air felt soothing on her skin.

Jack was already at the next grave. "And here. Annabelle Winthrop. Born 1847, died 1865. She was only eighteen."

An angel was carved into the top of the stone. "I wonder if she died in the Civil War," Hailey said. "I mean, like, maybe she starved to death on account of it or something."

"Did people starve to death around here?"

"I don't know."

Jack stood looking at her, and somehow just his presence was making her feel better. In the fog and the lowering dusk, his hair and eyes seemed darker, like they were catching shadows rather than light. "Close your eyes," he said, and when she cocked her head, questioning, he added, "Just trust me for a second."

She looked at him another moment, liking the angles of his face, then closed her eyes.

"Take a deep breath."

She inhaled. The damp air was thick with the scent of pine and pollen.

"Listen."

She heard leaves rustling in the slight breeze high above. A bird sounded a single note.

She felt him move closer. "I guess my point is the world's a really big place," he said. "And your life is going to be long. This is just one moment of it. A really shitty moment! But just a moment. I promise. Nothing lasts forever."

She opened her eyes, and he was close to her, looking at her softly.

What if everything were different, Hales?

She took a step back, her head pinging with pain again. *Stop,* she told herself. She thought she felt a tick crawling on her ankle, and she reached to brush it off, wrenching herself back to reality. "We need to go to town," she said. She needed to talk to Emma. Their dad *would* be back soon, and Emma and Eli and Cody needed to be here when he arrived.

Also, Hailey badly needed to talk to Noah. Patch things up, whatever it took. Because, when her dad got back, no way was Hailey going to tell him and her mom—in the middle of this unimaginable news about her grandpa, about Innisfree—that everything they'd done for her, everything they'd paid for, had been for nothing.

Jack nodded, looking into her eyes. "Lead the way," he said.

She let Jack drive her car so she could close her eyes. By the time he parked in the lot downtown, behind a row of old two- and three-story brick buildings and beside a wide spot in the tidal river, darkness had nearly fallen. The fog hadn't reached this far inland, and the sun was an orange ball sinking for the horizon in a darkening sky.

There were no missed calls from Noah, no texts. Jack, saying he'd give her some privacy, got out of the car and set out walking toward the town landing and dinghy dock at the other end of the parking lot. Hailey watched his silhouette for a moment, then caught herself and, from the passenger seat, clicked to dial Noah. She listened to the ringing in her ear. His voicemail picked up. The mechanical voice: "The number you have reached is *not* available." She said nothing, ended the call. He'd be back at the restaurant by now. She should really drive to Portland, be there to talk to him when he got off work, but she felt too sick to drive, and she obviously couldn't show up with Jack in tow.

Should she send a text? What would she even say? *Sorry my grandma threatened to shoot you, still wanna get married?*

Hailey rubbed her temple and dialed Emma, who answered and put Hailey on speaker with Eli, too. Hailey swallowed hard to think how they'd feel when they learned about Grandpa, about Innisfree. She'd always imagined she would spend summers at The Cove for the rest of her life. With her parents as they grew older, with the family she'd imagined she'd someday have, and with her brothers' and sister's families, too—just like Dad and Kate and Josh had done at the yellow cottage. Now none of that was going to happen, and that she was the only one of her siblings who knew it made her feel hollow and alone.

"I couldn't believe you guys just, like, left," she said. "You need to come back. Cody, too. Get him to drive you tonight, even if he has to drive back down to go to work tomorrow. Dad'll be back soon, and . . . and there's some other stuff going on, too." She wasn't going to tell them about Grandpa and Innisfree over the phone.

"We have some things we need to take care of here," Emma said.

A fresh knife of pain stabbed Hailey's head. She tried to get it out of them what they were doing, but they wouldn't say. "By tomorrow, you guys better be back up here," she ordered finally, in her best big-sister tone, though she knew the odds of them obeying her were slim. She said goodbye and ended the call, then she fumbled to open the car door, got out and ran the short distance over to the grass by the river, and threw up.

~

"I'm taking you home," Jack said a few minutes later, pacing near where she lay on a park bench beside the river, her knees drawn up, rubbing her head, wishing she could get rid of the horrendous taste in her mouth. Unfortunately, the noise of her getting out of the car and throwing up had drawn Jack's attention. At least he couldn't have truly *seen* the horror show, she told herself, since it was dusk and he'd been on the other side of the parking lot. He'd run to her, but by the time he got there, she'd been crawling to this bench, climbing up and stretching out. Normally, after she threw up, the pain would ease. Not this time. Of all her recent headaches, this was the worst by far, and she hated that Jack was seeing her like this. "You need to be in bed," he said.

Hailey kept rubbing her head. "I can't ride in the car," she managed to say. Even getting up off this bench was more than she could think of right now.

She sensed Jack's pacing stop. "Is this, like, a brain tumor? Do I need to take you to the ER?"

She almost would've giggled if things weren't all so dire, if she wasn't in so much pain. She'd never seen Jack wrought up like this. "No," she croaked. "I just get headaches."

"Are you sure? This does not seem right."

"Yeah," she said. "They're tension headaches. Sometimes escalating to migraines. Not a brain tumor."

More pacing. "Do you have anything in your car that you could take?"

"No." She usually kept emergency prescription pills in her glove box and purse, but she'd used the last out of the glove box and forgotten to replace them, and she hadn't brought her purse. "Actually. Grab me a mint? Out of the glove box?"

"Yeah, sure." She heard him leave, and she lay there rubbing her head. The pressure of the hard surface under her back and against the back of her head was helping ease the pain a little. When she heard him come near again, she opened her eyes, sat up partway, took the two mints he held in the palm of his hand, and popped them into her mouth.

"Thanks," she said.

He still looked worried. "Do you want me to go get you something? Migraine medication or whatever? The Rite Aid might still be open."

She lay back down. She didn't want him to leave her here alone. "No. Anyway, none of that stuff works. My prescription stuff is back at Innisfree." Even saying the name made tears pool in her eyes. She blinked and went on. "I just have to feel good enough to get in the car."

She felt Jack kneel beside her, felt the warm, gentle touch of two fingers against the side of her neck.

"I am still alive," she said.

"I'm checking your pulse. Like to see if it's too fast. Be quiet."

She waited, still rubbing her head. She had the odd thought that his nearness was going to make her heart rate speed up, and then he would think she was dying or something. What would happen then? Would he insist on taking her to the ER? She couldn't afford it; she would have to refuse. He'd probably offer to pay with his Silicon Valley money, and she'd have to refuse that, too. It would be a whole disaster. "What's the verdict, Dr. Westfield?"

"I think it's okay. Maybe some oysters on the half shell would help," he joked. "Wanna go to King Eider's?"

Hailey groaned as her stomach flipped. Some of the best oysters in the world came from this very river, and she usually loved them, especially in the cozy basement bar at King Eider's Pub, which was a two-minute walk away, through the parking lot and across Main Street. She wished she felt up to it. She wished a lot of things were different than they were right now. "Normally, yes," she said. "But. No."

Jack took pity on her. "Would it help if I rubbed your head for you?"

"That would be amazing." She rested her hands at her sides and waited. His fingers came lightly onto her forehead, tracing gentle circles. "No," she said, "you have to press really hard."

He scooted closer. The pressure increased. "Better?"

She sighed. "Yes."

"I can't think of a single thing that could be stressing you out," he said lightly.

She laughed, then moaned. "Stop making me laugh." With the pain in her head slightly eased, now the pain in her neck was overwhelming. She opened her eyes. The sky was black now, scattered with stars. Though lights illuminated the opposite half of the parking lot, this side, near the river, was fairly dark, which was a relief to her eyes. "Do you think you could rub my neck? The pain starts there."

"Yeah, sure. You want to sit up?"

With effort, she sat up on the bench, hugging her knees. He sat behind her back, facing the river, but as he tried to twist sideways to rub her neck, he realized he had no angle. "Okay if I sit behind you?"

She knew she shouldn't be that close to him, but the pain was terrible. "Yes."

He stood up and sat back down, this time straddling the bench behind her. Though he kept a few inches between them, she could feel the warmth of him surrounding her. She yearned to lean back into him; she kept herself upright. He gently moved her hair aside and began massaging her neck. The pressure of his fingertips made her want to moan, but she managed to confine herself to the occasional small gasp when he hit a nerve.

"You know," he said. "This is your body's way of telling you that something's wrong."

"You think?"

He laughed a little, moved closer, and pressed harder at the base of her neck, making her gasp again.

After a moment, he asked, "Did you get a hold of your fiancé?"

"No."

A pause. More pressure from his fingers. Another gasp. Jack spoke softly near her ear. "Maybe if you talked to me some more about what all is bothering you, it would help."

"Just this is helping," she said. She didn't want to think about Noah, or any of the rest of it. "Anyway, you know all about me, and I know nothing about you. Let's play the 'what if' game. It'll distract me. I get to start."

"Okay." He sounded amused as he massaged the top of her shoulders, making her gasp again.

She caught her breath. "Okay. What if your dad insists that your grandma has to sell Seabreeze?"

Jack's brief laugh had sorrow in it. "If my dad insists my grandma has to sell Seabreeze, I will buy it."

"Oh!" Her surprise quickly morphed to sadness, too. "I wish I could afford to buy Innisfree. I'm sure Emma and Eli and Cody don't have any money, either. Ow!"

"Sorry," he said, moving the pressure of his fingers to a different point on her shoulder.

"It's okay. It feels good." She sighed, leaning into his hands, forgetting for a second that she shouldn't. "Okay, so what if you lived in Maine all the time?"

He moved a little closer. "If I lived in Maine all the time, I'd have to travel to go surfing."

She laughed.

"I would miss my friends in California. I'd have to buy some winter boots. I would not be able to work for Google."

She was starting to feel better. "That's definitely true." She had an odd thought that she knew she shouldn't say, but she said it, anyway. "What about your girlfriend? Would you miss her? Would she move here to be with you?"

A pause. "I don't have a girlfriend right now."

"Oh." Whoops.

Jack patted her shoulder and stood up, and she wished she'd listened to the sensible part of her that had told her not to ask that question, because she didn't want the massage to have stopped. "All right, Hales," he said. "We'd better get you home. I don't think there's anything more you can do tonight about your fiancé, and you need your medication."

"Yeah," she said. "True." But the pain in her head was worse again already at the thought of leaving this peaceful riverbank and reentering the mess that was her life right now.

But when Jack held out his hand, she took it and let him pull her up, because of course she had to deal with things. Still, she wished she could go back in time about four minutes, experience that massage again, that moment away from her worries.

Jack let go of her hand and headed for the car.

"Jack, wait," she blurted. "I have one more question." He turned to her, a mild smile on his face.

And, yes, she knew again that it was reckless to ask what she wanted to ask now. She was just so tired of trying to do the right thing and be perfect all the time. And yes, life was long, the way Jack had pointed out in the cemetery, but somehow the news about her grandpa also made it clear that it could be far too short.

Also, she might have a brain tumor! Probably not, but it was possible!

"What if I wasn't engaged?" she said.

Jack's quick, reflexive smile was just visible in the dim light. "Hales." He drew out the sound of her name, admonishing her. "That one's not fair. Anyway, that's, like, a question for you, not for me."

She had to sigh at herself. Honestly. After everything that had happened today, she wanted to stir the pot a little more?

Yet, his response was somehow encouraging, and she went on. "No, it's a question for you, and I'm sorry, but you have to answer. That's the rule." It had been established years ago. No passes.

He laughed, then. "Dude. Seriously. You really have to ask?"

She wanted to laugh, too, hearing that, and her heart felt lighter, but she pretended to scold him. "That's not an answer."

He sighed and swung his hands together twice, his fist hitting inside the other hand. "Okay. Right. So. Here's my answer. If you weren't engaged, you could do anything you wanted to. And so could I." He stood still and let the words hang for a second between them, then said, "Now, come on. Let's get you home." He headed for the car, as Hailey stood watching him, trying to decipher what he'd said.

She decided: Okay, he'd just meant sex, right? Yes. Right.

Okay. She needed to get a grip. Focus on patching things up with her actual fiancé. The way Noah'd acted today had been an aberration, right? Probably brought on by stress.

Right. And, again, she could not disappoint her mom and dad about the wedding, especially not with everything else that was going on.

She hurried to follow Jack, trying not to wish again that she could go back in time, trying not to remember how consoled, how right, she'd felt when he was touching her.

CHAPTER 34

Lindy

Thursday, July 29, 2010
9 a.m.

Lindy spent the morning in the living room at Innisfree making calls, phoning everyone from outside The Cove who'd been invited to the anniversary party to tell them the party was off. People were disappointed, of course; concerned. She kept the calls short, the information to a minimum: "My father's not well, unfortunately."

She and her mother had argued for half an hour last night about the party alone, Lindy saying it was too late to cancel the food, the house cleaners, maybe they should try to go ahead? Maybe Tom could just say hello to everyone for ten minutes? Greta and Tom could stand still and smile and be toasted with champagne? It would be terrible, Lindy said, not to celebrate the anniversary at all, and so many people were planning to come.

But when her mother prevailed, Lindy found she was relieved. It was impossible to think of putting on a smile for a hundred people, given everything. She called Dorothy Severson, head of the SCPA committee this year, explained the situation, and asked, "Can we use the clubhouse Saturday night? I'd like to donate the food and invite everybody for a community party." Dorothy easily agreed and said she'd spread the word. Lindy called the caterer about the change in plans, saying the clubhouse door was always unlocked so they could just go in, and the caterer said no problem, they'd take care of everything. Lindy and her parents didn't even need to be there; they could just mail a check for the final fifty percent next week. "I'm so sorry about your dad," said the caterer, and Lindy thanked her, swallowing back the tears that welled.

After hanging up, Lindy walked over to the clubhouse through the pretty morning and posted a sign on the bulletin board out front saying that Tom and Greta Sanderson's anniversary party was now a community celebration at the clubhouse. *EVERYONE WELCOME! FABULOUS FOOD! BYOB!* There was no point stating a reason. Hailey had admitted last night that she'd told Jack about her grandpa's diagnosis, and Jack surely would've told his grandma, Marjorie, when he went home. Between that and Lindy's conversation with Dorothy this morning, all of Summerland Cove would know by noon—about the party, Tom's diagnosis, everything.

Honestly, Lindy realized as she walked along the sparkling blue cove back toward the yellow cottage and Innisfree, it was little wonder Greta had wanted to keep the news to herself for as long as possible. To try to contain the shock. For Lindy, having to process it at the same time as the rest of the neighborhood felt scathing, like her skin had been scrubbed raw.

As she passed the yellow cottage, Kate came running out. "Hey, what's this I hear about your dad?" Dorothy Severson had evidently called and told Kate everything, and now Kate hugged Lindy, wanting to know what she could do to help. For a second, Lindy wondered how Kate could seem so carefree. Then she remembered that Kate had believed Lindy's massive lie that David was on his own camping up north.

"Hey, I thought you would've gone back to the farm," Lindy said.

"Oh, no," Kate said firmly. "I drove up this morning and grabbed three littles and hustled back here. We're waiting for their Uncle David." Kate let out a small laugh. "And you can bet I'm going to give him a piece of my mind when he deigns to get here." Then she frowned and squinted, shielding her eyes from the sun. "Worrying about him shortened my mother's life, and it's shortening mine right now, too."

"Oh!" Lindy said, surprised Kate would come right out and say that.

"Do you really think he's okay? I mean, it's been a long time since he went off by himself, and the other times were usually—"

Lindy cut her off. "I remember." She couldn't stand to think about the old days, when Kate had been drinking so much, when David's mother had tried so hard, so constantly, to keep everything together. Nor could she stand to think about him off with Tiffany.

Even worse was to think—what if he wasn't off with Tiffany?

She wished she could confide in her old friend. But it was clear that Kate was unstable enough when it came to David. Joining Lindy in the land of betrayal and not-knowing-for-sure would likely unhinge her, send her down that slippery slope she'd traveled before with alcohol—and now she had her kids here to look after. Lindy squeezed Kate's elbow. "Listen, I've got to go, Kate." Now that Lindy had taken care of canceling the anniversary party, she was planning to head to Portland to talk with Noah and try to save her daughter's wedding. She simply could not let David ruin every last thing. "I'm sorry. Just . . . just don't worry, okay?"

Kate, still squinting under the shield of her hand, nodded, and Lindy hurried away, back toward Innisfree.

"Mom, I'm going to work it out with Noah," Hailey said, sitting at the kitchen counter in a pink tank and striped pajama bottoms. She'd refused Greta's offer of coffee and wanted only a spoonful of vanilla gelato to take her prescription pill with, which meant her headache was terrible. "You don't need to go talk with him."

Lindy, hating to see Hailey suffering, tried to keep her tone gentle. "Have you talked with him since what happened yesterday?"

Hailey rubbed her temple. "No."

"He didn't call you back?"

More rubbing; no meeting of the eyes. "I didn't leave a message. I didn't know what to say."

Lindy sighed. She hated to think of leaving her parents even for the afternoon, but she had to hope that an apology from her could help smooth the road for Hailey and Noah to reconcile. She also hoped to keep him from reporting Greta's actions to the police. "Okay, well, I'm going to drive down there and see him before he goes to work." She shot a look toward Greta, who was washing coffee cups at the sink. "Apologize on behalf of my mother."

Greta turned, eyes sparking. "That young man was threatening your daughter. He shows signs of becoming abusive, if he isn't already. He does not deserve an apology."

"Mother, that's ridiculous. And you need to tell me where you hid that gun."

"No."

Lindy decided to pick her battles for now. She turned to Hailey. "Honey, what really happened yesterday? Was Noah threatening you?"

"Excuse me," Hailey said, averting her gaze. "I need to get back to bed." She slid down from her stool and headed for the stairs.

"I hope you feel better, honey," Lindy called after her. "Need anything?"

"No, thanks, Mom."

Lindy, fretting, watched her daughter disappear up the stairs. Would Hailey even tell her if something was amiss with Noah? Probably not, because Hailey would no doubt believe that Lindy would be very disappointed if the wedding didn't go forward.

Had Lindy gotten so caught up in the planning—and so excited to think of Hailey settled and secure—that she'd failed to see other factors clearly? (Yes, Hailey had been getting stress-related migraines for a while, and cold feet were natural—but was throwing up right after you'd seen yourself in your wedding gown, and again later that same day?)

"Mom," she said to Greta. "You really believe he *threatened* her?" Lindy hated to think that her mother would've done and said what she had for no reason.

"Yes," Greta said. "I do."

"It's just . . . hard to believe," Lindy said, but she would be damned if she'd shove her daughter into marrying someone who wasn't going to treat her well. And Lindy truly did believe what she'd told Hailey yesterday in the car: Sometimes a path could be the exact right path—until suddenly it wasn't.

Also, she hadn't been able to help noticing, these past few days, how . . . *heavy* Hailey seemed in Noah's presence, in contrast to how light and at ease she seemed in proximity to Jack Westfield. This had been true even last night, when Hailey'd had a "killer" migraine and Jack had brought her home and said he was worried about her. Even Lindy, who'd long thought of Jack as simply a smooth operator, had to admit he'd seemed sincere.

She didn't want to think she could've been blind all this time, but, honestly, before this week, it had not even occurred to her that Hailey could be marrying the wrong man. Maybe because Lindy had always been so sure she had married the right one.

She sighed. "Okay, well, I'm going to go, Mom. I'm sorry to leave you and Dad, but I'll be back as soon as I can. I just need to get to the bottom of all this." Now she found herself hoping that, if she could talk with Noah alone, she could find something in his manner or words to reassure her that he was still the charming, kind young man she'd always thought him to be, that the incident yesterday had all been a terrible mistake, that there was some good reason why he hadn't stepped up to help search for David—and that he knew how lucky he was to be marrying Hailey.

Greta frowned. "You be careful, honey."

"He wasn't the one with the gun," Lindy said, then laughed to show she was teasing—even if she wasn't, exactly. Greta smiled weakly, and Lindy grabbed her purse and headed outside, the screen door banging shut behind her as she headed for the Volvo.

She lowered her sunglasses, put the car into gear, pulled out onto Summerland Cove Point Road, and headed for the world.

"To be honest, I feel sorry for you, Mrs. Kauffman," Noah said. They were standing just inside the door of his and Hailey's apartment in the small, dingy kitchen. Lindy had apologized for Greta's behavior and invited him out for lunch, her treat, but he'd said he was about to leave for work, and he hadn't invited her into the living room to sit down. Lindy had never been to the apartment before and would've liked to see it, but his distant manner precluded asking. "Because it's obvious your mother is not in her right mind."

On the bright side, it didn't seem like Noah was going to report Greta to the police.

But he sure wasn't acting like he felt lucky to be marrying Hailey.

"You never called Hailey back last night," Lindy said. "She's very upset. She has a migraine."

Noah was unreadable. Implacable. *No wonder Hailey gets headaches,* Lindy thought suddenly. *He's stressful to be around!* He acted calm—pleasant, even—but he looked down on her from his great height, arms folded, with an air of barely contained impatience, a balloon on the verge of popping. "I'm sorry to hear that," he said.

The words were close enough to right, but they rang hollow to Lindy's ears. There seemed little, if any, sense of empathy or care.

Lindy did not want to be seeing this, let alone thinking it. Was her mother right? Had David been right all along? (When David had said there was something he "didn't trust about the kid," Lindy had dismissed it as fatherly overprotectiveness, a cliché!)

Or maybe it wasn't so clear-cut. Hailey wouldn't be with Noah if he didn't have good qualities. Maybe he was just *changing*? He had been a boy three years ago when Lindy had met him. Now he was a man. He'd been living on his own in Portland for a year. He'd hardened, it seemed; gotten arrogant? Maybe. Self-involved, at least.

She was glad Noah had refused the lunch invitation. They did not have a great rapport going. Not that she could blame him for being a bit defensive today, after having a gun pulled on him yesterday at Innisfree.

Lindy needed to talk to Hailey, get to the bottom of how *she* really felt—and to the truth of the relationship, if possible. There was a lot at stake here. Maybe *everybody* was just having cold feet.

"Thanks for your time, Noah, and for being understanding about yesterday. I'll let you get to work now."

"Thanks for the apology, Mrs. Kauffman," Noah said pleasantly as he went to open the door. "I just hope your mother can get the help she needs. Tell Hailey to call me when she feels better."

Lindy, still not liking his responses, gave him a close-mouthed smile.

"Oh," Noah added. "Maybe you could get some of the boxes of wedding stuff out of here. They're cluttering up the place, and I know Hailey meant to take them up there."

Lindy hadn't thought about the boxes, and his request again only underlined what he could've done instead. (Driven them up to Innisfree himself!)

But she said, "Of course!" because when you came right down to it, the wedding was going to happen—*should* happen—right?

Back at The Cove, Lindy walked into Innisfree to find the kitchen quiet, though it was nearing suppertime, when Greta usually would be getting a meal underway. Hailey, on the living room couch writing in a spiral notebook, looked up briefly to give Lindy a little smile and wave, then went back to writing. She looked so content that Lindy didn't want to bother her, though it did seem strange that she wasn't jumping up to ask how things had gone with Noah. Maybe she'd talked with him already?

Well, Lindy was just glad the headache was evidently better—and that her lie about David's whereabouts was evidently sparing Hailey from worrying. Lindy didn't mind not having to discuss Noah right this minute. The boxes of wedding stuff could stay in the Volvo for now, too. She set her purse on the counter and went out onto the deck to join her parents, who were sitting side by side in the Adirondack chairs, holding hands.

Oh God, Lindy realized. *It's today!* Their fiftieth anniversary. How had she not remembered this morning, even as she'd made all those phone calls to cancel the party? And of course she'd planned the party for Saturday, because a party on a Thursday didn't make sense, but today was their actual anniversary. She should've bought them flowers, a cake, something. Of course, they had enough cake and food for a hundred and fifty people arriving the day after tomorrow. Even after sharing it with the neighborhood at the clubhouse, they'd surely end up with leftovers, since all the out-of-town people had been told not to come.

Well, she would take her parents out for dinner tonight, soon, and that would be their celebration. She would spring for lobster and champagne, the realities of her terrible financial situation and, no doubt, impending divorce—which were only just beginning to sink in, anyway—be damned.

"Happy anniversary, Mom and Dad," she said, and they both looked up at her and smiled. They seemed happy; at peace, even. She hugged them both, grateful that her father still seemed to know her today; determined not to pick another fight with her mother, not right now. She would not bring up Florida. She would not even mention the gun.

"Sit with us, pumpkin," her father said, so Lindy went to grab another chair, dragged it over beside him, and sat down. He reached to hold her hand, too, so that they were all connected, with him in the middle, and for a moment, looking out at the calm blue ocean, Lindy felt at peace, too. Whatever would come next would come. David would confess about Tiffany; they'd argue about money, about everything. Innisfree, unbelievably, might be sold to another family. Lindy's father would get sicker and sicker, her mother older and older, and Lindy would lose them both one day, and it would be unbearable.

But right now, in this moment, she felt lucky. She had been so lucky, all this time, to have the family she'd had. Her parents, David, her kids, Kate and the rest of the Kauffmans. And the entire community of The Cove. She'd been so very, very lucky to have The Cove, and Innisfree, for at least this long in her life.

If her marriage was really over, she thought, maybe she would move to Florida, too, at least for a little while. Or maybe, to stay closer to the kids, she'd see if her book club friend Samantha really would give her a job at the interior design studio.

Maybe it was a case of a different path suddenly coming clear for Lindy, too.

The thought was startling for a moment, but then she let it drift away, let her eyes sink closed, and she listened to the gentle waves, the seagulls keening, as she held on to her father's hand.

"Mom?" came Hailey's voice after a while, after the sliding sound of the door had broken into the quiet. "Mom, there's a phone call for you."

Lindy didn't want to let go of her dad's hand. She figured it was someone calling back in response to a message about the party. She didn't open her eyes. "Just—just take a message."

"It's Dad's assistant. Tiffany?" The name in Hailey's voice jarred Lindy out of the peaceful moment, back to the nightmare of David's being gone. And then Lindy thought, how dare that little tramp Tiffany call her now? As if she could justify her behavior!

And then Lindy thought, *If Tiffany was having an affair with my husband, would she be calling me?*

"Mom?" Hailey said. "She said it was important."

Lindy was getting a sick feeling in her stomach. She let her go of her father's hand, patting it absently as she scrambled to her feet. "Okay, I'll speak with her!"

"My boyfriend, Raj, and I have been camping in Nova Scotia, so I didn't have any signal!" Tiffany sounded worried, short of breath, as Lindy pressed the old plastic receiver to her clammy ear and Hailey stood by, watching, listening. "So, we just got to Bar Harbor and I just got your messages! I was so worried to hear that David didn't arrive the other day? He was so excited for his birthday party and your parents' anniversary and Hailey's wedding and everything. You must have heard from him by now? I just wanted to check and make sure he's okay?"

Lindy couldn't speak.

David wasn't with Tiffany?

He wasn't the secret boyfriend that Tiffany had been hiding from her coworkers?

If he wasn't with her, then where was he?

But how could Lindy be sure that the girl wasn't lying? What if David was standing right beside her, coaching her on what to say? (Was David *capable* of such a thing?)

Lindy didn't know. She couldn't think straight at all.

She didn't decide to ask; the words simply came out. "He's not . . . with you?"

"What? Why would he—Oh. God. No. David is like a *father* to me, he's a *mentor*—"

"Gina said you had a new boyfriend and you wouldn't say who he was," Lindy broke in, and she was gulping for air, she'd totally lost her cool. "And then I didn't hear back from you, and all, all the emails, the late hours, and at the Christmas party, I saw, saw, the, your coat, the, the picture—"

"Lindy, never, no! Oh my God." Tiffany didn't sound mad, just aghast, almost amused, so Lindy knew then that the girl was telling the truth, and that there was nothing at all to what Lindy had so vividly imagined.

"But you're so pretty!" Lindy wailed, realizing how badly she had wanted to be right about where David was; feeling the weight of the lie she'd told Hailey and Cody and Kate and everybody; thinking, *God, how could I be so wrong? Where is he? God, where is he?*

"Lindy, listen." Tiffany's tone had turned all business, lawyer-like. "You're telling me you haven't heard from David? He's been missing since you called me on Sunday? Do you have the police looking for him? What is going on, Lindy? Is David okay? Where *is* he?"

"I don't know!" Lindy cried, and somehow within the next three minutes she had agreed to Tiffany and her boyfriend coming to help with the search and given them directions from Bar Harbor to Innisfree, even as she couldn't stop herself from thinking, *No word from him in all this time and I called off the search and now he's probably dead of a heart attack or he slit his own wrists again and I had no idea anything was even wrong!*

"We'll be there in a few hours," Tiffany said, and when Lindy said goodbye and hung up, Hailey was standing there, looking at Lindy, pale, eyes wide. "Mom? Dad's still missing?" she said, and Lindy could feel it as the world came crumbling down.

PART THREE

Brand-New Key

CHAPTER 35

Hailey

Thursday, July 29, 2010
6 p.m.

"You lied? Mom! Why would you do that?" Hailey was aghast as she faced her mom, who stood in the living room beside the phone, looking like she'd just seen someone get hit by a bus.

Lindy ran a hand through her messy hair. "I just—I really thought the only explanation was that he'd run off with Tiffany. And I didn't want it to ruin your wedding. Emma and Eli and I all agreed—"

"You don't think my wedding is ruined now?" Earlier, Hailey's medication had quelled the worst of her migraine—enough that she'd indulged in working on her novel, totally ignoring the mess that was her own life. But now she could feel the pain lingering, ready to reignite, and her anger was going to make it worse even than last night at the river with Jack. She couldn't believe Emma and Eli had gone along with this stupid plan, too. To "save" her wedding? And then head for Cranston as if they were going to find some clue about their dad's whereabouts there, without Hailey and the rest of the family being the wiser? "Where is he, Mom? *Where is he?*"

Lindy blinked back tears. "I don't know. I'm sorry. I don't have any idea. I don't know what's happened to him."

"What if he's *dead,* Mom?" Hailey spat. "And what if, when you called off the search forty-eight hours ago, he *wasn't?*"

Lindy staggered. "Don't *say* that."

Hailey pressed her temples with her fingertips, but it was clear that her headache was about to tsunami again. "I need some air." She wheeled and ran, pushing her way out the screen door.

She hurried down the road toward the point. Looking at the ocean could help a lot of things. She wasn't sure it could help this. Her dad *missing* for days now, her mom and siblings liars, her grandpa sick, her grandma going nuts, Innisfree about to be sold, her fiancé being a jerk, her entire wedding a question mark—

Approaching the curve in the road, the ocean straight out ahead, she was about to step onto the rocks when she heard a familiar rumble. She stopped and looked. *Not funny,* she said to God, as the Z3 came around the opposite bend, Jack at the wheel wearing Ray-Bans.

He drove slowly to where she stood beside the road and stopped. "Hales! What's up?"

She burst into tears.

"Okay, don't get me wrong, this sucks." Jack squinted at Hailey from where he sat beside her on a rock facing the ocean. He'd pulled the car off the road, jumped out, hugged her till she got her crying reined in, then invited her to go for a drive. She'd refused—she needed to get back—but he asked her to sit for a minute and tell him what was wrong. So, she had, and it had helped. A little.

"It especially sucks that your mom lied," he went on. "But she was trying to protect you, right? And so were Emma and Eli? I mean, if they really thought all the evidence pointed to him having an affair."

Hailey shook her head. "She always told us there was no good reason ever to tell a lie. And she decides to tell one about *this*? I mean, we need to start looking for him right away. I mean, now! He could be out there somewhere, like, hurt." She suddenly recalled what her grandma had said yesterday when she was climbing upstairs with the gun and Lindy had asked if she was going to hurt herself. *I'm not David.*

What the hell did that mean? What did they know that Hailey didn't? And how could her mom seriously have stopped looking for him without knowing he was okay?

"I've got to get back," she said, and started to stand.

Jack grabbed her hand. "One more minute? Your own oxygen mask first, remember?"

She huffed and sat back down. "You're not my father," she said—which made her start to cry again. The sun was on its way down, softening the light. The air was cooling; the mosquitoes were about to come out. Time would pass whether she wanted it to or not. *Dad. 8/7/10.*

"Hales," Jack said. "We're going to find him."

"What if we don't, Jack?"

He was quiet. She wiped at her eyes, watching a gull wheel over the waves, which were a deep blue under the pinkening sky. The wind was picking up. *I'm not David.* Seriously, what the hell?

"Hey, Hales," Jack said. "I know you don't want to hear it, but, like, what if you put yourself in your mom's shoes for a second? What must it be like for her to have your dad missing? I mean, it kinda makes sense she'd be going insane, right?"

"You and your Zen," Hailey grumbled, but then she had to take a breath. Because, of course, he was right. If Hailey felt this hollow, this devasted, what must her mom feel like? Her mom and dad were, like, best friends. Two halves of one whole. Sure, they squabbled, they disagreed, but how much they loved and relied on each other had always been clear. Hailey sighed. "Okay, yeah."

"So maybe her lying is more a symptom of *that* than a sign of who she truly is?"

Hailey squared her shoulders. Brushed her hair away from her face, as the truth of this settled upon her. The whole thing still pissed her off, though. "Yeah, well, if that's true, then she should *not* be the one in charge of the search," she said, and stood.

"Can I come with you?" Jack said quickly. "Can I help?"

Hailey thought of Noah. He should be the one here helping her.

Well, she would have to call him. She would have to insist.

"I don't know if that would be appropriate," she said to Jack, keeping her tone very formal again.

His mouth quirked. Color came into his cheeks—or was that just a trick of the light? "Hales, I'm a concerned neighbor."

She huffed again. "Fine," she said, and held out her hand. He reached to take it, and when she helped him to his feet, he gave her a little smile that, in spite of everything, made her smile back, made her almost want to laugh. Maybe just to keep from crying, or maybe because life had gotten so ridiculously out of hand—or maybe because she was just so happy to have him there, even if she shouldn't be.

Still, she let go of his hand.

Jack had to drive the roadster back around the loop to park it at Seabreeze, so he dropped Hailey at Innisfree, saying he'd walk over in a few minutes. Hailey banged in the screen door to see her mom and grandparents out on the deck, seemingly just sitting there watching the light change over the water as the sun went down on the other side of the point. Doing *nothing* to try to find her dad.

Another sign Hailey needed to be in charge. *Damn it.*

At least for the moment she'd have privacy. She knew Noah's number by heart now. She picked up the phone and dialed the rotary, then pressed the receiver to her shoulder to go hands-free, twisting her diamond around her finger.

In her ear came the endless ringing again. For a second, she wondered: Had something happened to him, too?

Then she just wanted to scream. He *had* to recognize the Innisfree number, to know it was her calling. Yeah, he'd be at work this time of night, but still. She was mid-crisis, and he was ghosting her. A week before their wedding.

There came the automatic voice. The beep. Hailey swallowed—

her mouth felt dry—then took the phone in her hand, straightened, and said, "Hey, it's me." She told him the news, told him she needed his help. She said again that she was sorry about what her grandma had done. Then, she said, "Listen, I don't know if we should even be thinking about going ahead with the wedding as long as my dad's gone, but . . ." Another hard swallow. She didn't know what was getting into her, but she was tired of his bad behavior, and she was tired of trying to keep everything seeming perfect, when the truth was that everything was a fucking mess. "If I don't hear from you, like, tonight, I'm definitely calling it off." She hung up the phone in its cradle. She stood there for a second wondering if she'd just wrecked her life or saved it, then headed outside to get her mom.

CHAPTER 36

Greta

Thursday, July 29, 2010
8 p.m.

Greta was tired of keeping secrets. She was tired of taking the blame. But she would take the blame for *this*, for Lindy's giant lie, because Greta, after all, had been the one to show Lindy that the way to deal with intolerable things was to shove them down, ignore them, keep them secret, make them your own problem to deal with, and never ask for help.

Now, in the living room at Innisfree, Hailey, too, had evidently had enough. "I will try to understand why you lied, Mom," she was telling Lindy. The handsome young Jack Westfield sat nearby listening as if he was part of the family now, too, which made Greta fume. He would no doubt share everything he heard with his grandmother, Marjorie, who would spread it like a wind-fueled wildfire around the entire Cove, the way she'd been doing with gossip for seventy years. "But everybody has to tell the truth about everything now." Hailey turned to Greta, surprising her. "Starting with what you meant yesterday, Grandma, when Mom asked if you were planning to hurt yourself, and you said you weren't Dad."

Greta glanced at Lindy, feeling as if a silent grenade had just been detonated in the room; feeling on the defensive, suddenly. At the same time, though, it didn't seem right to tell what had happened long ago without David here to explain, and if this was the first time Greta understood that David had been a son to her all along, then that was to her shame. She sat up straighter. "I shouldn't have said that about your dad," she told Hailey. "I'm sorry."

"But you *did* say it, Mom," Lindy snapped, before her tone softened. "I think Hailey's right, though. No more secrets. Maybe if everybody knows everything, and we all put our heads together . . ."

Greta shuddered. Would she have to reveal her own old, terrible secret, too? She was tired of keeping it, yes—but what did it have to do with anything? It was nearly as old as she was; older than dirt, as the saying went.

Lindy turned to Hailey and spoke gently. "Honey, your dad, when he was young . . . well, he had some trouble with depression, and he . . . had to be hospitalized. We were all very worried about him, for a time."

Greta squeezed her hands together, remembering. She, of course, had been mostly worried about Lindy back then. She'd had so little sympathy for anyone outside her immediate circle. Her primary feeling about David had been suspicion, rather than hope that he might love her daughter in the way Lindy had wanted him to. Greta was ashamed of that now, too.

"Dad was hospitalized?" Hailey said, rubbing at her temple, her face flushing. "Like, you mean, he tried to . . ."

"He did try to hurt himself one time, when he was seventeen," Lindy said, and Greta, though proud of the unflinching way she spoke, wished the story of her daughter's first (and, yes, enduring) love could've been different; that Lindy wouldn't have had to be so strong. "Another time, later, he just . . . was thinking about it, I guess."

"Oh my God. So, do you think . . . now? That Dad might have . . ." Hailey's voice trailed off, and she covered her mouth with her hand. Jack was sitting up straight, looking at her with concern, and Greta found herself thinking better of him than she would've expected. Odd, too, that he didn't seem to know about David's past. Greta would've put money on Marjorie Westfield's having told him all about it.

"No, no, I don't!" Lindy said. "See, honey, from the minute he found out he was going to be a father, he really just . . . just *decided.* He wasn't going to let anything get the better of him anymore. Those old demons, you know? You saved him, you see? Just by being born! I've always thought so."

Hailey's eyes were wide. "*I* did?"

"Yes," Lindy said, and Greta wanted to believe it could be true that David had not wrestled with those demons again, that he hadn't been secretly wrestling with them all these years. But she wasn't sure. Did demons ever truly vanish—or, after twenty-five years, did they come back angrier than ever, furious they'd been stifled for so long?

Greta ought to know the answer to that, and unfortunately, she thought it was the latter. It wasn't as if her aversion to the attic had lessened, not in sixty-nine years.

Lindy continued. "He didn't *seem* to be struggling recently . . . I mean, to me, he didn't. And Gina and Tiffany both said he'd seemed normal at work. They said there'd been a lot of stress, though, and then—well, there's some money missing. A hundred thousand dollars."

Greta drew in a breath. Hailey said, "Oh my God."

"That's why I thought he'd run off with Tiffany," Lindy said. "Because the money is gone. And he applied to get a mortgage."

Greta had heard nothing about any missing money, a mortgage application. She felt caught out. Was everything her fault, after all?

Suddenly, she wished she'd made different decisions all along. When her father had died and left Innisfree to her, she'd wanted to sell it then. She'd told Tom and Lindy they could use the proceeds to buy another, possibly grander, place, possibly closer to the city—in Ogunquit or Kennebunkport, maybe! They wouldn't have to lose out on anything. Life could be easier, and probably more fun!

But the two of them had claimed heartbreak at the thought of giving up The Cove. (Lindy, eleven at the time, had sworn she would *die* without her best summer friend, Kate.) And Greta had succumbed. She'd swallowed her own feelings and kept coming here, summer after summer, half hating it, always wishing it could be different, how being here invariably made her want to rewind to back before the war, when her father and brothers had benevolently ruled the world. And yet, time just kept marching on, while, infuriatingly, the pain you wished would recede with the passing of it never seemed to.

Lindy went on. "And Gina said Tiffany had a 'glow,' so I thought—"

"Oh my God," Hailey said again.

Greta broke in. "David knew about Innisfree! I told him I needed to sell it. He was trying to figure out how to buy it, last I heard."

Lindy and Hailey turned to her, astonished. Greta stewed under their gazes, knowing she should have told Lindy about this when David had first gone missing.

And honestly, she should've sold the place in 1974 when she'd wanted to, and all of life would be different now! Lindy never would've married David; Lindy wouldn't even have *known* him. She would've had a career, maybe stayed in New York City, kept up with her music, her art, or all the other things she'd sacrificed to the cause of loving David and having a family with him. And Greta did not—oh, she did *not*—want to wish her grandchildren away, but just for a moment she thought, *If only! If only she could've been free!*

Lindy spoke first. "But, if he was putting together money to buy Innisfree, where did the money go? I mean, it seems to be totally gone. He hasn't given you any money, has he, Mom?"

Greta shook her head. The truth was, she did not want David to be gone. She loved David. She wanted Lindy and David and their children to have Innisfree and The Cove for decades and decades more. For all of them to spend the rest of the summers of their lives here, just as Greta and Tom, and Greta's parents before them, had done. That they might be able to do so was the whole reason Greta had plowed through all these years, despite her memories, her anxieties, her grief. Despite how she'd hated that returning here year after year had made it impossible to escape the past.

Oh, she *wished* that David had given her the money, that he'd been able to buy the place and secure his family's future, as she and Tom had been trying for so long to do. "Not a cent," she said.

Just then, a knock came at the door.

CHAPTER 37

Hailey

Thursday, July 29, 2010
8:45 p.m.

Lindy, nobody's going to take you seriously if they find out you lied." Tiffany paced in the living room, wearing a pink-and-green cotton flannel open over a white tank and khaki camping shorts, her hair back in a tight ponytail. Hailey had to admit it: Even just out the Canada woods, with no makeup, Tiffany glowed. Her boyfriend, Raj, a thirty-something anesthesiologist, sat nearby, admiring her. "This is the only way."

Tiffany was proposing that Lindy tell the police, media, even family, that she'd gotten a scam call Tuesday night, someone pretending to be David. Because of the TV coverage, Tiffany said, it was a realistic scenario, and claiming fraud would work to get people started searching for him again. Lindy could not, Tiffany insisted, admit that she had actually gotten no call at all.

The girl was ridiculous. Acting like this was some reality TV show that somebody could win or lose by cracking the code on where Hailey's dad was. Hailey had to put her foot down. "We are not telling any more lies."

Jack nodded in support, but Hailey's mom responded to Tiffany as if Hailey hadn't spoken. "But how would I have figured out that the call was a scam? Why wouldn't I have recognized it wasn't his voice? And why would anybody call pretending to be David and telling me he's fine?"

Tiffany shrugged. "People do all kinds of crazy things. That last part's not a stretch. And maybe you wanted so badly to hear from him that you convinced yourself it was his voice? So, you told your kids that it was him, and that was that. This lets your twins off the hook, too, see?"

Raj broke in, inspired. "You sent him money to get home, and now he hasn't come, so you realized it wasn't David!" He beamed at Tiffany, and she beamed back. It was evident they considered themselves geniuses.

"That could work . . ." Lindy said, apparently considering it for real.

"No way," Hailey insisted. She'd been having this weird feeling, ever since her mom had said that she had saved her dad just by being born, that it was up to her to save him again now—and she also had the sense that she didn't have much time. The fact that her mom and siblings had concocted this preposterous story so as not to "ruin" her wedding made her feel even more responsible. "Get serious," she said. "We have to review what we know. Make a plan. We need to get all the information together before we even think of calling the police. And we have to tell everybody the truth."

Lindy looked at her, then sighed. Rubbed her face with both hands. "Okay."

"Let's get Emma and Eli on the phone and start with the review." Hailey wished the twins had listened to her yesterday when she'd told them to get back up to Maine. Of course, she'd known they wouldn't, even though she hadn't known that *they* knew their dad was still missing, that they were down in Cranston searching for clues.

Had they found anything? Hailey hoped so. She was *not* ready to confront the maelstrom that was going to be let loose once Aunt Kate and Uncle Josh found out how Lindy, Emma, and Eli had lied. Maybe the group here could come up with a way to find David before everyone over at the yellow cottage had to know. "Jack, would you grab my notebook and take notes?"

Twenty minutes later, Jack read out loud the list they'd made: "Good husband and father. Called to say he was on his way. $109K missing. Applied to get a mortgage, was refused. Previously trustworthy. Left cell phone at home. Likes to hike. Old knee injury. History of depression. Stress at work. Knowledge of Innisfree sale. According to Reese: Lighthouse-slash-midlife crisis. No sightings of car by police. Was looking forward to family parties and wedding. Possible heart condition." A little glance at Hailey. That last bit had come as a complete surprise to her; another thing her mom had been keeping a secret. Jack looked back down at the list and finished, "Bought gas at Kennebunkport service plaza. No new charges on credit cards since."

Everyone was quiet, including Emma and Eli on the other end of the phone. The list did not add up to anything that sounded good.

Lindy spoke quietly, almost to herself. "How could I not have had any idea what all he was going through? I mean, none!" She inhaled, closing her eyes.

Raj spoke up somberly. "I think we need to consider the possibility that, if he was traveling with a hundred thousand dollars in cash, someone might've—you know—taken it."

Hailey shook her head; an ache had started up again. She'd been holding the phone out into the room so Emma and Eli could hear, but they'd been complaining they barely could, and now she hoped they *hadn't* heard that last part. She pressed the receiver to her ear and spoke into it. "Okay, guys, you keep looking on the computer, okay? We'll call back in a bit to let you know next steps." They grumbled but said goodbye and hung up.

Tiffany had started pacing again. "You know, bear with me one second here. I cannot tell you how many times that man heads out for lunch telling me he's going one place and then comes back having eaten somewhere else entirely. A different type of food! I'll tease him for it, and he'll just smile and say, 'The winds of change, Tiff. A man has to do what the spirit moves him to.'"

Hailey had never heard her dad say exactly that, but it definitely sounded like him. She rubbed her shoulder, trying to ease the pain that was in her head again. "What are you saying?"

"I guess I'm saying, what if he set out driving, intending to come here, and then he just . . . went somewhere else instead?"

Hailey swallowed, as her mom shook her head and said, "He wouldn't have done that without calling me first to tell me. I mean, I don't think he would. Or calling *someone*, anyway. And, even if he didn't call beforehand, he certainly would've called by now."

"But he doesn't have his cell phone," Tiffany said.

"He would have found a way," Lindy insisted.

"But if he has all that cash," Tiffany said, "he could be letting the wind blow him all over the place."

"I guess so." It was clear on Lindy's face that she didn't want to believe her husband would've just run off like that with their hundred thousand dollars. Hailey was finding it hard to fathom, too. "But if he had access to all that money," Lindy continued, "why would he have bothered to take three hundred dollars out of the ATM the day before he left?"

"He took out three hundred dollars?" Jack asked, and when Lindy confirmed it, he added a note to the list.

"You couldn't travel for six days on three hundred dollars," Tiffany said.

Lindy buried her face in her hands. Hailey had to bite her lip to keep from telling Tiffany to shut her mouth.

"I don't like her," Hailey proclaimed to Jack, as he led her toward the back door at a darkened Seabreeze in the moonlight. Even though Tiffany and Raj clearly wanted to help—they'd just taken off for town for signal so they could call all the hospitals in the entire state of Maine again—there was something about the girl's genius-reality-show-contestant vibe that plain rubbed Hailey the wrong way.

Jack laughed a little as he opened the back door, the Maine road atlas he'd just grabbed out of the Z3 tucked under his arm. Emma had insisted over the phone that Reese was never wrong and her clue about lighthouse/midlife crisis *had* to be included on their list, so, when it came time to decide where to start the search tomorrow, Hailey had proposed checking all the lighthouses from here to the New Hampshire state line. Nobody'd had a better idea. Jack had offered a book of his grandma's on Maine lighthouses, saying they could use it to make a plan, and Hailey had jumped at the chance to walk with him to grab it.

It was weird to realize, but she did *not* want to be in the room while her mom called Cody to confess what was really going on, then called Emma and Eli back to discuss the search. Hailey's usual MO would have been to try to manage everybody's emotions, but maybe right now she was just trying to do the whole oxygen mask thing. *Desperate times,* she heard her dad saying. She wondered if Noah would try to call while her mom was using the phone at Innisfree. He'd get a busy signal. Would he bother calling back in the middle of a long night at the restaurant? Would he leave a voicemail on her cell? She probably should've insisted on going to town herself to check . . .

"You just don't like that she was the reason why your mom thought your dad was having an affair," Jack said, as he flipped on the light inside the back hall.

"Who's having an affair?" came a voice from the kitchen. Marjorie!

"Oh, God! Nobody," Hailey called. Jack had said his grandma would be asleep. "Hi, Marjorie!"

Through an open doorframe to the right was the remodeled kitchen, stainless appliances and granite countertops gleaming. Marjorie was seated at the counter with a glass of white wine and a paperback, still dressed in her trademark crisp blouse and capris—blue and white, today—and statement necklace and matching earrings. She tucked her white bob behind her ear, closing her book as Jack went over to set down the atlas and hug her. "Hey, Grandma," he said, and Hailey saw the book's cover. *Change of Heart* by Jodi Picoult. Hailey hadn't read it, but it must be engrossing to keep Marjorie up so late.

"Planning your escape?" Marjorie said, with a lifted brow and a nod at the atlas, and Jack laughed and explained, as Hailey tried to keep from cringing at the thought of what her grandma would say about him telling Marjorie Westfield all the details of their family's private, terrible story.

"Oh, dear," Marjorie said finally, with a concerned frown at Hailey. "I'm so sorry. Are you all right? How is your mom doing? And your grandma?"

"As good as can be expected, I guess," Hailey said, though she was a little surprised at the unalloyed kindness. She would've expected probing for more information instead.

"Is there anything I can do to help?" Marjorie said, her blue eyes soft with concern.

"We need to use your lighthouse book," Jack said. "There's this psychic who said he might be near a lighthouse."

"Oh, by all means!" Marjorie said, not seeming the least bit taken aback by the mention of a psychic. She got up, went to the living room. The light flipped on. Jack gave Hailey a little smile. In a moment, Marjorie was back with a large coffee table book titled *Maine Lighthouses.* She handed it to Hailey. "Oh, what a pretty ring," she said, when she saw Hailey's diamond. Marjorie held Hailey's hand a second to study the ring, then looked up at her. "That wedding is coming right up, isn't it?" A glance at Jack, then back at Hailey. "Next weekend?"

Hailey swallowed as her eyes darted to Jack, too. Marjorie had a point. What was she doing spending all this time with her old flame Jack when she was marrying someone else next weekend? Hailey felt her face heating up. "Uh, yeah."

Marjorie's eyes crinkled. "Oh, dear, but with your father missing, how—"

"We're going to go upstairs," Jack interrupted. "Thanks, Grandma."

"Let me know what I can do," Marjorie called after them as Jack hustled Hailey out.

In Jack's room, he turned on the light and tossed the big Maine atlas onto the neatly made bed. Hailey, shaking off her embarrassment, saw it was all just as she'd remembered, down to the white comforter and shades-of-gray throw pillows on the bed. On the nightstand were copies of *The Art of Choosing, Kook, The Power of Intention,* and *The Stand.* Jack sat down at the desk in front of the window, where his laptop was open.

"You have internet here?" They could've been using it in the search!

Jack shook his head. "I'm trying to convince Grandma to get it, but she's saying it'll 'spoil the peace.'"

Hailey sighed, the pressure of her frustration punctured. "Oh. Well, she's probably right."

Jack laughed quietly. "She does like to think she is. Let me see that lighthouse book." She handed it over, and he opened it to a map of the coast with graphics marking the locations of the lighthouses along it.

Hailey peered over his shoulder. "That's a lot of lighthouses." At first glance, there appeared to be about twenty scattered between the New Hampshire border and The Cove. God, was it totally ridiculous to base their search on what Reese had said? Even Reese herself hadn't been sure if what she'd "heard" was "lighthouse" or "white house."

But again, what else did they have to go on? Hailey wished she understood why Emma had placed so much faith in Reese's clairaudience. And, if Emma *did* place that much faith in it, then why had the two of them argued and possibly—knowing Emma—split?

"We'll make a list," Jack said, getting up to grab the atlas again off the bed. "These maps are totally detailed, so we can look to see which lighthouses have hiking trails nearby. Maybe we expand the search to places a little more off the beaten path, away from the highway."

Hailey decided: They'd stay here half an hour, about as long as her mom was apt to be using the phone, then Hailey would insist on going back to Innisfree so she'd be there in case Noah called. "Okay, let's do it," she said, though it was suddenly hard to believe this task was anything but busywork designed to keep her mind off the fact that her dad could literally be anywhere in the world right now. Or even—especially considering Raj's theory regarding what might've happened if the wrong person had discovered David was carrying a hundred thousand dollars—nowhere at all anymore.

CHAPTER 38

Lindy

Thursday, July 29, 2010
9 p.m.

After Hailey and Jack, and Tiffany and Raj, set out for their designated tasks and Greta went up to bed, Lindy called Cody to confess. No answer. She left a voicemail just asking him to call, but he was no doubt out with friends and likely wouldn't call back till late tomorrow morning.

At least he'd be preserved from the worst awhile longer—and she would be preserved from what he'd think of her when he learned it.

Then she swallowed her pride and called the state police again. She was grateful it was a woman who answered, and that, when Lindy explained what had happened—her mistaken assumption about the affair—the officer made no comment, just took down the information about David's vehicle again and told her the same thing that other officers had before: Because David had not been known to be in distress prior to his vanishing, he wasn't eligible to be placed on the missing person's registry.

Lindy knew she should go over to the yellow cottage to confess to Kate and Josh, too, but it was late. If the kids weren't in bed yet, she might rile them up just as they were winding down. Either that or the whole house might already be sleeping. Or, if Kate was up, a confession from Lindy would definitely trigger her into drinking.

Lindy decided to wait till morning.

But Innisfree was quiet and dark, and she didn't know what to do. She wished her children would come back. She just wanted them in the same house, the same room . . .

But would they ever come back, truly, now? Would they ever trust her again? Emma and Eli had agreed to go along with her lie the other day, but now they were furious with her for having put them in that position. And who could blame them? She was their mom, so they'd trusted her to guide them to do the right thing—and she had steered them entirely wrong, instead.

She thought of Tiffany's theory that David could have simply . . . turned down a different road. On the spur of the moment, without letting anyone know?

In some ways, it was plausible. Often, he and Lindy would decide over dinner which Netflix DVD to watch, he'd go into the den to start it while she made popcorn, and by the time she got in there, he would have something else loaded up. It drove her totally nuts. So, sure, it was possible to imagine that, on his drive up to The Cove last Saturday, he could've just changed his mind and headed somewhere else.

But, alone in a room after dark, having heard nothing from him in nearly six days, it was almost impossible to believe.

She was grateful when Tiffany and Raj came back. They reported that none of the hospitals in the entire state of Maine had any record of David. Lindy's emotions were so dulled with shock that she felt only a slight flare of relief, a tiny wave of disappointment. She thanked them, said they should all try to get some sleep, and showed them to the attic, trying not to think about the gun she knew her mother had stashed somewhere in the storage area. Raj hauled in air mattresses and sleeping bags from their car, joking this was "certainly different" from camping in Bar Harbor as they'd planned, but "no doubt more interesting!" Then he sobered and said he hoped everything would be resolved quickly. "Pardon me, pardon me," he said, disappearing up the stairs loaded down with gear, and Lindy realized then that Innisfree was changing already, that the only people in the house now were practically strangers—other than her mother, who was making plans to leave her, and her father, whose mind was leaving him.

Innisfree. She had never dreamed she would lose it. Not once had she imagined even the possibility, and, as with her emotions over David, and over her father, the loss was too profound to be believed.

She got ready for bed, hoping Hailey would come home soon and praying that somehow, somehow, after all this time, David might just call out of the blue. It was possible, wasn't it? Trying to tell herself it was, she went back downstairs to the couch and, when the phone rang a few minutes later, her heart took off in a stampede.

Her hand trembled as she picked up the receiver. "Hello?"

"Mrs. Kaufmann?" As she recognized Noah's voice, her body collapsed with disappointment. He politely asked to speak with Hailey, saying he was at work and had only a minute.

"Oh, I'm so sorry, Noah," Lindy said, and her voice was shaking with the noise of her own broken heart. The last thing she wanted was for her daughter's heart to be broken, too, and she didn't think it would do anybody any good if Noah learned that Hailey was over at Jack's house right now. "Hailey's asleep, and I don't want to wake her if you don't really have time to talk." Only after the lie was out of her mouth did she realize: another one. They seemed to be coming easier and easier.

"Well," Noah snapped. "Tell her I called, and I'll talk to her tomorrow." In his voice was a barely contained rage. "Thanks," he remembered to say, then the line went dead.

Lindy hung up the receiver and lay awake a long time in the overwhelming quiet, stewing over whether the wedding that she'd been visualizing and planning all this time would actually happen (it was not seeming likely) and wondering if, after all these years, she was married to a stranger who would do incalculable harm intentionally, or to the boy she'd known a long time ago—and which was the more dangerous thing.

She'd been so hellbent on saving David all these years. She'd never imagined there would be a need to save herself—from him.

And she didn't know what she would do if it turned out David had truly left her for good and she was a widow, suddenly. She didn't feel old enough to be a widow, but nothing made sense right now, so it seemed anything could be true. And if David was dead—she had to admit it to herself, finally—it was the exact thing she'd been fearing since she was fifteen years old.

She was awake again in the dusky light of dawn as her mother came quietly down the stairs and headed to the kitchen to make coffee. Hailey hadn't come in yet from Seabreeze, which gave Lindy an unsettled feeling, and she was glad to think of seeing her mother, who was one of the few people in the family who didn't seem to be mad at her right now.

Lindy waited for Greta to cross to the front of the cottage, heading for the deck and the sunrise. "Mom?"

"Oh, I didn't mean to wake you," Greta said softly, with a mild note of alarm.

"You didn't." Lindy scooted closer to the back of the couch so her mother could sit beside her again, the way she had the other morning when Lindy had first told her that David was missing, that David hadn't shown up for his own birthday party.

That felt like years ago.

Greta sat down, set her coffee on the table, and reached to hold Lindy's hand atop the blanket. "My poor girl."

Lindy blinked back tears. "Poor you," she managed to say. "Your fiftieth anniversary." They'd never even eaten dinner last night, let alone had celebratory lobsters.

Greta smiled a little. "It's all right. As long as I still have Tom, everything's all right."

Lindy squeezed her mother's hand, wanting to cry again at the thought of her father slipping away, even as she remembered the sight of her mother with the gun.

Was everything "all right," really? To be losing your husband of fifty years this way must be simply intolerable. Just as bad, if not worse, as what Lindy was going through right now.

The gun, she had to think, must have been a cry for help.

But she didn't know how to ask her mother about the more profound things, so she just spoke bluntly about the most concrete. "Mom. Why did you pull a gun on Noah? Why do you even have a gun?"

Greta gave another small, involuntary smile and pulled her hand from Lindy's. She folded her hands in her lap and looked down at them.

Lindy propped herself up. "You said it's been here a long time. Does Dad know about it? Seriously, you're not planning to hurt yourself, are you? Or . . . hurt Dad?"

Greta looked at her then, still smiling slightly. "That's a lot of questions for so early in the morning after a night like the night you had." She spoke rhythmically, as if she were playing a sonata, and Lindy had a sudden flash of memory of Greta reading poems to her when she was a very little girl. She'd forgotten about that. Her favorite had been one about a witch. What was that? She would have to ask her mother. But not now. (Those words Greta had just spoken had *not* been reassuring.)

"Please answer me, Mom. No more secrets, remember? We agreed."

Greta sighed. Her eyes flashed to her coffee on the table and then to the deck outside, as if she was craving escape. Then she looked back down. "Your uncle Harrison gave it to me. For protection. Right after the war. We put it in the attic, and I hardly ever thought about it again."

Greta had said before that the gun had always been up there; still, Lindy's heart thundered. "Does it work? I mean, the boys have been staying up there since they were little. You had a gun up there that whole time?"

"I suppose it works. But it was in a place where they never would have found it."

"Who's to say they wouldn't have found it!" Lindy had managed to go a whole two minutes without being angry at her mother, but that was over now.

"Oh, please, Lindy. You don't . . . you don't understand."

"Was that the reason you didn't want me to go up there when I was a kid? Was that the reason you wouldn't let it be my room?"

"No. No, it wasn't."

There was something defeated-seeming in her mother's manner that made Lindy take pity on her, dial it down a notch. She reminded herself about the anniversary. About everything her mother was losing, the gradual eking away of it, which must have felt like a slow-drip torture. "Okay. Well. We have to get it out of there. Before the boys come back." Not that they were children anymore, but still. "Okay? You'll show me where it is, and we'll get rid of it?"

"I . . . I don't like to go up there . . ." Greta began, but then stopped herself.

"What is it, Mom?"

Greta didn't answer, just shook her head.

"Oh, Mom." Lindy sighed.

"I . . . I'm sorry," Greta said, and Lindy would have expected there to be more, but Greta said nothing else. And Lindy saw the shadow of something long-ago on her mother's face, and it spurred a new memory.

The firelight flickered on David's face. It was 1985, seven weeks after David had gotten out of the hospital in Blue Hill. He was studying hard for the bar exam, eating every hamburger and steak his mother put in front of him, and walking a mile or two a day on his aching knee.

Lindy had hesitated to go back up into the woods, to the old campsite, but David had insisted. Toby and Mike weren't around anymore; they hadn't been in a long time. Toby's family had sold their place, and Mike, having headed to college in Seattle some years ago, hadn't been back in four or five summers. The campsite was overgrown; Lindy and

David had had to clean fallen branches and leaves out of the old fire ring.

It had been seven years since David had slit his wrist inside the tent up here—so why did the place still feel haunted? Lindy was *not* going to spend the night up here, ever. She would insist he didn't, either.

"I still like it up here," he was saying. "It was never that I didn't like it."

Lindy shivered a little. She still loved The Cove, loved Innisfree more than any place else in the world, but she would really be glad to have seen the last of this old campsite.

David had seen the shiver. "I think it's important to confront things," he said. "Otherwise, they lurk. They attack you from behind."

Lindy flinched at the sounds of a branch cracking, leaves rustling, in the forest nearby. She could only hope it was a squirrel. "I don't like to think that's true," she said.

"I don't like to feel surrounded," David went on. "I like to be out at the edge of things. That's why I went all the way to Eastport, this last time. It's the first place in the United States to see the sun rise, you know? And I thought if I could get to the end of the road, and to the beginning of something else, I'd feel better."

This made no sense to Lindy. She cupped her hand over her belly. She hadn't told David yet; she wouldn't mention even the possibility of the baby till she was a hundred percent sure. "But, at the end of the road, you've got nowhere left to go."

"Exactly," David said. "It's where you make your last stand."

CHAPTER 39

Hailey

Friday, July 30, 2010
8 a.m.

"What do you mean, she left?" Hailey said to her grandma, who was stirring a pot of oatmeal at the stove, looking distressed. Four women in green polo shirts—the cleaning crew for tomorrow's now-canceled anniversary party—were hauling in vacuums, mops, and buckets loaded with cleaning supplies through the back door. Hailey'd just banged in through the side screen door. She couldn't believe she'd fallen asleep at Jack's house, and her guilty conscience conjured the wild thought that maybe her mom was on the way to snitch to Noah. "Is she going to Portland?"

"No." Grandma shuddered slightly. She was totally ignoring the parade of green-shirted women through the house. "Eastport."

"What? Where *is* that, even?" For a moment this morning, upon waking, Hailey's headache had been absent, but it was coming back in full force now. Just then, she spotted a note on the counter and recognized her mom's handwriting: *H, Noah called 10 p.m. Told him you were asleep. I assume you were? Love, Mom*

Crap, Hailey thought. *Crap, crap, crap.*

Her grandma was answering her question about Eastport. "All the way to the eastern edge of the state. She said she thinks it's about a six-hour drive. I didn't want her to go, but I couldn't stop her."

Tiffany and Raj came down the stairs, Raj calling out, "Good morning!" Hailey wondered where her grandpa was; the thought that he was probably upstairs "working on his book" sent a cascade of sadness through her.

"What's going on?" Tiffany said. She was wearing another brand-new camping outfit straight off the pages of the Eddie Bauer summer catalog. "We got some intel on David?"

"Oh my God," Hailey muttered. She grabbed her mom's note off the counter and crumpled it up before anyone else could see it.

"I started to think, what if he *did* just go camping?" Hailey's mom's voice sounded far away at the other end of the line, as Hailey pressed the old landline phone closer to her ear. The green-shirted women seemed to be everywhere—washing the windows, dusting the baseboards, carting a vacuum upstairs. Grandma, Tiffany, and Raj were all in the kitchen, eating oatmeal and pretending not to be eavesdropping on Hailey's conversation. Outside, gulls were crying over the calm blue sea, as a lobster boat with a bright red hull motored past.

"What?" Hailey said. She had thought, last night, that she had clearly put herself in charge of the search. Now her mom was going rogue?

"I mean, I didn't put it together last night when we were making our list of evidence," Lindy said, "but when the twins and I were down in Cranston earlier in the week, Eli looked for the camping gear, and it was gone. That was part of what made me think he was off with Tiffany."

Hailey interrupted. "Dad always puts the camping gear in the car anytime he's driving up to Maine. He always thinks maybe he'll just find some time." She thought her mom should have remembered that.

"That's true! But I was so fixated on the idea that he was with Tiffany that I didn't even think about that. I suppose I assumed that he certainly wouldn't have planned to go camping in the middle of everything we had going on!"

"Okay?" Hailey thought of Jack saying, *It makes sense she'd be going insane, right?*

Lindy went on. "And then, this whole time, we've all been so focused on thinking that, if he wasn't with Tiffany, he had to be hurt, or something must have happened to him. But when I thought of it early this morning, I realized he *could* have just gone camping by himself! I mean, I hate to think he'd have just gone off and done that thoughtlessly, but it is better than the alternative—"

Hope was flaring in Hailey. "That could explain why we haven't seen any charges on your credit cards! Remember how he's always restocking the dehydrated food supply, too?" Hailey and her siblings had always teased him about that, and about his excitement whenever REI introduced a new variety of beef stew or chicken noodle casserole that he could add to the stash that lived in the tote in the garage, waiting for its big day. *This stuff lasts for thirty years!* he would gleefully say. "Maybe he just went camping with supplies he already had. He would've had plenty of cash to pay for campsites for a few days, even if he was only using the three hundred dollars from the ATM."

"Yeah, that's what I was thinking!" Hailey's mom said.

Quickly, though, Hailey wondered: Would her dad really have missed his own birthday party? Not even called?

But they really needed some hope to hang on to. Hailey wouldn't bring up the implausibility of it all. "But, Mom, Eastport? Why are you going all the way up there to look for him? Grandma said it's, like, six hours away."

"I remembered something he said to me once about it. Call it a hunch, I guess. I mean, it doesn't explain the missing money, but . . . if he did go all the way up there and we haven't heard from him yet, I'm afraid he might be hurt in the woods somewhere, just like we'd been thinking, only in a different spot!" She actually sounded cheerful about the prospect that he could've blown out his knee or fallen off some cliff. Hailey's head was hurting worse again.

Lindy went on. "Do me a favor and let your brothers and sister know? I don't think I'll have signal much longer. Just so you know, I tried Cody but haven't reached him yet. I haven't told Kate and Josh yet, either. I think maybe I can find David before they're any the wiser! Kate was taking it so hard. I don't want her to suffer any more than she has to, you know?"

Hailey blinked back sudden tears. Her mom was totally abandoning not only her usual commitment to total honesty, but also her usual MO of making sure everybody was all right before she did anything else.

Had she seriously just taken off by herself, heading for the farthest, wildest reaches of Downeast Maine—on a "hunch"? Without even telling the rest of the family about it?

Was Hailey going to end up with *both* her parents lost in the wild?

"You should've waited for me, Mom. Or for someone. Where are you even going to stay once you get up there? It's too far to turn around and come back, and I can't believe—" Hailey cut herself off before she could say any more of the whole swirl of stuff that was in her head: *You're making such terrible decisions, you lied, you made the twins lie, you left me all alone when I'm supposed to get married a week from tomorrow and you've clearly forgotten all about the wedding and I don't know what to do!*

She took a breath, reminding herself that it made sense for Lindy to be acting insane right now.

"I've got a . . . No time . . ." was all Hailey heard, as the line had started to crackle.

"What, Mom?"

"Oh, honey, I think I'm losing signal—" Lindy said, then she was gone.

Hailey looked at the receiver in her hand for a second, then hung up and redialed her mom's cell phone.

No answer.

Unbelievable.

The lobster boat was out of sight now, but the gulls still wheeled and cried. Hailey glanced toward the back of the cottage, toward Tiffany, Raj, and Grandma in the kitchen. Caught at their eavesdropping, all pretended suddenly not to be paying any attention to her at all. Grandma grabbed the coffee pot and began to pour, as Tiffany and Raj exclaimed how delicious the oatmeal had been. Upstairs, a vacuum whirred into action, while from the next room came the squeak of a paper towel wiping a window clean. The scene—people acting like things were normal—felt jarring, unreal.

Hailey needed to call Noah. And Emma. But she wasn't going to get any privacy unless she left this house.

She'd arranged to meet Jack in an hour. They had their plan for searching the lighthouses of southern Maine . . .

But she was pretty sure now that she ought to follow her mom to Eastport instead—just to make sure Lindy had support, or didn't get lost herself? (Or else just to try to get her *back*?)

Or because a hunch from Lindy seemed to carry much more weight, suddenly, than what Reese had "heard" days ago?

Because it *was* true that Hailey's dad would've had all the equipment with him in the car that he'd need for camping. Hailey should ask Emma to check if the little tote with the camping food in it was gone, too.

Okay, so she didn't have privacy. She still needed to make these calls, and Noah had to come first, though she dreaded it. She turned her back on the kitchen, looking out the front windows toward the ocean and the morning sun. She picked up the receiver and dialed the number.

In her ear, Noah's phone rang and rang. It was still early; he must have his ringer silenced. *Damn it.*

The automatic voice came on. The beep sounded. "Uh, hey. Noah?" She didn't know what to say about the wedding, or about her threat last night to call it off. He *had* returned her call . . . "I'm sorry I missed you last night. So, now I need to go Downeast to help look for my dad. I need to get going right away, so don't worry about coming to help. I'll try to call you as soon as I can, but I might not have signal. Sorry," she said, and hung up.

Lame, she thought then, and the word applied to her, him, the message she'd just left, their whole relationship. *We're supposed to be getting married in eight days.*

She needed to actually talk with him. But right now, the truth was, making sure her mom and dad were okay was more important.

She could *not* invite Jack to come along Downeast.

But if she didn't, then she would be out there in the wilderness on her own, too.

Unless she invited Tiffany and Raj to come with her. Or Grandma and Grandpa.

No. And no.

What about Aunt Kate? No, because that would be betraying Lindy's hope of sheltering Kate and Josh from learning that David was still missing. Anyway, Hailey couldn't ask Aunt Kate to leave her kids.

Hailey could call her siblings, ask them to come up, wait for them. But for them even to get to The Cove would take hours—however long it took them to get their acts together, plus at least five hours of driving time—by which point who knew where their mom would be. And Hailey didn't exactly feel up to managing all their hurt feelings and fears. Her own were bad enough.

As it was, if Hailey got in the car right now, she'd be only about two hours behind her mom. Lindy had said she was heading directly for Eastport and that she thought it was a small enough town that she should just be able to find David's car, if he was there.

(Again: Lindy was definitely going off the deep end.)

But this also meant, if Hailey hurried, she'd likely be able to find her mom in Eastport the same way. If Hailey waited, and Lindy got there and couldn't find David, then Lindy would surely head off God knew where else on some other "hunch." Hailey would have no prayer of finding her, then.

Hailey pressed her fingers to her temple. It was clearly up to her to save *both* her parents now. She'd have to do whatever it took. Even if that meant driving up to the edge of the map alone.

She popped one of her prescription pills, threw together an overnight bag, and took off driving north through the woods on her own, over her grandma's protests. She would call Jack once she had signal and tell him to pass off the plan they'd written up last night for searching the lighthouses of southern Maine to Tiffany and Raj. The pair had already told Hailey enthusiastically that they'd be glad to execute it, still apparently believing they were contestants on *The Amazing Race* or something and that they might win.

Fifteen minutes after she left The Cove, as soon as she got into signal range, her voicemail dinged.

She struggled through dialing in as she drove. There was a message from Noah, from last night. She'd never heard him sound so angry. He also sounded drunk. "How dare you give me an ultimatum, after what your grandmother did to me? And then not even answer the fucking phone? You should be on your knees to me, after everything I've done for you, after everything I've put up with, after how long I've waited for you to come through for me and you not being there for me! You think your family is so much more important than I am, and I see now you're never gonna support me or care about me, you're always gonna be putting yourself and your family first . . ." It went on and on. Hailey couldn't really comprehend it all. But at the end she definitely heard him say that *he* was calling off the wedding and for her to come get her stuff out of his apartment ASAP.

She clicked off the call and tossed the phone onto the seat beside her. She took both hands off the wheel to remove her ring. She dropped it into the beverage holder, then inhaled deeply three times, managing to hold off tears of rage and dismay.

She was approaching a countryside church and slowed to pull into the parking lot. She picked up her phone again and texted Noah. *Got your message. Ignore the voicemail I left this morning. We're done. I'll text you about getting my stuff.*

She bit her lip, her finger hovering over the Send button.

She tried to remember what her mom had said the other day about how a path could seem like the exact right one until suddenly it wasn't. She tried to think, *Thank God this came out before the wedding and not after.* This . . . what? Narcissism? Had he really just been putting on the charm these last *three years*? Only to have it all unravel practically overnight just because she put her family first in a time of crisis?

God, it sucked, though. She really had thought she loved him.

Also, it was going to be embarrassing. A hundred and seventeen guests were on the way, expecting a lobster bake, Hailey in her gown . . .

Okay. That didn't matter. *What if you were married to an unsupportive asshole?*

She clicked Send and tossed her phone back onto the seat beside her. She rubbed her temple, trying to think of all the things she needed to do to let everybody—guests, vendors, bridesmaids, caterers, bakers, everyone—know that the wedding was off. The list seemed instantly endless. And she was not going to get her or her parents' money back on basically anything.

She let out a big breath. Okay, *none* of that even mattered right now. Right now, she had to go to Eastport and find her mom. And—hopefully, hopefully!—her dad.

She picked up her phone again and dialed another number. This one she knew by heart because she'd dialed it from Innisfree all the time, years ago.

Marjorie Westfield picked up on the first ring. "Hi, Marjorie," Hailey said. "May I speak to Jack, please?"

A minute later, she pulled out onto the road, turning south to head back for The Cove. Jack was coming with her to Eastport.

"Oh my God, she did what?" Emma barked, her voice emanating from Hailey's cell. The highway stretched out in front of Hailey's Protegé as she sped along tree-lined Route 1 North. Jack was in the passenger seat looking up something on his phone, the Maine atlas and lighthouse book at his feet. Hailey had her call on speaker; Jack knew all her secrets, anyway. Or most of them. Obviously, she hadn't told either him or her sister about Noah yet. How long before Jack noticed she wasn't wearing her ring? "And you're *following* her?" Emma said.

Hailey explained again, and, by the time she finished, Eli was back on the line from checking the garage. "Yeah, the camping food tote is gone," he said.

"Oh! Well, that's good, right? Maybe he *is* just off camping somewhere! Have you guys found anything else on the computer?"

"Not really," Eli said. "I keep checking the credit cards for activity, but there hasn't been any."

"That's a good idea. Keep doing that."

"Hell if you think you're gonna head up into the wilds of Maine looking for our parents and we're gonna sit here in Cranston," Emma said. "I'm calling Cody right now to get him to come up here, then we're all going to be on our way to fucking Eastport, Maine, in about an hour from now."

The pill Hailey had taken was keeping her migraine at bay, but for a second it thrummed at her temple, reminding her it could explode to full force again at any minute. "I think Jack and I have it covered. You guys should just keep checking the accounts."

"That doesn't take three of us," Eli said.

And shortly, it was decided that, as soon as Emma could get a hold of Cody to tell him so, Emma and Cody would be following Hailey up to Eastport to try to find their parents, while Eli stayed in Cranston to monitor the landline phone there, keep searching through their dad's files, and keep an eye on their dad's accounts on the computer.

When Hailey hung up, Jack was still clicking around on his phone. "It doesn't look like there are many hotels up there," he said, "and most of them are fully booked."

She rubbed her temple. Last night, she'd fallen asleep on top of Jack's white comforter while reading the lighthouse book, then woken up to find he'd covered her with a blanket and crawled in under the sheets and was sleeping beside her, his hands folded over his chest. She'd spent several minutes awake, telling herself she *had* to get up and get back to Innisfree—Noah would be calling, her mom would be worried—but she'd fallen back to sleep instead. She and Jack had slept side by side all night, and they had not touched each other at all.

If she'd known that Noah had already left her a message calling off the wedding, she might've . . . well. Rolled over to Jack's side of the bed and let him and Fate take it from there? Yeah, pretty much, she would've.

And now her heart had just accelerated at the thought of possibly having to share a hotel room with him tonight.

Just what she needed. A chance to act like an idiot, at just the moment her entire future had been shattered.

"Do you think your mom booked a place?" Jack asked.

"Oh! Yeah. Probably!" That would fix everything. Hailey could stay with her mom. Or, even if both she and Jack needed to stay with her mom, that would keep Hailey from doing anything totally stupid.

But thinking of her mom reminded Hailey: She was *not* supposed to have called off the wedding.

Well, she hadn't. Noah had.

Still, it was going to upset her mom for sure. Especially on top of everything else. Hailey rubbed her temple again.

"You okay, Hales?" Jack said. "Want me to drive?"

Hailey glanced over at him. "I'm okay for now," she said, amazed again at how he paid attention. She could really get used to that, she thought.

CHAPTER 40

Lindy

Friday, July 30, 2010
1 p.m.

Being alone—really alone—was weird. No kids, no David. Nobody. And, without cell signal, no possibility even of anyone calling to say they needed something.

Lindy turned on the car radio, and every station was playing songs from her teenage years or earlier. She sang along to "What a Fool Believes," "Lay Down Sally," "I Want to Know What Love Is," "More Than a Feeling." All made her think of her parents, of the nights both in New York and at Innisfree when her mother would put some new LP on the stereo and, always with a martini in her hand, pull Lindy's laughing father up to dance. Of the days when her mom would bring her to smoky-smelling record shops in the city and lift her up to file through the bins, telling her some piece of trivia about nearly every artist. Her mother was no classical music snob; she thought Dylan was a genius, and she loved The Jackson 5, The Moody Blues, Foreigner, Diana Ross, and on and on. Lindy had found it all very embarrassing.

Now she would've loved to see her parents dancing again, would've given anything to know they had years and years of dancing ahead of them.

When "Like a Rolling Stone" came on, she sang along until the line about being "on your own" made her start to cry. Her eyes already burned with exhaustion; the last thing she needed was more tears. She flipped off the radio, wiped her eyes, and drove in the quiet through the rolling blueberry hills. She'd never been farther east than Blue Hill before. The landscape was growing increasingly wild, rough, and beautiful, and the sky was broad and cloud-studded.

As the horizon stretched wider and wider, her decision to come up here—especially alone—began to seem more and more foolish. The odds of finding David up here were obviously slim.

What was beginning to seem more likely was that this vast wilderness would swallow Lindy up instead.

Eastport was definitely the end of the road. It was located on an island, accessible only by a causeway, according to the map. Lindy turned off the main highway onto a flat, broad road lined in short, leafy trees and tough-looking pines. Soon, she passed a sign that said Eastport was seven miles away.

Seven more miles! She had to pee. She'd had to for the last hour; there'd been no place to stop.

Seven more miles. And then, maybe, she'd find David's car.

She tried to convince herself it was possible. A small town on a small island. Of course she could travel every road! Of course their paths would cross, inevitably!

If he was there.

The sun was bright and hot. It was the middle of the day, and even this far north, everything shimmered in the summer heat. The road was lined in white bursts of wildflowers, with just the occasional small house punctuating the wilderness, quarter mile by quarter mile.

Lindy felt a million miles from Summerland Cove.

To her right, the beginnings of a marshy-looking bay came into view. This was Passamaquoddy country, a sign had said, and soon she was passing a cluster of low-to-the-ground houses, then a large maintenance building that announced itself as the Passamaquoddy Tribal Public Safety Building.

In the distance, past another small collection of neatly kept trailer and ranch-style homes, came the view of a larger bay, and then she was on the mile-long rock-lined causeway, blue water gleaming to either side. The tide was low, exposing mud flats; the expansive view was breathtaking. If she and David had been on vacation, she would've insisted they stop to take a photo.

He could be anywhere, she thought suddenly, shaken. A fresh stack of *MISSING* posters fluttered in the passenger seat, weighed down by her purse. *He might not be near here at all. And his heart. His knee. God knows . . .*

Was she just wasting time? *On a fool's errand,* as David would say?

She couldn't think that. She bit her lip, squared her shoulders, and kept driving.

Entering town, she stopped at a small IGA supermarket, used the bathroom, bought an iced tea. She posted a *MISSING* flyer on the bulletin board in the foyer, touching the picture of David's face lightly before she turned away. Did she know him anymore? How could she even begin to imagine, after all this, that she could predict what he would have done, where he might have gone?

But she was here now. She had to try.

She climbed back into the Volvo and drove slowly along the quiet street, passing a couple small, abandoned-looking warehouses, a pretty white church, a new-looking little bank, and a series of old frame houses. Some had gardens of phlox and coreopsis, daylilies and hostas. Most of the gardens looked overgrown, tired of making a stand.

A few blocks later, past a big building made of giant granite blocks—maybe an old customs house—the street ended at a row of brick storefronts labeled *1887.* The harbor was visible behind them. Lindy turned right and drove slowly along a downtown street lined with restored historic buildings. She searched for David's Subaru among the parked cars angled in toward the curb on the right-hand side. Families meandered the sidewalks in front of the shops and galleries, eating post-lunch ice cream cones. At a break in the buildings on the water side was a twelve-foot-tall statue of a bearded old salt in a yellow rain jacket and nor'easter hat clutching a giant fish. Another thing she would've stopped to take a picture of, in normal times.

She saw a few green Subarus, but none had Rhode Island plates. As the storefronts dwindled, she passed a diner where people sat on a deck under red-and-white striped umbrellas, enjoying fried seafood for lunch. Opposite the diner, on the crest of a slight hill, stood a stately old brick library. As Lindy crawled along another block, she spotted a two-story motel that faced the water, a *Vacancy* flag fluttering.

Now *this* was an end-of-the-line place. If David was using cash and *not* camping, this was exactly the kind of place he would likely choose to stay, she thought. She pulled into the parking lot. Her legs trembled as she got out of the Volvo. Heat radiated from the asphalt at the same time a cool breeze drifted in off the water. She got the feeling that this was a place where ghosts lived, and a shiver went up her spine.

"No, he doesn't look familiar," said the lady behind the desk inside the motel office when Lindy showed the picture of David on the *MISSING* poster. The office's brown-paneled walls were covered in framed images of lighthouses and lobsters, plus a variety of illustrated signs that all said the same thing: *Welcome to Maine, The Way Life Should Be.*

"Are you sure? Can you take a closer look?"

The woman peered in again. "No, I'd have remembered him. I like that curly salt-and-pepper hair." She shoved the poster back across the desk. "You need a room?"

Lindy was folding the poster into her purse, feeling defeated already. She had to remind herself: She was just getting started. He was probably camping, anyway. "Um, I don't—"

"We got just one left for tonight. A double queen. Probably the only room in town."

Lindy hadn't thought through where she might spend the night. She had a lot more searching to do in this area, and, even if she didn't, driving back to Innisfree tonight was out of the question. And there seemed to be few, if any, more towns within an hour's drive. "The last room in town?"

"I'd wager."

"I'll take it," Lindy said, pulling out her wallet.

After signing for the reservation—it was too early to get into the room—she drove up and down every street in town looking for the Subaru. She showed David's picture to shopkeepers and innkeepers. She drove the couple miles out of town to a campground on the northeast side of the island. One of the shopkeepers had told her about it, saying it was the only one nearby. Lindy spent half an hour walking the grounds, which featured beautiful waterfront sites with views of Canada in the distance. David would've loved the place, but she saw no sign of his car. She asked at the office, and the host graciously searched her papers from the past week but found no record of David or his Subaru. She said they'd had few vacancies, so if he'd shown up without a reservation, he probably wouldn't have gotten a spot. She also said she didn't remember seeing his face and that she was the one who was in the office most all the time.

It was six o'clock when Lindy gave up on the campground. If David really had set out to go camping, he probably would've chosen a wilder place, anyway.

She realized she was exhausted, ravenous. She'd been on the road since 5:30 this morning, and the campground host had told her to be sure to get dinner soon, because every restaurant in town was apt to close by seven. Lindy made her way back to town and the diner she'd noticed earlier and sat in a booth inside, making notes while she waited for her fish and chips.

What she'd learned today: Eastport would've been the perfect place for David to escape to, if escape had been his aim. But it sure didn't seem like he was here now, or like he'd been here at all this past week.

Did that mean he'd escaped to somewhere else?

Lindy still hated to think of him being so thoughtless. But what were the alternative scenarios? Nothing she liked to think about, either. Murder, injury, heart attack in the backcountry somewhere? All of those ended up with him dead in the woods and never being found at all.

Her fish and chips arrived in a paper-lined red plastic basket. She felt hollow now rather than hungry, but she knew she should eat. She forked into the breaded haddock, steam escaping as the white flesh was exposed. The fish tasted salty and fresh and restorative, and she tried to encourage herself: Even the police knew that a fifty-year-old white man on his own was no doubt fine.

Also, there were a lot of other places Lindy could still look, even if not in Eastport proper. She'd learned there was another significant town nearby, Lubec. Just a couple miles away across the water, it was an hour's drive on land—twenty minutes west back to the main highway from Eastport, then twenty minutes south, then another twenty minutes east down a peninsula from there. One of the innkeepers she'd spoken to had said that a point over there was actually the easternmost point in the continental U.S. because it was two miles farther east than Eastport.

So, maybe *that* was where David would've gone. It had been twenty-five years since he'd told her about Eastport being the first place in the continental U.S. to see the sun rise every day. It seemed likely he would've since learned that he'd been slightly mistaken about that.

LUBEC, Lindy wrote in her notebook in all caps, underlining the word three times for good measure. Yes. She would gather all the brochures and materials she could find about the entire area, and about Lubec in particular—any campgrounds, hotels, hiking trails, bed and breakfasts, anything—and spend the night studying them. She'd make a plan and set out fresh tomorrow.

She would try to keep her hopes up that David wasn't gone forever.

"Mom?" Lindy heard a familiar-sounding voice, and she looked up from her half-eaten haddock to see Hailey walking into the restaurant, trailed by Jack Westfield. For a second, she had the strange sensation that she might be dreaming. Or that maybe she wasn't actually in Eastport, because why would Hailey and Jack be in Eastport?

Hailey slid into the booth across from her, looking flushed, sweaty, and very real. "There you are! We've been looking all over for you. We saw your car parked outside." Jack slid in beside Hailey and gave Lindy a little smile in greeting.

Okay, you are not my daughter's groom, Lindy thought, but she didn't have it in her to ask questions right now. "It's a good thing I wasn't trying to hide out, I guess," she said, still feeling off-balance and strange. If they had found her this easily, why hadn't she been able to find David? And then she knew for certain: He simply was not here.

"Any sign of Dad?" Hailey said, in a tone that implied she would be speaking to Lindy seriously about Lindy's actions after the dust of all this had settled. It was a tone so like the one Lindy would sometimes take with her kids that it almost made her smile, despite the bad news she had to deliver.

"No, honey, I'm sorry." She slid her basket of remaining french fries across the table, but Hailey and Jack just looked at her with sad eyes, and Hailey let out a big sigh.

Lindy hated to see Hailey's sorrow, at the same time she hoped the fact that Hailey and Jack had followed her up here was a sign that at least Hailey might be in the process of forgiving her. But seeing them across the table also made her realize that she'd come up here on her own in hopes that, if she could find David, she could redeem herself in everybody's eyes for the lie she'd told—and even keep Kate and Josh from finding out about it at all.

Now that fantasy was over, and Lindy was stuck with the reality: She had not the first clue where David actually was.

Trying to keep the worst possibilities at bay, she told Hailey and Jack about Lubec. It was too late to search there tonight, she explained. It would be dark before they could get over there, and, if that town was like this one, everything would be closed, and there wouldn't be anywhere to stay. But, tomorrow, maybe they would find him there. "He told me he was looking for the end of one road and the beginning of another. He said he wanted to be in the first place in America to see the light!"

"Okay, Mom," Hailey said patiently, though the look she gave Lindy was the kind you'd give someone when you were wondering if they'd lost their mind.

CHAPTER 41

Hailey

Friday, July 30, 2010
7:30 p.m.

Back at the motel, while Jack studied maps up in the room, Hailey and her mom went to the office to use the pay phone, holding the receiver between them and leaning in. Greta, glad to hear they were all safe, reported that Innisfree was the cleanest it had ever been, and that Tiffany and Raj had called and, having had no luck with the lighthouses of southern Maine, were spending the night near Portland. Eli, in Cranston, had nothing to report from the computer end of things. Emma, on the road with Cody, said Cody hadn't been able to leave work till three, so they'd gotten stuck in Boston traffic and would be stopping at Innisfree for the night. Cody didn't say a word the entire call, as Hailey, Lindy, and Emma arranged a time to talk in the morning, landline to landline, to make a plan to meet.

"Cody must be furious with me," Hailey's mom said, shaking her head after they hung up. It was true he normally would've been throwing in his two cents at every opportunity, but Hailey, not wanting to hurt her mom's feelings, just shrugged. Lindy sighed, waved toward the phone. "I know we should call Kate, but I just . . . I just can't. I'll go now so you can give Noah a call."

Hailey's stomach whirred. She shook her head. "Can we talk outside, Mom?"

In the parking lot, she told her mom about the voicemail from Noah that she'd found this morning. About the wedding being off. Even about how, when she'd gone back to The Cove to pick up Jack, she'd stopped at Innisfree to stash her engagement ring upstairs, because she'd wanted it out of her sight. "I'm so sorry, Mom. I really wanted—"

Lindy broke in with a tiny smile. "I guess that explains why Jack is here."

Hailey's face heated up. This was not the reaction she'd expected. "You're not mad? All that . . . money. I don't know if we can get any of it back."

Her mom hugged her tightly. "I'm not mad, honey. I'm sorry you have to go through this. But I just want you to be happy. I mean, I noticed . . . when I visited Noah in Portland? Anyway, maybe this will be for the best. If you're okay?"

"Yeah, I'm okay, Mom," Hailey said, even if she did still feel shaken up like she'd been in a fender bender.

That it didn't feel like a ten-car pileup, she realized, was probably another sign that calling the wedding off had been the right thing.

Two hours later, in the motel bed beside her mom, Hailey couldn't sleep. She was conscious of Jack in the other bed. She didn't think he was sleeping, either.

Her mom definitely was, though, which was weird. Did Lindy truly believe that they were going to find Hailey's dad tomorrow way up here at the far edge of Maine?

And wasn't Lindy worried at all about Hailey, about Hailey's future, now that the wedding was off?

Impossible, Hailey thought. *She* was not going to be able to sleep. She crept out of bed and tiptoed across the moonlit room toward the balcony, past Jack's bed. When he propped himself on his elbows with a questioning look, she gestured for him to come outside with her, then slid the door open.

She was wearing a sweatshirt and boxers and hugged herself to stave off the chill in the air as she sat down in one of the chairs. Jack emerged and shut the door behind him. He sat beside her and softly asked how she was doing.

"My brain won't calm down," she said, then gestured to the horizon, the small lights of a boat out on the black water, Canada across the way. The damp air smelled of fish and salt. "I mean, where even *are* we?"

"It is a magical and very strange place," Jack said, in a tone implying agreement.

"And where the hell is my dad?"

Jack sighed, leaning back with his hands folded over his stomach. "You ever heard of the concept of surrender?" he said, and she felt chastised.

"Of course I have."

"So, if you surrendered right now to the flow of the universe, what would that look like?"

"I am not about to surrender to the fact of my dad being gone!"

Jack sighed. "I know, Hales. That wasn't what I meant."

She sighed, too, swallowing back tears. She looked out at the water, appreciating the cool breeze now, though her legs were covered in goose bumps. She realized her head didn't hurt at all. Also weird. It definitely *should* hurt right now, given everything.

"I think we're going to find him, Hales," Jack said. "I really do."

She looked at him. She'd spent so many years telling herself that Jack was gone and didn't care about her. Had it taken her till right this minute to understand that he *was* here—and he *did* care? And that maybe letting him in a little bit more might not be the foolish mistake she'd been telling herself all day that it would be?

"I hope you're right," she said. She looked back toward the horizon, the lights on the black water. She took a breath. "You know, I think what surrendering to the flow of the universe right now would look like is being right here. I mean, it's not like I planned this. It's not like this is somewhere I intended to go. Or like any of this is something I wanted to have happen."

Jack laughed. "True! Me, too, I guess. You're right, we wouldn't be here otherwise."

She knew then that the conversation had shifted from talking about her dad to talking about all that had happened to bring her and Jack together when everything inside her had been telling her—starting seven years ago—that it wasn't meant to be and the feelings she had for him weren't even real, or at least not destined to last. It seemed too much to believe that he might've been believing something similar? But he *had* recently told her that he'd loved her back then.

"I guess that's true," she said carefully, and a sense of peace came over her. She would not be marrying Noah next week. And it wasn't because of Jack. And the reason she felt peaceful now wasn't because she imagined she and Jack would "end up together," but simply because of the peace she felt in this moment at being with him. She realized that she had never felt this way with Noah—and that life was both too long to rush into marrying someone she didn't feel that way about and too short to live another day in a relationship where she didn't have that feeling.

"So," Jack said, clearly unaware that she'd just had an epiphany. "Then what would it look like to surrender a little more?"

She smiled, because it was funny how clear that answer seemed, too, and she reached out and took hold of his hand where it rested on the arm of his chair.

He smiled. "Hales," he said, like he was scolding her, but he didn't let go, and, despite everything, she laughed.

She looked out at the lights on the horizon again. "So. You might have noticed I'm not wearing my ring?"

A tiny pause, then: "I figured it wasn't my place to bring it up."

She glanced over just long enough to see his slight smile, then looked back at the water so she wouldn't lose her nerve. "Well, I'm not getting married! Noah called it off. I told him I was going to call it off if he didn't call me back and help search for my dad, then he called me and said *he* was calling it off because I thought my family was more important than him."

Jack squeezed her hand, a tiny, perfect show of sympathy. "That sounds like a very healthy relationship."

She laughed again. "Shut up," she said, and they sat there together looking out at the lights on the water and at Canada beyond, holding tightly to each other's hands.

CHAPTER 42

Hailey

Saturday, July 31, 2010
5 a.m.

Hailey awoke as the first rays of light began filtering in through the motel room's sliding door, and she propped herself up from where she lay in bed beside Jack. Last night, when they'd finally snuck back inside, she'd simply crawled in beside him, resting her head on his shoulder and her arm across his chest, while her mom slept on in the other bed. He'd sighed as he rested his hand on her forearm but made no move to hold or kiss her. *No kissing, that's good,* she'd thought, honestly just because her mom was right there, and because she was kind of relieved not to have to wonder what it would all mean. The sound of his breathing and his heartbeat had lulled her quickly to sleep.

Now, despite everything, she was thrilled to sense the oncoming sunrise. Whatever part of her dad or her grandma was in her would *not* allow her to miss being one of the first people in the continental U.S. to see it.

Besides, she didn't exactly want her mom to know that she'd slept in Jack's bed, even if it had been totally innocent.

She got up, being quiet so as not to wake anybody, and went out to the balcony. She pulled her feet up into the chair and wrapped her arms around her legs to keep warm, watching the horizon brighten by slow degrees, wondering where her dad could be, wondering how true it was that she'd saved him, years ago, just by being born. She remembered a time when she was about eight and she'd been brokenhearted over a bird that had crashed into a window and died, and he'd sat down beside her, put his big hand on her back, and said to her sadly, "The truth is you can't save everybody, honey, though your mother would disagree."

And just like that, her mind started scrolling through the list of things she needed to do, not just to cancel her wedding, but to totally rearrange her life.

If her dad never appeared, how would any of it even feel possible?

And then the top edge of the sun poked above the horizon, and Hailey held her breath, waiting for the whole globe of it to appear.

Jack went out in search of coffee while Hailey and Lindy took turns showering. As her mom finished up, Hailey went to the motel office to call Emma. The clerk gave her a message from Eli that had come in late last night, so she called him instead.

He answered sounding like she'd woken him up, but he didn't waste time with preamble. "There's a new charge on Dad's interest-free card," he said. "Made two days ago. I guess it took some time to come through. Forty bucks at a grocery store in Lubec, Maine. That's right by where you guys are."

"Lubec! We were planning to go there today! Oh my God, this means he's okay!"

"Unless his card was stolen. Otherwise, I guess Mom's hunch about him going way up there was right."

"Mom said Lubec's actually the easternmost point in the U.S.!"

"West Quoddy Head is, actually." Eli had clearly done his research last night. "It's a point a few miles south of Lubec. There's a lighthouse there and a state park. It sticks out a little farther east than Lubec does."

"A lighthouse? Seriously?" Hailey laughed. She said goodbye and hung up, then called Innisfree. Grandma answered, and Hailey told her not to wake Emma, just to tell her to stay put for now. "Because maybe he's camping right there by the lighthouse, so maybe we'll be able to find him right away! If we don't, then I'll call Emma to tell her what our next move is." Greta agreed and said good luck and to be careful. Hailey hung up and ran to find her mom.

They all packed up in a hurry while the coffee and cinnamon rolls Jack had returned with sat on the dresser getting cold. Hailey had thought her mom would be thrilled to have her hunch confirmed, but Lindy seemed stunned instead—happy, angry, and bewildered at once. "David really is just up here *camping*?" she said. "I mean, I guess I thought he *might* be, but it really doesn't explain about the money, or why . . ." She shook her head and went back to zipping up her bag. Hailey barely stopped herself from saying that his credit card might've been stolen, and the hundred thousand dollars might've been stolen, too, as if that—her dad still being missing, the victim of a crime—was a better scenario than him being up here camping all week and just casually going to the grocery store in Lubec for supplies.

They set out in both cars, Hailey following her mom's Volvo, Jack in the passenger seat beside her sipping coffee. A feeling of awkwardness began to set in. Out of habit, she rubbed her temple—only to realize that her head wasn't hurting.

"You all right?" Jack said.

"Yeah, I'm okay!" This was a surprise, even to herself, but the lack-of-headache evidence seemed clear. "I mean, if we find my dad, I will be." Now she didn't care how mad her mom was going to be at him. She wanted his credit card not to have been stolen. She *wanted* him to have casually bought forty bucks' worth of groceries in Lubec a couple of days ago, then headed back to wherever he was camping. She hoped he'd been enjoying some peace and quiet, if that was what he needed. She honestly didn't care about anything now except finding him alive and well.

In fact, she couldn't tolerate the idea that they might not, so she started talking as if they already had. "Except I don't know where I'm going to, like, live now. I'm supposed to start school in, like, three weeks."

Jack watched the highway for a moment. "I'm supposed to go back to California around then."

"Well, that sucks," she blurted, then bit her lip.

He laughed a little. "Yeah, it kinda does." He reached for her hand on the steering wheel and traced a line down the center of it with one finger.

She shook off the shiver that his touch caused, shook off the *what ifs* and *maybes* that it had set off tumbling through her brain. "Focus, Westfield," she said. "We're still looking for my dad."

"Right," he said, with a tiny quirk of his mouth, and then he reached for the map.

They'd already agreed Lindy would stop at the Lubec IGA to see if anyone remembered seeing David, while Hailey and Jack would drive the streets looking for the Subaru.

It didn't take long. The downtown here was even smaller than Eastport, and the number of residential streets even fewer. Some storefronts and houses looked abandoned; the whole place gave off a half-empty feeling. The Subaru definitely wasn't here. Jack pointed out the international border gate, the bridge that led to Campobello Island, Canada. Hailey was too busy looking for her dad's car to pay much attention.

Still—no luck.

They met Lindy downtown. After a quick conference between their cars—nobody at the grocery store had remembered seeing David—they headed for Quoddy Head State Park, where the lighthouse was. The flat highway that led out of town was lined with neat houses spaced widely apart and a few leafy trees. Otherwise, open fields provided distant views of the large bay they were traveling around, since Lubec was out at the end of one point and the state park was at the end of the next point to the south.

"I have a strong feeling now," Hailey said, thinking of Reese's certainty about the word *lighthouse*, and of what her mom had said about her dad's old desire to seek out the end of the road, the beginning of the light. "He's just *got* to be camping here."

"I hope so, Hales," Jack said, but his voice sounded uncharacteristically hollow, and she started to wonder if her mom's insanity was catching.

CHAPTER 43

Greta

Saturday, July 31, 2010
8:30 a.m.

Greta was surprised to hear a knock at the side door, and even more surprised when she went over and found Marjorie Westfield standing there holding a pie. It appeared to be blueberry, and apparently was straight out of the oven, as Marjorie wore oven mitts in a William Morris print. Where did a person even get such things? Also, there was no way Marjorie had baked that picture-perfect pie. The only thing she ever made was that insufferable "cookie cake." The pie was no doubt reheated, from Moody's.

"Marjorie," Greta said through the screen. She'd been enjoying the novelty of a quiet house, as Emma and Cody were still asleep upstairs and Lloyd Ralston had come to take Tom down to the SCPA for coffee with the group of neighborhood men who met every Saturday. Lloyd had promised to keep a close eye on Tom and bring him home if he seemed to be getting worn out or confused. Lloyd's manner—not to mention that this was the first time he'd ever stopped by to pick up Tom—made it clear that the entire Cove knew now about Tom's diagnosis. But Tom had been having a good morning and seemed happy to think of walking down to the clubhouse with Lloyd, so Greta hadn't objected.

"Hi, Greta." Marjorie tossed her coiffed silver bob. The William Morris–print oven mitts coordinated precisely with her periwinkle button-up shirt and sage capris. The mitts had golden birds and red berries on them, too, and Marjorie—was it coincidence?—wore dangling gold bird earrings and a necklace of berry-shaped beads interwoven with gold. "May I come in?"

It had been many years since Marjorie Westfield had darkened the door at Innisfree, and Greta supposed now that she had heard not only about Tom's diagnosis but also a lot more details from young Jack—about David's disappearance, possibly even about Greta and the gun. Marjorie was no doubt here to rake up whatever more dirt she could. "The party's canceled," Greta said. It had been scheduled for much later in the day, besides—but it would be just like Marjorie to show up wanting a front-row seat to the devastation.

Though it did seem if she were here for the party, she would've brought a cookie cake, not a pie.

"I know, I just—"

"It's not a good time, Marjorie."

"Just for a moment? Please."

There was an air of desperation about her that Greta had not seen before. She couldn't help being curious. She opened the door. Marjorie walked in, heading for the kitchen. "Do you have a trivet?" she said over her shoulder.

Greta went around to get one out of the drawer. She put it on the counter, and Marjorie set the pie down and gave a trembling smile.

What on earth was going on? Greta had never seen Marjorie not in perfect control.

"I just. Greta. Jack told me about Tom. And I just wanted to say how sorry I am. I'm not sure if you're aware. My husband. Years ago. He—Well, I know what you're going through, is all I wanted to say, and if there's anything I can do, anything at all." There were actual tears in her eyes.

"Thorndike?" Greta said, for this had been the name of Marjorie's husband, who had been dead now more than twenty years. He had been a good ten years older than Marjorie, and he had died over the winter one year, back in Connecticut, so Greta hadn't heard details. "Thorndike had dementia? He would've been so . . . young?"

Marjorie nodded urgently. "It's heartbreaking, just heartbreaking," she said, reaching to squeeze Greta's hand. "And Tom! Tom. He's always been so kind to you, and so obviously in love with you. It's so clear, just looking at the two of you. He's been such a lovely part of The Cove, all these years. Even if . . . even if we didn't see a lot of you two."

Greta could count on one hand the number of times over the past sixty-nine years that she'd spoken with Marjorie at all. After what had happened—the way Marjorie had faded away when they were twelve; the way she'd stopped speaking to Greta; the way she'd been almost cruel in how she'd made it clear to Greta that Rebecca Brock was her best friend now, *not* Greta, even if they'd been best friends since they were six years old before that—well, Greta had not felt friendly to her since then. Not in the sixty-nine years (but who was counting) since then.

"We all were always so glad you found Tom, after what happened to you. We were all so worried that you wouldn't—that you wouldn't get married at all, I guess!"

"What?" Greta said.

"Oh, I don't mean to bring up—I'm sorry. I just think . . . I've always thought . . . you're so *courageous*, Greta. I just wanted to say that to you this morning. I can't even imagine what a hard time your family is going through, between Tom and David . . ."

Greta put her hand on the counter, feeling the sudden need to steady herself. "What do you mean, 'after what happened to me'?"

"The thing with . . . oh, your brother's friend. I'm so sorry, I shouldn't have said . . ."

"How do you . . . how do you know about . . ." Nobody knew. Nobody knew. That was the way Greta had managed to get through her whole life. Nobody knew what had happened to her, what her brother's friend had done to her in the attic at Innisfree when she was twelve.

"Your mother told my mother. Oh, God, I'm sorry. I thought . . . Are you . . . okay? Maybe . . . sit down?" Marjorie took hold of Greta's elbow and guided her to one of the stools at the counter. Greta sank onto it just in time. Her knees had turned to water.

"I'm so sorry!" Marjorie said, and there were fresh tears in her blue eyes. "I shouldn't have said anything."

"My mother knew?"

"Oh, God," Marjorie said again, flinching. She stared for a moment, then turned and hurried to the cupboard and got down a glass. The glasses were in the same place they'd been for eighty years, so she knew right where to go. She filled the glass with water at the sink and set it before Greta on the counter, who was having trouble breathing. "You didn't know your mother knew?"

"No." Greta could feel her eyes filling with tears, her lip beginning to tremble, but she'd be damned if she'd cry in front of Marjorie Westfield. She'd be damned if she'd take a sip of that water, either, though she was suddenly dying of thirst.

Marjorie reached out and squeezed her hand. Greta tried to pull away, but Marjorie kept hold. "Oh, Greta. Didn't you know that anybody knew?"

Greta shook her head. "Nobody knows! Nobody knew!"

"Oh, God," Marjorie said again. She looked away for a moment and then back. She searched deeply into Greta's eyes. "Greta, everybody knew."

"How?" Greta managed.

Marjorie squared her little shoulders, lifted her chin as if about to do battle. But then she spoke very gently. "I guess your brother Harrison was up in the night? And he saw the guy coming down the stairs? Then he saw you looking strange the next day and he saw bruises, and then Cary confronted the guy? I mean, nobody knew details, but they . . . well, I suppose they put two and two together? And your father, I heard he wanted to kill him, and your mother restrained your father, and they sent the guy away first thing that morning? And then your brother Cary, he beat him up badly once they got back to New Haven." This last piece, she finally seemed to know for a fact. "He didn't kill him, but he put him in the hospital. Then I think the guy ended up dying in the war." She stopped, took a breath like a marathon runner, then finished, "That was what I heard."

"I knew he died," Greta spat. "My parents told me." He had been in the Navy, and Greta had seen it in her dreams: the sinking ship, a slick of oil, him screaming and drowning in it. Not less than he deserved, in her view.

She hadn't known anything about Cary beating him up, putting him in the hospital.

"Oh, Greta."

"How could they not ever say?" Greta said. "How could *you*—"

"Oh, God, I don't know! I—my mother told me I should give you space, or whatever the parlance of the day was, it wasn't that, but I was supposed to stay away from you. And it was like she thought you were contagious, like what had happened to you could happen to me, which was horrible, in retrospect, but I didn't know. I just saw you were sad and you had changed, and I didn't know what to say or do, and I didn't understand what had happened, not really. It was just whispers and then, 'Keep your distance; she doesn't want to talk to you right now.'"

This seemed ridiculous. Felt ridiculous. Yet, somehow, Greta believed it with her whole heart. She saw in Marjorie's eyes that it was all true. She saw in Marjorie's eyes that Greta's best friend, a child of ten, was still in there.

Marjorie blinked. Went on. "And then, the more time that passed, the more terrible I felt and the less I knew what to say or do. And I think now that I was just horrible to you. You must have been suffering so badly! And then to find out now that your mother didn't even let on that she knew? That your family and everybody in The Cove knew? I mean, I never told a soul, not even Rebecca, but I think it kind of traveled among the adults, you know, just because they wanted to watch out for you . . ."

Greta wanted to scream. Cry. Break things. She yanked her hand out from under Marjorie's. "I want you out of my house."

Marjorie stood up even straighter, as if invigorated by the challenge.

"No," she said. "I am not leaving you." She went to the cupboard and pulled down two plates. Greta couldn't object; she was busy trying not to vomit. She covered her mouth with her hands. Marjorie opened the drawer and got out a knife and two forks. "Where's your pie server?"

Greta lowered her hands. "Marjorie! Out!"

Marjorie was digging through a drawer and came up with the pie server, triumphant. "Here!"

Now Greta could only cover her face with her hands. She heard the clinking of utensils and plates, and when she lowered her hands and opened her eyes, a slice of blueberry pie waited before her on a plate, and Marjorie sat on the stool beside her, digging into her own slice. "Eat," Marjorie said. "It will ground you."

Greta wanted to pick up what was left of the entire pie and smash it into Marjorie's face, watch it ooze down over that perfect periwinkle shirt, send droplets onto those perfect sage pants. She wanted to sully her with irreversible stains.

"Moody's makes the best pies," Marjorie said, and Greta felt vaguely satisfied to realize she'd been right: Marjorie hadn't baked the pie herself. "Seriously," Marjorie said. "You have to try it. Just try it, Greta."

Marjorie sounded slightly desperate again, and she was shoveling her slice in so quickly, possibly out of nerves, that her piece was already half gone. And though Greta found some satisfaction, as well, in these observations of her perfect old friend seemingly undone now, she picked up her fork. She wasn't inhumane.

Not, apparently, like the rest of her family, the rest of The Cove. She took a small bite, and the blueberry flavor exploded on her tongue.

"Doesn't it make you glad to be alive?" Marjorie said, and the funny thing was, in spite of everything, it did.

They took a few more bites in silence. Greta wished she had a cup of coffee, but she didn't think her legs would hold her up to go make one, and she was damned if she'd ask Marjorie to do it. Also, she was damned if she'd drink the water Marjorie had gotten for her. It was just like Marjorie Westfield to barge in here and . . .

Her thoughts slowed down. What did she know about Marjorie Westfield, really?

Marjorie had never told *anyone*? Could that be true? Greta had always told herself Marjorie was an incorrigible gossip—but what evidence had she had? None.

"Does Lindy know?" Greta said then. "Does Tom?"

"Oh, God, I don't know about that," Marjorie said. She was to the crust of her slice now, and when she cut it with her fork, part went flying. She reached up like a major-league shortstop and caught it before it hit the counter, dropped it back onto her plate, and went on as if nothing had happened. "I wouldn't think so. It was just at the time, the adults talked about it and were concerned for you. But, you know, even the kids of our generation, I'd be surprised if . . . well, if anybody but me knew! As I said, I never told anybody. And I'm sure your brothers wouldn't have told a soul."

Greta felt the hollow loneliness of her life, of this secret she had kept, this shame of hers, her long-lost friendship with this woman-formerly-girl, wash over her.

And yet her parents and her parents' friends had been talking about it—about her shame, about that terrible young man—behind her back? "Why didn't anyone ever talk to me? I was so . . . ashamed. I thought that people would . . . cast me out, if they knew."

"Oh, God, no, the opposite! Your parents . . . I think they thought . . . you know, back then. People didn't know. They were just trying to protect you. They loved you. They were trying their best. People thought talking about things like that made them worse. They thought it was possible to just forget."

Greta actually laughed. "I can't even go up in the attic," she said, finding she didn't care a whit about keeping her secrets from Marjorie anymore. It was like they were eight years old again, the best of friends—only what was true now, too, was that they would both be dead before long, and all of this would cease to matter. "Not after all these years."

Marjorie set down her fork. She licked a tiny smear of blueberry from the corner of her lip. "Oh, Greta. I'm so sorry."

Greta felt again the sincerity of her old friend. It was odd to think—they could've been friends all these years?

"I'm selling the place, you know," Greta confessed brazenly. She *needed* a friend. She always had. She told Marjorie about Florida. How she wanted Tom to have the best care. How David had tried to put together the money to buy Innisfree from her but couldn't. He had good credit but so much debt, such a modest income. "His lofty ideals," Greta said sadly. "He's always cared more about helping people than making money. I'm sorry about it for Lindy's sake, and I *hope* it doesn't have anything to do with why he's gone missing. But for me, I'll be glad to never see the place again. Honestly!" she added, because of course that last part wasn't entirely true.

"Oh, Greta." Marjorie reached for her hand again, and in Marjorie's eyes Greta saw the sorrow, the long memories, the loss of *her* oldest friend, too. (Greta would not have imagined it had affected Marjorie at all.) Marjorie had known Greta's parents, her brothers. Everyone who Greta had loved and lost so long ago. Marjorie had known them well. They had been part of her life, too, when she was young. "No," Marjorie said, as if her heart was breaking.

CHAPTER 44

Lindy

Saturday, July 31, 2010
9 a.m.

"I'm sorry, ma'am, he doesn't look familiar," said the ranger in the small booth at the entrance to Quoddy Head State Park, shaking his head as he looked down at the *MISSING* flyer Lindy had given him. "And we don't have any campsites here."

"No campsites?" Lindy felt like her lungs had been punctured. She glanced in the rearview mirror, saw Hailey and Jack through the Protegé's windshield, and tried to regroup. "Are there any campgrounds nearby?" The ranger shook his head, said not really, not anywhere close. "Okay, well, can we look around the parking lot?" There were hiking trails; David could still be here. Lindy paid the entrance fee for herself, Hailey, and Jack, then drove into the gravel lot and parked. Only a few cars were in the lot, and David's Subaru wasn't one of them. Still, she needed a minute. She gripped the steering wheel, trying to breathe.

Because what she knew now, with Eli discovering the new charge on the new credit card, was this: Her husband was on an impromptu camping trip and, as of two days ago, had been in good enough health to go to town for supplies. He'd gone off on his own without bothering to let her or anyone know, setting into motion the worst week of her and her children's lives, even torpedoing their daughter's wedding.

It wasn't that Lindy had been hoping for death or injury. But to realize, after all this time, that this was how little regard David had for her, their marriage, their family, their daughter, was, in this moment, simply taking her breath away.

As Hailey's Protegé pulled into the parking spot beside the Volvo, tires crunching gravel, Lindy set aside the welcome brochure the ranger had given her, which showed a map of the park's trails. If the Subaru wasn't here, David wasn't here hiking, so there was no need to set out searching the trails, imagining a broken ankle, a blown-out knee.

If only, she thought—because she did not want to hate David, and right now she hated him more than she'd ever hated anyone in her life.

Hailey knocked on the window. "Mom?" Her eyes were full of tears. Jack stood off to the side watching her, looking distraught.

Lindy opened the door and got out of the car. She hugged her daughter tightly, then pulled back. "Let's check out the view." If David had brought them to the end of the road, she thought, the least they could do was try to see what it was that he'd been so hungry for that he'd left them all behind in search of it.

They walked together, the three of them, over toward the cliff's edge, the candy-striped lighthouse with the old-fashioned keeper's house attached. It killed Lindy to see Hailey so upset, her high hopes that her dad would be here at this park shattered. "There's a *lighthouse,* Mom," she'd said, as if she'd really placed faith in Reese's prediction.

There was nothing Lindy could think to say to make any of it better.

She looked out at the broad channel before them. The sky and water nearly merged in glistening shades of silvery blue as waves rolled in, crashing on the rocky cliffs below. The air was damp and clean. This had to be one of the most beautiful spots in the entire country; the world, even. And she realized then that David was right. A new sense of clarity was descending upon her, here at the easternmost edge of the continental United States: her marriage was over.

Because, even if David ended up being okay, how could she stay married to someone who would do this to her, to their kids?

She heard his long-ago words: *I thought if I could get to the end of the road, and to the beginning of something else, I'd feel better.*

Well, here we are, David! she thought, feeling suddenly viciously angry, feeling as if divorcing him would be easy. Easy! She thought of Hailey's canceled wedding. Ironic that she and her daughter were both at a fracture point at the same time. And her mother, losing her husband to dementia. They were all at the end of certain roads, the beginnings of others. They were all going to need each other, more than ever before.

She reached for Hailey's hand and squeezed it. "I really think we should get back to Grandma and Grandpa. And we need to take care of canceling whatever we can for your wedding."

Hailey shook her head, wiping tears from her eyes. "We can't give up on Dad. Even if he was okay two days ago, he might not be now! And we still don't know if that was even him who made the charge, or if his credit card was stolen."

Lindy tried to think what to say. The odds that David's credit card had been stolen seemed so small.

Jack interrupted. "So, like, I don't want to mention the obvious," he said, pointing across the channel, "but that's, like, Canada over there. And we saw a bridge in town, in Lubec, that goes right to it. Do you think he might've crossed over to camp over there?"

"You need a passport to get over there now," Lindy said. It was a reflexive argument. Because there was clarity here, too: If David had gone to Canada, she was going to kill him.

But Hailey seemed oddly excited by the prospect. "We should call Eli and see if Dad's passport is at home in Cranston! If it is, then we know he can't have gone over there. Do you know where he keeps his passport at home, Mom?"

"Sure, in his top dresser drawer," Lindy said, at the same time she was shaking her head. "But we don't have our passports, so it's not like we could follow him."

"But we could at least rule it out!"

Lindy wanted to refuse. How dare David do this to them—send them on this wild goose chase, worry them like this?

But Hailey looked at her, eyes filling again, and said, "Please, Mom?"

They drove back to town and found a pay phone. It was at a gas station right beside the IGA where David had charged his groceries, which made Lindy even more furious, to think he could've so easily called, at least to let them know he was alive!

If it was clarity he was looking for up here, it seemed he had found it. It seemed he had found that he didn't care about his family at all.

Hailey placed the call and reported back, her face ashen. "Eli says his passport isn't there."

Okay, I am divorcing him for sure, Lindy thought, because if he'd grabbed his passport, that meant premeditation. It meant he had lied when he'd called her at Innisfree on the morning of his party and said he was on his way. It meant he had caused all this pain—all this *searching,* all this heartbreak—on purpose.

She tried to unclench her jaw. "Let's grab some breakfast." She wasn't hungry, exactly, but she knew they'd all need fuel to get through the day—and get back to her parents, who actually needed her. "Then, we are heading back to Innisfree."

CHAPTER 45

Hailey

Saturday, July 31, 2010
10:30 a.m.

"I can't believe she wants to just give up," Hailey said, standing with Jack beside her Protegé in downtown Lubec, watching as her mom walked away down the street toward the one coffee shop they'd spotted. *Hailey Marie,* Lindy had said, in that tone you weren't supposed to argue with, but Hailey had insisted she *was* going to ask at the Canadian border about her dad, even if Lindy thought it was a "very bad idea." Now Hailey squinted against the morning sun, which was getting hot, and turned toward the cinder block building and the large gate in the distance. She had a *MISSING* poster in her hand to show the guards.

"Don't get arrested," Jack said.

"I'm not gonna get arrested," Hailey said. "Wait here." She put on her sunglasses and began walking, her sandals clicking across the hot pavement.

The officer who came out to meet her had a few questions for her, too. He made her remove her sunglasses, directed her into the building, and sat her down in a cinder block office that seemed designed to make her feel like a criminal. He asked to see her ID, then stood over her with his arms folded asking her a bunch of things, which she answered, feeling somewhere between terrified and irritated. She had been sweating in the sun, and the air-conditioning in the office made her shiver.

The longest ten minutes of her life later, after she'd basically bared her soul about her dad and, thank God, restrained herself from crying, the guard let her go, saying very seriously that he wasn't able, officially speaking, to give her any information about whether her dad had crossed the border there. But as he held the door for her on her way out, he kindly and quietly told her, person-to-person, that he didn't remember seeing him, and he wished her luck.

She made her way back across the hot pavement toward where Jack waited.

Ridiculous. All that whole ordeal had accomplished was to confirm there was definitely still a chance her dad could be over in Canada, possibly hurt or dead, and totally out of reach.

The coffee shop had a view of the water out big windows in the back, and fortunately it offered breakfast. "I guess I was wrong about everything," Hailey's mom was saying. "Maybe I've been wrong about everything my whole life." Lindy was evidently too angry to eat; she just kept stabbing at her scrambled eggs, as Hailey looked up in astonishment at hearing her say such a thing. *Oh, God,* Hailey realized, *I'm going to have to go back to Cranston and take care of her.* With Dad gone, Grandpa having dementia, and Grandma and Grandpa moving to Florida, Lindy was *not* going to be okay.

Hailey pushed away the veggie omelet she'd been only picking at. It was odd to realize that the idea of giving up law school, even to go back to Cranston, had made relief wash through her.

And, amazingly, her head still wasn't hurting, even after that grilling by the border guard.

Jack pushed his plate away, too. "I have an idea." He pulled from his pocket the brochure the ranger had given Hailey when they'd driven into Quoddy Head State Park behind her mom. Hailey had passed it over to

Jack without giving it another thought. Now he unfolded it, flattened it on the table, and pointed. "So, it says here under 'Nearby Destinations' that Cobscook Bay State Park 'offers a good base for exploring easternmost Maine with many waterfront camping sites.' I looked the place up on the map and it's, like, less than twenty miles away."

Hailey understood enough that excitement began to whir. "You mean, if he went to Quoddy Head to see the easternmost point in the U.S., then he would've gotten this brochure, too, and maybe he would've read this and gone to this park to camp?"

"Yep," Jack said.

Hailey looked to her mom, but Lindy was scowling, a forkful of scrambled eggs held aloft between her plate and her mouth.

Seeing her mom like this made Hailey want, more than anything, for Jack to be right. Her dad really *could* be at this park. Everything really *could* be okay, even after all that had happened. Sure, her mom was mad now, but if they *found* him, surely she'd get over it, right?

Hailey leaned on the table. "Mom, we know from the credit card charge that he was here in Lubec three days ago. We know from your memory that he had a fascination with the easternmost point in the U.S. We know he's probably camping." She tapped the brochure with her fingernail. "And we know that every visitor to Quoddy Head gets this."

"Cobscook Bay State Park is on the way back to Innisfree, basically," Jack put in. "Just a little off the main highway."

"It's our next stop, then," Hailey said.

"I don't know," Lindy said, still scowling.

"Mom, we can't just give up and go back without finding him. What would everybody think? Emma, Eli, Cody, Aunt Kate . . ."

Lindy set her forkful of eggs back on her plate and pushed the plate away. "Okay, fine. We can check there. As long as it's on the way back home."

"I don't know what I'll do if she just gives up after this," Hailey said, behind the wheel again as they drove out of Lubec. This time, they were taking the lead in the Protegé, since Jack was navigating. Hailey kept an eye on her mom's Volvo in the rearview mirror. "What if he really did go to Canada? What if he never comes back?"

"I don't think they let you stay forever or anything," Jack said, which didn't make her feel much better. She gripped the wheel tighter, frowning, picturing life back in Cranston with her mom, her dad gone forever.

Still, though, terrible as that scenario was, the notion of *not* going to law school was still surprisingly appealing. She thought of her mom the other day, swearing that she truly hadn't regretted giving up law school when she'd found out she was pregnant with Hailey; she thought of her mom just now at breakfast saying maybe she'd been wrong about everything her whole life.

Which was the truth? That Lindy marrying David and having a family was simply a "different path" that had come to seem "exactly right"—at least until now, twenty-five years later, when Hailey's dad had betrayed and disappointed her?

Or was the truth that Lindy'd had a family *instead of* pursuing the life she'd really wanted?

For the first time, Hailey wondered: Had her own plan to go to law school always been intended to make up for the fact that, just by being born, she'd ruined that chance for her mom?

Jack spoke up again. "You know, we could still stay up here and keep looking, even if your mom doesn't. I've found a few more campgrounds on the map within, like, a fifty-mile radius. We could call Emma and Cody and get them to come up, too."

Hailey sighed. "Yeah, maybe." She appreciated the thought, but Emma and Cody would be totally out of their element up here, and she and Jack weren't much better. Also, Hailey didn't relish the thought of her mom driving back to Innisfree alone—especially in the state Lindy was in.

But they couldn't seriously *give up* on finding her dad, could they? Hailey remembered again her mom's story about how, long ago, he'd tried to harm himself. *You saved him, just by being born!*

Well, what if that wasn't enough, anymore? Or what if her upcoming wedding had triggered him somehow? Like, if he'd thought he was losing her? Or if he was, like, totally stressed about the money?

What if Hailey was totally the cause of all of this? And now it was all for nothing, now that the wedding was off!

She had to fix it. She just had to. Her dad just had to be okay.

Reaching the end of the road that led to and from Lubec, they turned north onto Coastal Route I again, same as if they'd been returning to Eastport. Hailey's mom, back there in the Volvo, was no doubt fuming about this, since it was in the opposite direction of home, but Jack promised the turnoff to the park was just a few miles up the road. There were no houses along this section of highway, almost no side roads, just mile after mile of trees. Hailey drove biting her lip, feeling the isolation of where they were, remembering something the border guard had said: *A man could get lost in the woods pretty easy up here.*

She had not appreciated that nugget of wisdom one bit.

Finally, Jack directed her to make a right turn onto one of the only side roads they'd seen, which led them even deeper into the woods. "Are you sure this is right?" she said, checking the rearview again to make sure her mom was still following.

"Trust me, Hales," Jack said.

But Hailey's optimism was basically gone, and, as they got closer and closer to the campground, her stomach started to hurt. She didn't want to think ahead to the disappointment, to what it would feel like when her dad wasn't there.

Tall pines lined the park's entrance road, giving a peaceful feeling of shelter. At the gate was a booth—larger than the one at Quoddy Head—to stop to pay your entrance fee or reserve a campsite. As Hailey pulled up and stopped the car, a ranger stepped out and came to the window. "Hey, folks," she said. "Looking to camp tonight? We've got just a couple sites open."

"Actually, we're looking for my dad," Hailey said. Jack handed over a *MISSING* poster, and Hailey passed it to the ranger. "His name is David Kauffman. He's driving an old green Subaru with Rhode Island plates. We know he stopped for groceries in Lubec three days ago, so we think he's in the area." She didn't know why she'd added that last part; maybe just to try to prove they weren't on some totally wild goose chase.

The ranger looked up from the photo. "Yeah, he's here. A few days now. I mean, I don't think he's checked out yet. Want me to look up the site number and make sure?"

Hailey looked over at Jack. His eyebrows had shot up, and he grinned and grabbed her hand. She shook her head quickly to adjust to the new reality, grinned back, then turned to the ranger again. "Yes! Yes! He's okay? He's here, really? I—I have to go tell my mom! She's right behind us!"

The ranger backed up, nodding, heading for the booth. Hailey let go of Jack's hand, jumped out of the car, and ran back to the Volvo, yelling, "Mom! Mom! He's here! We found him!"

CHAPTER 46

Lindy

Saturday, July 31, 2010
11:30 a.m.

Lindy drove slowly along the winding road through the wooded campsites, every so often glancing down at a little map of the campground the ranger had given her after circling the site where David, according to the ranger, had been staying for the last five days. The park had more than a hundred sites spread across nearly nine hundred acres, and the speed limit on the one-way lane was ten miles per hour, so it was taking Lindy a few minutes to get there. She was glad for the time. She needed to adjust, to try to get her thoughts together.

Hailey had been eager to see her dad, but Lindy had asked her and Jack to wait back at the park entrance. She needed to talk to David alone first.

She still didn't believe he was really here. She was livid, aching with hurt. What would she even say to him? How would she explain what it had been like to spend these last several days in fear he was injured in the woods somewhere, or dead, or that he'd run off to start a new life? How would she make him understand the gravity of what he'd done and how the bottom had fallen out of their entire life?

How soon till she could mention the word *divorce*?

Words felt insufficient. She imagined herself simply screaming at the sight of him, shattering the quiet of these woods.

Just as the ranger had promised, there, at site 65, was David's Subaru. After all the time Lindy had spent looking for it—the hundreds, if not thousands, of miles she'd traveled in search of it—to actually see it, parked peacefully in the woods, felt disorienting. She pulled in behind it and turned off the Volvo's engine. She took a deep breath, clutching the wheel. The large site was shaded in tall pines and had a view of the shimmering bay. David's blue-and-gray nylon tent was set up fifteen yards ahead of where her car was parked, near a stone fire ring surrounded by log benches. She didn't see David anywhere.

She got out of the car and slammed the door shut. The noise was jarring in the silence. Her sandals made no sound on the pine needles that carpeted the ground. She heard a loon call in the distance, the chirping of songbirds above.

"David?" she said, approaching the tent. It was a different one from the canvas one he'd had all those years ago, but she felt fifteen again, her heart in her throat; she saw the fear in his eyes, the knife in his hand, the blood streaming from his wrist. *I love you,* she wanted to cry out. *Where are you?* "David?"

He appeared at the water's edge, rising from where he'd been sitting on a rock, it seemed. His beard had grown in, and to her surprise it was mostly gray. His curly salt-and-pepper hair was shaggy, and his white T-shirt and khaki shorts were smeared with dirt. He smiled at the sight of her. He was the most beautiful thing she had ever seen.

She hugged him first, tightly, for a full minute, then kissed him briefly and started yelling, swatting at his arm. "How dare you, how dare you, how dare you? I thought you were dead!"

"Honey, I called and told you where I was going." He was extraordinarily calm, infuriatingly so. But evidently, he'd spent the last five days here meditating beside this peaceful bay! Watching the birds flutter around! Why wouldn't he be calm?

"No, you didn't!"

"I did. I left a message on the machine at Innisfree. Saturday. I borrowed some guy's phone at a gas station before I drove out of signal range."

"No, you didn't!"

"I did."

"Nobody got a message! You've been *missing* for a whole week!"

"What?" David said, even as Lindy thought suddenly: *Dad.* Maybe her dad had listened to a message, deleted it, forgotten all about it.

"Oh, David." She started to cry. "So much has happened."

He took her hand and led her to sit down on one of the logs beside the fire ring. He held her hands. His familiar dark eyes were full of sorrow, regret, love. "How did you find me?"

"A statewide search!" she said, mustering anger again. "Everybody—I—you wouldn't believe—"

"Lindy," he said, like she was breaking his heart. Like *she* was breaking *his* heart!

"You—The kids—Hailey!" She could not form sentences. It still seemed like everything was lost, that it was too late to get any of it back.

David squeezed her hands. "I was planning to come back tomorrow. Monday, maybe, at the latest. I'm sorry you didn't get the message. Is everything on track for the wedding?"

She yanked her hands away. "Jesus Christ, David. You never seem to realize that we *need* you. Well, it's too late now!"

He appeared to falter, at that. He leaned back slightly and blinked. "What do you mean?"

"It's all ruined! Everything is ruined. If you want to take all our money and run away, see if I care. The kids just wanted to know you were alive! We know about your heart, David. And about the money. We searched the computer, we found everything, the missing hundred and nine thousand dollars, and, God, for a few days I thought you'd run off and were having a baby with Tiffany—"

"What?" he said, shocked now, then he laughed.

"It's not funny! Nothing about this is funny. Up till five minutes ago, we thought you might've run away to Canada! Why did you bring your passport? Were you *planning* on running away to Canada?"

"I didn't. It's in the safety deposit box."

"Oh. Right." Lindy had forgotten they'd agreed months ago to stow their passports at the bank. She quickly resurrected her outrage. "Well, Mom is selling Innisfree and moving Dad to Florida—she said you knew! Did you know Dad has dementia?"

"What?" His face said he had not.

"And now Hailey's not getting married!"

"What? What happened?"

Lindy shook her head. It felt too late even to explain. How, while he'd sat here soaking in the peace of the woods, their life had fallen apart. "It's all over. Our life together. Our family. It's over, David. If that's what you wanted, that's what you've managed to achieve! The kids hate me, and so will your sister and brother when they find out everything! And when they all find out you were just here, hanging out, *fine,* just not bothering to *call,* just selfishly *hanging out* without thinking of the impact it would have on everybody, they'll all probably hate *you,* too."

He sat up straighter, looking puzzled, shocked. "Honey, no. I just came up here for—you know, my head gets crowded. My head was getting really, really crowded. I couldn't face everybody at the party. I couldn't. It was really bad, but I'm doing better now. What happened with the wedding? Is Hailey okay?"

Lindy didn't want to hear it. And she didn't have it in her to try to explain. She covered her face with her hands. He squeezed her knee, then she felt him get up and leave. Behind her hands, she was crying now. The door of the Subaru squeaked open, then slammed shut again. Birds sang. He sat down again beside her and touched her arm so that she would lower her hands, and when she did, he was holding out a check for her to see.

She took it in her hands. It was a cashier's check made out to Lindy's mother for a hundred and two thousand dollars.

"I was going to see if she'd do owner financing. Take this as a down payment and then finance the rest. I wasn't sure it would be enough, but I was hoping . . ."

"What?"

"But then, on the drive up, I just got—Lindy. I guess you know now, if you looked at the computer." He pointed to the check with a dirty fingernail. "This is everything. It's all I've managed to save all our lives. And I felt like—like such a goddamn failure. My whole life adds up to this? And all I wanted was to make a good life for you and the kids. And I thought—it was going to destroy you to lose Innisfree, but if I do this, put this money toward it, we've got nothing left. We're starting from zero. Nothing even for the other kids' weddings, when the time comes. I mean, I had to take some money out of our savings account to pay the bills for Hailey's, and that isn't even over yet. I didn't know what to do. I felt I'd mismanaged everything. Failed at everything I'd ever tried to do."

Lindy stared at the check, blinking. She felt stunned, like something had exploded in front of her. Maybe it had. The money missing from their savings account had mostly gone toward Hailey's wedding. The rest of it, plus all their retirement money, was here in her hands. It seemed absurd, suddenly. No wonder he'd been stressed. "You didn't think of talking to me?"

"Not right now. I couldn't. Not with the parties. The wedding."

She looked up at him, knowing what he said was true. Regretting it. "Oh, God. I've been—obsessed. And it all fucking fell apart, anyway, you know? Because you did this!" She wanted to hate him. Looking in his eyes, seeing his earnestness, and remembering the husband he actually was—not the husband that, this past week, she'd been imagining him to be—hating him was hard to do.

Also, it was impossible not to see right now that, if she hadn't been so remote, so obsessed, so blind to him, so *unaware,* he probably *would* have talked to her.

"Lindy, you and the kids are everything to me," he said. "I needed to get my head right for you. I needed to be . . . the guy you've come to depend on. Not—not the version of me that loses his mind. The way I used to. I know you remember it! And I—I was getting close, it felt like. On the drive up, I just thought, I can't do this, I can't face all the people. I can't smile and pretend I feel normal when it feels like my skin is on inside out and my mind is screaming at me, and mostly I couldn't face you and tell you we might have to give up Innisfree, when I'd spent all these years assuring you I had everything under control. I just—I wanted to, Lin. I wanted to have it all under control. But . . . I guess I didn't."

"Oh, David." She felt her anger collapsing, falling away. She hated to think that he'd been feeling that way; that he'd thought running off alone was the only solution. "I wish you had told me."

"Well, I didn't want to admit . . ." He didn't seem to know how to finish his sentence. He rested his hand over hers, looked at her beseechingly. "I just didn't want to ruin anything for you, Lin. I just thought everything would go easier if I wasn't there. Even my birthday party. I guess I wasn't in my right mind. I mean, I know I wasn't. I'm sorry. I'm sorry you didn't get my message. I'm sorry I didn't try calling again. I didn't plan to stay gone so long. It just felt so peaceful here."

The loon cried again in the distance. She looked into his dark eyes, which she loved so much. (She would need to ask him about the EKG! Had he had it done?)

But now she was remembering being young with him. How desperate she'd been to make him see.

"David," she said, keeping a firm edge to her voice. "I need you to understand something now. If you've never understood it before, you *must* understand it now. Without you, the center does not hold."

"Things fall apart?"

She smiled slightly because she was happy he knew the poem she was referring to, and because if she didn't, her anger would fire up again, or she'd start crying recalling the events of the past week. "More than you can imagine."

He nodded slowly. "I will try to remember that. I'm sorry."

"It's a hole you've always had in you, David. You've never truly believed that your presence mattered. You always felt it was optional, a choice. And you believing that has done more than enough harm to our family now. Enough. It's *not* a choice. We need you! Never mind about the money. Your life adds up to so much more than some number in a bank account. We just need *you*."

"Okay, Lin. I'm sorry," he said again, and he appeared truly contrite.

She sighed. It seemed enough for now. And she knew then that she would not divorce him. She suddenly couldn't imagine even mentioning the word.

But she could imagine trying instead to begin a new chapter with him. She could imagine trying to learn to love him more loosely, to listen, not to assume. She found herself hoping they could actually save Innisfree. The owner financing idea might work. They could try to save everything. Maybe it wasn't too late.

Maybe they *were* at the end of one road—but it seemed possible now that they could be at the beginning of another.

She stood. "Okay. We have a lot more to talk about. But right now, I think your daughter would like to see you."

David smiled and stood beside her, and Lindy looked up at him and—she couldn't help it—smiled back. She would certainly be angry again—very angry—later. But right now, she was happy and relieved to see him alive, well, and the husband she'd always known him to be. Flaws and all.

He reached out his hand, she took it, and together they turned and began walking toward the car.

It felt strange to realize she had a husband again, after all the scenarios she'd imagined to the contrary. But it felt good.

"Is Hailey okay?" he asked again. "Why did they call off the wedding?"

Lindy shook her head, not sure she understood entirely herself, but recalling the sternness of Noah's face, and the way Hailey's face lit up whenever Jack was near. "I'll let her explain. But I do think it's going to turn out to be for the best." She laughed a little. "It's too late to get any of our money back, though."

"I don't care about that. Just as long as this is the right choice for her and she's happy."

"I knew you'd say that," Lindy said lightly, glad to think there were still some things she knew about her husband.

"I'm relieved, actually," David said. "I never liked that guy. But I didn't want to alienate her by arguing against it. Or you. You seemed to like him so much. I wondered if I was wrong."

Despite everything, Lindy smiled again, because she could've predicted he would say all that, too. "You weren't wrong, David. I'm sorry. Also, I should tell you, Jack Westfield is with her."

"Jack Westfield?"

She laughed, a release of tension at the strangeness of it all. "You missed quite a lot, honey. They're the ones who helped me figure out where you were. Hailey refused to give up, and I think Jack is at least a little bit in love with her. I think she might be in love with him, too."

"I always kind of liked Jack," David said thoughtfully.

"Oh, of course you did," she said, nudging him slightly with her shoulder as they made their way through the tall shelter of pines back toward the car, back toward the world.

CHAPTER 47

Greta

Saturday, July 31, 2010
2 p.m.

A slow parade of people had begun arriving at the side door of Innisfree in the late morning, most with casseroles or deviled eggs, potato salads or plates of cookies in their hands, so many that Greta was having trouble finding room in the refrigerator for everything. After his outing to the SCPA this morning, Tom was having a good day and spent an hour answering the door, greeting people, sitting at the counter to keep Greta company. He had just gone upstairs, and she was rearranging the refrigerator to fit a pasta salad from Dorothy Severson when the phone rang. Emma thundered down the stairs to answer it. She said a breathless hello, listened for a moment, then shouted. "Oh my God! Grandma, they found Dad! They're coming home!"

A key fit into a lock and turned. There was more screaming, hugs, yelling to Cody, a quick call to Eli, running upstairs to tell Tom, who probably wouldn't understand. Greta went into the piano room and put on an old LP to celebrate. "I got a brand-new pair of roller skates," the folk singer Melanie warbled. "You got a brand-new key . . ."

Greta couldn't wait for Lindy and David, and Hailey and Jack, to get back to Innisfree. She had such good news to tell them.

~

This morning, Marjorie had insisted, after Cody and Emma had woken up and come downstairs, on taking Greta up to the attic. She had held Greta's hand for the half hour it took until Greta stopped shaking. Then, she had asked Greta to tell her what had happened to her all those years ago, every detail of what had happened. "You've been keeping this secret for far too long. It's been taking its toll on you."

So Greta had spoken it out loud for the first time, to her oldest friend. How the young man had been so handsome, so charming, arriving with her brother like something out of a dream that Greta had hardly dared to dream—that someday, someday, a handsome man like that would notice her, pay her some attention. How he had flirted with her in front of her whole family, made her blush, and everyone had thought it was adorable, the older-brother kind of interest he had seemed to take in her. How, the night he came up to the attic, in the middle of the night when everyone else was sleeping—it was three steps from the guest room door to the entrance of the attic stairs—she had been flattered, at first. He had sat and talked to her for a while. Touched her hand, her face. Kissed her gently, thrilling her.

And then. And then.

"It's okay," Marjorie said, squeezing Greta's hand as Greta started to sob. "You can tell me if you want to. You can say the words. I understand. Greta, the same thing happened to me when I was fifteen."

At that, Greta's anger flared. How dare anyone do such a thing to Marjorie? "Who?"

Marjorie waved the question off. "We're not talking about me right now. I've had years of therapy, Greta. Years and years. It helps to talk about it. It really does. It helps to know you're not alone, and you have nothing to be ashamed of. It has happened to nearly every woman I know."

"But I—I flirted!"

"You were twelve! He was a grown man of twenty-three! He was a monster, Greta. You were his *victim*. And I'll tell you what—if he hadn't died in the war and he was still alive all these years later, he wouldn't be giving you a second thought right now. You'd probably be one of thirty girls he'd done this to."

Greta saw him again, drowning in that slick of oil. "I had . . . bruises. Afterward. He held me down. I tried to scream, but he put his hand over my mouth."

"I understand," Marjorie said, tears in her eyes.

And so, Greta, haltingly at first, and then more quickly as she began to feel more brave, told Marjorie everything, every terrible detail that had been flashing through her mind these last sixty-nine years. Marjorie squeezed her hands, gazing into her eyes, telling her over and over again, "You have nothing to be ashamed of. Nothing."

And then, when it was all over and Greta had cried in Marjorie's arms, Marjorie picked up the boys' Nerf basketball off the floor and handed it to Greta. "Throw this at the wall. Scream. Let it out. If you need heavier things, we'll find them."

Greta had ended up breaking an entire set of dishes Marjorie hauled out of the storage area that dated to the 1960s, a mustard yellow set Greta had always hated. ("Everything okay up there, Grandma?" Cody had called, from the foot of the stairs, sounding frightened. And Marjorie called down to him, "Your grandma just needs a minute!")

Afterward, Marjorie helped Greta sweep up the pieces. Even the way they clinked as they landed in the dustpan and jangled when dropped into the trash can was satisfying. Greta felt, oddly, better than she'd felt in years.

Marjorie linked arms with her, and they stood side by side looking out the big window at the ocean, which was calm today and a very deep blue. "I remember when this was your princess room," Marjorie said. "I loved it up here so much. And the way time flies, you're going to have great-grandchildren not long from now, Greta, I have a feeling. Maybe, if we're lucky, you and I will even share great-grandchildren, if my Jack will admit how he feels about Hailey. He was quite excited yesterday morning when she called to ask him to come with her to Eastport. And he said he suspected that her wedding might be off?"

At the actual twinkle in Marjorie's eye, Greta grinned. "Yes! It is off!" Hailey had been upset when she'd run in yesterday morning to leave her engagement ring upstairs, but Greta had been happy. And now she didn't think Hailey and Jack getting together was a bad idea at all. She'd seen the way Jack had looked at Hailey the other night, the way he was always there to help her when she needed it.

"Well, that is very good news, indeed!" Marjorie said, grinning, too. "And not only for that reason," she continued, "but because you're my oldest friend, I would really like to loan Lindy the money to buy this place from you. Then you and Tom can go to Florida, you can get your condo, and Tom can get the care he needs, and God knows I hope you'll still come back here for the summers, as long as you can, because I will miss you if you don't. But, Greta, I'll give her very favorable terms. Reasonable monthly payments, whatever she can handle. Because I would really, really like to see your great-grandchildren grow up here. Because, otherwise, that monster wins, Greta, after all these years. And we cannot let him win. He already stole seven decades of friendship from us! Well, that is more than enough! You have been so strong and so courageous all these years. We cannot let him win. We cannot let any of these bastards who do these things to us girls win."

Greta let all of that sink in. She thought, *Yes. Absolutely, yes.* She grinned. "Let me tell you about how I pointed a gun at Hailey's horrible fiancé the other day when he was threatening her," she said. Marjorie shrieked with laughter, and *this* incident she would no doubt announce at the next meeting of the SCPA, but Greta didn't care one bit about that. She was glad to think of it, in fact—of everyone in The Cove knowing her for who she truly was, after all this time—as she and her oldest friend made their way downstairs to have another slice of blueberry pie, because life didn't last forever, and it was long past time to forgive herself, and Marjorie, too, and whoever else she needed to. They'd all just been doing their best, all this time.

CHAPTER 48

Lindy

Saturday, July 31, 2010
8 p.m.

When Lindy walked arm-in-arm with David into the SCPA clubhouse, Hailey and Jack trailing them, everyone who'd gathered to enjoy the food from Greta and Tom's erstwhile anniversary party burst out in applause, laughter, tears. A telltale platter of cookie cake crumbs on the nearly empty food table, while Marjorie Westfield was nowhere in sight, spoke to the fact that some folks had clearly been there and gone, but those who remained didn't stint on cheering.

David finally held up his hands and, although he didn't want to, made a little speech. He thanked everyone for their support and concern and ended with, "I've promised my wife, if I ever go camping again, I'll be sure I speak with her *in person* to let her know my plans." More cheers, huzzahs.

Emma was the first in line to hug David, and she hugged him for a long time, seeming like a little girl again. When she finally let go, she said that Eli should be arriving any minute with Tiffany and Raj, who'd picked him up at the bus station in Portland. "Grandma and Grandpa are waiting for you back at Innisfree, but they said no rush," she added.

Cody came up next, shaking his head. He was taller than David by four inches, and the look on his face was stern. "Don't get me wrong, Dad, I'm glad to see you, but imagine if I'd done what you did," he said. "Did you think about the consequences your actions would have on everyone? On Mom, especially?" He began ticking off the damages on his fingers as he enumerated all that the family had been going through—the worry and speculation, the traveling and searching, the fear and lack of sleep and upending of plans, the way Lindy had gotten Eli and Emma to lie—and David's face grew pale.

"You could've at least called," Cody continued. "You call once and don't talk to anybody and just leave a message on the machine? And you think that's *sufficient* to be gone for an entire week, especially when we had so much going on and we were counting on you for it? And I'm not gonna say it's a bad thing that Hailey isn't marrying that douchebag, but how could you fucking disappear two weeks out from her wedding and not think it was going to totally fuck everything up?" He folded his arms, waiting for an answer.

Lindy was so proud of her youngest son in that moment. He had grown up. He saw things clearly. He was good and kind and thoughtful (thinking of his sister's wedding, for example!). And he was holding David accountable.

David glanced at Lindy and seemed about to say something to Cody, when Kate and Josh came up to take turns hugging him. "You'd better speak to *us* in person, too, if you go off on your own again," Kate told David, as Josh wiped away tears. Then Kate pulled Lindy aside.

"Goddamn it, Lindy," she said, glaring even as she, too, blinked back tears. "David told me over the phone that I shouldn't blame you for anything, he takes full responsibility and all of that. But what were you thinking, not telling me and Josh the truth?"

Lindy had ridden with David in the Subaru back from Downeast. Hailey had followed in the Protegé, while Jack brought up the rear in the Volvo. Nobody was about to let anybody else out of their sight, so when Lindy and David stopped to make calls from the first pay phone they could find, Hailey and Jack had stopped, too. They'd called Innisfree first, then Eli in Cranston, then, finally, the yellow cottage, where

David had spoken with Kate. (Lindy, standing by, could hear Kate's screams of joy and, after a moment, rage, at hearing her brother's voice.)

"I'm sorry," Lindy said now. "I just—what you said about your mother. And I saw you were taking it so hard. Drinking so much again. And I really thought . . . I really thought he was cheating! I was so . . . embarrassed."

Kate sighed, still frowning. But then she reached for Lindy's arm. "Well, we've been friends a long time, Lindy. And we've got a long way to go, hopefully. So, please. Let me in, next time." Then she laughed slightly, shooting a look at David. "Not that he's going to do *this* again. I'm going to be having a serious talk with him, let me tell you," Kate said, as if she were the older sibling. But perhaps she'd taken on that role decades ago, after all. "But, Lindy, seriously, let me in, okay?"

Lindy blinked back tears of her own. "Yes. Okay."

David came over and touched the small of Lindy's back. "Lin?" She turned to him, wiping her eyes. "Cody and I are going to take a walk," he said.

"Okay, honey," she said, and as he turned away, she met Cody's serious eyes and gave him a little nod that said, *Let him have it,* and Cody nodded back, still looking very stern, to say that he would.

"Ah, good," Kate said, noticing, too.

Lindy and David had made some decisions on the drive back. She had told him about her book club friend Samantha's offer to create a job for her at the interior design studio. If a hundred thousand dollars was enough to get her parents set up in Florida, Lindy told him, and her mother would agree to the idea of owner financing on Innisfree, Lindy was going to ask for that job so she could make the payments without putting additional strain on David.

Lindy had realized a few important truths in thinking about this potential job. First, there was no denying that she had been drawn to the importance of rooms—what they communicated, the way they shaped lives—ever since all the hours she'd spent in the period rooms at the

Met when she was a teenager. Redecorating at Innisfree and the Cranston house had always brought her joy. Clearly, working with Samantha would be the dream job she had never quite thought to dream of.

This led to her second realization: She had been setting aside her own natural interests for almost as long as she could remember!

Third—and most jarringly—no one needed her to do that anymore. The truth was, the kids were grown; they no longer needed her to manage their lives. David clearly knew far better than she did what he needed to do to take care of himself. And Lindy's mother had made it plain that she wanted to take charge of Lindy's dad's care—in Florida. So, Lindy would go visit as often as she could—maybe she'd work only part-time for a while. But she would do as her mother wanted, and she wouldn't let her dad's diagnosis stop her from moving forward with her own life.

If the events of the past week had taught her anything, it was that trying to control the lives of the people she loved had only led to wrong assumptions, blindnesses, too much left unspoken—and it had caused pain for everybody, including herself.

In the car, David had been—to her amazement—thrilled to hear about the job possibility, for reasons that surprised her. She hadn't known that he harbored regrets over things that had happened between them, things he'd said and done long ago. "I think I might've discouraged you," he said. "I might've made you think the things you cared about weren't important. When the truth was, what I fell in love with you for, from the start, was your ability not just to see beauty but to create it. It was something I didn't have a talent for, and I admired it. I wanted to soak it up. And instead, maybe I killed it in you. Or made you bury it, anyway." He laughed a little, sadly. "I gave you a life where the true you could only come out in little spurts here and there."

"We built our life together," she told him. "We built our kids. Our family. I don't regret one thing." He reached over to squeeze her hand. "But," she went on, "I am looking forward to a new chapter. To discovering who I am." She took a breath, then added, "And to who we are now, together."

"Me, too," David had said. "I'm really looking forward to that, too."

~

David and Cody returned to the party after about fifteen minutes, appearing to have come to some understanding. Cody went to grab a plate of food, and David brought Lindy a fresh glass of wine where she, Hailey, and Jack stood chatting with Lloyd and Anne Ralston. Lindy liked the sweet way Jack was looking at Hailey, and very much liked how Hailey seemed to have had a heavy weight lifted off her, for good this time.

"How'd it go with Cody?" Lindy asked David quietly, and he said, "Fine," in a way that said he'd tell her more later. He draped his arm over her shoulders, and the weight of it, mixed with the familiar scent of him, filled her throat with tears, as Anne and Lloyd chatted obliviously on.

When Eli walked in a few minutes later, trailed by Tiffany and Raj, everyone cheered again, and there were a lot more hugs all around. "We didn't have any trouble recognizing this boy as your son," Tiffany told David. "Man, you did give us a *scare,* though! You have to promise not to do anything like that again, okay? You don't even *know* how many people rely on you."

David smiled and thanked her, looking both surprised and dazzled by her being there. *Well, who could blame him?* Lindy thought, oddly glad to see that she hadn't conjured her suspicions from absolutely nothing, relieved to know that love could exist in a lot more forms than the stereotypical ones.

"Hey, Dad, what is your password for your phone?" Eli asked, running a hand through his messy curls. "I tried everything and couldn't figure it out."

David grinned, as if pleased to have stumped his brilliant son. "It's 'David.' Whatever numbers that is. I had it written on a Post-it in the desk drawer."

Eli groaned. "The Post-it! I can't tell you how long I looked at that thing trying to figure out what it meant or what it was for. The code. Three-two-eight-four-three. So obvious that it's a genius beard."

"Thank you!" David said, and everybody laughed.

Eli dug into his pants pocket, pulled out the old flip phone, and handed it to David. "Well, here it is. I charged it up and everything. We'll have the ceremonial gluing to your hand in a bit."

"There wasn't even any signal up there," David said, scowling down at it in his hand. "I'm telling you, the thing is useless."

"Nevertheless," said Eli, and Lindy, Hailey, Kate, Tiffany, Cody, Emma, and even Jack echoed him in an extravagant chorus, all saying the same word, "Nevertheless," until David finally laughed and said, "Okay, okay, I'll start carrying my phone."

It was late—past nine—when they all got back to Innisfree, but Greta was waiting up, and she hugged David, then insisted they all sit together in the living room. Lindy was excited to talk about the owner financing idea, and she needed to make sure they got the gun out of the attic, too. But, seeing how tired everybody looked, she said, "It's been a long day, Mom. Maybe we should talk in the morning?" The gun had been stashed upstairs for decades, apparently; it wasn't likely to start causing trouble right away now.

Greta shook her head. "I have exciting news," she said. Lindy couldn't imagine what could be more exciting than finding David, but she, David, their kids, and Jack, who hadn't left Hailey's side all evening, gathered around Greta in the living room. Tiffany and Raj had taken off to find a hotel so they could have a relaxing last night of vacation before heading back to Rhode Island tomorrow.

Greta folded her hands in her lap, cleared her throat, and said, "First, David, I apologize for confiding in you about my plans to sell Innisfree and then asking you not to tell Lindy. That wasn't right for me to do, and I regret any pain that it caused either of you."

"Thanks, Greta," David said, with a glance over at Lindy beside him, a little squeeze of her knee. Lindy pressed her shoulder to his just to feel the heat of it, to remind herself he was real.

"Mom, we—" she began, because it seemed like the right time to tell her they had a big check to give her, but Greta interrupted.

"I've had the most generous offer. Now, you know that I would give Innisfree to you if I could. But, if you will take her up on it, Marjorie Westfield would love to loan you the money to buy Innisfree, to keep it in the family. Just call Marjorie tomorrow and you can get it set up. She said she'll give you a very favorable interest rate, and perhaps even let you go a few months to start off without making any payment at all."

The room was silent for a second, as everyone looked to Jack, who smiled and shrugged to indicate he'd known nothing about this, then the kids all started cheering, hugging each other, taking turns hugging their grandma. Lindy glanced at David. The happy shock on his face mirrored her own, and even as she joyfully did some quick calculations on the earthly stuff—she'd get that job, and, if they didn't have to make payments on Innisfree right away, they could start paying off the rest of their bills, figure out reinvesting their retirement savings—in his eyes she saw the profundity of what was really true now.

In the end, though she would not be able to save her father, nor save herself from losing her parents to Florida, to Time, not everything was lost. In the end, she and David would be able to keep loving each other. To keep their marriage and their family intact. And they would be able to keep Innisfree for the next generations, for their children's children, and *their* children's children after that.

In the end, she was the luckiest woman alive.

CHAPTER 49

Hailey

Saturday, July 31, 2010
10:30 p.m.

That is so crazy that our grandmothers just, like, made up today after, like, a fight they had seventy years ago?" Hailey said, holding Jack's hand as they walked from Innisfree down the starlit road toward the point. Everyone else had headed to bed, but Hailey was too wrought up to sleep, and she'd wanted to hang out with Jack a little longer. Even after they'd spent most of the last two days together, it seemed there was still so much to talk about. (*What if you were a writer and not a lawyer?* Jack had asked her when they'd had a minute of privacy at a pitstop on the drive back from Eastport today, and she'd been thinking ever since about the answers that had come to her as easily as breathing: *I'd feel like myself; I'd stop trying to please everybody and be perfect; I'd live at Innisfree.*) "I didn't know they'd ever been friends."

"I didn't, either," Jack said with a tiny smile.

She squeezed his hand and sighed. Forty-eight hours ago, she would not have been able to convince herself that anything, let alone everything, was going to be okay. Now her dad was back. Her mom seemed happy, if still a bit miffed. Her brothers had offered to go to Portland to grab Hailey's stuff from Noah's apartment so she wouldn't even have to see him again. And her parents had agreed to sit down with her tomorrow to figure out the best way to divide and conquer duties to cancel what could be canceled of the wedding—and possibly refashion the rest of it.

None of it felt easy, but it did pretty much feel right.

Which, given everything that had been turned upside down this past week, was basically a miracle.

At the campground this afternoon, Hailey'd had enough of waiting at the entrance gate. With Jack in agreement in the passenger seat, she'd started up the Protegé and set off down the winding road through the tall trees toward the campsite where the ranger had said her dad was. The joy and relief of having found him was already wearing through to anger underneath. She had been planning to get *married,* and he'd just gone *camping,* without even bothering to let anyone know?

As she drove up to the site, she saw her mom's Volvo parked behind her dad's Subaru. "Unbelievable," she muttered. Jack said he'd wait in the car, and when she got out, there were her parents, walking up through the trees, holding hands.

She ran for them, hugged her dad, and immediately started to cry. He smelled earthy and sweaty after days out in the woods. "You've been gone for a million years!" she scolded. She was embarrassed to sound so childish, but she couldn't seem to stop herself. "We didn't know where you were!"

"I'm so sorry, honey," he said, and she pulled back. She'd never seen him with a beard before, but his eyes were jarringly familiar. She had really thought she might never see him again. The lawyer father she was used to, the Cranston father. And, yes, they'd gone hiking and camping many times. But it was still so strange to see him here in the woods in his dirty T-shirt, his beard.

Would he be mad at her about the wedding? She didn't want to wait to find out. "I'm sorry, too! I'm not getting married," she blurted.

He smiled sadly. The familiar eyes went soft. "That's okay, honey," he said. "Your mom told me. We just want you to be happy."

Yes, it was really him, she had thought then, and there was much more to say, but for that moment, Hailey had let it all go and hugged him again, while her mom had stood by—and the world, which had been tilted off its axis for these seven interminable, excruciating days, had begun to right itself again.

In the hours since, her dad, regarding the problem of canceling her non-refundable wedding, had had the idea to invite her grandparents' friends from away, the ones who'd been told not to come to the anniversary party, to come for a lobster bake at the wedding venue instead. If Grandpa had a good day, like Greta said he'd had today, maybe he could even join in. Noah's family and friends would, of course, be disinvited, but Hailey's dad said that, since they couldn't get their money back, they might as well have a great party. (Hailey's mom had nudged him and said maybe they could invite the people who'd missed seeing him at his birthday party, too, and it was hard to tell if she was teasing or simmering underneath her little smile. But he'd put his arm around her and kissed the top of her head, and Hailey and her brothers and sister had exchanged happy rolls of their eyes. Then Emma had called Reese, right there in the middle of all of them in the living room at Innisfree, to tell her that, thanks to her, they'd found their dad because they'd known to search at lighthouses, and maybe she could come up next weekend again, and they could start over?)

And not only did it seem like all this stuff was working out almost better than it would have if everything had gone according to plan, but now—thanks to the weird reconciliation between Hailey's grandma and Jack's, whatever that had been about—they were also going to get to keep Innisfree! Hailey wasn't sure what would happen with her grandparents, but she'd seen her grandma pull her mom aside just as everyone was heading to bed and say she had something to tell her in the morning, so maybe Grandma had changed her mind about moving to Florida. Hailey hoped so—but, if she hadn't, then lots of visits were in everybody's future.

Either way, when it was time for Hailey to have the family that she hoped to have someday, her kids—and her brothers' and sister's kids, too, if they had them—would get to grow up at Summerland Cove, just like she and her mom and her grandma had.

"God, it's so amazing of your grandma to loan my parents the money so we can keep Innisfree in the family," she told Jack, for maybe the twelfth time, but it truly was. "Isn't that wild, too, about my grandma deleting that staticky message last Saturday?" Greta had remembered it when Lindy and David had told everybody about the message David had left. They'd assumed maybe Tom had deleted it and forgotten about it, when in fact, Greta said, it must've been her. She'd explained how there'd been no voice discernible in the message, and she'd assumed it was someone calling about the party who didn't know their cell phone wasn't working. (In fact, that had been true—she just hadn't dreamed it might be the guest of honor.) "I mean, if the call had come through, if we'd gotten the message from my dad that he was heading Downeast to camp, like, none of this would've happened."

Hailey and Jack had reached the point and stopped, looking out to where the moon was reflected on the black water rolling gently in. The night was warm and pleasant, and the soft breeze ruffled Hailey's hair.

"I hate to say it, Hales," Jack said, with another little smile, "but I'm glad the call was staticky."

"You are?" she said, because even though it seemed like everything was going to work out for the best, it had still been the most painful week of her life, and it was hard not to think that somehow all that pain would've been best avoided. "Seriously? How can you be—"

"Because this," he said, and he leaned down and kissed her, and though it had been seven years since she'd last kissed him, it seemed suddenly as if no time had passed, and yet everything was brand new.

ACKNOWLEDGMENTS

I'm so grateful to have lived in Midcoast Maine for more than a decade now, and, although I'll always be "from away," I hope my love and appreciation for this magical place and its people come through in this story. That being said, I want to be sure to note that, though I was inspired by particular geographies and features of life here, the setting I've imagined as Summerland Cove and all the people in it are entirely and absolutely made up.

Thank you to my brilliant and extraordinary friend Terence Sullivan for always believing in and supporting me, for being there from start to finish on this book, for reading scenes and chapters along the way, and for giving quick and insightful feedback and encouraging me day by day. I couldn't be more grateful for our writing group of two, our friendship, and our collaborations.

Thank you to the marvelous Dustin Black for being my person, for always being there for and believing in me, for asking great questions, for challenging me and sharing in amazing adventures. Getting to do life with you is the greatest gift I could ever hope to receive.

Thank you to my parents, Bob and Marya Farrell, to the rest of my family, and to my friends all over the map for your unwavering love and support. Special thanks to Joyce Jones, Christine Skorjanec, and Carrie Sutherland for offering me your unconditional support and listening ears through the writing of this book and always!

Thank you to my amazing literary agent, Deborah Schneider, for guiding and believing in me and for your advocacy on behalf of me and this book. Special thanks also to Brian Lipson and Cathy Gleason for your enthusiasm, hard work, and support, and to Jonathan Saxon for your generosity.

Thank you to my fabulous editor Nicole Angeloro for asking all the right questions and for being this book's greatest champion from concept to completion. And a huge thank-you to the incredible publishing team at Mariner for all your wonderful work to bring this story to the world: Caroline Zancan, Lindsey Kennedy, Erin Merlo, Maya Horn, Lauren Grange, Stephanie Vallejo, and Yeon Kim.

Finally, thank you to my readers and to all of you booksellers, librarians, sales reps, social media influencers, and other passionate booklovers who make the book world go 'round. You're what makes this writing life of mine possible, and I could not be more grateful.

ABOUT

MARINER BOOKS

MARINER BOOKS traces its beginnings to 1832 when William Ticknor cofounded the Old Corner Bookstore in Boston, from which he would run the legendary firm Ticknor and Fields, publisher of Ralph Waldo Emerson, Harriet Beecher Stowe, Nathaniel Hawthorne, and Henry David Thoreau. Following Ticknor's death, Henry Oscar Houghton acquired Ticknor and Fields and, in 1880, formed Houghton Mifflin, which later merged with venerable Harcourt Publishing to form Houghton Mifflin Harcourt. HarperCollins purchased HMH's trade publishing business in 2021 and reestablished their storied lists and editorial team under the name Mariner Books.

Uniting the legacies of Houghton Mifflin, Harcourt Brace, and Ticknor and Fields, Mariner Books continues one of the great traditions in American bookselling. Our imprints have introduced an incomparable roster of enduring classics, including Hawthorne's *The Scarlet Letter,* Thoreau's *Walden,* Willa Cather's *O Pioneers!,* Virginia Woolf's *To the Lighthouse,* W. E. B. Du Bois's *Black Reconstruction,* J. R. R. Tolkien's *The Lord of the Rings,* Carson McCullers's *The Heart Is a Lonely Hunter,* Ann Petry's *The Narrows,* George Orwell's *Animal Farm* and *Nineteen Eighty-Four,* Rachel Carson's *Silent Spring,* Margaret Walker's *Jubilee,* Italo Calvino's *Invisible Cities,* Alice Walker's *The Color Purple,* Margaret Atwood's *The Handmaid's Tale,* Tim O'Brien's *The Things They Carried,* Philip Roth's *The Plot Against America,* Jhumpa Lahiri's *Interpreter of Maladies,* and many others. Today Mariner Books remains proudly committed to the craft of fine publishing established nearly two centuries ago at the Old Corner Bookstore.